Let It Crow!
Let It Crow!
Let It Crow!

ALSO BY DONNA ANDREWS

Let It Crow!
Let It Crow!
Let It Crow!

A Meg Langslow Mystery

Donna Andrews

MINOTAUR BOOKS

NEW YORK

First published in the United States by Minotaur Books, an imprint of St. Martin's Publishing Group

www.minotaurbooks.com

Title page illustration by Gabriel Guma

Library of Congress Cataloging-in-Publication Data

Names: Andrews, Donna, author.
Title: Let it crow! Let it crow! Let it crow! / Donna Andrews.
Description: First edition. | New York : Minotaur Books, 2023. |
    Series: A Meg Langslow mystery ; 34
Identifiers: LCCN 2023026717 | ISBN 9781250893963 (hardcover) |
    ISBN 9781250893970 (ebook)
Subjects: LCSH: Langslow, Meg (Fictitious character)—Fiction. |
    Women detectives—Fiction. | LCGFT: Detective and mystery
    fiction. | Novels.
Classification: LCC PS3551.N4165 L48 2023 | DDC 813/.54—dc23/
    eng/20230609
LC record available at https://lccn.loc.gov/2023026717

Our books may be purchased in bulk for promotional, educational, or business use. Please contact your local bookseller or the Macmillan Corporate and Premium Sales Department at 1-800-221-7945, extension 5442, or by email at MacmillanSpecialMarkets@macmillan.com.

First Edition: 2023

1 3 5 7 9 10 8 6 4 2

Chapter 1

"You can still change your mind, you know."

I closed my eyes and counted to ten. Then I opened them again. I crawled out from under the rough-hewn medieval-style trestle table I'd been repairing and looked up. Alec Franzetti was staring down at me with a pleading expression on his broad, bearded face. Both of his enormous, hairy hands were clutching a clipboard that held an untidy, inch-thick sheaf of paper. He gripped it tightly enough to turn his knuckles white. He looked so stressed that the temptation to snap at him vanished. I made sure my tone was gentle. Gentle, but firm.

"No, Alec," I said. "I'm very happy doing what I'm doing."

His face fell, and he sighed loudly.

"Is there anything I can help you with?" I stood up and gestured at the clipboard.

"Probably." He flipped through a couple of the top papers. "Let me think."

He glanced down at the clipboard, then wandered off, looking distracted and lost.

"Change your mind about what?" came a voice from behind me.

I jumped at the sound. Alec's anxiety was rubbing off on me. I turned and smiled when I saw my old friend Caroline Willner.

"Sorry," she said. "Didn't mean to startle you. Merry Christmas."

"Merry Christmas to you." I gave her a quick welcoming hug.

"And you don't have to apologize. How long have you been in town?"

"Only just arriving," she said. "Haven't even been to your house yet, because your dad said you were out here at Ragnar's farm, and could I drop by and try to rescue you? He wouldn't say from what. So who is this Alec person, and what does he want you to change your mind about? And for that matter, what is all this?" She made a sweeping gesture.

I glanced around, trying to see our surroundings through her eyes. We were in an enormous outdoor tent, the kind you'd get to hold a small circus or a really large outdoor wedding reception. We stood in the end that had been designated as the banquet hall, featuring the enormous oak table, four matching backless benches, and half a dozen tall, branching wrought iron candelabras. In the middle of the tent, taking up more than half of the floor space, was the forge area, featuring six assorted blacksmith's workstations, each complete with a forge, anvil, worktable, and a tall metal locker for tools, coats, and anything the director didn't want to see on camera. Beyond that, at the far end of the tent, was the production area, in which workers were setting up the lights, video cameras, microphones, and other tech gear needed to film what went on in the other two areas.

"Alec's an old friend," I began.

Not entirely accurate. But what was I supposed to call him? He certainly wasn't an old enemy. We'd never been all that close, and yet he was more than an old acquaintance. We'd known each other since our college days. He was someone I knew well enough to spend time with when we were thrown together, at craft fairs or blacksmith gatherings. Someone I rather liked when he wasn't being a complete pain in the neck. I vividly recalled that long-ago day when I'd met Alec, although I could no longer remember if it was in my sophomore or junior year of college. I'd ridden my bike from the UVA campus to the tiny, run-down building where William Faulkner Cates, my blacksmithing teacher, had his forge. I'd dashed inside, fired up for my next lesson, only to find that Faulk was working with another pupil. A much more traditional blacksmithing pupil—Alec was tall and burly like Faulk. He had brown hair to Faulk's blond, but apart from that they could have been brothers. I'd watched for a few minutes, unseen, as Faulk calmly guided Alec's faltering first attempts at blacksmithing. And felt a pang of—what? Jealousy, perhaps? Not sexual jealousy—even before I figured out Faulk was gay I'd realized we were meant to be friends rather than lovers. Still, I was more than a little resentful that someone else was taking up a part of my mentor's time and attention.

But it was more than that. Alec's arrival seemed at first as if it might slam the door I was trying to open—the door into a profession that wasn't exactly welcoming. Women blacksmiths were relatively rare, and the old guard treated us more as curiosities than colleagues. And apart from Dad, my own family members hadn't exactly been supportive. Oh, they were very encouraging about my taking lessons, but they seemed to see blacksmithing as a unique and interesting hobby to occupy my free time, once I'd taken up a suitable career as a doctor, lawyer, or professor. Something white collar and professional.

Faulk's forge was the only place where I could feel free from all those pressures—free from the disapproval of chauvinistic blacksmiths and the expectations of my family. And Faulk was, back then, the only person who really took my work seriously.

And then this intruder showed up. I was tempted to slink away, never to return. Clearly Faulk had only taken me on as a pupil because he hadn't found any men who wanted blacksmithing lessons. Alec would take my place and—

Just then Faulk noticed me, and his face took on such a look of welcome and relief that my urge to flee vanished.

"Meg," he said. "This is Alec Franzetti, our new pupil. Come show him how to tell when the iron's ready to work."

Our new pupil. My world fell back into place. There was a new pupil. But I was still the senior pupil—that post was mine to hold on to, if I could.

And I did. Alec might have looked more like most people's idea of a blacksmith, but he wasn't exactly Faulk's star pupil. He was a bit of a klutz, and bad at taking directions. Especially from me, which was unfortunate, since Faulk's original idea was to have me cement my knowledge of the blacksmithing basics by imparting them to Alec. We gave that up after a few weeks, and Faulk was more than half expecting Alec to quit his lessons entirely. But he never completely gave up, and over the years, Faulk eventually turned him into a competent blacksmith and then a bladesmith. But not a master at either.

I'd been overjoyed when Faulk and his husband, Tad, moved to Caerphilly, but relieved when Alec relocated to California. He was fond of bragging that "Cates taught me everything I know." Faulk tended to wince at this, and at least once I'd heard him murmur, "But unfortunately, not everything *I* know." Alec was much less annoying as an occasional visitor to the East Coast, and his change of career from journeyman bladesmith to TV impresario seemed like a good thing to me—as long as he stopped trying to drag me into it.

"An old friend who moved to California and has gotten involved in television," I went on. "They're making a TV series," I said. "*Blades of Glory.*"

"Ooh," she said. "So Michael's acting again? Some kind of swashbuckling heroic fantasy, I assume."

I could have pointed out that my husband had never exactly given up acting—although these days, as a tenured faculty member of Caerphilly College's Drama Department, he spent more time teaching and directing. I could have added that, since in his salad days he'd played a sinister though sexy wizard on a low-budget cult-hit TV show, appearing in yet another swashbuckling heroic fantasy was not a career move that would interest him. But I stifled the urge.

"Not that kind of TV series," I said. "This is one of those reality-TV competition shows. They start out with six blacksmiths—correction, bladesmiths; it's all about weapon making. Each episode, the judges will assign them a different weapon—a two-handed sword, or a Viking battle-ax, or whatever. And all the competitors have to go and make one. Then the judges test it for strength and sharpness and assess how aesthetically pleasing and historically accurate it is, and whoever does the worst gets kicked out of the competition. So by the last episode, they're down from six competitors to two and both the winner and the runner-up get nice cash prizes."

"Sounds interesting," Caroline said. "And you're going to compete?"

"No," I said. "Not really my thing."

"You're a blacksmith," she said.

"But not primarily a bladesmith," I pointed out.

"You've made plenty of weapons."

"Not compared to these guys." I waved at the forge area, although at the moment none of the competitors were there. "They're all specialists. Most of them members of the American Bladesmith Society. And Faulk *is* competing."

"And you don't want to show up your mentor." She nodded as if that explained everything.

"Since everything I know about making weapons I learned from Faulk, I'm smart enough to know better than to try to compete with a master bladesmith," I said. "And besides, although reality-TV competition shows aren't exactly my cup of tea, I've seen enough of them to know I don't want to be on one. I'm just helping out with some of the backstage stuff."

"Oh, you're no fun," she said. "Is there a reason they're planning to film here in a tent in Ragnar's goat pasture?"

"Ragnar invited them to film here," I said. "And offered to put up all the cast and crew during filming."

"Very generous," she said. "And just what you'd expect from him."

I nodded, although I wasn't sure if Ragnar was being generous or whether he thought the filming would be a lot of fun and wanted a ringside seat. Ragnar had retired from a lucrative career as the drummer for several heavy-metal bands that had evidently been wildly successful—although I'd never heard of any of them. He'd bought a large estate in the Caerphilly County countryside and was busy turning what had started out as a sprawling mansion into a veritable castle, complete with stone walls, towers, a moat, and enough wrought iron to keep both Faulk and me busy for the rest of our careers.

"But for some reason, none of the hundred or so rooms in the castle quite works for filming the main blacksmithing scenes," I went on. "So here we are."

"Hope they get some space heaters for this tent," she said. "It's a bit chilly now, and the temperature's going to get colder, not warmer, over the next few days."

"I've suggested that," I said. "And the forges will help warm things. Here's hoping the snow holds off."

"And the arctic polar vortex. And— Wait. No. That would doom us all to not having a white Christmas. I take it back. Let it snow! They can just cope with it."

"If you have any influence with the snow, please tell it to hold off until Friday afternoon," I said. "They're going to film the first episode this week, then take next week off."

"That's nice," she said. "Everyone can celebrate the holiday and then pick up again in the new year."

I nodded. Actually, I doubted if the production team would have time for much celebrating. I'd overheard enough to know that they'd spend the holiday creating a rough cut of the first episode and showing it to some of the higher-ups in their company—higher-ups who, if not sufficiently impressed, might pull the plug on the whole project. Which meant Alec wouldn't be doing much celebrating, either, since he'd invested more money in this crazy project than he could afford to lose. He'd spend the whole Christmas break worrying, and I was afraid he'd go bonkers if the show didn't get green-lighted. Bonkers, and maybe even bankrupt. But I kept this to myself, since I only knew any of it from the eavesdropping I'd done while helping to set up the six blacksmithing stations. So far all of the production people tended to overlook my presence, as if I were merely a non-stationary part of the set. I wanted to keep it that way.

"Will you be here much longer?" Caroline began to sit down on one of the benches, but I grabbed her arm just in time to stop her.

"Don't sit on that just yet," I said. "The idiots who assembled the furniture didn't bother to tighten any of the bolts. That one's safe."

I steered her to the one bench I knew could hold the weight of even a small, roundish person. It had collapsed about an hour ago, spilling the assistant director onto the straw-covered floor of the banquet area. I'd reassembled it, making sure the hidden bolts were good and tight, and was now working on ensuring that the table and the rest of the benches were structurally sound.

"Thanks for the warning," she said. "And if there's something you need to be doing, don't let me interrupt you."

"You can amuse me while I work," I said.

So while I made sure the other three benches and the table were safe to use, she chatted away, relating some of the recent happenings at the wild animal refuge she ran. She was in the middle of telling me about the success she was having raising several orphaned Virginia big-eared bat pups when an officious young woman in a mustard-colored mini-skirted suit and stiletto heels strode over. Her clipboard was much tidier than Alec's. Jasmyn, the production assistant, was organized—I liked that in a person—but she never brought good news.

"Those simply won't do." She pointed toward the two folding tables we'd set up for the judges. "They're not in period."

"They're not finished yet," I said.

"But they need to be finished today!" Jasmyn sounded stressed. "We start filming tomorrow at eight!" She proceeded to rant and rave on the subject, and I'd have cut her short except that I spotted something happening behind her back. Ragnar had appeared, carrying what looked like an armload of star-spangled darkness. Unfolded, the darkness was revealed as two large expanses of black velvet, embroidered in silver. While Jasmyn continued to revile me, he spread the velvet over the tables, and then stood back to admire the result.

"You're right," I said, finally interrupting my tormentor. "They need to be covered with something, so they look in period. I'll take care of that immediately." I snapped my fingers, then pointed to the tables. "How's that?"

She turned to look. I saw her nod slightly. Then, clearly in the mood to continue venting at someone, she turned back to me, frowning.

"Well, why wasn't it done already?" she asked. "What are we *paying* you for?"

"You're not," I said. "I'm one of Alec's people. The guys you're paying went on break an hour and a half ago, and I have no idea where they are."

She pursed her lips, and I suspected she was trying to think up a sufficiently snide reply. But just then a large splotch of gooey white liquid landed on top of her sleek auburn pageboy. I looked up to see a crow sitting on one of the guy wires near the ceiling of the tent. He cawed raucously.

It took Jasmyn a second or two to realize what had happened. Then her face crumpled.

"Oh, gross!" she screamed. And then she ran out of the tent, shrieking. The other workers in the production end barely looked up in spite of her noisy exit.

"He must like you." Caroline was staring up at the crow with an expression of approval. "Have you been feeding him?"

"Only helping Ragnar," I said. "He feeds them all the time."

"Crows notice," she said. "They're very intelligent."

"Yes, I know," I said quickly. Caroline, like my grandfather, was fond of sharing little tidbits of information about her favorite creatures. Little tidbits or great long lectures. And they were both particularly fond of corvids—crows, ravens, and even jays. Caroline had been a nurse before retiring to found her wild animal sanctuary and often put her medical knowledge to good use rehabilitating injured creatures—including corvids.

"I'm worried about this one, though," she said. "It's starting to get dark outside. He should be out finding a good place to roost for the night. Getting his rest. Not in here where some idiot who doesn't like corvids might try to chase him."

As if he'd heard us, the crow cawed twice, then took off and flew out through one of the tent openings. Caroline nodded in satisfaction.

"Caroline! Have you come to watch the filming?" Ragnar loomed over us, six and a half feet tall and looking almost as wide in a bulky down coat. He hugged Caroline. Given the foot-and-a-half difference in their heights, he had to bend over almost double to do so.

"I've come to spend Christmas with Meg and her family," she said. "But I'd love to eavesdrop on the filming if it's allowed."

"Of course!" Ragnar exclaimed. "You can even stay here at the castle if you like. Plenty of room. And arriving today—perfect! You can help with the Christmas decorations. I've been too busy to put them up!"

"But Mother's coming over today to take care of it," I reminded him.

"Yes." Ragnar beamed. "And I know she would love to have Caroline's sharp eye to help her."

"Sounds like fun," Caroline said. "Do you—"

Just then the crow flew back in, cawing. He headed directly

for where the three of us stood. He circled us three times, still cawing, and then flew out the tent opening again.

"He must want us to see something." Ragnar began striding after the crow.

"Either that or he flew around us three times as part of casting a spell on us," I said, falling into step behind him. "What if we suddenly transform into crows?"

"Then Ragnar will feed us until we figure out how to change back." Caroline sounded out of breath. Even though at five-ten I have long legs, I had trouble keeping up with Ragnar. She was flat-out running behind us.

When we emerged outside the tent, we found three or four crows circling overhead, seeming to indicate something on the ground. No, someone.

It was Faulk. He lay on the close-cropped grass, clutching his right arm to his side and breathing heavily. Enough light fell on him from the tent opening that I could see that his face and his shaggy mop of blond hair were streaked with blood.

"Call nine-one-one," Caroline said as she scrambled to Faulk's side, all of her retired nurse instincts kicking in. "And get me a first-aid kit."

Chapter 2

"It's broken." Faulk had been saying that ever since we found him. Now that we were racing along in the ambulance, instead of saying it to me, he was telling the EMT. If he was hoping for a diagnosis, he'd have to wait a little longer. The EMT wasn't going to preempt the doctor, and the doctor wouldn't give a definitive diagnosis until they'd taken an X-ray.

My phone dinged. I glanced down. A message from Tad, Faulk's husband.

"Tad beat us to the ER," I said.

Faulk's face lit up briefly. Then it fell again.

"Did you tell him what happened?" Faulk asked.

"Yes," I said. "While we were waiting for the ambulance."

"Nobody's told me," the medic said. "And I need it for my report. And I want to hear it from the horse's mouth." He frowned sternly at Faulk.

Did he really need to know what happened? Or was he just trying to distract Faulk from the pain? Because no matter how hard he tried to tough it out, Faulk was definitely in pain. His forehead was beaded with sweat and his jaw was set in a grim expression.

"I don't want a whole lot of fuss about this," Faulk said. "It could hurt the show."

"I'll keep my mouth shut, then," the EMT said. "But the docs will need to know what happened."

Faulk sighed and closed his eyes. I thought he was going to say he didn't feel up to talking. Then he opened his eyes again and seemed to brace himself.

"I was walking down from the castle to the tent to see if there was anything I could help with," he said. "And I had my earbuds in, listening to some music. Which I wouldn't have done if I hadn't thought it was pretty safe out there on Ragnar's farm. And suddenly something whacked my arm, hard. Felt like a baseball bat or something like that. From behind, so I didn't see who it was. And then whoever did it took a swing at my head, but I was already falling down, so I didn't think it hit me all that hard. Guess I was wrong."

He glanced ruefully at his bloody shirt.

"Only a minor scalp laceration." The EMT looked up from the blood-pressure cuff he was once more inflating. "Head wounds always bleed like crazy. But don't worry—they'll be checking you out for a possible concussion." He sounded cheerful, as if Faulk's injuries were the sort of interesting occurrence that made his job worthwhile.

"Great," Faulk said. "Possible concussion. Possible broken bone. Who's going to break the news to Alec that maybe I won't be in any shape to do blacksmithing tomorrow?"

"No maybe about it," the EMT said. "Even if it's not broken, you probably have some kind of serious soft-tissue injury. I wouldn't count on using that arm for at least a few days. Maybe longer."

"Meg—you'll have to step in." Faulk made a gesture as if to reach for my hand, then winced and lay back. "They can't possibly find another blacksmith on such short notice. I know you aren't all that keen on doing it—"

"Understatement of the year," I said. "I hate the idea of doing it. I know it's going to be hard on Alec if this thing falls through—"

"Hard on me and Tad, too," he said. "A big chunk of the money Alec's going to lose if the show fails is money he borrowed from us."

"Damn," I said softly. I'd turned down Alec's pleas that having a woman blacksmith would make it easier for the production team to sell the show. I'd already been steeling myself to turn a deaf ear to his pleas that I step in to help make the show a success. No one had told me that Faulk's and Tad's finances also depended on the damned thing.

"I know, I know," Faulk said. "I should have known better. But Alec was so keen on it, and his producers talk a good game. If you gave me a do-over, I'd use it to go back and say no another fifty times, until Alec gave up and found another sucker to lend him money."

"If I were you," the EMT said, "I'd use it to go back and take my earbuds out before wandering around in the dark."

"Also an excellent idea," Faulk said, with a quick grin that looked more like a grimace. "But I don't think I'm going to get the chance to do either. Unless, by some chance, Josh and Jamie are working on a time machine for this year's science fair."

"Alas," I said. "They're doing something with DNA." Though I was sure if my twin sons knew their honorary uncle Faulk needed one, they'd absolutely try to invent a time machine. "I'll need to ask Michael," I added. "If he's not okay with it—"

"Understood," Faulk said. He looked reassured. He probably knew as well as I did that Michael wouldn't say no if he knew the situation.

"Here we are," the EMT said. We were turning in to the Caerphilly General Hospital's parking lot. "You stay put on the stretcher and let us wheel you in."

Faulk lay back with a resigned expression on his face.

We pulled up at the hospital doors and the ambulance came to a stop. The EMT's partner jumped out of the cab and raced around to open up the back doors. I hopped out and made sure I was not in the way as they began maneuvering the stretcher out of the ambulance.

"Meg!" My dad appeared at my elbow. "I raced over when I heard it was Faulk. What happened? How is he?"

I filled Dad in on what little I knew. Then I followed him and the stretcher inside and repeated the whole explanation for half a dozen medical personnel. I sat with Tad while Dad accompanied Faulk back to what they now called the Medical Imaging Department. Did Dad not yet trust the relatively new doctor on ER duty this evening? Or was he intent on managing the case because it was Faulk? Either way, he had taken charge and ordered X-rays for Faulk's arm and whatever tests were needed—CAT scan or MRI or both—for his head. The rest of the hospital staff seemed happy to have Dad there.

I managed to slip away long enough to call Michael and brief him on what had happened.

"Faulk wants me to fill in for him," I added. "I told him I needed to run it by you."

"The boys would be over the moon if you competed," he said. "You know how crushed they were when you turned Alec down. And it could be fun. But if you still don't want to do it—"

"I don't," I said. "But I think I need to, for Faulk's sake. What do you think?"

"Whoever went after Faulk might still be out there," he said. "I don't like the idea of you going into danger like that."

"I'm not sure there's any real—" I began.

"So the boys and I will come, too," he said. "I'm sure Ragnar can find us a couple of rooms at the castle. I'll call him now. And frankly, I think it might be a good idea for someone with television experience to keep an eye on what this production company is doing. I mean, quite apart from the fact that they're non-union, it doesn't exactly sound as if they're top drawer. For all we know they could be total crooks. And they'll want you to sign some kind of contract—don't even think of doing that until I've reviewed it. I'll give my old agent a call and have him standing by, just in case I see anything that worries me."

I returned to keep Tad company while Faulk went into surgery to treat what was, indeed, a badly broken arm. Tad tried to persuade me that he'd be fine on his own, but I insisted on staying.

"If I go back to Ragnar's, I won't get anything done," I said. "I'll end up having to explain what happened another twenty or thirty times, and I won't be able to answer them when they ask if he's well enough to compete."

"I think we both know the answer to that." Tad's slim brown face was drawn with anxiety.

"I gather you and Faulk have a lot riding on this wretched show. Financially."

Tad nodded.

Damn. Appearing on *Blades of Glory* was absolutely the last way I wanted to spend even part of my holiday season. But if its failure was going to hurt Faulk and Tad . . .

"Once Faulk gets out of surgery, I guess I'll have to head back and tell Alec that, yes, I can fill in for him," I said. "The show must go on."

"That would be incredible," Tad said. "Thank you."

"Don't thank me yet," I said. "Alec still wants me to compete, but I have no idea if the producers are open to the substitution."

"Pretty sure they will be." Tad's smile looked genuine for the first time since I'd arrived. "They've been driving Faulk and Alec crazy, trying to get them to think of another female bladesmith they can recruit. The only reason they finally stopped bugging you is that Faulk put his foot down. They've probably called every female blacksmith on the East Coast. Not enough diversity in the contestants."

"They've got diversity," I said. "Victor is Black and Andy Kim's Korean American."

"Yeah, but apart from that even Victor and Andy are a whole lot like the rest of the crew. Five big, hairy, burly guys, and most of them tattooed and bearded. You'll stand out in the crowd. Probably be a fan favorite."

I stifled a sigh. I didn't want to be a fan favorite. Maybe I'd luck out and get eliminated in round one. Not that I had any plans to throw the contest, but I shouldn't have to. From what I had heard, the other five contestants were all full-time blade-smiths. Thanks to the demands of children, extended family, and my part-time job as the Mayor's Assistant in Charge of Special Projects, I didn't have nearly as much time as I liked these days for blacksmithing. And what time I did spend at the forge was mostly focused on the kind of extravagant gothic ironwork needed to carry out Ragnar's vision for his castle. I could hammer out a wrought iron raven or gargoyle with my eyes closed, but it had been a while since I'd made a blade. I should be a shoo-in for elimination in the first round.

"We'll figure it out when I get back to Ragnar's," I said. Just then a scrubs-clad figure bounded into the waiting room, strip-ping off his surgical mask. "Look—here comes Dad. Faulk must be out of surgery."

Tad bolted to his feet and raced over to meet Dad.

"He did great!" Dad exclaimed. "We're going to keep him overnight, just to watch for concussion, but so far everything's just great. They're taking him up to his room now. We can go and meet him."

I followed them down the hall, but as we were waiting for the elevator, I decided it was time for me to bail.

"I should head back to Ragnar's," I said. "Before Alec suc-cumbs to despair and leaps off one of the castle towers."

No one argued with me, so I waved at the two of them until the elevator doors closed. While waiting out Faulk's surgery with Tad I'd noticed my phone buzzing from time to time, signaling an arriving text. I'd been ignoring it, but now I checked. One text from Michael. Fifteen from the annoying Jasmyn. Several from other people whose names I didn't recognize.

Michael's text assured me that he and the boys were on their way to Ragnar's. I was taking a deep breath and preparing to see what Jasmyn wanted when—

"Good evening, Meg."

Chief Burke strolled up. His khaki uniform was as neat as if he'd just stepped out of his house, though I could see a few rain-drops beaded up on the hat. I hoped the precipitation stayed rain—I wasn't ready for snow. Not for a couple of days. The chief glanced at the elevator button, then turned to me.

"How's Faulk doing?" he asked. "I hear they're keeping him overnight."

"To watch for signs of concussion," I said. "You know Dad and head injuries. If it were just the broken arm, I think they'd be sending him home. You're coming to interview him?"

"If he's up to it." He frowned. "And if he'll let me."

"Why wouldn't he let you?"

"Vern happened to be patrolling downtown and was passing by the hospital when I got the news, so I sent him in to take an initial report. Faulk seemed reluctant to talk. Said something about bad publicity. Not sure how letting people know you've been mugged is bad publicity."

"I think he means for the show," I said. "He was fretting about that on the way in."

"Very likely," the chief said. "Tad called to ask me to come down. I'm hoping that means he's going to do his darndest to persuade Faulk to talk to me."

"If anyone can change Faulk's mind, Tad can," I said. "But Faulk can be stubborn."

The chief rolled his eyes slightly and nodded.

"So I'll give you something else you might be able to use to change Faulk's mind," I said. "Remind him that I'm filling in for him in the contest."

"You are?" His face brightened with interest. "I thought you'd turned them down."

"I did," I said. "Repeatedly. And I'd have turned them down again this evening, except that apparently the show won't go on without another blacksmith and I'm the only one available on such short notice. If the show gets derailed, Alec will lose not only all his money but also everything he talked Faulk and Tad into lending him. Which was more than they could easily afford."

The chief winced at the thought.

"So if Faulk is still reluctant, point out that I'm subbing in for him," I said. "And that I'd feel a lot better about it if I knew he'd done everything he could to help you find whoever jumped him. Because in the meanwhile, I'm going to be so focused on watching my back that I probably won't make it past round one of the contest."

"I'm sure you'll do fine," he said.

"All I need to do is fill in for Faulk until I'm eliminated," I said.

The chief thought for a moment.

"Is there any way you could arrange for Vern to spend some time out at Ragnar's without it being blatantly obvious that I'm assigning him to keep an eye on things?" he asked.

"No problem," I said. "If I'm going to be competing in the show, Alec will need someone to do all the things I've been doing—a little light carpentry and general handyman and go-fering work."

"Right up his line."

Yes, although Vern Shiffley was the chief's senior deputy, he'd grown up in a clan that performed most of the carpentry, plumbing, electrical, and construction work in the county. He was probably a lot more qualified for the job of Alec's handyman than I was.

"But don't they have strict rules about hiring only union workers?" the chief asked.

"This is a non-union production," I said. "Or they wouldn't be letting me onto the set. I gather this is fairly common for reality shows. I'll tell Ragnar Vern will be coming out. He'll be fine with it—he likes Vern."

"And we'll be pretending Vern's off duty," the chief went on. "No need to arouse their suspicions."

"I will feel all the safer with him around," I said. "And Michael will approve—he plans to bring the boys and settle in for the duration, so they can keep an eye on me."

"Good," the chief said. "It's a plan. I'll tell Vern to change into his civvies and show up at Ragnar's door as soon as possible. You going back there?"

"Eventually," I said. "I was about to head for the parking lot, but I just remembered that I rode here in the ambulance. My car's out at Ragnar's. I'm about to start looking for a ride."

"Hold that thought."

The chief pulled out his cell phone and punched a couple of numbers. Whoever he called answered almost immediately.

"Have you taken off for Ragnar's yet?" After a short pause, he went on. "No, that's good. Meg's here at the hospital. Give her a ride out there, and she can show you where they found Faulk. Thanks."

He shoved his phone in his pocket and turned back to me.

"Horace is going out to see what evidence he can find," he said. "He'll pick you up in a couple of minutes."

"Perfect." Not only was I happy to get a ride, I was also pleased to know that my cousin Horace Hollingsworth, the chief's lone evidence technician, would be doing his forensic thing at the site where Faulk was attacked. Not that I'd ever doubted that the chief would take the attack seriously, but I also knew the department was shorthanded—as usual this time of year.

The chief finally pushed the elevator button and headed up to Faulk's room. I sat down in the lobby, as close to the entrance as possible. I pulled out my phone and texted Ragnar that Vern would be coming out to fill in for me.

Then I braced myself and checked the texts from Jasmyn.

"Alec says you can step in for Faulk—can you confirm?" was the first one. Repeated, verbatim, five minutes later. Then followed by "I NEED TO KNOW IF YOU'RE SUBBING FOR FAULK!!!" Hadn't anyone ever told her that it was rude to shout at people, even in a text? After that she'd either heard that I'd agreed to fill in for Faulk—perhaps she'd been texting him as well—or assumed it, because she began first asking and then ordering me to come back to the set for an emergency cast meeting.

"Will return as soon as possible," I said. "Still at hospital making sure Faulk okay."

Jasmyn responded with a few hysterical orders to come back now, *now*, NOW! I suppressed several possible responses that would have been more satisfying than diplomatic. No sense alienating someone I'd have to work with, now that I was subbing for Faulk.

"I have good news," I texted instead. "I think I've almost convinced Faulk that suing the production company would be a bad move. Making sure that's settled before I leave here."

As I hoped, that silenced her.

I was reading Ragnar's rapturous response to the news of Vern's impending arrival, and warning him that Vern would be working undercover, pretending to be off duty, when Horace strode into the lobby. I hopped up to meet him, put on my winter coat, and we went outside to his waiting cruiser.

Chapter 3

"How's Faulk?" Horace asked as he pulled away from the curb.

So I filled him in on Faulk's arm, and his head, and then what little I knew about how he'd gotten his injuries.

"When we get there, can you show me where you found him?" Horace asked.

"I could," I said. "But my presence seems to be required at an emergency cast meeting—whatever that is. I'll get Caroline to show you."

I texted Caroline, who agreed to guide Horace to the scene of the crime. And then I texted Jasmyn to say that I was on my way and to ask where the meeting would be.

"In the library," she texted back. She began to give me elaborate directions on how to find the library.

"It's okay," I texted back. "I know where it is."

And a good thing I did, since following her directions would have led me to Ragnar's favorite bathroom, the one with the gargoyle-shaped faucets on the enormous black-and-gold soaking tub.

We stopped at the front gates for Horace to lift up the panel that concealed an electronic keypad and punch in the access code. I noticed a new sign posted next to the gate that read RAGNARSHJEM—which was Norwegian for "Ragnar's home." Evidently, he'd grown tired of people like me misspelling it as Ragnarsholm, which wasn't Norwegian for anything.

We drove slowly down the lane. Earlier in the day, a camera crew had been out filming bits of local color—views of the castle, the grounds, and Ragnar's goth menagerie. His horses, cows, goats, sheep, llamas, alpacas, ducks, chickens, geese, and swans were universally either all black or black-and-white. The director had gone crazy over this. But now it was dark, with only a sliver of a moon. Most of the animals, if they were still outdoors, would be merely blobs of greater darkness on the shadowy fields. Or, occasionally, blobs standing in the middle of the lane, which was why we went so slowly.

We spotted Caroline waiting at the foot of the wide marble steps that led up to the castle's front entrance. She was so bundled up against the growing cold that only her eyes were visible below her knit hat and above her woolly scarf.

"Hurry in," she said, as she stepped forward to take my place. "The television people have been driving everyone crazy, asking how soon you'd be here."

She and Horace drove off toward the production tent.

I braced myself for whatever was waiting for me inside and trudged up the steps.

When I reached the top, where a broad terrace lay between me and the front door, I spotted a man in black standing by the balustrade. No, make that posing—posing so obviously that I looked around to see if I was interrupting a photo session of some kind. But there were no lights or cameras in sight. So why was he standing there, coatless, in this cold? I pulled out my phone and checked the temperature—it was down to twenty-eight. Should I chase him indoors before frostbite set in?

The man turned his head slightly—just enough to let him see who was arriving without spoiling the perfection of his heroic pose. But it seemed I was not whoever he'd been hoping to see—he frowned slightly, then returned to gazing moodily over Ragnar's rolling acres.

But the slight change in position had shown me enough of his face that I recognized him—Marco d'Antonio, the well-known martial artist who'd be serving as one of the judges. I'd seen him often enough when he'd guested at science-fiction/fantasy conventions where Faulk and I were selling our ironwork. More than once I'd watched his dramatic swordplay demonstrations. But I wasn't sure we'd ever been formally introduced, or that he'd even remember me if we had. Since I didn't know what the etiquette was for interacting with the judges—particularly one who was notoriously touchy and temperamental—I smiled, nodded, and strode on through the open front door.

Ragnar was waiting.

"They're going crazy," he said. "I'm supposed to bring you to the library immediately! But quick, tell me how Faulk is."

Reassuring him that Faulk was on the road to recovery and answering all his many questions took up the whole hasty trip to the library. I wouldn't have minded except that it left me no time to prepare my mind for whatever the emergency cast meeting would involve. Ragnar flung the heavy library door open and, with a gallant bow, gestured for me to enter. I took a deep breath to center my mind—my cousin Rose Noire, patron saint of yoga and mindfulness, would have approved—and stepped into the library.

Normally just being in Ragnar's library lifted my spirits. It was—according to Dad, who was picky about such things—a proper library, with an impressively large and varied collection of books. Bookshelves covered every inch of wall space, up to the double-height ceiling, with several wrought iron library ladders running on tracks along the walls to give access to the upper shelves. It was furnished with a variety of comfortable black leather sofas and red velvet chairs, each flanked by a bright reading lamp—most of them wrought iron lamps made by Faulk or me. Nearly every chair or sofa had a table at its side—the sort of table that had enough dings, dents, and water rings that you knew you didn't have to worry about coasters. At the far end were several black-painted chairs and tables for anyone who needed a work area for homework or writing. Altogether a very inviting and comfortable space. Even people made uncomfortable by Ragnar's trademark black-and-red color scheme usually found the library welcoming, thanks to the rainbow of otherwise forbidden hues added by the thousands of books it held.

But normally the library was quiet and mostly empty, not populated with a tense knot of people impatiently awaiting my arrival.

So I dashed in and grabbed the closest seat I could find. The other five competitors were already settled on the various sofas and chairs. A couple of them smiled and murmured greetings. A couple scowled or ignored me. Tad was right. It was going to be five big, burly, bearded, tattooed men—and me. Most of them were holding heavy glass beer mugs. A small table nearby held several more mugs and a cluster of beer bottles and cans, including several of Ragnar's beloved pricey craft beers. There were also a few Diet Cokes, but I decided neither beer nor caffeine was a good idea at the moment. I was hoping the meeting would break up soon so I could go to bed. It had already been a very long and tiring day.

One of the two producers stood in a central position along one wall, tapping his foot with impatience. No one had introduced me to him yet, or to his near clone—both of them thirty-something men of average height with blandly attractive features. I'd come to think of them as Tweedledee and Tweedledum. Sam Wilson, the director, and Alec, whose fault it was I had to do this, were sitting a little farther off, as if to keep some distance between them and the competitors. Alec would have blended in with the crowd—he had the bulk, the beard, and the tattoos. Sam was short, skinny, clean shaven, balding, and devoid of dermal ink. He seemed to be eyeing the contestants warily, like a dog trainer encountering new pupils whose temperaments were as-yet unknown.

"Sorry," I said to the assembled group. "Just got back from the hospital."

"How's Faulk doing?" asked one of the competitors—the twentysomething Andy Kim.

"His arm is pretty badly broken," I said. "He also had a head wound, so they're keeping him overnight to watch for signs of concussion. But the doctors think he'll be fine."

Murmurs of "good" and "that's a relief" and similar sentiments went around the room.

"But he won't be picking up a hammer anytime soon," I added.

"That's okay." Tweedledee beamed at me as if I'd done something really clever. "We've got you."

He didn't have to look so pleased about it. And seeing renewed scowls on the faces of a couple of the others didn't thrill me, either.

"I thought we were going to have these meetings out in the tent at the banquet table." This was from Victor. I couldn't tell if he was one of the scowlers. His face was so impassive that I found his expression hard to read, even if he hadn't been sitting at the shadowy end of one of the sofas. "Not that I mind being indoors in weather like this. I just like to know what to expect."

"For the meetings we film, we'll be out in the tent," Tweedledee said. "And we're bringing in space heaters. But this is an unofficial, practical meeting, to make sure you're all up to speed with what's going on. For starters, I wanted to make sure you all knew that, thanks to Meg Langslow here for agreeing to step in for Faulkner Cates, filming this first episode can go forward as planned."

"Could have gone on just fine with five of us." This muttered comment came from the tallest, broadest, burliest of the contestants, the one with the bushiest beard and the most tattoos. Who also happened to be the one doing the most scowling at me. He was wearing black jeans and a black T-shirt—had someone clued him in to Ragnar's favorite color scheme?

"I hear you, Duncan," Tweedledee said. "But it really wouldn't work out. We have the whole thing—well, scripted isn't exactly the right word with a reality show. We've got . . . a plan. A template. And we need six contestants for the template to work. We've done a few of these shows before, you know. You let us take care of the production side, and just worry about making the best sword."

"We could postpone until Faulk's well," said another contestant, a big blond man whose close-cropped beard contained hints of red. He spoke with a strong Southern accent—Tennessee was my guess. "I'd be open to that."

"I'm afraid if we did that, the production team and financing we've been able to put together would fall apart," Tweedledee said. "But I appreciate your flexibility, Brody."

I appreciated how he seemed to be deliberately calling the other contestants by name. Of course, it might get annoying if he always did that, especially if he kept using the same expression of transparently false warmth. But right now he was definitely helping me learn the cast of characters.

"So, Meg." Tweedledee beamed at me again. "Just in case you haven't already met them—Duncan Jackson's from the L.A. area."

Duncan crossed his arms and grimaced.

"Andy Kim, also L.A."

Andy waved to me.

"Victor Noone, Fresno."

Victor raised his right hand to his temple in a mock salute.

"John Dunigan, Martinez, California."

John smiled and nodded at me. I'd already mentally dubbed him "the quiet one." He was also, at not quite six feet, the smallest of the company—well, apart from me—and the most normal looking. While he was muscular, it wasn't the pumped-up, overdefined muscle a couple of the others had. Duncan, in particular, looked almost like a cartoon. John's brown hair and beard were neatly trimmed and I could only see one tattoo, a small and rather faded one on his forearm.

"Brody McIlvaney, Murfreesboro, Tennessee."

Brody tipped an imaginary hat to me. There was something flirtatious about his manner. I made a mental note to introduce him to Michael as soon as possible.

"For those of you who haven't yet met her," Tweedledee went on, "Meg learned blacksmithing and bladesmithing from Faulk, and Ragnar tells me that she's done a lot of the ironwork here in the castle and on its grounds."

He gestured up at the wrought iron chandelier overhead, an elaborate piece that depicted two dragons fighting over the central glass globe.

"Dragons! Cool!" Andy exclaimed, and touched his wrist, where you could see an intricately detailed tattoo of a dragon's claw emerging from his sleeve—part, I suspected, of a complete dragon we'd be seeing if he shed his shirt. Make that *when* he shed his shirt. In my experience, people with really elaborate tattoos were always shedding garments to show them off.

Brody pretended to marvel at the chandelier. Duncan barely gave it a glance. Both John and Victor studied it and then nodded slightly. Okay, it was ornamental ironwork rather than weaponsmithing, but at least I seemed to have made a favorable impression on some of the competition.

The library door opened, and Tweedledum, the other producer, walked in. Tweedledee nodded at him before turning back to us.

"So much for the introductions," Tweedledee said. At the far end of the room, Sam Wilson, the director, sighed and looked put upon, but said nothing. Maybe Tweedledee assumed I'd already met Sam. "Let's go over what's happening tomorrow and review the ground rules."

Ordinarily, I'd have been whipping out my notebook-that-tells-me-when-to-breathe and taking copious notes, but my mind rebelled at the idea. Maybe I was still feeling a little resentment at even having to be here. Or maybe I was being influenced by my male competitors' nonchalance. They were all sitting back, either relaxed or doing their darndest to appear relaxed. Maybe they'd heard it all before and this was a review for my benefit. Or maybe they all shared the common male assumption that if anything was really important, someone would remind them of it.

I paused for a moment and made a conscious attempt to clear my mind. So I didn't want to be here. Nothing I could do about it now. I could keep sulking or I could look on the bright side. Make lemonade, as Dad always said. I'd be spending time blacksmithing—always a good thing. The boys would be delighted. I'd have the inside scoop on how the contest was going, instead of being outside wondering. I'd get to know my fellow contestants, some of whom might turn out to be interesting new friends.

With my mood considerably improved by this mental pep talk, I focused back on the instructions the Tweedle was giving us.

We were all supposed to show up at the tent tomorrow at 8:00 A.M.—in our work clothes but looking as presentable as possible. Sam, the director, would film us arriving, setting up our work areas, and getting to know one another.

I did my best to ignore the way Brody smirked at me at that point.

Then we'd film the first meeting with the judges, which would be complicated, because there would be ten of us on camera— six contestants, three judges, and Alec, who'd be acting as the host or emcee.

"And then Alec will give you the mini-assignment." Tweedledee beamed.

"Mini-assignment?" Victor growled. "I thought we were making swords."

"Weapons," Tweedledee said. "Weapons, generally. You'll be spending most of this week making your first sword, but tomorrow you'll be working on a small weapon."

"You mean a knife," Duncan said.

"Or some other small weapon," Tweedledee said.

"A knife." Duncan sounded dismissive. "What else is small? A Barbie broadsword, maybe?"

Brody found this hilarious.

"Could be a dagger," Andy said. "A dirk."

"A poniard," Victor put in. "A stiletto."

"An anlace," John suggested. "A skean."

"Or a bayonet," I added to general approval.

"A small weapon." Tweedledee seemed to find this conversational thread unnerving.

"So does this mini-competition count for anything?" Duncan asked.

"It's kind of a warm-up thing," Tweedledee explained. "So you can get used to working with the cameras. It only lasts one day—the rest of the week, you'll be working on your swords."

Muted grumbling from Duncan and Brody.

"Oh, and did I forget to mention that whoever wins the mini-competition has immunity at the end of this episode?" Tweedledee said. "Meaning even if he makes the worst sword, he won't be eliminated. He or she," he added, bowing in my direction.

"That's good," Andy said.

"I don't plan on needing any damned immunity," Duncan said.

"So you'll be working on your knives tomorrow," Tweedledee said. "Er . . . your small weapons. Sometime later in the week we'll be pulling each of you out for an hour or so to do your individual interviews, but most of tomorrow you'll just be working at your anvils, so Sam can get a lot of nice action shots."

Sam sighed as if he found the mere thought of filming half a dozen blacksmiths at work unutterably depressing. I made a mental note to look him up online. I was getting the distinct impression that directing *Blades of Glory* wasn't his dream assignment. Was he slumming between more palatable jobs? Or had he spent most of his directorial career in what I suspected he thought of as the reality TV ghetto?

Tweedledee then went over some of the rules. No cursing on camera. No smoking in the tent. And no, that rule came from their insurance company, so there was no chance they'd relax it. No interfering with other contestants' tools or materials. And absolutely no talking about anything that went on to anyone outside the production team.

"We don't want the identity of the winner to leak out prematurely," Tweedledee explained. "So what happens in the tent stays in the tent. Got it? And, naturally, those of you who get eliminated will be staying around until we finish filming."

"I thought we were getting to go home for Christmas," Andy objected. "My parents—"

"Yes," Tweedledee said. "Once we've finished filming this first episode, you all get a break—so assuming we're able to finish on schedule, you'll all be going home for Christmas."

"And keeping your mouths shut," Tweedledum added.

"Right," Tweedledee said. "And then coming back for the several weeks it will take us to film the remaining episodes. Any questions?"

They both looked around. I got the distinct impression they were eager to leave. And relieved when we all either shook our heads or just remained silent.

"Great!" Tweedledee exclaimed. "Get a good night's rest, and we'll see you tomorrow."

They scurried out.

No one spoke for a few long seconds. Then Sam stood, drained his mug, set it down on the nearest table, and strode out without a word.

"Real sociable gent," Victor observed.

"He probably doesn't want to get too involved with us," Andy suggested. "Needs to keep his impartiality."

"And doesn't want to get too attached to people who might be going home all too soon," John observed.

"Speak for yourself," Brody said.

"Early start tomorrow," Duncan said, not looking at anyone in particular. He stood up and slung a black leather jacket over his shoulder with what struck me as a well-practiced air of casual unconcern. Then he glanced down at Brody before strolling toward the door.

"Yeah, time to get some shut-eye." Brody sprang up and followed Duncan out of the library.

"Although I doubt we'll be seeing eye to eye about many things, Duncan has a point there," I said. "I need to find where Ragnar has put me and get settled in."

"Let us know if you need anything," Andy said. "I mean—"

Just then we heard voices from the hall.

"Bunch of losers," Brody said. "Am I right?"

Chapter 4

"Losers?" Victor muttered.

I turned to see that Duncan and Brody had left the library door open.

"Yeah, it's totally bogus," Duncan was saying out in the hall. "Whoever mugged Cates didn't do us any favors."

"Totally," Brody said. "He may have been a little . . . um . . . my dad would have called him light in the loafers. But at least he looked the part."

"Just barely. And now we're stuck with this . . . chick."

Evidently, Duncan was an equal-opportunity bigot.

"That might not be too bad." Brody's voice suggested that he was leering as he spoke. "At least she's something of a looker, ya know?"

"Whatever floats your boat," Duncan said. "Not my type. Producers seem happy. I wonder if they had anything to do with the mugging."

"I can't imagine them doing it," Brody said. "I mean, Faulk's a big guy, and I don't see either of them getting the drop on him or anything. Besides, I heard they were off having dinner with the director guy when it happened."

"I don't mean they did it themselves." Duncan was clearly impatient with what he probably saw as Brody's cluelessness. "They'd have it done. They'd know people. And it makes sense it was them. They waited until the last possible moment, when there was no way Alec could find another real bladesmith, and stuck us with this bitch. Makes me sick the way she's pretending she doesn't want to compete when she's obviously dying to."

"Well, it's not like she's gonna win, is it?" Brody said. "We'll see to that."

"Damn right."

Then the library door slammed closed, the way it some-times did when a draft came through, cutting off their voices. I glanced around. The remaining three blacksmiths were still there. Andy's mouth was hanging open in shock. John was frowning slightly. Victor was, as usual, inscrutable.

"They probably don't realize how well their voices carry," Andy said.

"And I'm sure they don't really care," I said. "In fact, I bet they were doing it on purpose, to undermine our morale. Could be part of their strategy for winning the contest."

"I can believe that," Victor said. "Duncan has already made it pretty clear he's not happy about having me and Andy around. Brody's more of a talk-behind-your-back kind of fool. He'd be embarrassed if we called him on it." He grinned broadly, as if looking forward to the fun of calling Brody on his words.

"Interesting," John said. "I don't think their theory is all that plausible."

"You don't think the producers would sic someone on Faulk to clear the way for a contestant they want more?" It sounded paranoid to me, but I'd only just met the Tweedles.

"I don't think they'd hesitate if that was the only thing they could do to get their way," John replied. "But they don't have to. Duncan should reread his contract. They can fire any of us at any time. Or more likely, keep us under contract but just not use us in the show."

"But firing one of us wouldn't convince Meg to fill in," Andy said.

"It would if they lied and said he quit," John said. "Or ordered him to fake an injury."

"Wow," Andy said. "You really don't like the producers, do you?"

"I can take them or leave them," John said. "But I don't trust them, and they have all the power."

"All that starts to change at eight A.M. tomorrow." Victor stood up and stretched. "Once the filming starts, they're kind of stuck with us for the duration. And the more film they shoot, the less eager they'll be to waste it all by canning one of us."

"I think they use videotape these days, rather than film," Andy said.

"Whatever." Victor's voice was amiable. "I don't pretend to know anything about the TV business. I just know weapons. I'm going to go get my beauty sleep."

He ambled out of the library.

"I should go, too," Andy said. "I have enough trouble getting to sleep in ordinary times. Don't let those two throw you, Meg. Some of us are happy to have you. Not that we're glad to see Faulk go, of course. Faulk's great."

"If only our mugger had chosen Duncan instead of Faulk," John said. "Then we could have Meg and Faulk."

"Yeah!" Andy clearly liked that idea. "Too bad. Anyway— night."

He hurried out.

"I should follow his example," I said. "And you should, too. Start the contest in good shape."

"For what it's worth." John glanced at his mug, which still held an inch and a half of Ragnar's craft beer. I gathered he was planning to stay put and finish it. "I have no illusions. I'm only here 'cause they needed a sixth contestant. I might be the first out the door. I've only been bladesmithing for three years or so. I can't hold a candle to some of these guys."

"Odds are we'll be duking it out for last place, then," I said. "I'm not a seasoned bladesmith, either. I'm not even blacksmithing full-time these days."

"Faulk seems to have confidence in you."

"Bias," I said. "After all, he taught me. Would he want to admit that one of his pupils wasn't up to competing in this circus?"

He looked thoughtful for a few seconds before answering.

"From what I've seen of Faulk, he wouldn't do that," he said finally. "He'd be just as tough on you as on anyone else. Maybe tougher. 'Cause his rep's on the line, too. He wouldn't build you up if he didn't believe in you. So I'm not counting you out."

"We'll see tomorrow," I said. "You've had more chances than I have to assess your fellow contestants. How do you see this playing out?"

"You're asking who I think will win?"

I nodded.

"Well, before Faulk got eliminated, I was betting on a big showdown between him and Duncan. A showdown I was hoping Faulk would win."

"Duncan's good, then."

"Yes." He winced as he said it. "I know he comes across like a braggart, but he really is almost as good as he thinks he is. Depressing, considering that he's also such a thoroughly miserable human being."

I nodded and bit back the harsh words I was tempted to say about Duncan. There might not be cameras and microphones here in Ragnar's library, but there would be plenty of them around tomorrow. A good idea to practice holding my tongue.

"And with Faulk out?" I asked instead. "Who do you see in the final round now?"

He studied me for a few moments.

"Probably Duncan and Victor," he said. "Though I wouldn't put money on it. Brody—from what I've seen, he's not amazing, but he's no amateur. And Andy could surprise us. He's new at this—almost as new as I am—but he's good. And very talented. If he can keep his head and gets a few breaks, Andy could pull it off. And then there's you. Our dark horse."

"I wouldn't put money on me," I said.

"Yeah, but maybe you've got that impostor thing going on," he said. "A lot of women do, especially if they're in jobs people think are mainly for men."

"You sure you don't have a bit of it yourself?" I asked. "You don't see yourself as having a chance?"

"A chance?" He chuckled. "Yeah. An outside one, but a chance. You know the one thing I've got going for me?"

I shook my head.

"Temperament. I don't let things bother me. I just keep my head down and do the job."

I nodded. It was how I planned to get through the contest myself.

"Which is the same thing I thought would probably give Faulk an edge," John went on. "Faulk strikes me as someone who doesn't rattle easily. Duncan, Brody, Andy, even Victor—they could lose it on temperament. Some silly accident happens, someone makes a negative comment—it could throw them. They'd get mad or anxious or just lose focus at the wrong moment and completely blow it."

He had a good point. I'd learned long ago that however satisfactory it might be to pick up my biggest hammer and punish a piece of hot iron when I was angry, I should stick to rough, uncomplicated projects until I cooled down. Trying to do anything complex or difficult at times like that was guaranteed to backfire.

And tomorrow wouldn't be ordinary blacksmithing—not even demonstration blacksmithing in front of an audience, which I was sure we'd all done at least a time or two at state fairs and craft shows. Tomorrow would be intense and high pressure, and temperament would definitely be a factor.

Which meant it would probably be a mistake to count out John as a competitor. If I were trying to win, I'd be well served to keep that in mind.

"Duncan's floated the theory that you're not a blacksmith at all," John said, breaking the thoughtful silence we'd both fallen into. "Just a ringer brought in to please the woke crowd, as he put it. He says we should keep an eye on you. Make sure you're doing your own ironwork."

"I wouldn't put it past the producers to slip in a ringer," I said. "Guess you'll have to wait till tomorrow to find out."

"Oh, I already know you're not a ringer," he said. "You've got blacksmith's hands."

He held up his right hand and slowly turned it to show both back and front. I saw what he meant and held up my hand beside his. His was bigger and hairier, but both of us had the same telltale scars and calluses.

He chuckled as he pulled his hand away again and wrapped it around his beer mug.

"Tomorrow should be interesting," he said.

"And I'm going to get some sleep so I'm ready for it." I turned to go, then thought of something and turned back. "This may sound stupid, but do you know the producers' names?"

"The ones who briefed us just now?" He shook his head slightly. "I think they're Pierre and B. J. But I wouldn't put money on that, either, and damned if I know which is which."

"Yeah," I said. "I've taken to thinking of them as Tweedledee and Tweedledum."

"Thing One and Thing Two," he said, with a chuckle. "If winning requires being able to tell those two apart, we're both doomed."

With that, we wished each other a good night. I left him sipping the last of his beer and headed up the grand black marble staircase to the second floor. Time to join Michael and the boys.

Ragnar had put my family in the Van Helsing Suite, which was the first door you came to if you turned right at the top of the stairs. It included a small sitting room, an oversized bathroom, and two bedrooms. The boys were in their room, bouncing on the spiderweb-patterned velvet spreads that covered the two twin beds.

"Mom! You're going to be a TV star!" Josh exclaimed.

"Go, Mom!" Jamie echoed. "You're a shoo-in."

"I appreciate the vote of confidence," I said, "but I'm not going to be at my best if I don't get a good night's sleep. Can we plan to settle down soon?"

"Right!"

"No problem!"

They began creeping around, trying their best not to make any noise, and being about as successful as such attempts usually were. But at least they'd stopped bouncing on the beds. I could probably fall asleep in spite of whatever ordinary noises they made.

In the other bedroom, Michael was stretched out on the black velvet spread that covered the black-canopied, king-size bed. He held a sheaf of papers and a red pen.

"Correcting papers?" I said.

"Reviewing your contract." He looked over his reading glasses at me. "There are only a few bad clauses, and I've pretty much browbeat the Dynamic Duo into crossing them out."

"If you mean the gentlemen I've been calling Tweedledee and Tweedledum, their names are B. J. and Pierre." I pulled out my phone and checked the various texts I'd received while at the hospital. Yes, as I expected, the producers had texted me. "B. J. Zakaryan and Pierre Duval. But I probably won't remember that tomorrow, and don't ask me which is which."

"Good to know." He sat up and rolled off the bed. "And you should get some sleep, so you look fresh for the cameras. Rose Noire's coming by in the morning to do your hair."

"Do my hair? Can't I just tie it back, the way I usually do when I work?"

"She'll put it in a French braid, which will be just as efficient and much more decorative. I'll take this out to the sitting room, so I won't keep you up if I have to argue some more with B. J. and Pierre."

He gave me a quick kiss and exited. I opened up the suitcase he'd brought for me and pulled out my toothbrush and my pajamas. Although Ragnar's castle was well heated, I was still glad he'd packed flannel pajamas instead of a nightgown—the Christmas pajamas, red with reindeer prancing all over them. I changed into them, ducked into the bathroom to brush my teeth, and crawled into bed a few minutes later.

I had just settled in comfortably when I heard a scratching noise on the door.

"Hey, Mom," Josh called. "The dogs want to sleep with you. Is that okay?"

Of course they'd bring the dogs. And unlike Michael and the boys, the dogs probably wanted to turn in early.

"As long as they're quiet," I said.

The door opened. Josh and Jamie tiptoed in. Josh was carrying Spike, aka the Small Evil One, our nine-and-a-half-pound Tasmanian Devil in canine guise. Jamie had a Pomeranian—I couldn't tell which. All seven puppies from a rescued litter had been adopted by friends or relatives, and the ones that didn't live with us often stayed with us while their humans worked.

Josh set a pillow on the foot of the bed and ceremoniously deposited Spike there.

"Stay," he said.

Spike glanced around like a king surveying his domain and curled up on the pillow. The boys had actually managed to get him into a red-and-green doggie Christmas sweater.

Jamie set the Pomeranian down on the bed.

"Good girl," he said as she scampered over, wormed her way under the covers, and curled up next to me.

The bed shook as Tinkerbell, my brother Rob's Irish Wolfhound, leaped up. She curled up over and around my feet. Better than an electric blanket.

The boys tiptoed out. I surveyed the bed. It was king-size. There was plenty of room for Michael. There would have been room for half a dozen more people, or possibly another wolf-hound.

I fell asleep to the comforting sounds of Michael and the boys talking quietly in the sitting room and the soft snoring of the dogs.

Chapter 5

"Rose Noire is here!"

I opened my eyes and blinked blearily up at Josh and Jamie.

"That's nice," I said. "Tell her to go away and come back later."

No, I am not a morning person.

"Just sit up so I can do your hair," Rose Noire said. "They want you on the set in half an hour."

On the set? My morning mind hadn't kicked in yet, so it took me a few seconds to remember why they were waking me up so very early.

The blacksmithing contest. *Blades of Glory.* I was so not ready for this.

I sat up and blinked. I was in unfamiliar surroundings—in a tent. No, a king-size bed furnished with red satin sheets and a black velvet bedspread and surrounded with black velvet curtains. Unfortunately, my cousin had pulled back the curtains, allowing a flood of bright gray winter light into my sleep-gummed eyes.

"Turn around."

I liked that idea, since turning around let me put my back to the horrible daylight. I remained upright but closed my eyes while Rose Noire did things to my hair. She was humming cheerfully, but at least she didn't try to start a conversation with me. I pondered, not for the first time, how I could possibly share DNA with someone who was such a complete morning person.

"I've got your clothes." Michael handed them over in a neat pile. "And since you're probably not ready for breakfast yet, the boys will bring you something over in the tent in an hour or two. Here."

I heard the familiar pop of someone opening a can of soda. Michael lifted my hand and closed it around the cold metal cylinder.

"Caffeine," he said. "Sip it; you'll feel better."

I sipped and savored the familiar taste, the bite of the caffeine cutting through the sweetness of the cola. Yes, even in winter, I like my caffeine cold and bubbly.

"There! Perfect!" Rose Noire exclaimed. "Now get dressed."

I slipped into the bathroom to make what limited beauty preparations I could cope with while still half asleep—some mouthwash and a quick face scrub. Rose Noire had done a good job on my hair. I looked . . . well, elegant and sophisticated were probably stretching it. Still. I looked a lot more civilized and pulled together than I felt.

When I emerged from the bathroom, Michael and Rose Noire nodded their approval, and the boys announced that they'd be taking me down to breakfast. They were probably afraid I'd find a corner to curl up in and go back to sleep unless they kept watch over me. So I headed downstairs, following Jamie and trailed by Josh.

A buffet breakfast was set up in what Ragnar called the Great Hall, and a few people were sitting around with plates on their laps. It was exactly the kind of over-the-top buffet I'd expect from Ragnar—he had any number of those metal pans with the little burners under them, filled with bacon, sausage, ham, Canadian bacon, eggs, hash browns, oatmeal, French toast, and waffles. Several dozen assorted little boxes of various kinds of cereal. A fruit bar with strawberries, raspberries, blackberries, blueberries, cantaloupe, honeydew, pineapple, apples, peaches, kiwis, kumquats, persimmons, grapes, and mangoes. Four different kinds of toast. A dozen different jams and jellies. A dozen yogurt flavors. A wide assortment of freshly baked pastries.

Okay, I wasn't keen on competing in *Blades of Glory*, but I could get used to staying at Ragnar's and being fed by Alice, his fabulous cook. I could tell in an hour or so, when my stomach was more awake, I was going to enjoy my breakfast.

The boys, distracted by the spread, abandoned me and began heaping plates for themselves. I drifted toward the French doors that led out onto the terrace, then hesitated. Should I take the time to fill a plate?

"Morning."

Caroline Willner was sitting on a black velvet sofa, nibbling a slice of bacon.

"Morning," I said. "What are you doing here in what I would call the middle of the night?"

"I've been up for hours." Surely she was exaggerating. "I'm meeting your mother in a few minutes. We're going to decorate the castle for Christmas."

"It still amazes me that Ragnar's okay with that."

"He's delighted to have us do it," she said. "He's been so busy with this TV show of yours that he hasn't had a chance to do more than set up that tree." She pointed to the far corner of the room where a huge Christmas tree stood. It was such a dark green—nearly black—that I wondered if that was the natural color or if Ragnar'd had it spray-painted to better suit his color scheme. So far the only decorations on it were hundreds of tiny twinkling lights.

"That should be very nice when it's finished," Caroline said, nodding at the tree. "But the place needs a little more something, don't you think?"

I nodded. Of course, if Mother was involved, the place would be getting a lot more something. Minimalism wasn't a concept Mother understood.

"He knows what you're planning, right?" I said. "I mean—"

"Don't worry," she said. "We know his color scheme. Everything will be red, gold, silver, or black. He's approved the plans."

"All good, then." I blew out a breath. "Sorry to interrogate you, but at the moment Ragnar's a little protective about his decor. Downright touchy."

"Why?"

"Did I already mention that the original idea was to film *Blades of Glory* here in the castle?" I explained. "Using the Great Hall and the dining hall and that huge blacksmithing shop Ragnar had installed for me and Faulk."

"What happened?"

"At first the producers loved how the castle looked," I said. "But then the lighting designer said everything was too dark and wanted Ragnar to paint all the walls white, and the camera crew wanted him to knock out a few walls to give them more room to maneuver, and after a couple more requests like that, even Ragnar lost it. So he rented a tent and told them to film there."

I glanced around to see where the boys were. I spotted them sitting cross-legged by the hearth, devouring vast platefuls from the buffet.

"I should go," I said. "I'm already going to be late." I put on my coat and a knitted hat, made sure my heavy gloves were in my pocket, grabbed a bear claw pastry for the road, and stepped through one of the French doors onto the back terrace. A stairway leading from the terrace down to the pasture level would be the fastest way to get to the production tent.

The day was bright but overcast, and the sky was that sullen, luminous gray that suggested precipitation might be in our future. And cold as it was, anything that fell would be either snow or sleet. I hoped the space heaters in the production tent were good.

Still, the view was nice. Fog shrouded the pastures, beginning to break up on bits of high ground but still clinging thickly to the low places. Ragnar's black cows were either grazing or slowly ambling toward their favorite winter cud-chewing spots. Farther off, in another pasture, I could see the black sheep and goats. The two black swans were gliding slowly and elegantly across the pond, as if they knew a camera crew was filming them from the shore.

The temptation to zone out and gaze at the landscape was almost insurmountable.

Just then a crow landed on the stone balustrade that surrounded the terrace and stared at me. Or maybe at my bear claw.

"Were you the one who dive-bombed Jasmyn yesterday?" I asked him.

The crow cocked his head as if asking a question of his own and cawed softly.

"Yeah, it could have been you." I pulled off a small chunk of the bear claw and tossed it onto the balustrade beside him. He cawed again, then began pecking and nibbling at it. I pulled out my phone and got a few nice close-ups of him. Then I noticed the time on my phone screen.

"I was due at the tent five minutes ago," I said. "Give my regards to the rest of the murder."

I crossed the terrace and was about to take the stone stairway heading down to ground level when a voice startled me.

"Dammit, how soon can you get it here?"

I paused and looked around. I didn't see anyone, and I didn't think whoever said the words was talking to me. But something about the voice caught my interest. It was a stage whisper, half furtive, half anxious. And I'd be the first to admit I'm nosy. I stood, one foot still raised to take the first step down, and listened.

"Get it here as soon as you can, then. . . . No, I'm stuck here all day. Let me know when you get there and if I can't come out, I'll send someone else. . . . Yes, same as last time."

I waited a few more seconds, then spotted Brody scurrying

away from the house and back toward the tent. Evidently, he'd been standing beside the stone stairs to hold his telephone conversation, not realizing that anyone coming down the outside stairs would overhear him.

Just what was he so eager to have delivered here to Ragnar's house? Nothing nefarious or illegal, I hoped.

I'd worry about it later.

"Mom!"

I turned to find Josh and Jamie standing in the doorway to the house. Josh was holding a covered plate.

"You can't skip breakfast," he said as he handed it to me.

"And juice." Jamie gave me two thermoses. "Cranberry and orange. You can take your pick."

"Actually, you should drink them both," Josh informed me.

"Thank you," I said. "Now go inside where it's warm."

They nodded and disappeared. I set out again for the production tent.

As I approached the tent, I noticed that half a dozen crows were perched atop it, keenly watching as various people approached the entrance flap. I couldn't help imagining that the crow who'd dive-bombed Jasmyn last night had gone home and told all his friends what fun he'd had. There was something mischievous and expectant about them.

I kept my eye on them as I entered the tent.

Inside, things were humming. And chaotic. Michael, with all his experience on TV and movie sets, could probably have made sense of it all. I just plodded through, sipping my soda, nibbling my bear claw, trying to avoid being run into as I made my way to my workstation.

Faulk's workstation. That finally jarred me out of my customary morning stupor. As I set my plate on the worktable and stowed my wraps in the locker, I reminded myself that I had a mission. Not the same mission as the rest of the people swarming through the tent. The crew members were intent on getting today's filming done. The contestants were out to win the competition.

I needed to figure out who had attacked Faulk. And why. And then make sure Chief Burke had enough evidence to put him away for . . . whatever the penalty was for breaking someone's arm with a baseball bat. I had no idea how much that would be, but I hoped it was a good long time.

Vern would know. And Vern would be here today, helping out. I glanced around. Sure enough, he was nearby, appearing to watch the chaos around him with placid unconcern, but ready to step in when something needed doing—and almost certainly taking in every detail.

He noticed me noticing him and strolled over to wish me a good morning.

"You need anything?" he asked.

"I'm good," I said. "The boys fixed me breakfast. Eventually I'll need more caffeine, but I'll worry about that later."

"Your boys already took care of that," he said. "Couple of sodas stashed in your locker. And I'm supposed to tell them when the supply runs low so they can bring you more. Dig into that breakfast."

Good idea. As I nibbled a slice of bacon, I glanced around and dropped my voice.

"Did Horace find any evidence last night?" I asked.

"Found where it happened," he said, matching my low tone. "And retrieved a baseball bat hidden in some bushes. Probably the weapon. Keep your fingers crossed that whoever did it wasn't wearing gloves and we get some touch DNA, because so far nothing we've found helps us finger the culprit."

"Yeah. Please tell me if you catch him, he'll rot in jail."

"Up to the county attorney, but it'd probably be malicious wounding. Class three felony. Five to twenty years."

"Good." And then a thought hit me. Clearly, the caffeine was working. "What if it was a hate crime?"

"Penalty'd be even more serious," he said. "We were just assuming someone wanted Faulk out because he was going to be tough to beat. You think they had other reasons?"

"It's possible that some of the other contestants aren't thrilled to have a gay blacksmith on the show." I repeated the gist of the conversation I'd overheard last night between Brody and Duncan.

"That's . . . despicable," he said. "Brody and Duncan . . . that would be Blondie and the Hulk, right?"

I smiled and nodded.

"Bet they aren't too fond of some of the other contestants, either," Vern said. "Victor and Andy and you."

"That's what I was thinking. John's probably the only one they actually like, though I suspect it isn't mutual."

We both glanced around. The workstations were laid out in two rows of three. I was in the middle of row one, with John on one side of me and Victor on the other. Andy was across the center aisle, flanked by Brody and Duncan.

I liked the layout. I couldn't exactly avoid interacting with Brody and Duncan, but at least I'd be as far from them as possible while working.

"I'll let the chief know about that conversation. Let me know if you pick up on anything." He nodded and crossed the aisle to where Andy seemed to be having trouble with the power strip into which all of his electrical equipment was plugged.

"Everyone to the banquet hall! Take your places in the banquet hall!"

It was Jasmyn. Today she was wearing another short-skirted suit, this one in deep maroon. And she had donned a broad-brimmed black felt hat with a maroon scarf tied around it, in a not-entirely-successful attempt to make it look like a natural part of her outfit. In spite of the hat, she kept looking nervously up toward the top of the tent. And clutching her clipboard to her chest as if to protect its contents.

Score one for the crows.

Chapter 6

I joined my fellow contestants in the banquet hall area, and we all took seats along the sides of the oak trestle table. And then got up and switched our seats around a half-dozen times under Sam's direction, until he was satisfied with our placement. He wanted the biggest contestants, Duncan and Victor, farthest from the judges' table—and the camera—so those of us who were shorter could be seen.

This put John and me in front. I suspected he wasn't any happier about the arrangement than I was.

"Okay, contestants." Jasmyn stood at the head of the table and beamed at us. "This should be easy. Alec's going to introduce the three judges. You just sit there and sip your coffee and applaud when each judge comes out. We'll probably be filming this bit a couple of times, to get a lot of good reaction shots from you. Got it?"

We all nodded.

She hurried away, and Sam came to take her place. He stared at us lugubriously, as if he'd never filmed a less prepossessing group of subjects. He sighed, and was about to turn away when—

"Stop! You there—the . . . um . . . lady blacksmith. Why are you drinking a Diet Coke? Get her a coffee."

After a long, awkward pause, Jasmyn scurried out holding a cup of coffee. She tried to hand it to me while reaching for my soda can. Was there some kind of rule against showing brand names on the show?

"No thanks," I said, fending off the coffee cup with my elbow while jerking the can out of her reach. "I don't drink coffee."

"But this is a morning meeting," Sam said. "You can't be drinking a Diet Coke. People don't drink soft drinks in the morning."

"This people does," I said. "But there's an easy fix."

I held out my hand for the cup. Jasmyn smiled and surrendered it. I poured out the coffee onto the dirt-and-straw floor of the tent—taking care to stay clear, though just barely, of Jasmyn's elegant open-toed maroon suede shoes. I pulled a napkin out of my pocket, shook a few bear claw crumbs off of it, wiped the cup clean, and poured my soda into it. I handed the empty can to Jasmyn and looked up at Sam.

"Okay now?"

He looked at me, frowning, for a few seconds. If he was trying to play that Hollywood cliché of the powerful director, dictatorial tyrant of the set, striking fear into the hearts of his cast and crew . . . he didn't have the chops for it.

Someone behind me snickered. Brody, probably.

"Good enough," Sam said. "Okay. We're about to start rolling."

"What do you want us to do?" Duncan asked.

"Keep your traps shut and look like you're paying attention. Got it?"

We all nodded.

"Okay. Action!"

We all settled back, holding our mugs and looking with unnatural eagerness toward the empty table where the judges would sit. After a little bit of stage-whispered coaching, Alec strode in from one side and turned to face us, smiling, but looking a bit nervous.

"Welcome, combatants," he said. "I mean contestants." And then, realizing he'd mangled his line, he dropped an F-bomb.

"Cut!" Sam shouted.

Evidently, this was Alec's first appearance on camera. And

unfortunately, he wasn't a natural. He was visibly nervous and kept flubbing his lines. After about half an hour of doing take after take of his three-sentence introduction, Sam finally called a halt.

"I think we've got enough, thank you," he said.

"He hasn't managed to get through the whole thing right," one of the Tweedles protested. "Not even once."

"We'll put it together in the editing room," Sam said. "Intercut it with the reaction shots. It'll have to do. We need to move on."

Then we filmed the introduction of the judges. A short, balding, barrel-chested man with the arms—and hands—of a veteran blacksmith. A white-haired older man with a twinkle in his eye and an elaborate handlebar mustache. And Marco d'Antonio, elegantly dressed in all black, moving with the sinuous grace of a dancer. Not hard to guess that he was a swordsman and martial artist rather than a blacksmith—he looked like a whippet among bulldogs.

I noticed Marco and Duncan eyeing each other with mild distaste. I suspected they both wanted to be the mysterious man in black and resented encountering a wardrobe clone.

Alec repeatedly mangled the judges' names. A good thing I already knew Marco's name. I'd work later on figuring out which versions were the right ones for the other two. Or maybe I wouldn't need to. Our instructions were to steer clear of the judges, to avoid even the appearance of impropriety.

After a whispered conference between Sam, Alec, Marco, and the two producers, we proceeded with the next bit of filming—issuing instructions to the competitors. Which I knew Alec was supposed to do, so I braced myself for another long wait while he struggled through his lines.

But it was Marco who stepped forward to give us our instructions. Which was probably a good thing—we might actually finish filming this scene before Easter. But I felt bad for Alec, who was relegated to sitting in a chair behind the judges' table, look-ing on as Marco did his lines.

And did a very fine job of them.

"We'll be judging you on completion, of course," Marco said, with a smile that suggested that as a judge he had no intention of being a pushover. "If you've got an excellent blade but ran out of time to make a hilt for it . . . you'll lose points. And historical accuracy. If we tell you to make a Malay kris and you hand over a medieval broadsword . . . you'll lose points. Aesthetics counts. We probably won't be giving a whole lot of points for making something pretty, but if your final product is rough and ugly . . . you'll lose points."

Was it just my imagination that he glanced at me while saying "making something pretty"?

"But the two final and most important tests—strength and sharpness!" He strode dramatically over to a side area where two techies had rolled in a couple of props during the last break. One prop was a battered but sturdy-looking steel trash barrel. The other was rather like a miniature gallows, but instead of a hangman's noose, it supported two lengths of heavy manila rope, at least an inch and a half in diameter.

"Your blade must be sharp enough to cut this rope," Marco announced. "If it fails to cut cleanly . . . you'll lose points. And finally, your blade must be sharp and strong enough to pierce this steel barrel. If it fails to penetrate—or breaks . . . you'll lose points."

Alec was doing a brave job of smiling as if he appreciated Marco's dramatic performance. I felt bad for him. The whole show was his brainchild and now someone else was taking the spotlight.

"For your first assignment, you will be making . . . a knife!" With a flourish, Marco whipped out a sleek, elegant weapon, holding it in his right hand and drawing it in a line in the air above his left arm in a curiously menacing gesture. Its slightly curved blade of darkened steel flowed naturally into a graceful, understated handle of the same material. "The style of the knife and the hilt is up to you. But the knife must be at least six inches long, and no longer than eight inches. And you must use the steel we provide—it's a good, high-carbon steel. I think you'll like it."

I frowned. Was that it? I wanted to know the exact composition of the steel. All steel was an alloy of iron and carbon, but the amount and kind of carbon made a huge difference in how the metal performed. For that matter, so did the trace elements that either occurred naturally or were added in the manufacturing. Chromium, for example, increased resistance to corrosion. Important in a knife or sword intended for use in wet conditions, like duck hunting or fighting orcs in the Dead Marshes. But the judges wouldn't be testing how rust-proof our knives were. And chromium reduced hardness, which would be a bad thing in our contest. And while high-carbon steel was ideal for forging strong blades, too much carbon would decrease the blade's ability to resist cracks and chips when the judges tried using it to poke holes in a steel barrel. The more we knew about the metal they gave us, the better our odds of avoiding such problems.

I looked around to see if anyone else was troubled by how little they were telling us about the steel. Everyone else looked intent. None of them looked worried. Maybe they'd already been told more about the steel. Or already knew we'd be working with limited information and had grown accustomed to the idea.

I decided to ask for more information—but not until the cameras were off.

Marco wrapped up with a rather eloquent few sentences about how we were carrying on the tradition of bladesmiths throughout the centuries and around the world. Alec, poor thing, could never have pulled it off. At the end of his speech, Marco raised a sword—a thin, elegant rapier—and saluted us with it, intoning "To *Blades of Glory*." He held the pose for a few seconds.

"Cut!" Sam yelled.

Marco relaxed, putting his left hand on his hip and pointing the sword at the ground.

"They should be cheering," one of the Tweedles said. "Why aren't they cheering?"

"Because you didn't tell us you wanted cheering," Victor said. "I seem to recall being told to keep my trap shut."

"We can edit in the cheering later," Sam said.

"Fine," the Tweedle said. "But let's film it now."

So Marco did his final few lines several more times, until Sam and the Tweedles were satisfied with the fervor of our reaction. I hoped we wouldn't be judged on the caliber of our cheering, since Duncan and Brody would have been the clear winners. In addition to cheering, Brody added a few noisy war whoops, and both of them pounded their mugs noisily on the table. Of course, both of them had brought along heavy pewter mugs that could handle the pounding. I wasn't going to risk breaking my china mug—a Christmas present from the boys that read THAT'S WHAT I DO—I HIT METAL AND I KNOW THINGS.

It only then occurred to me that Jasmyn had brought me coffee in my own mug. A mug that had been tucked away in my locker. I wasn't sure I liked the idea of just anyone rummaging through my things.

"Okay, it's a wrap," Sam said. "Fifteen-minute break. Blacksmiths, when that's over, we need you to start doing things at your forges."

People scattered. Alec was still sitting at one end of the judges' table, looking forlorn. The judges were chuckling over something at the other end.

I approached Alec.

"I have a practical question," I said. "And apologies if I'm supposed to know this already, but I'm still catching up."

"Ask away." Being asked a question visibly improved Alec's mood.

"High-carbon steel," I said. "Nice to know that much, but do we get any other data on the composition of the steel we'll be using? Or is figuring that out part of the challenge?"

"Very good." Alec grinned as if pleased with me.

"Do we get to give her points for that?" the white-mustachioed judge asked. "Because she's the first one to ask."

"Only one to ask," Marco corrected. "Give her the spec sheet."

Alec fished something out from under the table and handed it to me. A manufacturer's specification sheet for the steel. Not only did it give additional bits of information that could be useful, I also recognized the manufacturer's name and product number. I'd used this particular steel before, plenty of times.

"Thanks," I said.

"Do what you will with it," Marco intoned.

Initially, that struck me as an odd thing to say—until I realized that he was leaving it up to me whether or not to tell my fellow contestants that the spec sheet was available.

Or maybe just saying something dramatic for the camera. Because yes, one of the cameras was still running.

"Good," Sam said. "We can use that."

A useful reminder that nothing I did would be very private for the next few days.

I headed back for my workstation, still pondering whether or not to share the spec sheet with the rest of the contestants. And while part of me protested that it would serve them right if I didn't share—after all, I was the one who thought to ask—I decided to share it with anyone who was interested. Because if I did win—or at least did well in the contest—I wanted it to be fair and square. Because of my abilities, not because I had some bit of information that the others didn't have.

So when I got back to my workstation, I set the spec sheet on top of my worktable and set the actual steel bar on it. Then I added my mug, since in a few minutes I'd be starting to use the bar. Though not until after I did justice to the breakfast the boys had packed for me. As I munched, I gave some thought to the best way to call the other contestants' attention to it. Should I just visit every workstation and show it to them? Or would that come across as bossy? Or—

Just then Andy wandered across the aisle to my workstation.

"This is gonna be great!" he said. "Do you think— What's this?"

"Specs on the iron we'll be using," I said.

"Are you sure? How did you get it?"

"I asked for it."

Andy looked at me as if I'd done something amazing.

"They'd probably give you one if you asked," I said. "Or you can just look at mine whenever you need to."

"Great!"

"And spread the word," I said. "A level playing field's better for the contest."

Within a few minutes, Victor and John had both dropped by my workstation to cast their eyes over the specs. Even Duncan and Brody eventually showed up. Duncan pretended to be scornful.

"That's nice for anyone who needs it," he said. "Me, I think the best way to figure out how to handle a piece of iron is to work with it. Of course, I've had a lot more experience than some of you."

"Yeah," Brody said. "We don't need no stinkin' cheat sheets!"

At this, they both laughed raucously and strolled away.

Chapter 7

"Jerks," Andy muttered.

"They can do what they like," Victor said. "I think I've had at least as much experience as either of them, and I find this useful."

"Who has the copies?" John said. "I might go get one for myself."

"I'm just going to keep a copy of it in my phone," Andy said.

Victor and John agreed that this was a good idea. So did I, actually. We all took pictures, which meant I could tuck it away, where it wouldn't be in danger of catching fire once we all started heating and hammering metal and maybe sending off sparks.

Although before I did, I noticed that Brody stopped by and made a big fuss over my mug. The mug that was sitting atop the spec sheet.

"This is a hoot," he chortled. "Where did you get it?"

"Christmas present from my kids," I said. "I could ask them where they got it."

"You have kids? Who knew?"

But he spent a good long time staring at the spec sheet, which got to be rather annoying since even when he wasn't trying to talk to me, I could hear his annoying persistent sniffle. I hoped it was just his reaction to being out in the below-freezing air, not a sign that he was coming down with a cold that we'd all end up catching. I was relieved when he finally took advantage of my back being turned to whip out his phone and take a picture of the spec sheet.

I could hear hammering to my right—Victor was getting off to a fast start. John was currently coping with one of the camera crews—I could hear him patiently explaining various objects in his workstation. Andy had turned on his forge and was arranging his tools.

Duncan and Brody seemed to be vying to catch the cameras' attention. They flourished their tools dramatically. They called out playful insults to each other up and down the line of workstations and even strolled to each other's forges a time or two to continue the banter. They also occasionally lobbed mild insults at the rest of us, in what I was sure they'd claim was a friendly manner if we called them on it. Victor answered back occasionally, and I was already starting to appreciate his skill at delivering a blunt, unambiguous, yet amusing put-down to some of Duncan and Brody's more annoying efforts.

John and I just ignored them. And I had a lot more to ignore than John, since Brody had taken to dropping by my workstation and trying to strike up a flirtatious conversation. After the third or fourth such interruption, I checked with Jasmyn to see when we'd be breaking for lunch and texted Michael an invitation for him and the boys to join me then. Of course, since Brody was the kind of clueless jerk who considered double entendres a form of flirtation, he might not be discouraged by the fact that I was married. Maybe I'd have to get the boys to sic Spike on him.

And at least I was across the aisle from Andy, not Brody. Andy was actually a joy to watch, though I couldn't spare much time to do it. He was visibly nervous but also elated. The whole time he was working—so far only arranging his tools and sketching ideas for his dagger design—he talked to himself under his breath, alternating between chiding and encouraging, which got him a few dirty looks from Duncan when he passed by. I could see that Andy needed to settle down a bit. He'd wear himself out at this rate. Or make a silly mistake from being too nervous.

Still, it cheered me up to see someone this excited about his blacksmithing work. And if a chance came along to help one of my fellow competitors—to lend them a tool, say, or offer a bit of advice—I'd happily do it for Andy. Or John or Victor, for that matter, though they were less likely to need it.

Duncan and Brody, now . . . call me petty, but they were on their own.

And they weren't my problem. Whatever any of the other five was doing wasn't my problem. I could feel free to tune them out—the other competitors, the sound and camera crews, the hovering producers, the ubiquitous Jasmyn—even Sam, unless he barked any more directorial orders at me.

To my surprise, I realized I was happy. I was getting to spend the whole day at my anvil and forge. I tried to remember the last time I'd managed that.

So I set to work. Some of the competitors were busily sketching out the daggers they planned to make, and waving the sketches around to make sure the cameras caught them. I already knew what I was going to make. A couple of years ago, when Michael had directed a production of *Macbeth,* he'd requested that I make "a seriously creepy dagger" as a prop for the production—something whose very appearance would make the audience shudder slightly when one of the Macbeths waved it around onstage. I'd actually made half a dozen creepy daggers, several of which appeared on-stage. One dagger, inspired by watching *Lord of the Rings* with Josh and Jamie for the millionth time, had a big red eye on the hilt. Another had a hilt that appeared to be made of a blackened human finger bone. A third had a snake winding its sinuous coils around the hilt and the cross guard. Michael's favorite was one inspired by a fungus we'd found in the woods, something called the Dead Man's Fingers, that actually looked like a withered human hand emerging from the soil.

And one had a hilt that looked like a bird of prey. I'd make something similar today. Some of the creepy daggers were a little awkward to grip, which would almost certainly cost me points in this contest. But I'd worked doggedly to make the bird's head hilt fit smoothly and naturally into the hand. And maybe I'd even change the bird a little bit. Not a hawk or a falcon, but a crow, in honor of the flock that seemed to be keeping watch over our project.

So I tuned out my surroundings and went to work. I reached to turn on my forge and took a moment to be grateful that it was a good one. The producers had planned to give us small, cheap tabletop forges that even an apprentice blacksmith would turn up their nose at. Predictably, Alec had caved on the issue, but Faulk had dug in his heels and won. I admired the resulting forge—a sleek two-foot-long black metal cylinder on sturdy legs. It had two propane burners, so you could use one for a short project and both for a long one, like a sword blade. It was open-ended, which meant if need be we could work on a blade too long to fit into it. Apart from being brand new, it was almost identical to the two forges Ragnar had installed in the castle blacksmith shop for Faulk and me to use. In fact, now that I thought about it, I wondered if Faulk had actually won his argument with the producers or if Ragnar had stepped in and contributed the forges.

I'd worry about that later. For now, I turned it on and set it to the temperature I wanted—2000 degrees Fahrenheit, a fairly high temperature that would be optimal for the first, rough stage of working the metal.

Farther down the way, Duncan was holding forth on this very subject, presumably for the cameras. When you used high heat and when it was counterproductive. The twin perils of not working your metal enough and overworking it.

"It's tricky, selecting the right temperature," he pronounced. "Too cold and the steel won't move when you try to work it— could even crack. Too high, and you burn it—it gets brittle and crumbles."

As he continued to lecture, I noticed that it was good information, all of it. If he could lose the condescending manner, he wouldn't make a bad teacher.

While my forge was heating, I laid out my tools and inspected the piece of steel they'd given me, to make sure I was happy with it. And then I mentally went over the steps ahead of me. First—

"So what will you be making!"

I glanced up to find that Alec was standing just outside my workstation. One of the camera crews stood behind him and a little to the side, busily filming me. I glanced over my shoulder and saw another crew behind me, filming Alec.

"A dagger," I said. "With a six- to eight-inch blade."

"Well, obviously," Alec said. "Let's see your sketch."

"Don't have one," I said. "It's all up here." I tapped my forehead.

Alec faltered for a second, then smiled broadly.

"Then it will be a big surprise!" He flung out his arms in a dramatic gesture, almost whacking one of the camera crew in the nose.

I smiled, nodded, and went back to testing and studying my assigned length of steel. Alec didn't lob any more questions. And since nothing I was doing looked particularly exciting on camera, after a few minutes he and the camera crews moved across the way to interrogate Andy. I stifled a sigh of relief.

While my forge was heating up, I decided to pay a visit to the crows. Over on the banquet hall table, several people had left paper plates behind with scraps of their breakfast. I dumped all the scraps onto a single paper plate and ducked out the nearest tent flap. To my amusement, lined up along the outside of the tent were a dozen battered metal trash barrels, brothers to the one Marco had displayed when laying out the rules. Evidently, it had occurred to someone that a single barrel could only take so much testing. I walked halfway down the line and set the plate on the lid of one of the barrels. Then I retreated to the tent flap and looked up into the sky.

Some of the watching crows had already taken off and were circling the feast.

I pulled out my phone and took a couple of shots for reference. Then I shoved my phone back into my pocket.

"Have fun, guys," I said, as I hurried back inside where it was warm. Well, at least warmer than outside, thanks to half a dozen space heaters scattered throughout the tent.

Back at my station I put on my gloves and used my tongs to pick up my length of steel. I turned to the forge. I checked, mechanically, to make sure it was ready.

And swore under my breath. It was at the wrong temperature. I'd set it for 2000 degrees Fahrenheit—I needed a pretty high heat for the first step. Now it was blazing away at a mere 1500 degrees.

I set down my tongs, pulled off my gloves, and twisted the dial back up to 2000 degrees. I could already hear at least three of the other contestants hammering. I reminded myself that this was a long process, and it didn't matter that much if they got a slight head start. At least, thanks to the good work habits Faulk had taught me, I hadn't gone ahead and started work at the wrong temperature. Trying to shape the blade at too low a temperature would, at best, take longer and tire me sooner. At worst, the blade might be flawed from the start.

I stared at the forge as its temperature gauge slowly rose. Was I sure I'd set the dial for 2000? Had I had a moment of absentmindedness when setting it? Or had my fingers accidentally jogged the dial after I set it?

I didn't think either of these had happened. I'd taken a couple of minutes to mentally calculate the best temperature for my first round of working the steel, then turned directly to start the forge. No way would I have set it for 1500. And as for accidentally jogging the dial . . . it would take quite a sharp tap to move the dial down a whole 500 degrees. I'd have noticed that.

Someone had tampered with my forge.

Chapter 8

I looked around. No one else was watching me—even the camera crews were focused on someone else. But someone had definitely tried to sabotage me.

Duncan and Brody were the most likely suspects, I decided. They were the ones who'd seemed least pleased at my addition to the contest. They were the only ones who had repeatedly left their workstations to walk past the rest of us. And they were among the small number of people who would know that if they tricked me into starting my knife at too low a temperature, they'd be sabotaging my efforts. The other three competitors would also know, of course. And Alec and the judges.

And anyone who'd listened to Duncan just now, holding forth on the importance of getting your forge temperatures just right. So, technically, Tweedledee and Tweedledum and Sam and Jasmyn and all those busy tech workers could have known.

But what motive could any of them have? Sam, taking revenge for my rebelliousness over the Diet Coke? Jasmyn, resentful of my hobnobbing with the crows?

No. Odds were one of the other competitors had done it. Just as one of them had probably broken Faulk's arm.

I'd keep my eyes open. Check my tools and check them again. And watch to see if anyone looked surprised if my knife turned out okay.

When my knife turned out okay. In fact, better than just okay.

For someone who had declared her hopes of being eliminated in the first round, I was showing a curiously strong competitive instinct.

I spent most of the morning working diligently. And kept an eye on my forge as much as possible—though I couldn't watch it every minute. Not if I wanted to do a good job on my bladesmithing. So I just made sure to check the temperature gauge every time I wanted to heat my dagger. And a good thing I did. Something—or someone—changed the temperature again, this time raising it from 2000 to 2500. Even though I caught the dangerously high temperature before sticking my dagger into the forge, I wasted an annoying number of precious minutes waiting for it to cool off again.

And I was distracted by the thought of what else our saboteur could do if he decided to escalate his efforts. I could think of any number of things he could shove into our forges that would have disastrous consequences. Explosive things. Things that would give off poisonous fumes. Having a vivid imagination can sometimes be a curse.

I was relieved when Jasmyn walked up and down the aisles, notifying us that our lunch break would start in ten minutes. By that time I had my dagger roughed out, a long slender blade with a straight piece at the end that I'd shape into the tang—the part of the blade that went into the hilt. I'd hammer out and attach a crow hilt if time allowed, and I could always go with a plain wooden hilt if time got away from me.

I texted Michael that we were breaking for lunch. Kibitzers in the production tent were discouraged but the lunch, served in a smaller tent now set up beside the big one, was open to all, since Ragnar was providing it. And I was delighted to remember that Alice, Ragnar's chef, was catering it. I set my unfinished dagger carefully on my worktable, turned off my forge, and left my workstation. But even as I walked over to what I supposed we'd be calling the mess tent, my mind was on my dagger. I was looking forward to the afternoon's work—making the cutting edge, normalizing the blade, smoothing it, quenching it—

"Wow, you're really concentrating." Andy appeared beside me in the chow line.

"And if you're suggesting maybe I should take a break, you're probably right. With luck, my husband and sons will show up soon to distract me."

"Mind if I join you in the meantime?"

"Please do."

Lunch was only soup, salad, and sandwiches, but with Alice in charge, that was like saying dinner was only filet mignon. We heaped our plates high with artisan bread, gourmet cheeses, and generous slices of locally raised ham, beef, and turkey. I managed to balance a plate full of Caesar salad atop my sandwich fixings, along with cups of both chicken noodle and potato leek soup.

"No dessert?" Andy asked as we settled at one end of a picnic table.

"Not sure I'll have room," I said. "And I can always send the boys back for it."

"Hey, Andy-san." It was Brody. "No rice on the buffet! That's not going to bother you, is it? But I guess they left it out so you wouldn't have an unfair advantage."

He guffawed at his own words. Fortunately, he didn't wait for an answer, but continued on to the table he was sharing with Duncan and several of the production crew.

"Jerk," I said.

"Yeah," Andy agreed. "He also told me this morning that he hopes I get eliminated before they ask us to do a katana, because then I'd have an unfair advantage. Unfair advantage—baloney. He doesn't even know that Koreans don't make katanas."

"No," I said. "Jingums, right?"

"Very good!" He grinned broadly. "The *jingum*—it comes from *jin-geom*, or 'true sword'—is one main type of Korean blade, and probably the best equivalent to a katana. Points to you for knowing. I'm impressed."

"Don't be too impressed," I said. "That's almost literally everything I know about Korean sword making."

"Well, it's more than Brody knows."

"Are *jingums* at all like katanas?"

"Actually, they are." Andy set down the sandwich he was about to bite into and sat up straight. Obviously, I'd hit on one of his favorite subjects. "Not surprising, since the two countries are so close, and did a lot of fighting back and forth. Both katanas and *jingums* have long, slightly curved one-sided blades, and the hilts are similar. As a general rule, a *jingum*'s blade is slightly thinner and wider than a katana's—although not always. Depends on the individual bladesmith. But usually—and that's the reason some martial artists prefer *jingums*—they say they feel lighter. More maneuverable."

Andy went on telling me more about Korean swords and only occasionally losing me in the technicalities. He was particularly keen on something called the *ingeom,* or tiger sword, which could only be forged in the year of the tiger, giving it the ability to ward off evil—especially if it was a *sa-ingeom,* or four-tiger sword, forged not only in the year but also in the month, day, and hour of the tiger.

"I tried making one of those last year," he said. "Wasn't entirely a success. But I'll try again next time."

"Won't that be twelve years from now?" I asked. "Long time off."

"Yeah." He chuckled. "I figure by that time maybe I'll have enough practice. And if I don't manage it in 2034, well, there's always 2046. I might still be kicking around."

I decided I liked Andy. He was smart and courteous and had a wry, self-deprecating sense of humor. I was hoping *Blades of Glory* would be all about the weapon making, without the intrigue, backstabbing, and snide remarks that seemed to fuel drama on most of the reality shows I'd seen. Not that I'd seen all that many, but they were hard to avoid these days. Still, if for some reason our show degenerated to the point that we started forming alliances to watch each other's backs, Andy seemed like a good potential ally.

At that point, Michael and the boys arrived, carrying their plates and bowls, and settled in with us. I'd finished by this time, but Andy, who'd been doing a lot of talking, still had most of his second sandwich.

"How's it going?" Michael asked.

"Meg's doing great," Andy exclaimed. He related my small clash with Sam over the coffee, and the boys were exuberant at the thought that the mug they'd given me might appear on-screen. And Andy made it sound as if I'd done something both heroic and self-sacrificing by liberating the spec sheet on the steel and sharing it with the rest of the competitors.

"Go, Mom!" Jamie said.

"I bet a couple of those guys would have kept it to themselves if they'd got their hands on it," Josh said.

"You've got that right," Andy agreed.

"How's your knife going?" Michael asked Andy.

Andy's face fell.

"I'm a little worried," he said. "I made a stupid mistake this morning—set my forge temperature at twenty-five hundred instead of two thousand. I'm hoping I caught it before I did too much damage."

"But that could make it brittle, couldn't it?" Josh asked.

"Exactly," Andy said. "I'm impressed that you know that."

"Mom's been teaching us blacksmithing," Jamie said. "And Faulk, too. Just the basics."

"But we're pretty good at it," Josh added.

"Are you sure it was your mistake?" I asked Andy.

"What else could it be?" Andy looked puzzled.

"I can think of a couple of possibilities," I said. "The same thing happened to me this morning—a couple of times my forge was exactly five hundred degrees off, either higher or lower than I remember setting it. And maybe we're both just rattled by the pressure of the competition."

"As if," Josh scoffed.

"Is there maybe something wrong with the forges that makes them hop around?" Jamie asked.

"Maybe." Andy sounded dubious.

"Maybe someone came along who had a different idea about what temperature you should be using and changed it, thinking they were being helpful," Josh suggested.

"Yeah, but why would they dial one up and the other down?" Andy said.

"Just maybe someone doesn't want us to win and is messing with our forges to sabotage us," I said.

Andy nodded and looked thoughtful. He took a big bite of his ham and Swiss sandwich, chewed it slowly, and swallowed before speaking.

"If it was just me, I'd say I messed up," he said. "But if it happened to you, too . . ."

He shook his head and took another bite.

"That means someone's cheating," Josh said.

"Who would do that?" Jamie asked.

Andy didn't answer, but I saw his eyes dart quickly to the part of the tent where Duncan and Brody were sitting.

"Check and double-check the temperature gauge every single time you put your knife in the forge," I said. "And if you see anyone hanging around your workstation, don't assume they're just being friendly."

"Yeah." Andy nodded. "Pretty hard, trying to get your best work done when you have to watch your back the whole time."

"We can watch each other's backs," I said.

He gave me a thumbs-up. As did Josh and Jamie.

"Five more minutes!" Jasmyn was striding through the tent, clipboard in hand. "Everyone back on the set in five minutes!"

"Maybe you could get Kevin to help watch your backs," Michael suggested.

"Good idea," I said.

"Who's Kevin?" Andy asked through a mouthful of salad.

"I'll explain later." I stood and looked around. "Finish your lunch—you need fuel for this afternoon's work."

Andy nodded and focused on his food.

"Kevin's our cousin," Jamie said.

"A grown-up cousin," Josh added. "He lives in our basement with all his computers and does programming and stuff."

"He's like a genius with computers," Jamie said. "Or any kind of tech."

Just then I heard a commotion from the other end of the tent.

"Miserable birds!" someone shouted.

I turned to see a crow flying away from the picnic table where Duncan, Brody, and a couple of the film crew guys were sitting. And the table's occupants were trying to pelt the departing bird with whatever objects they could grab—a mug, a soda can, a half-eaten apple.

"I should do something about that." I gave Michael a quick kiss and strode over to Duncan and Brody's table.

"I wouldn't do that if I were you," I said.

"But you're not," Duncan said. "Maybe you don't care if some filthy bird's trying to steal your food, but I'm not going to stand for it."

"Chase them away if you like," I said, "but don't try to hurt them."

"Why not?" one of the tech guys said. "I mean, who cares?"

"Ragnar does," I said. "He feeds them and calls the vet out to take care of them if they're injured. He wouldn't like it if he saw you throwing things at the crows. For all I know, he might kick you out of the castle. He's done it before."

"Yeah, right," Duncan muttered.

He couldn't say he hadn't been warned. I wouldn't be upset if Duncan or Brody got evicted. Or, better yet, Duncan *and* Brody. I wouldn't be the only one celebrating if that happened.

"And quite apart from how Ragnar would react, the crows resent it," I said. "They've been known to retaliate when people hurt them or try to."

"What's it gonna do?" Brody guffawed, then sniffled and wiped his nose with a paper napkin. "Poop on my head like it did to Jasmyn?"

The others snickered.

If my grandfather were here, he'd have insisted on explaining that birds do not produce liquid urine the way mammals do, and that the white goo the crow had deposited on Jasmyn's head was actually solid pee, not poop. But I didn't think Duncan and Brody cared.

"They've been known to do that," I said. "I'd rather not have to watch the sky every time I step out of the tent. They've also been known to dive-bomb humans. En masse. Ever seen Hitchcock's *The Birds*?"

"I'll do my best not to kill any of them while Ragnar's watching," Duncan said.

Brody found this hilarious. The crew members didn't seem to find it nearly as amusing. Maybe, being in the film industry, they'd actually watched *The Birds*.

I'd tried. As my grandmother Cordelia would say, you can't fix stupid.

I put on my coat and headed for the tent exit. On my way, I scooped up the half-eaten apple.

"Five minutes!" Jasmyn said as I passed her.

"Fresh air break," I said, in case she or anyone else cared what I was doing.

When I got outside, I spotted three crows sitting nearby. I held up the apple so it was visible, then sent it rolling along the ground in their general direction—rolling so it would be obvious I was giving it to them, not attacking them with it. They cawed, and then, when the apple came to a stop, they flapped down and began feasting on it.

"Isn't that dangerous?" I turned to see John coming out of the tent, pulling his coat collar up against the bitter cold.

"In what way?"

"What if you get them used to accepting food from humans, and then one of those jerks in there decides to poison them?"

"Crows are intelligent," I said. "And they learn how to tell different humans apart. I doubt if they'd eat anything Brody or Duncan gave them. And my grandfather the zoologist is convinced they can detect many common poisons."

"How?" John asked.

"He doesn't know yet," I said. "Kind of hard to figure out unless you want to risk killing some of the crows, which he's not. They also use tools, you know. Grandfather did an experiment once where he took tall, narrow beakers, put water in them, then added bits of meat that floated too far down for the crows to reach. The crows figured out that if they dropped enough stones in the beakers, they'd raise the water level so they could reach the meat."

"Cool." He watched the crows for another second or two, then shivered and looked up at the sky.

"So is it going to snow?" he asked.

"Not for a day or so, according to the weather service," I said. "Though it sure looks as if it's going to, doesn't it?"

"I wouldn't know," he said. "In California, you usually go to the mountains to see snow—it doesn't come to you. Doesn't get anywhere near this cold, either." He ducked back into the tent.

I strolled far enough from both tents that no one inside either one could possibly hear what I was saying. I ended up down by the pond, where the black swans were still posing for the cameras that were no longer there. I took a seat on a wrought iron bench, pulled out my phone, and called my nephew Kevin.

Chapter 9

"I thought you were busy filming today," Kevin said, instead of hello.

"I am," I said. "But I need your help. I think one of the other contestants is trying to sabotage me." I explained my suspicion that someone was raising or lowering the temperature in my forge while my back was turned.

"And you want to figure out who it is. Gotcha. I'll send someone down with a little wireless spy cam you can set up in your work area."

"Send two," I said. "Because I think they might be doing the same thing to another of the contestants."

"Can do. But just playing devil's advocate here—don't they already have a lot of cameras on you guys?"

"Good point," I said. "They do. But I have no idea if anyone is reviewing all the footage they're capturing, not yet. And what if . . ." Another more unsettling thought had occurred to me, and I paused to consider it more thoroughly.

"What if . . . ?" Kevin prompted.

"What if whoever's looking through the camera sees it and isn't doing anything? What if they just think whoever's changing the temperature setting is being helpful? Or what if they do see it, but they like it? What if they think it's good for the show? You've seen these reality competition shows—"

"Not really," he said. "Not my thing."

"Not mine, either," I said. "I've seen an episode or two all the same. They're looking for drama. Feuds. Competition. Backstabbing. What if the production people see what someone is doing to sabotage the other competitors and like it?"

"I can see it," he said. "I can even see them talking someone into doing it, saying it's for the good of the show."

"So can I," I said. "And if I decide I need to confront the producers with this, I want evidence. My own evidence, under my own control, that they can't delete if it embarrasses them."

"I'll send you a bunch of little cameras," he said. "You can do whatever you need to with them."

"Send them to Vern," I said. "He's hanging around, working undercover and doing handyman stuff. He can probably install them without anyone paying much attention."

"Word."

"Thanks," I said—but he had already hung up. And was already gathering cameras, I suspected.

I put my phone back in my pocket and looked around. A crow was sitting on the other end of the bench, studying me. Two more were perched in the bare branches of a nearby flowering cherry tree, looking hopeful.

"Sorry." I held up my hands to show that they were empty. "The apple's it for now. I don't have any more food with me. But I'll bring you something later today."

As if he understood my words—and given what I'd heard about the intelligence of crows, I wasn't entirely discounting the possibility—the nearest crow ruffled his feathers slightly, as if to express his disappointment, then took wing and headed back toward the tent. The other two followed him.

I headed that way myself, trudging more slowly. I wasn't sure which idea I hated the most—that one of the other blacksmiths could be deliberately sabotaging his colleagues' work, or that the show's producers might be allowing—or even encouraging—the sabotage. Either way, I needed to watch my back.

And help Andy watch his.

Back in the production tent, I threw myself into my work. The dagger was shaping up. I was sighting down my blade, deciding if it needed another round of the delicate strokes that fine-tuned the blade edge when—

"Hey, Meg."

I started. It was Vern. I had to suppress a feeling of mild irritation at the interruption. But I reminded myself that it could have been worse. It could have been Brody interrupting me. Or Jasmyn. Or Sam. Or—

"Just ignore me," he said. "Got to install these carbon monoxide detectors near each of the forges."

"Carbon monoxide detectors?" I looked up and yes, he was holding a round disc, just like the ones scattered all over our house.

"County ordinance," he said. "Kevin from the fire department's going to come down later today or tomorrow to inspect the premises. Don't want the production to get cited and fined."

If there were any Kevins in the Caerphilly Volunteer Fire Department, it was news to me. So presumably these were the cameras my nephew Kevin had sent. That was quick. And they really did look like carbon monoxide detectors. In fact, as I watched Vern fiddle with one of them, I decided Kevin had probably gutted half a dozen genuine ones and replaced their innards with his tiny web-enabled cameras. I made a mental note to inspect our household carbon monoxide detectors when I got back home.

Vern found a spot on the side of my locker where he could attach the faux detector and, I presumed, aim it at the controls of my forge. He was wearing an earbud in one ear, and seemed to be muttering to himself and listening to something inaudible to me. I deduced that Kevin was helping him fine-tune the camera's aim.

"That's got it," he said, after a few minutes of adjusting. "Try not to mess with it or jar it. They're kind of fiddly, and if the alarm goes off, it'll really interfere with our shooting schedule.

And worse, for all I know, the fire department could order us to evacuate the tent until they can inspect and clear it."

"That would be a disaster," I said. "I'll be careful."

Actually, I was already being careful. I'd taken to standing to one side when I opened the door to my forge, and then peering in to make sure there was nothing dangerous inside. At least if our saboteur did something nasty and blew up the entire production tent, the chief would know who to blame.

Over the next half hour, I heard Vern go through the same routine at all the other workstations. I wondered if Kevin would be merely recording what the little cameras saw or if he was curious enough to watch for a while. I could easily imagine him in his basement lair, with six of the many computer monitors mounted around the room tuned to the six cameras. No, he wouldn't be in the basement—at least he shouldn't be. My brother, Rob, and his wife, Delaney, had gone on a cruise to the Galapagos with Grandfather and wouldn't be back until Friday. Since they'd left Kevin in charge of Mutant Wizards, Rob's company, in their absence, I hoped he was at least paying some attention to what needed to get done at the office.

Not my circus, not my monkeys. I focused back on my dagger. It was taking shape now. I allowed myself to feel a moment of satisfaction, then reached for the tools I'd need for the next step.

"You're making it hard for yourself, aren't you?"

Enter Alec and his twin camera crews.

"Hold that thing up so we can see it," Alec ordered.

Obediently I held up my dagger. I stifled the thought that it was only the first day, and I was already getting tired of having Alec show up to interrupt my work. After all, the filming was the whole reason for being here, wasn't it?

"The mission was to make a knife." Alec seemed to have recovered from his initial stage fright. "Meg's making a dagger—which is why I said she's making it hard for herself. See if you can figure out why."

I looked around to see who he expected to answer. I noted one of the Tweedles shaking his head lugubriously, as if he was giving up hope on Alec.

"Damn," he said. "I did it again. Don't tell Sam I'm asking the camera questions again. Can we try that again?"

"Just start over," the cameraman said. "We'll keep rolling."

"Meg's making a dagger," Alec repeated. "Which is why I said she's making it hard for herself. Meg, tell us why."

"Because a dagger, by definition, is double-edged," I said. "Twice as many edges to sharpen."

"Exactly," Alec said. "Which means twice as many edges that have to pass the sharpness test. And more than that—not only should both sides of the dagger's blade be perfectly symmetrical—both edges should be, too. Was there a reason you chose a dagger rather than a single-edged knife?"

"I like daggers." I shrugged.

"She likes daggers." Alec seemed charmed by this. "Keep on working so we can watch you for a while."

Fine with me, as long as they let me work and didn't keep making me talk. I preferred to concentrate on the next step in the process, which was to hollow out the fuller, a groove running down both flat sides of the blade.

"She's making what some people call the *blood groove*." Alec said the words in such a melodramatic tone that I actually winced.

"Only people who have no idea what it's really for," I said. "Everyone always assumes it's to help blood flow out when you stab someone."

"And it's not?"

"No," I said. "It makes the blade both lighter and stronger. The same way corrugated cardboard is stronger than flat cardboard. Nothing to do with blood."

"Fascinating!" Alec exclaimed.

I tried not to roll my eyes. Alec knew all this. Why was he

pretending not to? And even more important, how had he gotten this gig as the show's host when he was so bad at it? I didn't think his performance was going over well with Sam and the producers. Every so often I'd catch a glimpse of them wincing when they overheard what Alec was saying. Was his stage fright back? After all, serving as host was a form of acting. Was he one of those actors who aced his audition and fell down during the actual performance? Or had they, perhaps, not done any kind of audition or screen test on him? Just taken his money and given him the job?

He had the good sense to keep quiet while I hammered the groove along most of the knife blade. I had nearly finished—and was trying hard not to whack the camera that had zoomed in and was almost touching my right ear—when we heard shrieking from somewhere else in the tent.

"No, no, no, no!" It was Sam, the director, bellowing.

Alec and the cameras raced away toward the commotion—which seemed to be coming from the banquet hall area. If I hadn't been in the middle of fullering my blade, I'd have stepped out of my cubicle to see what was up—but blacksmithing was where the cliché "strike while the iron is hot" originated. I kept working. Out of the corner of my eye, I saw Brody heading toward the banquet hall, passing between my area and Victor's.

"This is completely unacceptable!" Sam roared. "What were you thinking of?" Followed by a string of epithets that would need to be bleeped out if anyone was filming him.

Across the way, I saw Andy finish up with a bout of hammering and put his knife aside. In fact, when Sam had first shouted, at least five of us contestants had been hammering. Now I heard only one apart from myself.

"Don't let it distract you," I muttered. So I kept going until I'd finished the groove and held it up to inspect it. Not bad. I'd do a little fine-shaping at one end, but it was almost perfectly symmetrical. I squelched the brief temptation to do that fine-shaping now. I reminded myself that it was probably better to wait until I wasn't distracted by whatever Sam was up to. Let the iron tell you when it's time to stop, as Faulk was fond of saying. The iron or your common sense. I made sure the knife was safely stowed and turned off my forge before going over to the banquet hall area to see what was happening.

Sam stood there, glowering at Jasmyn. She was holding two limp strands of tinsel garland in her hand, one gold and one metallic red. The judges' table had been festooned with a modest-size artificial evergreen wreath, and two more lengths of tinsel garland, one gold and one red, were looped along the edge of the table from the wreath to one of the ends.

"Well? Well?" Sam stood, hands on hips, glowering up at Jasmyn—up, because in her spike heels she was half a head taller than he was. "What do you have to say for yourself?"

"But it's Christmas!" She burst into tears and went running out of the tent, trailing the tinsel behind her.

"Aw," Brody said. "Let the little lady have her tinsel, why don't you?"

"If we were filming a Christmas special, that would be perfectly acceptable," Sam said. "Although if that were the case, I think the set crew could find some more impressive decorations. Remember, we don't know when this will be shown. It could air at Christmas. It could air in the middle of the summer. Or maybe it won't even air at all if we can't come up with something a little more professional than that."

He pointed scornfully at Jasmyn's wreath. Well, it wasn't a big, impressive wreath. But I was willing to bet she'd bought it with her own money—it was identical to the smaller wreaths sold at the Caerphilly Drug Store. In her naïve way, she was just trying to help make the season jollier.

I wasn't the only one scowling at Sam.

But maybe I was the only one who didn't give a damn about offending him.

"You didn't have to be so nasty about it." I stepped up to the table and removed the wreath—it was only held on by a bit of two-sided tape. "You could have just told her to keep the holiday cheer for offstage," I added, as I detached the two tinsel garlands from the table and rolled them up into balls.

"She's completely incompetent," Sam muttered. "She has no idea what she's doing. The things I have to put up with—"

"Then why is she even here?" Duncan asked. "I mean, she's decorative to have around, but if she's incompetent—"

"She's Mr. Zakaryan's niece," John said.

Silence. It took me a second to remember that Zakaryan was one of the Tweedles. Oops.

Sam was starting to look a little worried. Maybe he'd lost it when he saw the Christmas decorations and was only now realizing that one of the show's producers might not be all that happy to learn that his niece had run off the set in tears.

"We will not speak of this," Sam said. "Everyone, back to work."

If he thought this wasn't going to get back to the Tweedles, he was dead wrong. Not that I planned to tell them. But someone would. My fellow competitors all began drifting back to their forges.

"Back to work! Back to work!" Sam repeated.

I hesitated for a moment. Then I grabbed my coat and strode out of the tent, heading for the castle.

Chapter 10

Behind me, I heard a few voices calling me back, but I ignored them. As I walked—briskly, because the temperature was definitely dropping—I pulled out my phone and texted Rose Noire.

"Are you here at Ragnar's?" I asked.

"In the kitchen helping Alice," she answered.

"Do you know who Jasmyn is? The production assistant?"

"Yes. Why?"

"She needs comforting. Help me find her."

I reached the stairway at the bottom of the terrace and half ran up to the main level. One of the French doors was open slightly, so I ran in.

And stopped dead in my tracks. The Great Hall had been transformed. The walls were bedecked with what looked like evergreen garlands that were either the darkest green I'd ever seen or had been spray-painted a glossy greenish black. And the garlands were festooned with tinsel in Ragnar's favorite colors—red, gold, and glossy metallic black. Really nice tinsel, much thicker and glossier than poor Jasmyn's little garlands.

"Who even knew they made black tinsel?" I muttered.

And then I reminded myself that I was looking for Jasmyn. She'd probably run up to her room—one of the several dozen bedrooms scattered around the castle. I'd probably save time if I found someone who knew which one was hers. Ragnar might remember. Alice definitely would. Or Rose Noire.

I dashed out into the entrance hall, almost running into a ladder on which Ragnar was standing. He was draping metallic black tinsel over the wrought iron chandelier, under Mother's direction. In a corner, surrounded by a protective delta of old newspapers, Caroline was spraying black paint on a bunch of evergreen boughs.

"Have you seen Jasmyn?" I asked.

"That young woman in the unfortunate hat?" Mother asked.

"That's her," I said.

"She went thataway," Ragnar called down. He was pointing at the black marble stairs to the second floor.

I raced up and, on the top landing, stared down the hallway to my left and right. No sign of Jasmyn.

Only the closed doors of a lot of bedrooms.

I pulled out my phone and texted Rose Noire again.

"Do you know which room Jasmyn's in?"

"The Bon Temps Room."

I knew approximately where that was. On this floor, all the suites and rooms were named after people and places associated with vampire books and movies. Rooms and suites named after people were to my right, while ones named after places would be to the left. I turned left. Behind me, I could hear the elevator in motion. Probably Rose Noire coming up to help. She loved having an excuse to ride in the elegant Art Deco elevator, but it was so slow I rarely bothered with it.

Nice that Ragnar had installed little nameplates outside each door, although they were so tiny you had to be right at the door to read them. I passed the Whitby Suite, and the Pointe du Lac Room, then—finally—the Bon Temps Room.

The door was partly open. And there was no one there. I took a quick look around, just to be sure. Not in the overstuffed closet. Not under the bed. Not in the en suite bathroom. The whole place was a mess, with discarded clothing and empty soda cans and food containers everywhere, but no Jasmyn.

And why did it make me feel a little weepy that she'd set up a miniature Christmas tree on the cosmetics-laden dresser and wound a few thin strands of red and gold tinsel around the bed-posts?

My phone buzzed. A message from Rose Noire.

"She just ran out of the elevator. Heading for the back terrace."

"I don't have time for this," I muttered. But at least the terrace was on my way back to the tent. If she wasn't there by the time I got downstairs, I'd leave her to Rose Noire. Who, with luck, had already found her.

I raced downstairs. Both Mother and Ragnar pointed toward the Great Hall and shouted "Thataway!" in cheerful tones, as if they were enjoying the drama. Nice that someone was.

Jasmyn was standing on the terrace, leaning on the balus-trade and staring into space. Or maybe she wasn't just staring into space—maybe she was contemplating the idea of commit-ting suicide by hurling herself over the parapet. If that was her idea, she wasn't going to succeed. Although the view looked dra-matic from here on the terrace, the ground was only about four feet below us, and then sloped rather gently in a series of shal-low terraces to the pasture level. On warm sunny days, Josh and Jamie and their friends had always loved playing games here on the terrace—knights, ninjas, or superheroes were the most pop-ular, and all of them sooner or later involved posing heroically on the parapet, then falling—or being pushed—over the side and rolling all the way down with shrieks of laughter. Jasmyn would have a hard time even injuring herself here.

But just because she was lacking the common sense needed to do away with herself efficiently didn't mean she wasn't thor-oughly miserable enough to try. And with my luck, she'd be the one-in-a-million klutz who did manage to injure herself jump-ing from a height of four feet. Where was Rose Noire? I needed to get back to my forge, but I didn't want to leave Jasmyn alone.

If nothing else, I should lure her back inside before she got frostbite. So I strode over to her.

"Sam's a jerk," I said. "I get why he wanted you to take down the Christmas decorations, but he could have told you nicely."

"I told Uncle Brad this was a bad idea," she said. "Not the Christmas decorations—I mean, yeah, that was probably a bad idea, too. I just thought it would cheer people up. Everyone's so tense. I should have thought. But it was totally a bad idea, me working on the show. I know I should be grateful that he's giving me a chance to break into the television business, but I'm not really interested in the television business. Not that I want to tell him that."

"Yes," I said. "That would probably sound like heresy to him. If you're that miserable, why don't you quit? Tell him you don't like working for Sam."

"I wish I could." She sighed. "They do need a production assistant. I don't want to do anything to hurt the show."

I pulled out my phone and called Michael.

"How's it going?" he asked.

"My dagger's going well," I said. "Can't say as much for the production. If Jasmyn has to quit her production assistant job in protest, could you rustle up a replacement? Someone qualified to take her place and too tough to let Sam bully them?"

"No problem," he said. "Got a couple of grad students who'd jump at the chance. Want me to have one standing by?"

"Please," I said. "Tell whoever they'll get room and board at Ragnar's all week even if we don't need them."

"Can do."

I turned back to Jasmyn.

"You're replacing me," she said, her tone sullen.

"No," I said. "I'm giving you an escape hatch. Sometimes feeling you have no way out makes a bad job worse. Michael will have someone standing by, so if you want to quit—if you *need* to quit to take care of yourself—you can do it without feeling guilty about what it does to the production. But we won't do anything unless you say the word. And if you do, I'm sure Ragnar would be fine with you staying here for as long as you need to while you figure out what you want to do next."

"You really think he would be okay with it?" She sounded wistful.

"I know he would. Ragnar's always taking in—" I had been about to say "strays," but realized she might find that insulting. "Always taking in people who are going through hard times. See that guy over there with the easel?"

I pointed to a couple of fields over where a figure, well bundled up against the bitter cold, was painting a pastoral landscape on a large canvas. Even from this distance, I could tell he was depicting a clump of cows looking small and stoic in a beautiful though bleak midwinter field.

"That's Erasmus Winkelman," I said. "Just Winkelman to his friends. Moderately well-known artist. Ragnar invited him here for Christmas, found out he was about to get kicked out of his apartment, and told him to stay as long as he wanted to. That was six or seven years ago now. He does a little light work with the sheep and goats to earn his keep."

Jasmyn peered out at the painter with a hopeful expression.

Suddenly Winkelman threw down his brush, rummaged in the battered rucksack at his feet, and pulled out a camera. He began taking pictures—of the cows, the crows perched on the fence, and especially the luminous gray sky.

"Why's he doing that?" Jasmyn seemed startled by this burst of frenzied activity.

"He works from photographs if the weather turns really nasty," I said. "Which the weather service predicts it will in a day or so. And I expect he wants to capture the color of the sky right now. He's famous for his skies. So what would you do if someone gave you a sabbatical?

"What's that?" She looked slightly anxious at the unfamiliar term.

"A chunk of paid time off to do whatever you want."

"Oh!" She started to say something, stopped herself, then took a deep breath and persevered. "I'd study to get qualified as a yoga instructor. And I'd find something to do with animals. Puppies and kittens. I'm really good at socializing feral kittens."

She and Rose Noire should hit it off like crazy. Assuming Rose Noire ever showed up.

"Not birds, though." Her face went all anxious as she glanced up to see half a dozen crows circling as if about to land on the balustrade. "And here they come, those horrible things."

Two of the crows touched down not far from us. Jasmyn flinched and glanced over at the terrace door as if planning to escape inside. Then she bent down, picked up a stone, and was pulling her hand back to throw it at the crows.

"Don't do that!" I grabbed her arm to stop her.

"I'm not trying to hit them," she said. "I would never do that. I just want to chase them away."

"And how are the birds supposed to know that?" I asked. "To them, it probably looks as if you're trying to hurt them and just have bad aim."

"They're only stupid birds." She dropped the stone but sulked a bit.

"Actually, crows are very intelligent birds," I said. "Some scientists think they're as smart as a seven-year-old human. And if you think a seven-year-old human isn't going to take a dislike to someone who throws rocks at them, you haven't spent much time around children."

"What does it matter if they like me or not?"

"For one thing, they don't deliberately dump their droppings on people they like," I said. "They haven't ever done it to me, for example. Watch."

I strolled down the terrace to where Ragnar kept his bird-feeding supplies—a big, closed container of shelled sunflower seeds for the small birds and a similar container of unshelled peanuts for the bigger ones. I carefully undid the latches—which were designed to be too strong for a crow to move yet small and complicated enough to foil bears. I grabbed the scoop and filled a small metal bowl with peanuts. Then I locked up the bin again and returned to where Jasmyn was standing.

The crows knew what the bin was for. The airborne ones began landing on the parapet or the terrace. They all began inching closer, their bright, beady eyes focused on me.

"Watch this," I said.

I began tossing peanuts toward the crows. Some of them liked to flutter up and catch the nuts in their beaks. The others just picked them up from the stone surface of the terrace and gobbled them down. More crows began showing up, thanks to their infallible radar for food. The terrace was starting to look as if we were filming a remake of *The Birds.* Jasmyn looked anxious, but to her credit, she stood her ground. Then she gasped and pointed to something behind me.

Rose Noire had arrived and, seeing what we were up to, had filled another bowl with nuts. But instead of throwing them to the crows, she was hand-feeding them. One enormous crow was perched on her left wrist, gently picking up the peanuts she was holding in her palm. She was holding up peanuts for another crow who was perched on her right shoulder.

I noticed that sitting on the stone pavers near her was a tray with a teapot on it. Not just a teapot—cups, saucers, knives and spoons, cream, sugar, a plate of scones, and a small crock that almost certainly contained Alice's homemade clotted cream. Even though I wasn't hungry, my mouth watered.

Rose Noire, seeing we were looking at her, tossed her last few peanuts to the crows. She must have made some kind of signal visible only to birds, since they all cawed a few times before flying off. She strolled over to join us and matter-of-factly took a blanket she was wearing as a makeshift coat and draped it around Jasmyn's shivering shoulders.

"Why don't you take a little time off?" I said to Jasmyn. "Go do some yoga with Rose Noire. Help Ragnar put up his Christmas decorations. If Sam complains, tell him Ragnar asked you to and remind him whose hospitality we're all enjoying."

"That sounds like a wonderful idea," Rose Noire said. "First let's have some tea."

"And didn't one of Ragnar's Norwegian forest cats just have a litter of kittens?" I asked. "Show her those."

"Kittens?" Jasmyn's face lit up at the thought.

"Norwegian forest kittens," Rose Noire said. "They don't come any cuter."

I watched as they went back inside, happily discussing the relative merits of jasmine and matcha tea. Then I hurried down the stairway to ground level and headed back to the production tent. Time was ticking away, and my knife wouldn't make itself.

Chapter 11

John and Andy looked up as I returned to my workstation. Andy, who was in the middle of hammering on his blade, smiled and nodded. John put aside what he was doing and came over.

"She okay?" he asked.

"I think she will be," I said.

"Probably help if we keep God's gift to women away from her." He nodded ever-so-slightly toward Brody's workstation. "Or at least make sure she's not left alone with him."

"He's been harassing her?"

John's jaw clenched and he nodded.

"I'll keep that in mind," I said.

John grinned, saluted, and went back to his workstation.

I turned back to my worktable and studied everything on it for a few minutes, getting back into the mindset I needed for working on my knife. Which now looked, to the inexpert eye, as if it was almost complete. If I were only making it as a decoration, I'd sharpen the edges, add on the hilt, and call it finished. But since the judges would be testing its performance—and since Faulk had taught me never to do anything halfway—I had several more steps ahead of me. I'd be heating it to specific temperatures and then either air cooling it or quenching it in water, steps that would change the physical structure of the steel, making it as hard and strong and flexible as possible.

And the precise temperatures I used would matter even more

with these steps, so I'd be keeping a close eye on my forge's temperature gauge.

I finished normalizing the blade—a process that did useful things to the consistency and texture of the steel, but one I hoped Alec didn't ask me to explain to the home viewer. While waiting for it to air-cool enough to go ahead with the next step, I decided to start working on my crow's-head hilt. I was laying out my tools and materials when my phone dinged a couple of times, signaling that a couple of texts had come in.

I pulled it out and looked. Kevin.

"Got the goods on the blond guy," his text said. "Messed around with the Asian guy's forge. Tried it with yours, but you were too alert for him."

He sent a couple of screenshots. A shot showing the temperature gauge of Andy's forge set at 1500. Brody with his hand on the temperature dial. Another shot of the gauge, now at 1840. Brody reaching out his hand toward the dial on my forge. Brody with his hand snatched back from my forge and a suspiciously innocent look on his face.

"Great," I texted Kevin. "Any chance you could put some of this up online someplace where I can easily show it to someone?"

He answered by sending me a link. I clicked it, and instead of screenshots, I could see a whole video collection of Brody's sabotage attempts, both the successful ones and the close calls.

"Bingo," I said to myself. And then I texted my thanks to Kevin and went back to work.

The afternoon wore on. The six of us kept working, but the camera crews seemed to be paying fewer visits to us. Not surprising. The first steps of any blademaking project were a lot of fun to watch. The glowing metal being pulled out of the forge. The smith hammering an iron rod into a blade. Sparks flying. But now we were down to a lot of finishing steps that were probably pretty boring for the camera crew. They'd make all the difference in how our blades performed in the strength and sharpness tests, but they didn't make any visible difference in the look of the blade. In a movie, they'd have shown this phase with a quick montage of the six of us repeatedly sticking our swords into our forges, quenching them, and holding them up for inspection. And then they'd skip to the next exciting bit.

At one point I overheard Alec explaining as much to one of the Tweedles.

"It's like . . . like cooking something," he said. "It gets kind of boring to watch, but if you try to cut the cooking time short, you get meat that's raw on the inside, or a cake that's still liquid at the center."

I had to smile, remembering when Faulk had been teaching the basics of bladesmithing to Alec. He hadn't been the world's greatest pupil.

"I wish, just once, he'd listen to me," Faulk had complained. "He always wants to do everything in a hurry. He heats his metal too hot, hammers it past when he should, and he's had to learn the hard way that normalizing and tempering aren't just old blacksmith superstitions—they really make a difference."

Alec had eventually become a capable bladesmith—though not, I gathered, a top-rated one. He was still, according to Faulk, too impatient for that.

And I suspected the producers, who hadn't learned the hard way why the steps we were doing were necessary, were even more impatient.

It was really a culture clash, I decided. The TV people were in a hurry—maybe because they were used to thinking of things in minutes and seconds. For them, an hour-long show was never more than about forty-five minutes, to leave room for commercials. And here they were, tapping their feet impatiently, as they watched a group of people do something by hand. Something that couldn't really be hurried. Something people had been doing in much the same way for centuries, if not millennia.

Something that didn't look interesting enough to take up even one of those forty-five minutes.

And then I stopped worrying about how I was probably boring the producers and focused on my blade.

I finished my dagger a good hour before the absolute deadline. Not that I wanted to brag about it or even let anyone find out. The other five contestants could probably tell who was as good as finished and who was sweating the deadline. I remembered doing a similar thing in school. At least in the subjects I liked and was good at, I'd sometimes finish a test well before the time was up. I always fretted about the proper etiquette in these situations. It seemed silly and a waste of time to sit there, pretending to work, but I didn't want to discourage my friends who were still working. And no one liked the people who were ostentatious about finishing early. Not even me. So I always pretended to work until the teacher called time.

Not much had changed. I got a generally relaxed and confident vibe from Victor and John, but they were continuing to putter in their workstations. Andy was clearly anxious. At some point, the tip of his blade had broken off, and he'd had to scramble to reshape a new point. Luckily he'd started out making a knife near the maximum length of eight inches, so his blade should have no trouble beating the minimum length. But if it was brittle enough to break while he was working on it, that boded ill for the strength and sharpness tests.

I didn't have as good a view of what Duncan and Brody were up to. Brody was clearly sweating it. And not coping well, to judge by the erratic hammering and cursing I could hear. I wondered, not for the first time, if he was on something. At first I'd just put it down to nicotine craving—he grumbled from time to time about not being able to smoke in the tent and was constantly running out for a cigarette break. But I was starting to suspect he might be on something worse. Cocaine, possibly? I could remember a few of the symptoms, thanks to Dad's annual lectures on drug and alcohol awareness for the Caerphilly Parent-Teacher Association. Cocaine users were restless and jittery. Check. And they eventually developed a chronic runny nose. Check. I'd assumed Brody's constant sniffling was a reaction to the cold weather, but maybe not. After lunch, he'd grown listless and irritable, and seemed to spend a lot of time simply staring at his work instead of doing anything. He also took more and more cigarette breaks as the day wore on, and after one particularly long cigarette break, he'd suddenly erupted into a frenzy of energy and good humor. The good humor had faded, but the energy continued.

I remembered the conversation I'd overheard in the morning, the one where he'd said, "Dammit, how soon can you get it here?" I'd been too unawake to think about it at the time, but to my admittedly uninformed mind, those words did sound rather like what a user might say to his dealer. And his disappearance and return with such an astonishing surge in energy also seemed suspiciously like what someone on cocaine might do.

If this had happened in another situation—like at a craft fair or a blacksmiths' hammer-in, I might have sicced someone on Brody. Vern or Dad, depending on whether I wanted him arrested or sent to detox. But if I did either of those now, I could bring the whole production crashing down. And Faulk and Tad would get hurt along with Brody.

I decided I'd find a chance to bring this up with Alec. He had a vested interest in making sure any wayward behavior from Brody wouldn't torpedo the show.

So I focused on my work. Well, on cleaning up my workstation and doing a little more smoothing and polishing on my blade.

Around four-thirty, Alec went around reminding us that we had to finish by five. Then he gave us a fifteen-minute warning, then ten minutes, then five. And finally—

"Time!" Alec was walking up and down the central aisle, ringing a handbell. "Time! Hammers down! Grab your knives and come to the banquet hall for the judging!"

The two camera crews were circulating, looking for a few candid shots of us finishing up. Or maybe hoping to catch anyone who tried to squeeze in a few more minutes of finishing work. Everyone looked reasonably cheerful except for Andy and Brody. Andy was aiming for cheerful but couldn't quite pull it off. Brody looked seedy and out of temper.

We all trooped into the banquet hall area carrying our knives and, since no one knew how long this phase of the filming would last, our mugs, filled with our beverages of choice. Mostly hot coffee, since the tent was a bit on the drafty side. In spite of the temperature, I stuck to my familiar Diet Coke. I caught a brief whiff of what smelled like alcohol from Brody's direction. I suspected he had spiked his coffee. Or maybe he hadn't even bothered with the coffee.

The judges were standing over by the production area, chatting and getting ready to make their entrance. Following Alec's instructions, we all set our knives on the velvet-covered head table, hilts toward the side where the judges would be sitting and points toward the audience—which was us. Then we all took our assigned seats, tallest in the back, as before. I brought my iPad with me, so I'd have a way to show Kevin's video clip when needed.

Alec came up and swapped the knives around a bit, saying that he wanted to make sure we weren't all sitting directly opposite our knives. I wondered if he'd deliberately moved my knife to the right-hand end of the table. If the judges took them in order, mine would be judged either first—or last.

I rather hoped it would be first, so I could get it over with.

The knives made quite a varied collection. Duncan's knife looked like something you'd expect a terrorist to wave around to intimidate a group of hostages. It was stubby and thick, with a strong point, an impressively sharp edge, and wicked-looking serrations along the top of the blade. The hilt was odd—it looked more like the butt of a gun than a typical knife handle. It even had a hole or loop on the bottom side, shaped rather like the trigger guard on a gun—although I expected its purpose was to help the user avoid dropping it in combat. Because, yeah, this was definitely a combat knife.

Andy's knife was slim, elegant, and minimalist, with the hilt formed out of the same steel as the blade. The shape of it was rather reminiscent of a katana and the only decorative note was that he'd worked a lanyard hole into the end of the handle, with a black silk cord threaded through it and tied in a knot of studied casualness.

Victor's knife was as thick and solid as Duncan's, but less aggressively warlike. No serrations, no pistol-like grip. Just a sturdy, solid, well-made hunting knife with a leather-wrapped handle. It looked like a strong entry to me.

As did John's, also solid and sturdy, though less bulky than Victor's. A deceptively simple and classic design with a gracefully curved single-edged blade and a smooth cherry-wood handle.

Brody's was kind of a mishmash, with a shortish, stubby blade and a disproportionately large handle. He'd put fine serrations on one edge of the blade and coarser serrations on the other, which looked . . . odd. Unbalanced. And the grind, the flat part of the blade that sloped down to the sharpened edge, was visibly narrower on the finely serrated side than the coarse one. Had he started off making a single-edged knife and then encountered some problem that made him pivot and turn it into a double-edge? Or was his aesthetic sense . . . well, I was about to say terrible, and amended it to "very different from mine."

I thought my dagger looked just fine as a part of the collection—and damn good sitting where it was, right next to Brody's. The blade was simple and very satisfyingly symmetrical. The crow-themed handle had come out particularly well—the main part of it was the stylized body of the crow, swelling slightly in the middle to make a more solid and comfortable grip. Then, after enough room for even a very large hand, the crow's head was done in much more realistic detail, complete with tiny black stones for eyes and a sharp little beak pointing upward, so, in theory, you could even use the hilt to do a little surprise stabbing. It was, I hoped, a nice melding of drama and practicality.

The camera crews had filmed us placing our knives, and were now filming the knives themselves, doing medium shots to show the entire lineup and close-ups of each individual blade. Off to the side, where we could see it—although the cameras could not—Sam was watching the screen of a monitor that let him see what the main camera was seeing, and issuing instructions to fine-tune the closeups of our blades. Eventually, he nodded and turned back to us.

"I think we've got enough on the knives." Sam's tone suggested that the only thing drearier than filming our knives would be filming us. "Let's get on with the judging."

Chapter 12

We all settled in our seats, and the three judges marched in—with Marco in the lead, of course. He stood by the table while the other two took seats. And Alec also took a seat beside them, looking a little out of sorts. It quickly became obvious why. As with the initial introductions, at this point the original plan had been for Alec to be the emcee or ringmaster or whatever you called the one who did most of the talking. But now Marco was taking center stage, gesturing dramatically at the knives and setting the proceedings in motion.

The judges quickly agreed that yes, all of our knives were finished, and since the directions for this first challenge didn't specify any particular kind of knife, historical accuracy wasn't really a big concern at the moment. Marco whipped out a steel ruler and carefully measured all of our knives, even the ones that were obviously well within the six-to-eight-inch range. Duncan's knife came within a hair of being too long, and Brody's was about an eighth of an inch too short. He blustered that it was exactly six inches on *his* ruler. After some discussion, and an inspection of the ruler in question—which did appear to be a little worn down at the ends—Marco sternly told him to get a better ruler next time and allowed it to pass.

"We'll be discussing who gets points for aesthetics later." Had Marco's eyes darted involuntarily to my dagger as he said that? "Now it's time for the tests of strength and sharpness."

He picked up the first knife in line—John's—and stood holding it while two stagehands—Vern and a scrawny young man with a perpetually startled expression—rolled out a steel barrel and the rope-holding gallows. Marco moved his hand up and down a few times, as if assessing the weight and feel of the knife. Then, with a dramatic flourish, he made a blindingly fast sweeping cut at one of the lengths of rope.

I wasn't the only one who blinked or started at the speed, power, and sudden sheer violence of his action. I wondered if I was the only one whose imagination conjured up a picture of Faulk, cut down by much the same kind of blow, though from a bat instead of a knife. And while I had no reason to suspect Marco of the attack on Faulk—I didn't even know if he'd been in town at the time—I made a mental note to find out if there was bad blood between them.

It took me a few seconds to realize that John's knife sliced into the rope, not cutting it entirely, but getting more than half-way through.

"Not bad," Marco said. "Not bad at all. And now for the test of strength."

He strolled over to the barrel and paused dramatically for a few seconds. He was holding John's knife with what I'd have called a high underhand grip, poised for either an upward slash or a straightforward thrust.

He went for the forward thrust, again with blindingly fast speed, although we were expecting it by now and weren't as startled. John's knife pierced the metal side of the barrel with a scraping noise. Marco pulled it out and held it up with a flourish.

"John's knife passes the tests," he said in a solemn tone. He held the knife out on both palms, bowed slightly to John, then set the knife back in its place at the far-left side of the table.

Sam called "Cut," to give the stagehands a chance to turn the barrel so the hole made by John's knife was invisible. Then, with the cameras rolling again, Marco repeated the process with the next knife in line—Duncan's. Impressively, Duncan's knife cut clean through the second length of rope. It punctured the trash barrel with the same ease.

"Duncan's knife passes the tests," Marco said, repeating the slight formal bow.

Another break while the stagehands turned the barrel and hung two new lengths of rope on the little scaffold.

Next up was Victor's knife, which cut the rope a little better than John's, though not as well as Duncan's.

Andy's knife only made a slight dent in the rope, and when Marco thrust it into the barrel, it only went a little way through the steel side before the tip broke off.

A slight murmured reaction ran through the tent. Marco bent, picked up the fragment, and held out the two pieces on his palms in the now-familiar gesture.

"I'm sorry, Andy," he said. "Your knife did not pass the strength test. You are in danger of elimination."

Sam called "Cut" again, and while the stagehands again turned the barrel and hung new lengths of rope, Andy shook his head, clearly crushed.

"It was that temperature fluctuation in the forge," he muttered. "Burned the metal. Made it brittle."

John, who was sitting next to him, patted his shoulder in sympathy.

I wondered if now was the time to reveal the video Kevin's cameras had captured. No, not quite yet. Better to wait until they'd finished the strength and sharpness tests.

I was really beginning to wish my knife had been farther toward the left of the table instead of the last one in line. I hadn't wanted to appear on *Blades of Glory*; I didn't, in the long run, care if I won the grand prize; and I had initially been thinking how great it would be if I could just get eliminated in the first round and be done with this nonsense . . . but right now I didn't want to lose. Not now. Not in the very first round.

Not to jerks like Duncan and Brody.

Filming resumed.

Marco picked up Brody's knife. Was it just my imagination that he frowned as he did it? Only the barest ghost of a frown—hardly more than a slight twitch of one eyebrow. His face remained calm and impassive, but something made me think he didn't like the feel of this knife. He shifted his grip a little bit. He hadn't done that with any of the others. Brody's knife had looked unbalanced to me, but I had told myself it was my imagination. That I was deliberately trying to find fault with it because it was Brody's. Something about Marco's attitude suggested that no, it wasn't my imagination.

Marco slashed at the rope. Brody's knife made a slight cut in the right-hand rope—about as deep as Andy's knife had done. And then, to our surprise, Marco made a backhanded slash at the second rope.

Of course. Brody's knife had two edges. They'd want to test them both. They'd do the same with mine.

The second edge—the one with the coarse serrations—only made a slight dent in the rope.

On to the barrel.

At first, it looked as if Brody's knife had passed the strength test just fine. But then Marco frowned—a definite frown this time—and brought it up to his face for a closer look.

"Some of the teeth in your serration broke off," he said. "I'm sorry, Brody. Your knife does not pass the strength test. You are in danger of elimination."

"What! Let me see."

Sam left the cameras running while Brody leaped up to inspect his knife and make a great fuss about when the broken serrations had happened. Whiny is never a good look. About the third time Brody insisted that Marco must have done something to break off the serrations even before stabbing the barrel, Marco snapped at him,

"Mr. McIlvaney! If the serrations broke due to anything I did before your knife even touched the barrel, then I think it fails the strength test even more decisively. If you continue to dispute the judges' decisions, we will impose a penalty."

He frowned at Brody. So did the other two judges.

Brody subsided and slouched back to his seat.

Andy looked a little less lugubrious than he had. His expression showed that while he definitely felt sorry for Brody, he was relieved not to be the only one in danger of being eliminated.

And now it was my turn.

The stagehands rotated the barrel one last time and hung two new lengths of rope.

"Action," Sam yelled.

Marco strode over to the table and picked up my blade. He held it up so everyone could see the crow's head before taking his customary underhand grip. Was it my imagination, or did I detect a slight smile as his hand closed around the hilt? I'd taken trouble over the hilt, making sure it offered not only a solid grip but a comfortable one. Faulk had drummed that into me all through my bladesmithing lessons—it didn't matter how sharp the blade was if the hilt was difficult or uncomfortable to hold.

Marco stepped up to the ropes and slashed at the first one. My knife cut all the way through. And the backslash with the other side of the blade came very close to doing the same thing—the rope wasn't completely severed, but it was dangling by maybe a dozen fibers.

I nodded and tried hard to look as if this was only to be expected. I imagined how Michael and the boys would react—with cheers, fist pumps, high fives, and a few exclamations of "I knew you could do it!" We'd do all that later. For now, though, I wanted to stay—or at least look—cool, calm, and collected.

Marco turned to the barrel and again made that lightning-quick stabbing motion. My knife seemed to pierce the barrel just as easily as anyone else's. And after he withdrew it, Marco lifted the knife to his eyes and, while he scanned the blade, ran his finger in a line, half an inch above the edge, going from the hilt to the tip, as if emphasizing that my knife had neither chipped, cracked, nor broken. Then he placed it on his out-stretched palms and gave his ceremonial bow.

"Meg's knife passes the tests," he said before placing my dag-ger back on the table.

Back in the offstage area, I saw Vern give me a wide grin and a thumbs-up.

"The judges will now consider their verdict," Marco intoned. "We will be discussing the results of the strength and sharpness tests and doing our own close examination and assessment of your work."

I glanced around. Everyone looked a little tense. Understand-able. From what I'd seen, Victor, John, Duncan, and I were all four very much in contention to win this first challenge. And Andy and Brody were both in danger of being eliminated. Every-one was in suspense.

I decided that maybe now was the time to share my video. I stood up.

"Before the judges retire to consider their decision," I said, "I would like to share some information that they may find helpful."

Chapter 13

Marco glanced over at Sam, who nodded slightly. Sam looked wide awake for the first time all afternoon, suggesting that he didn't mind my interruption. In fact, he might even be hoping this interruption would lead to the kind of drama the producers were hoping for.

"And just what is this information?" Marco asked.

I picked up my iPad and turned it on. I'd made sure Kevin's video link was on screen when I turned it off, so it would be handy to click when the power came back on. I walked up to the judges' table, set the iPad down, and clicked the arrow to start the video.

"Hang on a sec," Sam said. "Get a camera on that thing."

I stopped the video and stepped aside so the main camera could zoom in on the iPad's screen. Sam nodded. I clicked the arrow again to start the video and then got out of the way. I could see my five competitors craning their necks to watch Sam's screen as the close-up of my iPad began playing on it.

Brody was the first to realize what was going on. He shot me a thunderous look and growled a few highly bleepable words.

Kevin had done a very good job of editing together the highlights of the footage his little cameras had captured. His video started with a shot of Brody dropping by Victor's work area, reaching toward the temperature dial, and then snatching his hand back quickly when Victor turned around.

"Were you trying to do what I think you were?" Victor growled.

Next was a shot of Brody turning up Andy's temperature gauge. Followed by Andy inserting his partially completed knife without noticing the change.

"I thought *I'd* done that," Andy exclaimed. "It kept happening again and again, and I was kicking myself for being stupid enough to set it way too high and then not even notice."

A shot of Brody dialing up the temperature in John's forge, followed by him approaching the forge, noticing the too-high temperature, and then dialing it down and tapping his foot as he waited for the forge to cool.

Another shot of Brody interfering with Andy's forge, this time setting it much too low. And then the same with John's forge. Then a series of close calls—shots of Brody loafing past various workstations, clearly on the lookout for more moments when we were not paying attention. The only competitor whose forge he hadn't been caught tampering with was Duncan. Maybe he'd spared Duncan because they were friends. Or maybe Duncan had put him up to it. I wouldn't be surprised.

"A pity you wasted so much time messing with us that you could have spent on your own blade," Victor said. "Maybe you could have made something halfway decent."

John glanced at Victor and shook his head, as if to suggest that no, Brody would still have failed even if he'd spent twice as much time on his knife.

The video ended. I turned to see how Brody was taking it. So did everyone else, including the judges. He sat with his arms crossed, clearly trying to hide his anxiety with a fierce scowl.

Marco bent and exchanged quiet words with the other two judges. After a minute or two they all three nodded. Marco picked up Brody's knife and turned back to us.

"Brody McIlvaney. Stand, please."

Brody hesitated for a moment, then stood, hunching his shoulders as if to ward off blows. I knew I'd rather have suffered blows than the humiliation he was about to receive. Although he'd earned it.

"Brody McIlvaney," Marco said. "You have not only broken the rules of the *Blades of Glory* competition, you have trampled on its spirit. It is the decision of the judges that you are the loser of this first challenge."

I heard Andy let out his breath in relief.

"Moreover, you are hereby disqualified from any further participation in this or any future *Blades of Glory* competitions. Leave the tent."

He held out Brody's blade, hilt first. After a long moment of standing there, mouth open, eyes shifting around as if seeking some kind of support, Brody reached out, took his knife, and stumbled out of the banquet hall area.

"Andrew Kim."

Andy jerked his head back to look at Marco.

"Although your blade failed its strength test, the judges recognize that you were the unwitting victim of sabotage. You will remain in the contest."

Andy tried to smile but couldn't quite manage it. He stood and bowed deeply to the judges. Marco bowed back, and the other two inclined their heads.

"Thank you," Andy said. "I'll try to do better."

He sat down again, and both Victor and John thumped him encouragingly on the back.

"And now for the winner of this first challenge," Marco announced. "A difficult decision, considering that all four of the contestants who were not sabotaged have completed excellent blades that passed the strength and sharpness tests and are aesthetically pleasing in their own different ways. But one blade excelled above all the others in a criterion that is often overlooked, and yet is absolutely critical in a weapon. The balance."

He turned back to the table, swept his eyes across the line of knives, then leaned over and picked up my knife.

He turned back and held it out on his flat, outstretched palms.

"Meg Langslow. You are the winner of the first mini-challenge."

Andy let out a whoop, turned around, grabbed my hand, and pumped it furiously. John gave me a thumbs-up, and Victor added an approving nod.

"Deserved," Victor said. "And we owe you one for showing up that creep for what he is. But game on! We'll be coming for you in the next round."

"Bring it on," I said. "And may the best blade win."

And then the four of us—Andy, John, Victor, and I—lapsed into laughter, exchanged high fives, and generally behaved as if we'd all won the contest as a team. Marco and the other judges smiled as they looked on. Sam actually looked cheerful for a change, glancing back and forth from his monitor to his live view of our celebration. From the sidelines, most of the tech crew were smiling and giving us the thumbs-up.

Only Duncan wasn't joining in the fun. Oh, he was trying. But he was visibly having a hard time smiling. I found myself wondering—was he upset because he'd lost? Concerned because his main friend and ally had been eliminated?

Or was he thanking his lucky stars that he hadn't helped with the sabotage?

"It's been a long day," Victor said. "We off duty now?"

Marco, Sam, and one of the Tweedles put their heads together briefly for a murmured conversation. Then they all nodded, and Marco turned back to us.

"Contestants," he said. "You may take your knives and leave the banquet hall. Please stay at your workstations for a few minutes while we make sure there's nothing else we need to do today."

We all went up to the judges' table and grabbed our knives. Duncan just strode off with his, looking irritated. The rest of us strolled back to our workstations as a group.

Vern ambled over.

"Ragnar says congratulations," he said. "And you've got about an hour to clean up and rest up for the feast."

"Feast?" Andy echoed.

"He's had his staff cooking all day," Vern said. "Whole castle smells heavenly."

"Lunch was a feast," Andy said. "If dinner's going to be better than that—"

We all hurried to set our workstations in order.

"Dammit, did someone borrow my jacket?" Duncan was standing in the center aisle, glowering at the rest of us.

We all variously shrugged or shook our heads.

"I left it right here in my locker." Duncan stormed off to look elsewhere. After chivying the sound and camera crew for a few minutes, he stormed over to where Marco was standing.

And Alec was still standing nearby, with an expression of mingled pleasure and exhaustion, listening as Duncan interrogated Marco about the missing leather jacket.

I headed that way. Maybe I could avert a quarrel between Duncan and Marco, and I wanted to talk to Alec anyway.

"Think what you like," Marco was saying as I drew near. "But if your jacket is missing, don't look at me. Not my size, not my style, and I don't do hand-me-downs."

Duncan glared at Marco, and then turned his glare on me when I drew near.

"Alec," I said. "Can we talk for a sec?"

"Sure," he said.

I glanced at Duncan and Marco—the sort of glance that was an unsubtle invitation to give Alec and me some space. Either they didn't pick up the hint or they were both pretending not to notice.

"Privately." I grabbed Alec's arm and led him out of the tent.

"So what's the deep dark secret?" he asked when we were ten feet or so away from the tent flap.

"We have a problem," I said. "It's about Brody."

"What about him?" Alec looked rattled.

"He's using something. Cocaine, maybe."

"Yeah, possibly," Alec said. "I'd even say probably. There were rumors he had some problems with that a few years ago. Of course, we wouldn't have let him compete if we hadn't thought he was clean. Maybe the stress of the competition got to him. But at least we got through the first event without it causing a problem. Should be smooth sailing now that he's out of the running."

Curious. Alec had looked so rattled when I'd said Brody was a problem. I'd expected him to argue with me. Blame Brody's mood swings on too much nicotine and Red Bull. But he wasn't arguing and actually seemed calm again. Positively philosophical about the possibility that one of his show's cast members—presumably one of his friends—was using drugs on set. What more dire problem had he thought Brody might be causing? Or was it just his stressed-out condition that made him react so strongly, rather than knowing—or at least suspecting—that Brody might be up to something even worse?

"It won't be smooth sailing if he gets arrested," I said. "That wouldn't exactly be good PR, would it? Maybe it wouldn't hurt your chances of selling the show, but I wouldn't want to count on that. And besides, don't they need to keep him around for things—like retaking anything that didn't turn out right? If he won't cooperate—or isn't in any shape to film—the producers won't be able to get all the shots they need."

"Damn. You're right." Alec was looking anxious again. "That could hurt the show. What should I do?"

"Talk to your producers about what they can do," I said. "He's still under contract, right? I let Michael do all the analyzing and nitpicking on my contract, but I did read it, and I seem to recall it had a fairly typical moral turpitude clause. Something about not doing anything that 'might tend to reflect unfavorably on *Blades of Glory*.' That should cover it."

"Yeah, but what incentive does he have to follow the contract now? He's out of the competition—why would he even care?"

"He hasn't been paid yet, surely."

"Oh, true." He looked a little less anxious. "And I bet B. J. and Pierre have probably dealt with this before. I mean, Hollywood—right?"

I decided not to share my suspicion that B. J. and Pierre might not be quite the successful and seasoned producers he imagined.

"Maybe they can cut a deal with him," I suggested. "He agrees to go into a treatment program and behave himself until they get a good deal for the show, and they won't release the video of him cheating. And Andy and I don't sue him for what he did to us."

"Can you sue him for that?"

"Why not?" I asked. "As one of my lawyer cousins is fond of saying, you can sue anyone for anything. You can sue because it's Monday. Or because it's raining, and you woke up on the wrong side of the bed. Winning your suit is another thing, but even a suit that gets thrown out of court is a major hassle and worth avoiding."

"Suing Brody wouldn't do you any good," Alec said. "He's broke. I had to lend him gas money to get him here. Pretty sure he's hoping to hang around Ragnar's for the free food as long as he can."

"Then he might want to shape up," I said. "Ragnar's very down on drugs. And for that matter, enlist Ragnar's help. He's had experience doing drug interventions—he might be able to help Brody. And you might want to think about coming clean with Chief Burke. Let him know you have suspicions, but no proof. If Brody really did get ahold of a controlled substance here in Caerphilly, the chief might be more worried about the dealer than a single user. Maybe if he felt that Brody—and the production team—were doing what they could to help him catch the dealer, he might do what he can to keep it low-key. Cut Brody some slack and keep *Blades of Glory* out of the news stories."

"You really think he might?" Alec's face wore a pleading expression. "Could you maybe talk to him?"

"You talk to him," I said. "Don't worry. He's a fair man. And he knows how important this show is to Faulk and Tad. And you, too, of course," I added hastily.

"I'll talk to him, then."

"Let me know if there's anything I can do to help." I was anxious to bring our conversation to a close and duck back inside where it was warmer.

He nodded and stood looking down for a few moments. Just then a crow landed on the ground nearby.

"What if— Dammit! Get that thing away from me!"

He began backing away while flailing his arms as if to fend off the crow. But since he was a good six feet from the bird when it landed, and getting even farther away with every backward step he took, the crow barely noticed him.

Then Alec bent down, picked up a rock, and pulled back his arm to throw it at the crow.

"Stop it!" I shouted, stepping between Alec and the crow. Either Alec didn't notice or it was too late for him to stop his throw. The rock, about the size of a golf ball, flew in my direction, and I had to duck slightly to the left to avoid getting hit in the face.

I lost it.

"Stop that!" I shouted. "I'm tired of dealing with stupid, ignorant, cruel people who think it's perfectly fine to hurt animals. If I ever catch you doing that again, I'll come after you with a rock. One the size of your head."

"Sorry," he said. "I wasn't aiming at you. I—"

"Go do something useful with yourself," I snapped.

Alec turned and almost ran away.

I turned to make sure the crow was okay. And to see how he reacted. He looked up at me with those curiously bright, intelligent eyes. I couldn't help thinking he was studying me. Considering something.

"You can't fix stupid," I said, not for the first time today.

I noticed he was carrying something in his beak. He stalked forward, head bobbing with each step, until he was only about a foot away. Then he opened his beak and dropped the object he was carrying. Whatever it was glittered slightly as it fell.

"For me?" I asked.

He flew up a few feet and landed a little farther away, as if deliberately backing away to make sure I felt safe picking up whatever he had dropped. Whatever he was giving me.

I bent down and found it. A prism, about an inch long, with a tarnished brass hook through the top. I picked it up and twirled it slightly, sending off bits of light in every direction, like frozen sparks.

"Thank you," I said.

The crow cawed and flew away.

I studied the prism for a few more seconds, then tucked it into my pocket and went back inside the tent.

Chapter 14

When I reached my workstation, I found Michael, Josh, and Jamie there. Spotting me, the boys set up a cheer.

"Go, Mom," Jamie said.

"I told you so," Josh said.

"Congratulations," Michael said. "May we touch the prize-winning dagger?"

"Yes," I said. "But be careful. It's wicked sharp."

The boys examined the dagger and pronounced it "the best one yet." Then I found a makeshift sheath for it. After I checked to make sure everything valuable in my workstation was either locked up or too heavy to steal easily, we donned our wraps and left to hike up to the castle.

"Ragnar's having a feast tonight," Jamie exclaimed, accompanying the words with a leap into the air, as merely thinking of the delights ahead inspired him to become airborne.

"Ragnar almost always has a feast," I pointed out.

"Yes, but this is in honor of Faulk getting out of the hospital," Josh said. "So we're having all of Faulk's favorite foods."

"Wasn't that supposed to be a surprise?" Michael asked. "Faulk being here?"

"No," Jamie said. "The surprise is—"

Then he clapped his hands over his mouth.

"You nearly blew it," Josh complained.

"No more talking about surprises," I said. "I'm fine with waiting until whatever surprise you're planning is unveiled."

Although the boys assured me that no, it wasn't part of the surprise, I was bowled over by the transformation Mother and her crew of helpers had brought about in the castle. Apart from bits of evergreen, obviously chosen for their unusually dark color—or possibly enhanced with a bit of black paint from Caroline's spray can—nothing in it violated Ragnar's black-red-and-gold color scheme. And while the effect was obviously a little different from most people's idea of holiday décor, it was undeniably festive. Mother had seen to that. A good thing we had ten months to go before Halloween. It would probably take that long to replenish the East Coast's entire supply of black tinsel, black ribbon, and black velvet roses.

The walls were hung with black or dark green wreaths and garlands, festooned with red and gold ornaments. A large black onyx nativity scene filled the mantel over the outsized fireplace, where a yule log blazed merrily. The only thing not yet completely decorated was the enormous tree. The top was so covered with ornaments that you could barely see the dark evergreen branches. In addition to black tinsel garlands and glass balls in red and gold, it also sported quite a few black ornaments. Black glass balls. Black glass icicles. Penguins and black dragons in blown glass. And dozens and dozens of tiny feather-covered ravens and black velvet bats perched on the tips of the branches.

But the bottom of the tree was bare except for a black tinsel garland and a few hundred tiny white lights. And strategically positioned around the base of the tree were half a dozen black-painted wicker baskets containing Christmas ornaments. Red and gold glass balls. Red cardinals. Gold coins. Blown glass ornaments painted mostly black, including owls, reindeer, donkeys, bats, knights, and dragons. Black-and-red glass candy canes. And faceted mirror ornaments like tiny disco balls, whose reflections multiplied all the shiny bits of red, gold, and black around them.

The dozens of friends and family members who'd showed

up for the feast were doing their best to make sure the bottom part of the tree would soon be as full of ornaments as the upper reaches, moving back and forth between the tree and the baskets with glittering ornaments in their hands. Children were crawling around the base of the tree, alternating between hanging ornaments—unbreakable ones, I hoped, that far down—and shaking some of the wrapped presents that were already under it—black boxes with red or gold ribbon, and red or gold boxes with black ribbon. Probably fake presents for decoration only, but they'd still be interesting to shake, since when Mother decorated for the holidays she always insisted on putting something in the empty boxes her crew wrapped, to make shaking them more interesting—bells, beads, stones, rattles, marbles, sand—anything that would make an enticing sound.

"Congratulations, dear." Mother came up, kissed my cheek, and handed me a squat black stoneware mug with something steaming hot in it. "I know we're technically not supposed to know you won the first challenge, but . . . word does get out."

Especially when Mother was determined to uncover it.

"Wassail?" I asked, lifting the cup and inhaling the cinnamon-and-clove-scented steam.

"Children's version," Mother said. "I thought you'd rather start with that. If you'd rather have one with hard cider—"

"This should be fine," I said. "As tired as I am, hard cider would be too much. You deserve congratulations, too," I added. "I'm sure Ragnar is delighted, and it actually looks Christmassy."

Mother beamed, and then, with a wave, sailed away to where several visiting relatives were calling for her.

Michael and the boys had joined in the tree decoration. I made my way slowly through the crowd, greeting friends and being introduced to the few unfamiliar faces. It would be nice—well, not so much to forget about *Blades of Glory* for the rest of the evening . . . After all, I'd won the first contest. But to stop worrying about it. Enjoy my success, and then focus on enjoying

Ragnar's holiday festivities. Add a few ornaments to the tree. Nibble a few Christmas cookies—but only a few, because the gala feast would begin soon.

Only two things spoiled the perfection of my mood. One was that I hadn't yet spotted Faulk. I wanted to check for myself that he was okay. Or if not okay, at least on the road to it. I reminded myself that Dad would have moved heaven and earth to keep Faulk in the hospital if he wasn't well enough to come home. But I knew that even Dad occasionally lost a battle against the dreaded insurance companies. Or against patients who insisted on leaving the hospital against his orders.

Of course, Faulk was probably avoiding the Great Hall, which was so crowded that he'd have a hard time keeping people from jostling his broken arm. He'd probably taken refuge in some other more lightly populated space. He might be resting in his room, or in the library. Ragnar might have admitted him early to the dining room, to make sure he got a choice seat near the buffet. I'd find out later—so far I'd barely made it halfway across the Great Hall. Yes, being here would be too tiring for Faulk. I was feeling a little tired myself. And while I appreciated Ragnar's Renaissance- and medieval-themed Christmas music playlist, the effort of shouting over it took a lot of the little energy I had left.

The other thing annoying me was the weight of my tote— not surprising, since it contained not only my dagger but also about fifteen pounds' worth of hammers. Call me paranoid, but I hadn't wanted to leave my favorite tools in my workstation in the tent, protected by whatever low-cost security the Tweedles had provided. So I was slowly but steadily working my way toward the entrance hall, from which I could nip upstairs to lighten my load.

As I picked my way through the Great Hall I ran into Duncan, who still seemed to be in a foul mood.

"This place needs something like a lost and found," he said.

"Actually, there is a lost and found," I said. "Go out to the entrance hall and look for a door with a small portrait of St. Anthony of Padua hanging on it. Lost-and-found closet."

"St. Anthony of Padua?"

"Patron saint of lost items," I said.

"Maybe you could just show me where it is?"

"Just follow me and I'll point it out. Still looking for that leather jacket?"

"Yeah." He scowled. "I'm going to be seriously ticked if someone stole it. Damned thing was expensive."

"It'll probably turn up," I said. "And tell Ragnar. He'll keep an eye out for it. But check out the lost and found first. This way."

But we got separated while pushing through the crowd. I looked back. Like Michael and Ragnar, Duncan was tall enough that you could easily spot him in a crowd. Instead of following me, he'd trailed after a young woman carrying a tray of cider mugs.

Well, I'd told him what to look for.

I made it, finally, to the foot of the black marble stairs and—

"Mom! Where are you going?" Jamie asked.

"Dinner starts in a couple of minutes," Josh added.

"I'm going to drop by the suite," I said. "Stow my tote bag and freshen up a little." I didn't add that I was looking forward to using a bathroom that didn't have a long line at its door.

"Hurry back!" Josh said.

I raced up the stairs and was delighted when I arrived at the second-story landing and spotted a familiar shaggy blond head at the far end of the left-hand corridor. Faulk!

"Hurray! You're back!" I shouted.

The figure ahead of me turned.

It wasn't Faulk. It was Brody. Looking both surprised and pleased that I was calling him. Had I just undone all the efforts I'd been making to discourage him?

"Sorry," I called. "Wasn't talking to you." I realized to my relief that I had my phone in my hand. I lifted it to my mouth. "No, it's fine," I said as if talking to someone on it. "I think I just startled one of Ragnar's other guests. Are you downstairs? How are you doing? I'll meet you down there."

I turned and headed back to the stairs. I could haul my heavy tote around a little while longer. Send one of the boys to take it to the suite. And I could wait my turn for one of the bathrooms downstairs. I had no desire for a close encounter with Brody. A pity the show had to keep him around for the rest of the week, especially since I doubted he'd be all that cooperative with the requirement to keep quiet about who was in and who was out. It wasn't going to be fun, watching him sulk.

And I kept thinking about my mistake. Did Faulk and Brody really look that much alike? Not from the front. Faulk was clean-shaven while Brody had a full beard—close-cropped, but very visible. And he needed the beard—if you looked carefully, you could tell it was camouflaging a weak, almost nonexistent chin. Faulk had handsome, regular features, while Brody's face looked as if it had been assembled from slightly mismatched parts. Brody had quite a few visible tattoos, while if Faulk had any they weren't anywhere I'd ever been invited to see. And Faulk had very nice blue eyes; Brody's, though technically blue, were small, rather pale, and a little too close together.

From the back, though, my mistake was understandable. They were about the same height, with broad shoulders and hair that was remarkably similar in color and cut.

What if I wasn't the only person to make that mistake? What if whoever had attacked Faulk had actually been aiming for Brody?

I tucked the idea away to ruminate on. And to share with the chief when I saw him.

Chapter 15

As soon as I went downstairs, I was sucked back into the party. A giant buffet had taken over the dining hall so completely that Ragnar had had to set up tables outside in the hall for diners, and even then many people were taking their food back to the Great Hall to eat. And from the glimpses I caught of passing plates, Ragnar wasn't just serving Faulk's favorite foods—he was clearly aspiring to serve everybody's favorites. No wonder Rose Noire was volunteering in the kitchen to help Alice out.

I squeezed into the dining hall, caught sight of Josh and Jamie, and was initially appalled. They seemed to be pushing their way to the front of the buffet line.

And Ragnar and Michael were helping them. What in the world—?

I slipped through the crowd to get a better view of what they were doing—trying to make it obvious that I was stealing a peek at the buffet, not jumping the line.

"He definitely likes roast beef," Josh was saying.

"And he likes that sauce on it," Jamie added. "But on the side."

"Right," Ragnar said. "Gravy on the side."

"No, not gravy," Josh said.

"He does too like gravy," Jamie protested.

"But he also likes that white stuff," Josh countered.

"If you're talking about Faulk," I said, as I stepped closer, "I think he also likes horseradish sauce. On the side."

"Of course," Ragnar said. He grabbed a small bowl and put a heaping dollop of horseradish sauce in it.

"Why don't you go keep Faulk company for a little while?" Michael said, turning to me. "We can bring up a plate for you, too."

"As long as he's up to having visitors, I'd love to," I said.

"Tad doesn't think he's up to dealing with this much of a crowd." Michael waved his arm at the cheerful chaos around us. "But selected visitors are allowed."

"Tad's wise," I said.

"See if you can help Faulk remember who attacked him," Josh said.

"Grandpa says it's normal to get amnesia after a blow to the head," Jamie explained. "And he might never remember what happened to him."

"But that's no reason not to try." Josh sounded impatient.

I could actually think of a very good reason for Faulk not to work too hard at remembering—maybe even a reason to pretend he remembered next to nothing about the attack. Whoever did it could still be here at the castle, ready to strike again if he thought Faulk was about to identify him.

Or was I starting to think a little too much like Dad, whose avid consumption of mystery and true crime books made him sometimes a little too ready to suspect plots and crimes?

"I'll try to help him remember once Dad says it's okay," I said. "Remember, Faulk's recovering from injuries. So where is he?"

"The Whitby Suite," Jamie said.

"Turn left at the top of the stairs, and it's the first door on the right," Josh added.

"Sounds great," I said.

"You can take him some appetizers," Josh said, handing me a plate.

"And there should be enough for you," Jamie added.

"And when we go back through the line for ourselves we'll fill a plate for you," Michael said.

"Perfect." I took the plate they handed me—a rather large plate complete with a glass cover to keep things warm. Had they appropriated a serving platter for Faulk?

At least the cover helped me restrain myself from nibbling any of the ham biscuits, samosas, pot stickers, meatballs, sliders, crostini, wings, spring rolls, potato skins, bruschetta, bite-size quiche cups, prosciutto-wrapped melon balls, and mini pigs-in-a-blanket it contained. Would any of us make it past the appetizers? Hauling around a serving platter made me look as if I were helping out with the dinner arrangements, which made it easier to thread my way through the crowd of family and friends who all wanted to congratulate me, catch up on family news, or maybe just wish me a Merry Christmas. And I did want to talk to them. All of them. Well, most of them. Just not right now. Right now I wanted to sit down somewhere quiet and decompress.

And reassure myself that Faulk was really going to be all right.

The anxious look on Tad's face when he opened the door of the Whitby Suite wasn't reassuring. But some of the strain eased when he saw me.

"It's Meg," he called. "With food."

"Okay," Faulk said from inside. "Her you can let in."

Tad stepped aside and invited me in with an exaggeratedly low bow. I stepped inside. Faulk was half sitting, half lying on the enormous Victorian fainting couch upholstered in black velvet. Much as I appreciated Ragnar's color scheme, it wasn't flattering to anyone who was under the weather. Faulk looked alarmingly pale.

But with luck, I kept my face from showing my worried reaction.

"It's only the appetizers," I said. "Michael and the boys are gathering the main dishes."

"And desserts, I hope," Faulk said. "Let's not forget dessert."

"Have you ever known the boys to forget dessert?" I had to laugh at the mere idea. "But let me know if you're not up to having too many people, or any people at all for too long. Especially energetic young people who probably have several million questions. We can cut the visit short."

"Michael and the boys are fine," he said. "And I'm sure if I say I'm too tired to answer questions tonight, they'll listen."

"Unlike some people we know," Tad said in an ominous tone.

"Tad just chased Alec out," Faulk explained. "I know Alec's worried about me and upset that the attack on me might have something to do with the show—"

"He's worried about his stupid show, that's all," Tad said. "He's a self-centered user and—"

"And now that you've kicked him out, we can forget about him for a while," Faulk said. "And now that Meg's here, why don't you run your errands? She can keep an eye on me while you're gone."

"If you're okay with that," Tad said to me. "I want to get a few things from the house, and I've been down at the hospital with Faulk since it happened and there's stuff at the office I need to pick up and—"

"We'll be fine," I said. "If I have to leave before you get back, I'll make sure someone else responsible is here. Preferably someone with medical credentials like Dad or Caroline. Or maybe even Rose Noire, if Faulk doesn't mind drinking the herbal tea she'll insist he needs."

Faulk made a face, but he was smiling. Tad looked relieved.

"Thanks," he said, and dashed out of the room.

There was a comfy-looking red velvet chair across the coffee table from Faulk's fainting couch. I set the hors d'oeuvres down on the table, grabbed a pot sticker, and plopped into the chair with a sigh of contentment.

"Long day?"

"If I'd known they started shooting at eight in the morning, I'd have had one more reason to turn Alec down when he tried to talk me into this," I said.

"I know." He chuckled. "I don't hate mornings quite as much

as you do, but that was still a tough one. We really owe you for doing this. I know how very much you didn't want to."

"Well, it has had its compensations," I said.

"Like winning the first challenge of the competition." He grinned and held up his left hand for a high five.

"There's that." I leaned over and managed to smack his hand rather than his face—high fives are awkward with your non-dominant hand. "But explain to me just how your budget got so tangled up with Alec's TV project."

"Stupidity." He picked up a samosa and nibbled its edge. "We really shouldn't be investing in something that . . . uncertain. You probably know that our financial situation has been rocky ever since my cardiac problems started."

"I knew the whole thing was expensive," I said. "I guess I didn't realize how expensive."

"I make a good living from my blacksmithing," he said. "But I had to cut back a lot in the couple of years leading up to my surgery. Only just hitting my stride again when this happened." He gestured at his cast. "Not that Tad doesn't make good money—Rob sees to that."

"Tad totally earns it," I said. I knew what a key employee Tad had become at Mutant Wizards, the multifaceted computer software company that had grown out of my techno-challenged brother's curious talent for inventing mega-popular computer games.

"And the health insurance is top notch," Faulk said. "No complaints there. But even the best insurance doesn't cover everything. And what it doesn't cover has completely eaten up our savings, and paying back what we had to borrow is eating up most of what we're earning. Ironic, isn't it, that modern medicine literally gave me the rest of my life back . . . except I may spend the rest of it working like a dog to pay for the miracle. And having chosen life with debt over certain death, we're more aware than ever about how hard it is to make money unless you already have some. And then Tad's great-aunt died and left him a small legacy. The smart thing to do would have been to just use it to pay off some of our debt, but somehow we fell for Alec's pitch that investing in *Blades of Glory* was a once-in-a-lifetime chance to get in on the ground floor of something big. Stupid."

He shook his head.

"Not your fault," I said. "I'm sure Alec made it sound . . . incredible." That sounded rather mild. Maybe even condescending. "I mean, he's so . . . excited about it."

"Unfortunately, being excited about something doesn't make you any better at assessing its chances for success," Faulk observed. "Rather the opposite. I've been asking Michael some questions the last few days. Asking him to be brutally frank and tell me what he thinks of the show. It's been eye-opening. Wish we'd been smart enough to do that before investing in it. I mean, we sat in on the producers giving a sales pitch to some wealthy potential investors. It was amazing. They had all these charts and graphs about the exploding market for reality television and the projected cash flow for the project, and a list of the other shows they'd been involved with. We thought we were on board for the next *Great British Bake Off*. Michael was the one who figured out that their cash flow plan was a joke, and they weren't the producers on any of the shows they listed. Just minor members of the production team."

I nodded. Another time, when he was more recovered, I'd read him the riot act about not asking for help. Not just from Michael on things like whether or not *Blades of Glory* looked like a TV show that had a good chance of success. The Hollingsworth clan, Mother's extended family, was full of people with useful expertise. We were particularly well supplied with lawyers, doctors, and members of the teaching profession at every level from kindergarten to graduate school. If I ever needed advice on a subject and didn't know where to turn, I'd eventually ask Mother if anyone in the family was an expert in the field, and she'd never yet failed to deliver. I had cousins who were professional gam-

blers, Buddhist monks, disbarred jockeys, and forensic philate-
lists. We even had a convicted murderer in the family tree—on
a very distant branch, of course, and whenever his name came
up Mother insisted that he didn't look at all like a Hollingsworth
and perhaps there had been a mix-up in the hospital. Still, whenever Kevin needed information for *Virginia Crime Time,* his true
crime podcast, like the straight scoop on how something really
worked inside a prison, our wayward cousin was always eager to
oblige. For that matter, nearly everyone in the family was eager
to oblige when Mother was doing the asking.

And if Faulk and Tad's debt was that bad, maybe I should
figure out a way to help. Organize some kind of fundraising
event. We'd done it over the summer to help a local dairy farmer
whose high-tech milking shed had been struck by lightning and
burned to the ground. Amish farmers had nothing on Caer-
phillians when it came to pitching in for the common good.
Between the benefit concert and the live and online auction of
donated items, we'd raised more than enough money for a new
milking shed.

I could worry about fundraising later. When I was safely past
the contest.

"Hindsight is twenty-twenty," I said for now. "Let's talk about
something more useful."

"Such as?" Why had he tensed slightly?

"What do you know about these guys?" I asked. "My fellow
competitors."

"Ah." He relaxed again. "For a minute I thought you were
going to ask if I could think of anyone else who had a grudge
against me and might have attacked me."

"That sounds like one of Alec's questions," I said.

He nodded.

"And I gather you already told him that if you could think of
anyone, you'd have told the chief about it," I said.

"Yup." He bit into a ham biscuit and chewed thoughtfully.

"So if you're not saying anything, either you have nothing to say or the chief told you to say nothing, so there's no use in Alec asking a dozen times."

"Exactly." He grinned. "Though just so you know, I can't think of anyone with a grudge against me. Been racking my brains. And in case your mind works the same way as Alec's, no, not only did I not see who attacked me, I didn't hear him or smell him or . . . anything. I don't even remember it happening. I was just walking along listening to the Moonfruits' latest album, and the next thing I knew a million crows were flying overhead while you and Caroline stared down at me. Your dad says it's probably a mild case of retrograde amnesia. Mild, because I only seemed to have lost maybe five minutes."

"That's good," I said. "And I'm sure Dad pointed out that with retrograde amnesia, you could get back the memory of those five minutes any second now, or they might be lost forever."

"Yeah." He shook his head. "It creeps me out, just thinking about it. That you can lose a part of your life like that. Even a small part. Your dad thinks even if I do get those minutes back, I probably couldn't have seen my attacker. The blows would have come from directly behind me."

I wanted to ask if he really didn't remember anything or if he was pretending to keep whoever had attacked him from trying again. Maybe he and Dad had agreed that faux amnesia would be his best protection against another attack. And maybe they weren't paranoid—just realistic. The attack had happened. Maybe Tad wasn't being overprotective when he insisted that someone stay with Faulk.

"So what do you need to know about the other four competitors?" Faulk sounded more cheerful.

"Everything," I said. "Like, is there a reason most of them are from California?"

"Well, Alec moved out there a few years ago, you know," he said. "He mostly tapped people he knew. And they were originally going to film out there, so maybe he thought having mostly

West Coast contestants would keep down travel expenses. I think they only added me and Brody when they ran out of California bladesmiths willing to ruin their holiday season by appearing on the show. And it's a good thing Brody's out of the running so you probably don't want any scoop on him, because I couldn't give you any. Never heard of the man until he showed up on Alec's cast list, and I think the same went for the other four. Which doesn't mean he's no good, of course."

"No," I said. "But we figured that out today."

"How bad was he?"

"His knife didn't pass the strength test," I said. "Neither did Andy's, but it wasn't Andy's fault."

"Why not?"

Just then someone knocked on the door.

"Come in!" Faulk called out.

Michael and the boys entered. Josh was pushing a small cart, the kind hotels use for room service. Both its top and bottom shelves were crammed with bowls and plates.

"Save room for dessert," Jamie advised. "There's crème brûlée," he said, looking at me. "And *krumkaker* and *trollkrem*," he added, glancing at Faulk, who had grown fond of Alice's Scandinavian desserts.

"And Ragnar says if there's anything you're in the mood for that isn't here, let him know and Alice will make it," Josh said.

"We should be fine with all of that," Faulk said.

"Did you hear Mom won the first challenge?" Josh asked.

"Did Mom show you her winning dagger?" Jamie asked.

"No. Do you have it with you?" Faulk looked over at me.

By way of an answer, I reached into my tote, pulled out the dagger, unwrapped it, and handed it to Faulk. Hilt first, of course.

He sat up a little straighter as he reached out his hand to take it.

I held my breath as he examined it. So did the boys, I think. We all knew Faulk wouldn't pull his punches if he didn't think my knife deserved to win.

Chapter 16

Faulk looked up from my knife and smiled.

"Not bad," he said. "Not bad at all."

The boys, who knew that coming from Faulk those words were high praise indeed, let out their breath rather noisily and grinned at me.

"So spill," Faulk said. "How did the day go? I want the blow-by-blow account. Including why it wasn't Andy's fault that his knife broke."

So while the five of us demolished the contents of the room service cart, I told them about my day. The knife challenge. Brody's sabotage. Jasmyn's flight. The judging, and my revelation that I'd captured the sabotage on film.

"Awesome," Josh said. "Serves them right."

"Some of them," Jamie added. "They weren't all nasty. Is there any more crème brûlée?"

We heard a knock on the door, and the boys both ran to answer it.

"It's Grandpa," Josh called.

"We ate most of the food," Jamie said. "But we can go get more if you're hungry."

"No, I've eaten." Dad dashed in and set his medical bag on the coffee table. "I came to check on Faulk. How's the head? Headache gone? Any more dizziness?"

"If you're going to do a full medical examination, the

boys and I should take off," Michael said. "We have shopping to do."

"Anyplace fun?" I asked.

"No!" they all said, in unison.

"You'd be bored," Josh said. "Really bored."

"And you've had a long day," Jamie said. "You should rest. You'd be really tired if you went with us to—"

He clapped his hand over his mouth, while Josh gave him a look of exasperation.

"Yes," Michael said. "In case you have not already deduced it, we are going out to shop for your Christmas present. So you can stay and keep an eye on Faulk."

With that, they dashed out.

"Or if you like, you can go join the party for a while," Faulk said. "I expect your dad will be here. Tad may think I need a babysitter—"

"More like a bodyguard, I think," I put in.

"I'm the one who told Tad not to leave him alone just yet," Dad said. "Concussion symptoms don't always show up immediately. They can develop up to forty-eight hours after a blow."

"Whatever," Faulk said. "If Tad isn't back by the time your dad wants to leave, he can text you to come back."

"Good idea! And don't worry—I won't leave him alone!" Dad drew himself up as if he were Gandalf battling the Balrog in the mines of Moria.

Faulk glanced at me and nodded in Dad's direction, as if to say, "See? You can stop worrying."

"If you're sure," I said.

Dad and Faulk were already discussing how well his arm was healing, and how soon he'd be able to start physical therapy. I'd been planning to talk to Dad about Brody's possible drug problem. Enlist his help. But tomorrow would do. Brody might have lost, but he wasn't going away just yet, and neither was his problem. I grabbed my tote and slipped out into the hall.

The lighting in the hall wasn't all that bright. Ragnar said he liked the moody atmosphere created by the dim lighting. I pulled the door shut behind me and—

"Well, lookie here. Little Miss Tattletale."

I turned to find Brody standing in the hallway behind me. He was holding a black pottery mug. Ragnar brought out dozens of them for parties, on the theory they were cheaper in the long run and more environmentally sensitive than paper cups. Brody took a gulp of his mug's contents, and I caught a whiff of alcohol.

"If you're trying to make me feel guilty that I caught you cheating, don't bother," I said.

"Pretending you don't want to be on the show," he said. "And then you go all out and manage to win it. Explain that, why don't you?"

"I wasn't crazy about going on the show," I said. "But if I agree to do something I'm going to do it as well as I can."

"Bull," Brody said. "I know you were really crazy to get on the show. Don't eshpect me to buy that crap about only shtepping in to help out. You did everything you could to get on it, didn't you?"

"Good night, Brody." If he was drunk enough to be slurring his words, I saw no reason to continue the conversation.

"Wass your hurry?" He made a noise that was half laugh, half snarl. "Don't you realize you should be nice to me?"

"I thought I was pretty nice," I said. "I didn't whack your fingers with a ball peen hammer when I caught you fiddling with my forge."

"Yeah, you need to be really nice to me." He struck a pose familiar to any woman who's ever encountered a lecherous drunk in a bar. "Because I know what you were up to Sunday night."

"Sunday night?"

"The night your friend got what was coming to him. The man who was standing between you and your chance to get on the show. I saw what happened Sunday night. So you better be really nice to me. I'm gonna make the producers put me back on the show—and you're going to help me."

I couldn't quite suppress my laughter at that. He took a step forward and reached for me with one huge, ham-fisted hand. I stepped back and smacked his hand down with a well-placed blow from my heavily laden tote bag. He swore and stepped back.

"Good night, Brody," I said. "Go try that nonsense on someone more gullible."

I took another couple of steps away from him before turning my back and striding down the hall to the Van Helsing Suite. I didn't hurry, but I didn't waste time, and I was alert to any sign that he might be trying to follow me. I made sure my fingers were ready as I punched the key code into the door lock and breathed a sigh of relief when I heard the door latch behind me.

What was that all about? What could possibly make Brody think I'd had anything to do with the attack on Faulk?

Maybe he was fishing. Pretending to have seen or heard something in the hope that I had something to feel guilty about.

Or maybe he had seen what happened to Faulk and mistook the attacker for me.

Who could he possibly have mistaken for me? Probably not Duncan or Victor, who were both considerably taller than me and quite burly. Even with John or Andy, it seemed unlikely. Although maybe it wasn't quite as unlikely, given the extremely cold weather we'd been having. Most people bundled up like arctic explorers before stepping outside.

And visibility would have been bad. The sun was still setting when we found Faulk—but the castle cast a huge shadow, and at sunset, any place on its east side, where we found him, was already quite dark. And the attack on Faulk hadn't taken place that much earlier. Brody could very well have witnessed the attack on Faulk without being able to tell who had done it.

Still, if I had to put money on it, I'd bet he was fishing.

I made a mental note to tell the chief about all this. But later.

I stowed my tote bag, used the bathroom while I had the chance, then opened the door and cautiously peered out into the hall. No sign of Brody.

Good riddance.

I headed downstairs and flung myself into enjoying the party. The buffet lines had died down, but there were still people feasting in nearly every room on the ground floor, and Ragnar was noisily encouraging people to come back for a doggie bag when they had to leave. In the music room, a dozen or so local musicians were accompanying an enthusiastic carol sing-along. In the game room, Rose Noire and several other aunts and cousins were organizing Christmas games for the smaller children—Pin the Red Nose on Rudolph. Tinsel Limbo. A candy cane hunt. The Jingle Bell Toss, which was like Pong with jingle bells instead of coins.

In the Octagon Room, a crew of volunteers was wrapping presents—toys destined for underprivileged children and children living at the Women's Shelter. Books, candy, slippers, and bed jackets for the residents of the nursing home. And quite a lot of packages that would be slipped stealthily into the collection boxes for the Clay County Christmas Angel program, since we'd figured out years ago that without our clandestine contributions, the needy residents of our neighboring county wouldn't get much help from the angels.

In the Great Hall, a handful of diehards was trying to find room on the tree for the last few ornaments. I saw John, Andy, and Victor lounging by the fireplace, sipping mugs of wassail and looking more relaxed than I'd seen them all day.

"Hail to the champ!" Andy called out, raising his mug.

The other two raised their mugs, and I gave them a thumbs-up.

"Got to play while the cats are away," Victor said.

"He means the producers," Andy said.

"They're not around?" I was a little surprised, but not displeased. The Tweedles did not strike me as people who would be the life of a party.

"They probably went back to their hotel," Andy said. "And it's a nice hotel, but Ragnar's place is more fun."

"I don't think fun is their thing," Victor said.

"They're still here somewhere," John said. "One of them raced through a few minutes ago, looking as if he was about to have a cow about something."

Suddenly Ragnar appeared.

"Meg! Just the person I was looking for! I hate to drag you away from the festivities, but could you do a small repair in the library? I'm keeping everyone out of there until it's fixed. Don't want any problems. But I'm sure it won't take you any time at all."

He was thrusting a toolbox into my hands. Technically his toolbox, but since Ragnar's clumsiness with tools was legendary, Faulk and I were usually the ones who made use of it.

"No problem." I took the toolbox. "But what do you want repaired?"

"Oh, well, most people wouldn't even see it," he said, with a chuckle. "But you will, right away. It will be obvious to you!"

With that, he dashed away.

After the long day I'd had, repairing something was the last thing I wanted to do. No, make that the next to last thing—the absolute last thing was trying to guess what I was supposed to repair. But I could take a look, figure out what needed doing, and see if I had the energy to deal with it tonight or if I wanted to beg off and tackle it tomorrow. Better yet, get Vern to tackle it tomorrow.

"Duty calls," I said to my fellow competitors as I headed for the library. They lifted their cups in salute.

The library's enormous doors were closed, with a small OUT OF ORDER sign hanging from one doorknob. I went in, set the toolbox down, and stood in the middle of the room, looking around, trying to figure out what Ragnar wanted fixed. Nothing looked broken or out of place. Why couldn't he just come right out and tell me what he wanted done? Why was he so secretive?

And then the reason dawned on me: Ragnar probably wanted me to perform some kind of repair to the secret passage.

Chapter 17

Along with building towers at the corners of the house and digging a moat across the front of it, with a working portcullis and drawbridge, Ragnar had become obsessed with creating secret rooms, passages, and hiding places. His favorite was the secret passage in the library. You pulled out a specific fake book, which triggered a lever so that an entire section of bookshelves swung open. Behind that, a secret passage led, via a sturdy, circular, wrought iron stairway, to a small closet near the kitchen.

I'd set up the fake book. Originally I'd used the one that Ragnar had provided, a beautiful leather-bound replica of the *Necronomicon*—which, in the works of H. P. Lovecraft, was a mythical tome of arcane and forbidden lore, its contents so shocking that to read it was to risk madness. Ragnar's idea of an in-joke. Unfortunately, his guests tended to be people who'd actually read Lovecraft and knew about the *Necronomicon*, which meant they were always trying to take that particular book off the shelf and examine it, revealing the increasingly less and less secret passage. At my suggestion, we replaced the fake book with a real one that we hoped would prove much less enticing—volume XX (Renden-Schinkel) of the 1919 edition of *Salmonsens Konversations Leksikon,* a Danish-language encyclopedia. Anyone who didn't speak Danish would have little or no reason to take it out, and the occasional Danish speaker who stumbled upon it could see at once that it wasn't anything they'd ever want to read, so the passage was once more reasonably secret.

I picked up the toolbox and carried it over to the bookcase that was actually a secret door. Volume XX was there, looking innocent and boring, just as it always did. I pulled out my phone and took a minute or two to finally answer a question that always sprang into my mind when I saw it. A quick visit to a Danish-English translation site revealed that "renden" meant "gutter" and "schinkel" was "ham." Curiosity satisfied, I gave volume XX a firm pull.

The secret door lurched open, its hinges squeaking like a cave full of bats.

Easy to see what Ragnar wanted me to fix. There was an oil can in the toolbox. I grabbed it, stepped into the secret passage, and went to work on the hinges—which were, of course, hidden on the inside. A few minutes later I had them oiled up nicely. I pushed the button that opened and closed the door when you were inside—no need to hide that behind a fake book. The door swung shut almost noiselessly. The bottom hinge still had a little bit of a squeak. I bent down and added a little more oil. I was about to press the button to open it and see if I'd achieved perfect silent running when I heard voices in the library. Books make good insulation, so very little sound made it through the bookshelf door and I had no idea if the new arrivals were people with whom Ragnar had shared the secret of volume XX or the very sort of people he used the secret passage to avoid.

But at least I had a way to find out who was outside. While setting up volume XX as the handle to open the secret door, I'd also hollowed out volume XIX ("Perlite–Rendehest"—from "perlite" to "draft horse") and inserted a well-camouflaged peephole. I stooped slightly, slid open the little door that covered the peephole, and peered through it. Damn. It was Tweedledee and Tweedledum. Not quite the last people I wanted to run into— Duncan and Brody headed that list. But the two producers or executives or whatever you called them were not far behind.

Luckily I didn't have to run into them. I could just take the stairs down and—

"Dammit, talk to me. What's so damned urgent and secret that it can't wait till we get back to the hotel? Or were you just looking for an excuse to get away from all the Merry Christmas hype?"

Okay, maybe I'd eavesdrop a little bit before taking the stairs. I moved my ear closer to the peephole, making sure to keep my breathing slow and quiet. As long as it was dark inside the secret passage, you couldn't see through the peephole into it, only out, but noise would travel both ways.

"It's that damned McIlvaney."

"What now?"

"He's pitching a fit about having to stay around for the rest of the filming."

"Tell him to read his contract. He leaves now, he doesn't get a cent."

"I told him that. He's drunk as a skunk. Says he doesn't care. Says he's been spied on and humiliated and if we don't let him go he'll sue our asses off."

"Yeah, right. Just tell him . . . tell him whatever you think will keep him around till morning."

"I took away his car keys."

"Good."

"Wasn't hard. He kept dropping them. And Ragnar's going to have someone babysit him. Talk him down, or even hold him down if he tries to leave."

"Good. Because a guy like that probably knows how to jump-start a car. Taking away his keys might not be all that effective."

"Yeah, and he might try to shake the babysitter, so Ragnar's going to put a volunteer out at the gate. If McIlvaney takes off—in his own car or anyone else's—they'll notify the local cops to pull him over for a DUI."

"That takes care of tonight. What about tomorrow?"

"Tomorrow, when he's sober, we'll try to reason with him.

Make sure he understands that if he walks now, he leaves with nothing."

"Up the ante. Tell him that if he walks, we sue him for breach of contract."

"Can we?"

"How should I know? Get the lawyers on it. But it doesn't really matter—you think he knows if we can sue him or not? Just scare him enough so he stays put for a couple more days and we're home free."

"I'll try. By the way, if you decide to go and talk to him—"

"God, let's hope neither of us has to do that."

"If you do, remember Ragnar's moved him to a different room. Someplace pretty far away from the other contestants and the rest of the production team. In a wing where it should be easier to keep an eye on him."

"That should help, not having to run into all the people who know he cheated and still lost."

"Actually, they did the move this afternoon, while the contest was still going on. Before we even knew he was going to be the big loser. Apparently, he was hassling some of the women."

"Which ones?"

"That blond camerawoman. And . . . um . . . your niece."

"I'll kill the bastard." Evidently this Tweedle was B. J. Zakaryan.

"Don't worry," said the other one—presumably, Pierre Duval. "Jasmyn's fine. He was just, you know, making her feel uncomfortable."

"I don't care. No one bothers my niece. Keep him away from her, or I will kill him."

"Ragnar's taking care of it. He's got an in with the local sheriff or something. He sort of hinted that he could get a deputy out here undercover to keep an eye on things. If he bothers any of the women—"

"We don't have any room in the budget for—"

"There's no charge. Or if there is, Ragnar's taking care of it. He's done a great job handling the whole situation—he and our woman blacksmith."

"Meg? What did she do?"

"Seems to have brought her cousin out here to keep Jasmyn company and fend off McIlvaney. And found that girl who's filling in for Jasmyn."

"We owe her one. I owe her one."

"We owe her another one. She noticed Brody's little problem."

Zakaryan's reaction to this was unprintable.

"It's okay," Duval said. "She didn't go to the cops. She told Alec about it. Kind of gave him an ultimatum to fill us in so we could do something about it before Brody got up to anything that would bring the cops down on his head."

"So we're not out of the woods yet."

"Now that he's out of the contest, we should be okay."

"If you can keep him under control."

"Working on it."

"How come we ended up with him? Why couldn't we find someone who wasn't a druggie?"

The other Tweedle didn't answer—perhaps recognizing this as a rhetorical question.

A pause.

"What do you think of her?" Zakaryan asked.

"Meg? We're damn lucky we got her to fill in. And that whole thing with the mini cameras hidden in the carbon monoxide detectors—brilliant. It's going to absolutely make the first episode."

"No one's going to believe she thought of that herself. They'll all claim we rigged the whole thing."

"Still makes for good drama."

"Did she really make the best knife? Or did the judges pick her because they liked the hidden camera stunt?"

"Marco says it was legit—they'd pretty much decided her knife was the winner before she outed McIlvaney as a cheat. Says it was just what he said in his speech—the balance. You remember when the judges were all picking up the knives and hefting them and waving them around and all? Marco says they all noticed it. Except for Brody's, none of the knives felt unbalanced—not even Andy's. But hers was exceptionally well balanced. Who knew that was a thing?"

"That's good, then. Marco has a pretty good social media platform. He'll get the word out. But what if we can't manage Brody? What do you think she's going to do? Tell the cops?"

"Alec says she probably won't unless she thinks we're ignoring the problem."

"So we don't have the luxury of hoping nothing happens."

They were silent for a minute or so. I decided I'd heard enough. I could sneak away the next time they started talking, so there would be enough noise to cover any little sounds I made while easing away from the door and down the spiral staircase.

"Let's go try to find the bastard again," Zakaryan said.

"I'm not sure I'm ready to go out there again," Duval said. "If I have to listen to one more Christmas carol . . ."

"We'll have a quick look around, and then head back to the Inn. At least their Christmas decorations are tasteful."

If Mother heard that . . . I tried not to imagine her reaction. Of course, Mother had also done the Inn's decorations, but still. She was a firm believer in the notion that a designer's work should reflect the client's taste, not the decorator's. Her decorating for Ragnar absolutely did that, and if you asked me it was all in perfectly good taste. Take that, Tweedles.

"Going to be hell, getting a cab at this hour," one of them was saying. "Maybe we should call one now."

"Alec can drive us back. Or Ragnar can find someone."

I heard the library door open and close again.

"Well, that was interesting," I said to myself. And then I stood still for a couple of minutes, listening for any noise that might indicate that one of the Tweedles had lingered in the library—or had left something behind and had to come back for it. Satisfied that it was empty, I was reaching for the button to open the secret door when I heard the main library door open.

"We can talk in here." I recognized Brody's voice.

"Make it fast." John's voice. He sounded impatient. "I have better things to do."

Okay, maybe I'd eavesdrop a little while longer.

Chapter 18

"Why so hostile?" Brody asked. "But okay. I'll cut to the chase. I know."

A silence.

"You know?" John said. "Know what?"

"What you were up to."

"This is like watching paint dry. Up to?"

"Sunday night." Brody's tone became sly and insinuating. And while he was slurring a little, it wasn't that bad. He appeared to have sobered up a little since my encounter with him. "You didn't know I was there, of course, but I went out for a bit of fresh air. And I saw."

John said nothing.

I pulled out my phone and texted Ragnar. "If anyone's looking for Brody, he's in the library." And then I sent the same thing to Alec.

"It's completely understandable," Brody went on. "I mean, he was the strongest competition, right? The biggest danger. And you weren't putting him out of the picture permanently. Just . . . making sure he wasn't in your way."

"You think it was me who attacked Faulk." John's tone was flat.

"And I'm just as glad as you are to have him off the show," Brody said. "Maybe even gladder. Because I think maybe you're going to want to keep me quiet."

"Am I, now?"

John didn't sound worried. He sounded like someone who was being deliberately calm and patient. If Brody had any sense, he'd be starting to feel a little worried.

I pulled out my phone and started a text to the chief.

"Yes, you are." Brody was trying to sound menacing. He wasn't very good at it. "You don't have to do much. Just join in when I make my pitch to get back on the show. You know it wasn't fair. They weren't supposed to eliminate anyone until the end of this week's filming. And once I'm back on the show, I'll be so happy I'll probably forget all about what I saw."

I couldn't see either of them—they were out of range of my peephole. But I'd bet anything Brody was wearing that smarmy smile.

I glanced down at the text I'd been typing: "Brody McIlvaney is telling various people he'll turn them in for attacking Faulk if they don't help him get back on the show. Including me, so I don't think he really knows anything. Just fishing." I hit SEND.

"Go to hell," John said.

"Come on—don't be like that."

"I don't know what you think you know, but I had nothing to do with the attack on Faulk. And if you think you know something about what happened, you should go to the police with it, instead of trying to blackmail me or anyone else into helping you."

"You can't really—"

"And I hope they tell you to go to hell when you ask to get back on the show. You cheated. You don't get a do-over. Good night."

I heard John's footsteps—a little heavier than usual, suggesting that he was working to control his temper. The library door opened and then slammed closed.

"Shoot," Brody said, though without venom. "Well, I knew he was a long shot."

He waited a minute or so, as if to make sure John was gone, then crossed to the door and left, shutting it carefully behind him.

My phone vibrated. A reply from the chief: "Thanks."

I felt relieved. If Brody really knew anything about the attack on Faulk, the chief would get it out of him. And if he didn't, maybe the chief would shut down his blackmail gambit.

Should I lurk here a while longer, to see if Brody tried it on anyone else?

Not necessary. I knew he'd tried it on me and on John. I didn't need to hear him tackle the other three competitors to know what he was doing.

And no reason for me to continue eavesdropping. I opened the secret door long enough to grab the toolbox, then closed it again and took the circular stairway down to the kitchen level.

Halfway down, I got a text from Ragnar.

"Brody not in library."

"No." I paused on the stairway to text back. "Left a few minutes ago."

"We must find him! I've had his possessions moved to the Renfield Room so we can take care of him."

I couldn't decide if this was sad or funny. The Renfield Room might sound elegant—for that matter, it probably even looked elegant. But it was named after the fly-eating lunatic from *Dracula* and had been designed as a comfortable but secure lodging for what Ragnar referred to as "difficult" guests. This usually meant friends he was helping kick a drug or alcohol addiction, but on occasion, it had been used to safely house acidheads on bad trips as well as would-be suicides. It was very far from all the other guest rooms, soundproofed, with bars on the windows, contained nothing that even the most determined occupant could use to harm himself or others, and was the only bedroom in the house where the door could not be opened from the inside. I hoped Ragnar found Brody and introduced him to the enforced joys of the Renfield Room before he could harass anyone else.

"Will let you know if I see him," I texted back.

When I got to the bottom of the stairway I waited for a minute or so, listening for sounds and peering out of a peephole that gave me a view of the corridor outside. As far as I could tell it was empty. I hurried out, shut the closet door behind me, and quickly made my way to the larger corridor that led past the kitchen and the storerooms. That corridor eventually led to the large blacksmith shop Ragnar had installed for Faulk and me to use when we were making iron things for the castle. If anyone questioned my being down here in the basement level, I could claim I had gone there to look for something. I took a deep breath and looked up and down the corridor.

Once I was sure the secret of the library was safe, I relaxed and began strolling down the corridor, to the upbeat sounds of "Jingle Bell Rock." As I passed by the door to the main kitchen, I glanced in. Alice, Rose Noire, and several other kitchen helpers were there, performing a sort of Rockette-style precision dance number to the tune. I watched, bemused, for a few bars. Then a timer went off, and they all raced to grab potholders and pull batches of cookies out of the kitchen's several ovens. Scattered around the kitchen I could see multiple batches of cookies cooling on the several dozen tiers of wire racks.

Alice's traditional holiday cookie bake was off to a good start.

I continued down the hallway until I got to the elevator. I punched the button and then, given how slow it was, I leaned against the wall to wait for it. And found my mouth opening in a wide yawn.

Maybe instead of going back to the party, I should head up to bed. It wasn't that late for a night owl like me. But I'd gotten up earlier than usual this morning, and I was going to have to do it again tomorrow.

The elevator arrived. I punched the button for the first floor. I closed my eyes during its slow ascent.

The elevator lurched to a stop and the doors slowly opened. The noise of the party startled me into opening my eyes. The two Tweedles were standing there in the front hall, looking expectantly at the elevator. Their faces fell when they saw me.

"Where's Alec?" one of them called.

I raised my shoulders in an exaggerated shrug. Then I spotted Alec coming up behind them, so I pointed.

"Sorry," Alec said. "I left my backpack on the terrace—just let me grab it and then I'll bring the car around."

He dashed away again. I punched the button for the second floor. The doors slowly closed and after another eternity the elevator stopped again.

When the elevator doors opened I could hear the noise of the party, but a little muted by distance. I sighed with relief. Then I stepped out of the elevator and was surprised when I almost ran into Rose Noire. She must have run up the stairs from the kitchen while the elevator made its slow ascent. She was standing by the elevator but gazing back down the hallway.

"Are you okay?" I asked.

"Oh, yes," she said. "I'm fine."

Was that a slight emphasis on the "I"?

"How's Jasmyn doing?" I asked.

"Better." Her voice sounded tentative.

"But . . ." I prompted.

"I'm worried about her," Rose Noire said. "She's doing better, but she still seems . . . well, haunted."

"Do you mean literally?" I asked. "By a ghost? As in possessed?"

"No, of course not." She rolled her eyes. "Haunted as in suffering from the aftereffects of some traumatic experience. Her whole aura is . . . sad and damaged."

I nodded. I wasn't sure I believed in auras—and even if they did exist, I didn't share Rose Noire's ability to detect and assess them. But I'd long ago figured out that she was a good judge of character.

"Just what did this Brody person do, anyway?" she asked.

"I have no idea," I said. "All I know for sure is that he's the sort of smarmy, self-centered jerk who doesn't pick up on social cues, and thinks leering is a form of flirting. If he's done worse with anyone, I haven't heard about it. Not yet anyway. Has she said anything?"

"No." Rose Noire pursed her lips for a few moments. "But she seems reluctant to be in the same room with him, even if there are plenty of other people around."

Not good. I'd merely assumed Brody was a nuisance. What if—

"Try to get her to talk," I said. "If he's harassing women, or worse—"

"They've moved him to another room," she said.

"I've heard," I said. "Does that make Jasmyn feel better?"

"I don't know," she said. "I came up to invite her to join Alice and me but she's not answering her door."

"Maybe she's gone to bed early," I said. "That's my plan. And I bet she had to get up even earlier than I did this morning."

"You're probably right," she said. "Well, those cookies aren't going to bake themselves."

She pressed the button to call back the elevator.

"Night," I said, and headed for our suite.

The suite was dark and quiet. Mostly quiet. As soon as I stepped inside, I heard the clicking of canine claws on the marble bits of the floor. Tinkerbell, Spike, and three Pomeranians came out to greet me. The three Poms were so excited by my arrival that they kept whirling around in circles, yipping excitedly. Tinkerbell wagged her tail in a slow, dignified manner. Spike scowled glumly at me as if to say, "If you're not Josh or Jamie and you're not bringing me a treat, what use are you, anyway?"

"I hope nobody needs to go out," I said. "Because I'm too tired to take you."

I pointed to the room door. They all stared at me. Tink let out a "whuff."

I assumed that meant they were all fine for the moment.

I handed out treats all around, which seemed to satisfy everyone. I glanced around and was relieved to see that someone— Michael, no doubt—had brought along a portable version of the family task whiteboard. According to it, the boys had taken the pack for a long walk at 8:00 P.M. I pulled out my phone and checked the time. Only 10:30. The dogs could last until the boys were back.

All five of them followed me to the bathroom and observed me solemnly while I peed, brushed my teeth, and washed my face. Then they followed me into the bedroom. Tinkerbell leaped up onto the huge black-and-red king-size bed. I had to lift up Spike and the Pomeranians. Spike curled up on Michael's pillow. Tinkerbell sprawled across most of the rest of what would eventually be Michael's side of the bed.

I'd let Michael and the boys deal with it when they came in.

The three Pomeranians waited until I'd curled up under the covers, then glued themselves to me—one against my back, one against my stomach, and one across my feet.

"I'll never get to sleep like this," I muttered.

The dogs ignored me. Several of them were already snoring.

And that was the last thing I remembered.

Chapter 19

"Good morning!" Rose Noire trilled.

"There's no such thing," I muttered.

"You'll feel better when I've braided your hair."

I probably wouldn't, but I wasn't awake enough to argue. Déjà vu all over again, as Michael often said.

"And I'm going to lay out your clothes." An unfamiliar voice.

"Jasmyn's going to help, too," Rose Noire said. "Isn't that nice?"

I reserved comment.

"Gotta win the next challenge, Mom!" Josh.

"I've got your soda." Jamie.

I opened my eyes. I was surrounded by five dogs and four humans. That was about nine beings more than I wanted to share the bed with at this disgustingly early hour.

Jamie popped the top on my Diet Coke and handed it to me. I managed to mumble my thanks.

Michael appeared. "Bundle up and take the dogs out for a nice, long walk, guys," he said, "and we'll meet you downstairs for breakfast."

Boys and dogs vanished. I closed my eyes and caffeinated while Rose Noire and Jasmyn worked on my hair. Even in my early morning stupor, I was struck by the difference in Jasmyn. She was . . . nice. Human. Kindly and considerate. She even looked like a different person in jeans and a T-shirt with NAMASTE across the front. Liberating her from the *Blades of Glory* set had been a great idea. Later, when I was feeling more articulate, I would enlist Rose Noire to make sure she didn't ever return to what was obviously, at least for her, a soul-draining job. Better yet, I could enlist Ragnar to convince her she needed to stay at the castle for a few months until she found herself.

I was feeling closer to human by the time we went downstairs. I actually decided to eat breakfast before heading down to the production tent.

"I'm not sure eight slices of bacon constitute a balanced breakfast," Michael said as I turned to leave the buffet.

He had a point. I went back to add two small sausages and a bear claw.

I found a place on one of the black leather sofas and began nibbling my bacon. Michael brought me a bowl of fruit, and I decided that looked good, too.

Around the room, I could see other members of the cast and crew filling their plates, or maybe just mainlining coffee.

"Thanks," I said. "The fruit's a good idea."

When we'd cleaned our plates, Michael suggested that a little fresh air might help me wake up. Considering that any air meeting the definition of fresh would probably be chilled to about 25 degrees Fahrenheit, he was probably right. But it sounded like a good idea. I had to go outside soon anyway.

We donned our coats and went out onto the terrace. There we sat on the stone parapet and gazed over the rolling fields, with me sipping my soda and Michael drinking his coffee. A little sanity before I had to immerse myself again in *Blades of Glory*.

"What are you and the boys doing today?" I asked.

"We're starting off with a cross-country ride," he said. "Ragnar's going to let us borrow some of his horses."

I felt a brief pang of envy. I'd enjoy the day's blacksmithing work once I got into it, but at the moment, riding around the country on one of Ragnar's beautiful coal-black Friesian horses sounded like a lot more fun. The enormous creatures might look like fiery battle steeds, but they were actually gentle, docile, and very well-trained.

"Let's do that sometime soon," I said. "Sometime when I'm not tied up all day."

"Absolutely," he said. "And you should probably head down to the production tent soon."

"I will," I said—a little absently. I'd just caught sight of something odd out in one of the pastures. "I'm waiting till the last minute. Can you tell what's going on out there?"

"Where?" Michael's brow furrowed as he peered through the morning mists, trying to see what I was pointing at.

"In the cow pasture," I said. "Why are the cows all standing around in a semicircle?"

He shook his head.

"Never seen them do anything like that before," he said. "Of course, I don't spend a lot of time watching cows. Especially not at dawn. Maybe this is some ritual they do every morning. The bovine equivalent of Rose Noire's sun salutations. We could go down and check it out."

"Let's take a closer look first," I said. "Ragnar keeps binoculars handy."

I went over to the bird-feeding area where, beside the bins, there was a little waterproof cabinet in which Ragnar kept a couple of bird identification guides and several pairs of binoculars. A delicate Art Nouveau–styled pair and several ornate steampunk contraptions—all black or black and gold, all looking like elegant toys, but all fitted with top-quality lenses. I grabbed two pairs, handed one to Michael, and focused the other on the cows.

"They seem to be looking at something in the middle of the circle," Michael said. "A dead calf, maybe?"

"No calves this early," I said. "I think it's a person."

"I think you're right."

We both took the binoculars down from our eyes and exchanged a look.

"I think maybe someone should go check it out," Michael said. "I'll go."

"I'm coming with you," I said. "They'll have to put up with me being a little late."

We stowed the binoculars, hurried down the stairs, and began walking as fast as we could across the field behind the terrace. It normally served as a pasture for the sheep and goats, but they'd all been exiled to a more remote field for the duration of the filming, both to reduce the amount of baaing and bleating that had to be edited out of the soundtrack and to make it harder for the always-curious goats to invade the production tent.

From ground level, we couldn't actually see the circle of cows anymore—not until we had nearly reached the fence separating the pasture we were crossing from the one where the cows were. They were all still there. In fact, a couple more might have joined the circle.

There were also a few crows around. Of course—there were nearly always crows at Ragnar's. Several of them were circling overhead, and several more were sitting on the fence. When we arrived at the fence—one of the elegant wooden fences that had recently received a new coat of glossy black paint—the sitting crows rose into the air and settled down a little farther along the rail. The crows circling overhead joined them. I wondered if, like llamas, crows just enjoyed watching what humans were up to.

If I'd been a stranger to Ragnar's, I'd probably have hesitated before jumping over the fence into a pasture with his cows. The Belted Galloways were merely big, but both the Lakenvelders and the Scottish Highland cows had long, wicked-looking horns. Fortunately, I knew that, like the Friesians, all of them were as mild-mannered as you could possibly want. The only real danger they posed was that some of them weren't particularly careful about not stepping on humans' feet when they came up to beg for treats and have their heads scratched. And once Michael and I climbed over the fence, they seemed to know this was no time for head scratching.

About fifteen of them were standing in the circle. Several of them moved courteously aside as if they knew we wanted a better view of what they were looking at with such obvious curiosity: a crumpled figure sprawled on the grass.

A figure with a shaggy head of blond hair. Not Faulk, though. The figure's head was turned just enough to show a bit of the close-cropped reddish beard.

"It's Brody," I said. "Call nine-one-one."

Michael pulled out his phone.

I walked over to Brody's side. One of his arms was flung out as if he'd stuck it out to break his fall. I took hold of his wrist to check for a pulse.

Even before I got my fingers in the proper place I could tell that he was dead. His skin was surprisingly cold. Still warmer than the chilly air around us, but way too cold for a living person.

I did the pulse check anyway. Nothing. And the arm was stiff. Rigor mortis. He'd been dead for a while.

Behind me, Michael was talking to Debbie Ann, the dispatcher.

"Out in Ragnar's cow pasture," he was saying. "We'll have someone meet the ambulance at the gate to show them where . . . Meg, what's his full name? And how bad off is he?"

"His name is Brody McIlvaney," I said. "And I'm afraid there's not going to be much the ambulance can do. He's dead. Probably been that way for a while. He's cold." I almost said, "cold as ice," but that would be an exaggeration. "Cold and stiff," I added instead.

While Michael relayed this, I pulled my hand back and stepped away from Brody's body. I was curious to know what had happened to him, but I was content to let the EMTs figure it out when they got here.

Then I noticed something. There was blood on the ground beside Brody's head. And a few smears of blood in the matted blond hair.

"And let Chief Burke know about this," I said. "There's blood here. Brody may have been attacked."

As Michael repeated my words into the phone, I realized that "attacked" wasn't accurate. If there was blood in Brody's hair and on the ground around his head, maybe he hadn't just been attacked. Maybe he'd been murdered.

"Vern's helping out with the show," I said. "He's probably here by now. Let's notify him."

"Good idea," Michael said. "I'll let Debbie Ann know. And once you do that, tell Ragnar about sending someone out to guide the ambulance."

I nodded.

Vern answered on the second ring.

"What's up?" he asked. "Things are about to get started over here. They're not looking for you just yet, but they will be soon."

"I'll be there when I can," I said. "Something more urgent's come up. Brody's dead. Possibly murdered. Can you come out to the cow pasture and take charge of the crime scene till the chief gets here?"

"Holy hell. On my way."

Next, I called Ragnar.

"Good morning, Meg," he said. "Are you coming down for breakfast? Today's filming starts soon, you know."

He sounded uncharacteristically anxious. Well, at least that meant the bad news I was about to share wouldn't ruin a good mood.

"I'm already down," I said. "I've got bad news. Something's happened to Brody."

"I know," he said. "I'm sorry. I know you were counting on me to keep him out of trouble. I recruited a couple of volunteers to keep watch and make sure he stayed in his room, but we never found him last night, so I told them to stand down and we'd start looking again in the morning. And I had one of them stationed in the hall outside his old room, in case he came back. But don't worry. We're looking everywhere for him. We'll find him sooner or later."

"Michael and I already found him," I said. "Out in the cow pasture."

"The cow pasture? What is he doing there? He's not . . . up to something, is he?"

"Not anymore," I said. "He's dead."

A brief silence.

"Oh, dear," he said. "The poor man. Was he . . . did he . . . ?"

"It's not suicide, if that's what you're thinking," I said. "Probably murder. Chief Burke will be coming, and probably some of his officers, and the ambulance. Can you get someone to show them back here?"

"Of course. I will do it myself. I was supposed to be watching over him, you know. Protecting him. And instead, someone kills him? Here? If I find who did it—"

"If we find who did it, we will turn them over to the chief," I said. "And don't feel bad. You were supposed to be protecting him from himself. How were any of us supposed to know someone had it in for him?"

"But still. He was under my protection. I'll go down to the gate myself."

We rang off, and I went over to where Michael was still talking to Debbie Ann.

"No," he was saying. "Meg checked him for a pulse, but apart from that, we've tried not to disturb anything. Vern's here. I'm going to sign off if that's okay."

I turned to see Vern approaching at a rapid clip, thanks to his long legs and ground-covering stride.

"Chief notified?" he asked.

"Debbie Ann's notifying him," Michael said. "And Horace and Meg's dad."

Vern nodded. He took out his phone and began taking pictures of Brody's body and the surrounding pasture.

"Any idea what happened?" he asked. "No chance the cows trampled him, is there?"

"I doubt it," I said. "I think we'd see some more visible damage if that had happened. And you know Ragnar's cows. They're all gentle. Almost housebroken."

"Yeah." Vern was leaning over to get a better look at Brody without moving closer, his body almost at a 45-degree angle. "I can see one of them hauling off and kicking him if he was tormenting her. But even that would take a lot of provocation."

I nodded.

"I can stay here with Vern if you need to get over to the production tent," Michael said.

"I'd rather stay here until the chief arrives," I replied. "Not sure how well I can pretend that nothing's happened, and he might like to be the one who breaks the news to the cast and crew."

"And sees their reactions," Vern said. "Good thinking."

So we stood around. I felt awkward, torn between my curiosity about what had happened to Brody and the feeling that it was rude and somehow intrusive to stare at him. After all, he wasn't a friend, and I couldn't pretend to be feeling any great sorrow. In fact, now that I had recovered from the initial shock of finding him, I was feeling a mixture of curiosity about who had killed Brody and worry that perhaps someone I did consider a friend might have done it. He had certainly managed to provoke enough people. Not that provocation excused murder, but I could definitely see Brody causing someone to lose their temper and lash out.

"The crows are certainly curious." Michael pointed down the fence, where several more of them had landed. They were all surveying the scene with their bright, beady eyes. "Do they eat carrion?"

"If they can get it," I said. "They're opportunistic feeders."

"Good thing we got here so early, then."

I nodded and glanced around. In addition to half a dozen crows on the fence, there were at least another dozen in the trees. Yes, a good thing we'd found Brody before they had.

My friend Aida Butler was the next deputy on the scene.

"You got here fast," I said.

"Actually, I was already on my way here when the call went out," she said. "Was going to pick up my puppy from Josh and Jamie's doggie daycare. Looks like maybe I should leave her here a little while longer—I'm probably going to be pulling a double shift, thanks to this."

She nodded toward Brody's body.

Horace and Dad arrived next, closely followed by the chief. Dad went over to pronounce Brody officially dead, and then he and Horace began their medical and forensic examination of the crime scene. Which I knew from past observation would take a long time and be not nearly as dramatic and fascinating as it looked on TV.

"Unless you need me, I'm going to take the boys out on that horseback ride," Michael said. "Before everyone up at the castle hears about this and the misinformation starts flying around. I'd rather keep them away until the first round of morbid curiosity dies down."

"Good idea," the chief said. "Meg, I'd appreciate it if you could stick around. Just for a little while. I know they probably want you down there where they're filming—"

"They definitely do." I'd silenced my phone and stuffed it into my pocket, but I'd started to feel the buzzes that alerted me to incoming texts and voicemails. "But if they haven't already heard about this, you probably want to be the one to break the news to them—considering that the people involved in the show, especially the cast, are probably going to be your prime suspects."

"A good point." The chief turned to his deputies. "Vern, maybe you could go back to the tent and continue your under-cover assignment for a little while longer. Keep an eye on the

Hollywood folks. I'll come down there to talk to them as soon as I've finished interviewing Meg, but if rumors get out before then, take charge of the situation, make sure they don't start talking to each other about it, and let me know."

"Right, Chief." Vern nodded and began striding back toward the tent.

"Aida, someone from the funeral home's bringing their hearse out to pick up the deceased when Horace and Dr. Langslow give the go-ahead."

"Not the ambulance?" Aida asked.

"They were already out on a run," the chief said. "And from what Michael told Debbie Ann, it was pretty obvious that Mr. McIlvaney was past their help. So I told them to stand down and called Maudie at the funeral home. You take charge here until they're finished."

Aida nodded.

The chief walked a little closer to where Horace and Dad were at work.

"Dr. Langslow," he said. "I realize it's early, but can you give me even a rough time of death?"

"So you can start checking alibis." Dad stood up and turned to us. "Of course I can only give you a very rough one, though. Based on rigor and body temperature, and making allowances for the cold temperature overnight—at least six hours, but probably no more than eleven."

"So between eight P.M. and one A.M.," the chief said. "That's helpful. Thanks."

The chief gestured to me, and we turned to head away from the pasture. I wasn't sorry to leave the crime scene behind.

"So tell me about this Brody McIlvaney."

Chapter 20

"Where should I start?" I asked.

"Wherever you like." The chief set a slow pace, and I fell in step beside him. "I assume his death's going to play havoc with this TV show you're filming."

"Not really," I said. "He was eliminated late yesterday afternoon—first one out."

"Interesting." He had taken out his little pocket notebook and was scribbling in it. "So the other competitors might not be my prime suspects after all, if eliminating him to improve their chances in the competition would no longer be a motive."

"They still might be suspects," I said. "Just not for that reason. Even before the end of the first challenge, I don't think any of us were too worried about him as a competitor. But he's done plenty of other things to annoy people. Nothing that would inspire me to do away with him, of course."

"But you think others might feel differently?"

"Possibly," I said. "In fact, I can think of one really good reason why someone might have knocked him off."

The chief cocked his head to indicate that he was listening.

"Last night, after dinner, Brody made an opportunity to talk to me alone," I said. "And he dropped a very thinly veiled hint that he knew what I'd been up to Sunday night, and if I didn't want him to tell everyone, I should be really nice to him and help him get back on the show."

"And just what were you up to Sunday night that he thought you wanted to conceal?"

"Nothing," I said. "Nothing I'd have any qualms about seeing on the front page of the *Caerphilly Clarion*. Or *The New York Times*, for that matter. I went to the hospital with Faulk. I had a meeting with the producers and the other contestants. I turned in early, and Michael and the boys can testify that I didn't go anywhere until I had to wake up at seven-freakin'-o'clock Monday morning."

"This was the fishing you notified me about." The chief scribbled some more. "I'd have called it attempted extortion, myself. I was planning to tackle him today—make sure he really didn't see anything. But why would he approach you? You weren't yet a competitor when Faulk was attacked."

"Yes, but he thought I wanted to be," I said. "And was seeing if I showed any signs of guilt. I was trying to figure out why he had approached me until I overheard him trying the same thing on John."

"And Mr. Dunigan didn't rise to the bait?"

"He pretty much said he knew Brody was fishing and told him to buzz off. But I'd bet anything Brody tried the same thing with some or all of the other competitors—pretending he had something on them and trying to talk them into helping him get back into the contest. For that matter, he might have tried it on anyone else he thought might be a suspect, but apart from the competitors, I can't think of anyone else involved in the production who has an obvious motive for wanting Faulk out of the picture. But if you figure out who attacked Faulk, maybe that person had a reason to want to shut Brody up."

"Interesting," the chief said. "It's a very plausible motive, what you're suggesting. Strange how it never seems to occur to extortionists what a risk they're taking."

"Does it count as extortion?" I asked. "He wasn't asking for money—he wanted us to help him get back in the contest. Am

I remembering wrong, or doesn't extortion need to involve money?"

"According to the Code of Virginia, it counts if you extort money, property, or pecuniary benefit," he said. "There's a cash prize for this contest, right?"

I nodded.

"Pecuniary benefit," the chief said. "So Brody was attempting extortion. And one of his targets may have silenced him. What's your take—who benefits from sidelining Faulk?"

"Not me," I said with a sigh. "I'd much rather be on the sidelines watching Faulk compete. Although a couple of the other competitors probably think I'm lying about that."

I thought for a few more moments.

"Okay, I think Faulk was considered a leading contender," I said. "Possibly *the* leading contender. John thinks it would most likely have come down to a battle between Faulk and Duncan in the final episode, though he thought he had a chance, as did Victor and Andy."

"And not you?"

"He was talking about how it looked before Faulk was attacked," I reminded him. "I was just a gofer then."

"That's right. But even though you weren't in the picture, Mr. McIlvaney was."

"In the picture," I said. "But not generally considered in the running. Victor thought it was going to be him—Victor himself, I mean—against either Faulk or Duncan. He was complimentary about John and Andy, but pretty dismissive of Brody. I think all the competitors were."

"So none of the competitors were likely to think knocking off Brody would improve their chances."

"No. But they all saw Faulk as tough competition."

"Fair enough, but can you see any of them trying to eliminate the competition by attacking Faulk?"

"Well, yeah," I said. "Brody."

"No one else?"

"Remember, I don't know them all that well," I said. "Except for Brody, they're all from California. And all five of them mostly do bladesmithing, so it's not as if I've gotten to know them at craft fairs."

"Understood. But your impressions?"

I thought about it.

"Not John or Andy," I said. "They know they're not considered front-runners, but they think they have a chance, and I don't think they'd value winning the contest if it wasn't fair and square. And the same goes for Victor, except that he's a lot more confident about his chances, and I get the feeling he's disappointed not to be able to go toe-to-toe with Faulk."

"And the fifth one?" The chief looked thoughtful. "Mr. Jackson?"

"I know him even less than the others," I said. "I was avoiding him. Him and Brody."

"But . . ." he prompted.

"If you told me one of the competitors had attacked Faulk, I'd have said it was either Duncan or Brody. Brody because he realized his chances of winning were remote, and he wanted to improve them. Or Duncan, because he knows he's good and thinks he deserves it and will probably win it—but he's a pragmatist and I don't imagine he'd be squeamish about bashing Faulk if it helps ensure he gets the win. If he loses, I bet he complains that the judges are biased or aren't really knowledgeable enough, or something like that."

"So you see Duncan as a plausible suspect for attacking Faulk, and then killing Brody under the belief that Brody witnessed the attack and was trying to blackmail him."

"Plausible?" I sighed. "I'm not sure I find any of them all that plausible as suspects. Let's call him the least *im*plausible. But Brody's extortion attempts aren't the only reason someone might want to do him in. I can think of a couple of others, and probably should have brought them up before now. Although I don't think any of them are as likely as him trying to blackmail whoever attacked Faulk."

"Go on."

"Brody had reportedly been harassing a couple of women involved in the production," I said. "I have no idea if he was just a nuisance or if he might have provoked one of them to retaliate. Also, he may have been a drug user, which tends to put you in touch with dangerous people. And the reason he got kicked out of the contest in the first round was that in addition to turning out a pretty shabby excuse for a blade, he tried to sabotage the other competitors. Did manage to sabotage at least one. Maybe someone wanted revenge for that."

"Good grief," he said. "Let's stop here for a bit. I need to hear all of this before I tackle that tent full of suspects."

We were passing a bench—one of the decorative black wrought iron benches scattered about the grounds, most of them my handiwork. We took a seat, and while the chief filled page after page of his notebook with notes, I explained about the sabotage, my suspicion—shared by the producers—that Brody was using some kind of drug, and what I'd overheard talk about Brody harassing at least two women members of the production crew.

"Maybe three, if you include me," I said. "But I shut him down pretty quickly. Not sure I let him get as far as anything you'd call actual harassment."

"I have no doubt." The chief was suppressing a smile. "So to sum it all up, the other four competitors might have had a grudge against Mr. McIlvaney because of his attempts to sabotage them. One of the producers might have been enraged by the harassment of his niece. At least two women—possibly more—might have felt sufficiently threatened or outraged by his sexual harassment to lash out at him. Both producers, and potentially other members of the production crew, might have resented the risk his alleged drug use posed to the success of the project.

And since the people from whom a user acquires his illicit substances do not tend to be peaceful, law-abiding citizens, we have the wild card of an as-yet-unidentified local drug dealer who might have had a reason to kill one of his customers—a customer who tried to get away without paying, for example, or one he suspected might turn him over to the authorities. Have I missed anything?"

"Not any suspects," I said. "But there is one more thing. What if whoever attacked Faulk Sunday night was actually trying to wound or kill Brody?"

"And attacked the wrong man in the dark?"

"It could happen easily," I said. "Last night I was running up to my room, and I thought I saw Faulk at the far end of the corridor. I've known Faulk since our college days, and I absolutely thought it was him. But when I called out to him, saying how great it was that he was back from the hospital, he turned around—and it was Brody. And the hallway lighting was a little on the dim side, but it wasn't anywhere near dark. Outside, at dusk, in the shadow of the castle, and with only a quarter moon—someone could absolutely mistake one of them for the other."

"True." He sighed. "If your dad were reading this in one of those murder mysteries he loves so much, he'd be a happy camper, with all these possible suspects and motives. It's giving me a headache."

"Sorry," I said.

"Not your fault. Is there anyone who actually likes Brody? Might be useful to talk to someone who can tell me about any redeeming characteristics he might have."

I thought for a second.

"Ragnar, maybe," I said. "Ragnar liked him enough that he was going to try to keep him sober and out of trouble last night."

"Ragnar likes everyone," the chief said. "He was also drinking, then? McIlvaney, that is."

"Yes," I said. "One of the producers—I forget which one—said he was drunk as a skunk. But I think he was exaggerating. It was only a few minutes later that I overheard Brody talking to John, and he didn't sound as drunk as all that. Slurring a little. I think you need a little more than that to qualify as skunk-level drunk."

"He didn't spend time with anyone in particular?"

"He hung out with Duncan," I said. "I don't know either of them well enough to say if they were really friends. If I had to guess, I'd say it was more that Duncan liked having a sidekick and Brody . . . Brody probably wasn't in any position to be choosy about who he hung around with. He annoyed people."

"I imagine he did if he was in the habit of attempting extortion and/or sexual harassment of them," the chief said dryly. "And given your father's estimate of the time of death, it's entirely possible that his encounter with Mr. Dunigan was the last anyone saw him."

"I'm afraid I don't know what time it was," I said.

"Ah, but I do." He grinned. "While Ragnar was showing me the way back here, he mentioned that you texted to notify him of McIlvaney's presence in the library."

"That's right," I said. "Him and Alec."

"I got Ragnar to show me the text—it was at nine forty-four."

"And he never did find Brody?"

"No," he said. "In spite of what sounds like heroic efforts, first by Ragnar himself, and then by several of his . . . I don't suppose staff is the right word. Semi-permanent guests. So it's entirely possible Mr. McIlvaney came out here soon after the conversation you overheard."

"If anyone else volunteers that he talked to Brody—he or she—I'll let you know. But before you say it, no, I won't try to bring up the topic if they don't."

"Thank you," he said. "I should probably go down to the tent and meet all these suspects. I think it might be a good idea to break the news to them before the hearse shows up—which could be any minute now."

We both stood up and headed for the tent, walking side by side, but both lost in our thoughts.

The second I stepped inside the tent, one of the Tweedles ran up to me.

"You're late!" he said. "Go over to the banquet hall immediately so—"

He noticed the chief, who looked very authoritative now that he'd shed his overcoat to reveal his neat khaki uniform.

"Is there something wrong?" he asked.

"Yes," the chief said. "Please assemble your people. I need to make an announcement."

The Tweedle dashed back to the production area. From where the chief and I stood in the tent entrance we could hear him fussing.

"The police are here! Why has she brought the police here? We should have started filming half an hour ago."

"Maybe I should go over and point out that the sooner he rounds up everyone for an all-hands meeting, the sooner he can get back to filming," I said.

But then I noticed a tall redheaded young woman heading our way with purposeful strides. And she was carrying—no, not Jasmyn's clipboard. But she was holding an iPad in much the same position. I recognized Roxanne Ballinger, one of Michael's grad students.

"I gather you're filling in for Jasmyn as production assistant," I said when she was near enough that I could do it without shouting.

"For my sins. Is something wrong?"

"Yes," the chief said. "I'm afraid I'm about to throw a monkey wrench into your life. Any chance you could gather everyone associated with the production? I need to make an announcement."

"Can do. Five minutes in the banquet hall." She strode off.

"We don't really need to drag everyone back to the castle," the chief said. "If—"

"Not Ragnar's banquet hall," I said. "This way."

I led him there. He glanced around, nodded, then took one of the middle seats behind the judges' table. I stood to one side—I didn't want to look as if I were an official part of the program. But I didn't want to take a seat in the audience, either. I wanted to see the looks on people's faces when the chief gave them the news.

Roxanne was efficient. She had almost everyone there by the five-minute mark. It took her a few more minutes to round up Sam, Duncan, and one of the Tweedles. When she'd done that, she nodded to the chief and came to stand beside me.

The chief stood and took a moment to study the assembled crowd. As if following some kind of well-established rule of etiquette, the contestants, the Tweedles, Alec, and Sam took seats at the oak table while the various crew members stood in clumps around the periphery.

"Thank you all for taking time from what I know is a busy day," the chief began. "I'm Henry Burke, Chief of Police for the town of Caerphilly and Sheriff of Caerphilly County. Unfortunately, I have some bad news to share."

He paused for a moment. I wondered if he was looking to see if any of the upturned faces showed signs of guilt or anxiety.

"Mr. Brody McIlvaney is dead," the chief said. "At present, we are investigating his death as a possible homicide."

Chapter 21

A ripple of exclamations ran through the crowd. The chief waited until everyone quieted down, his eyes moving back and forth as he watched people's reactions.

Finally one of the Tweedles stood up.

"This is all very sad," he said. "But I hope this isn't going to interrupt our project. I'm sure Brody himself would be the first to say that the show must go on."

Roxanne snorted softly at that.

"I understand your concern," the chief said. "Mr. . . ."

"Zakaryan," the Tweedle said. "B. J. Zakaryan."

"Thank you, Mr. Zakaryan. I can assure you that I will do what I can to help you keep on schedule. But a human life has been taken. Finding out how it happened and who is responsible will have to take priority."

"But Brody's no longer a member of our cast." Zakaryan's cheerful tone suggested that he thought this exempted the cast and crew from any involvement in the investigation. "He was eliminated yesterday. From the competition, that is. Only from the competition." He laughed nervously as if worried that the chief would interpret his words as a confession of guilt.

"I'm aware of that," the chief said. "Unfortunately, it is quite possible that his death resulted from his activities and associations while he was participating in the competition."

Zakaryan sat down, looking cowed.

The chief looked around, spotted Vern, and nodded to him.

"Vern," he said. "Come on up and let me introduce you to these good people."

More muted comments and exclamations as Vern strode up to the front of the room.

"This is Vernon Shiffley, my senior deputy," the chief said.

Vern nodded pleasantly at the assembled crowd.

"After the attack on Mr. Faulkner Cates, I assigned Deputy Shiffley to come out here and keep an eye on things. I thought it would be less disruptive if he did it in plain clothes."

"You had someone spying on us," Duval, the other Tweedle, exclaimed.

"You can see it that way if you like," the chief said. "At the time I thought it would be a good idea to provide some additional security out here. Try and keep all of y'all safe until we caught whoever attacked Mr. Cates."

Duval didn't seem entirely mollified, but I saw a good many people nodding with approval.

"Additional security?" Victor said. "News to me that we had any security in the first place."

Murmurs of agreement from some of the crowd. The chief smiled, and I could almost hear him saying "Precisely."

"Deputy Shiffley will be assisting me with my investigation," the chief went on. "He and I will be interviewing all of you."

Spluttering noises from the Tweedles, but they thought better of protesting.

"If you think you have some information that might be important to the investigation, please make yourself known to Vern or to me," the chief went on. "We're particularly interested in anyone who saw Mr. McIlvaney last night after, say, seven in the evening. And until you've been interviewed, please refrain from discussing this case with anyone else. And—pardon me for a second."

Horace had appeared in the doorway of the tent. He looked

around, then hesitated when he saw the chief was holding what appeared to be a formal meeting.

"Come on in," the chief said. "This is Deputy Hollingsworth, my top forensic investigator."

Last I'd heard, Horace was the chief's only forensic investigator, but I kept a straight face.

Looking self-conscious, Horace hurried over to the judges' table. He was carrying a large brown paper bag. To the uninitiated, it probably looked like a grocery bag. Thanks to having a forensic specialist as my cousin, a deputy as one of my best friends, and the local medical examiner as my father, I knew an evidence bag when I saw one.

Horace and the chief exchanged a few whispered words. The chief nodded.

"Deputy Hollingsworth has found an object that may be the murder weapon," the chief said in a solemn tone. "Can anyone identify this object?"

Horace stuck his gloved hand into the paper bag. Maybe he was making sure he had a good hold on the object. I suspected he was pausing for a moment to heighten the drama. Then he pulled out his hand to reveal—

"It's a cross peen hammer," I said.

"A big one," Andy added. "Probably a three pounder."

"Very common smith's tool," John said. "I expect we all have one in our workstations."

"Well, I don't," Victor said. "I did yesterday morning, but it disappeared either yesterday afternoon or overnight. Couple of you probably heard me complaining about it already."

"Could this be yours?" the chief asked.

"Looks like it," Victor said. "If it is, it'll have my initials burned into the wood right up near where the handle meets the head. Or I could come up and check it out."

Horace peered more closely at the hammer.

"If you're either VN or NA, it's yours."

"VN. Yeah." Victor nodded and clenched his fists as if choking back anger that someone had used his tool as a murder weapon. "Got some nerve," he muttered. "Stealing my hammer and using it for that."

"I'm afraid we'll have to hold on to it for a while," the chief said.

"Keep it as long as you like," Victor said. "I don't want it back. Not after what someone did with it. Rather get me a new one that's never had blood on it."

The chief nodded as if he thought this an eminently sensible reaction.

"You need one for what you're doing today?" Vern asked. "Some cousins of mine run a metalworking shop—I'm sure they could spare one for a few days."

"I'd appreciate that," Victor said. "Thank you."

Horace carefully replaced the hammer in its evidence bag and dashed off. I could see Vern texting on his phone. One blood-free cross peen hammer coming up.

"My deputies will be taking all of your fingerprints," the chief said. "For exclusion purposes."

"What about DNA?" one of the camera crew asked. "Are you going to be asking us for DNA?"

"Not at present," the chief said. "We don't yet know if we're going to find any DNA evidence to compare it to. If we do, we'll come back and ask for your cooperation in that. For the time being, I'm afraid I'm going to ask all of you to vacate this tent."

Both of the producers stood, clearly about to protest.

"Only for an hour or so while we do an initial search of the area," the chief said. "With your cooperation, we'll get this over with as soon as we can so you can go on with your shooting."

I could see that both Tweedles wanted to protest, but the chief's tone made it obvious that they'd only be wasting time. Vern said a few quiet words to the chief, who nodded.

"Let's all move over to the mess tent in an orderly fashion,"

Vern said. "Don't bother going back to your work areas—we'll have deputies here to make sure nothing happens to your personal possessions."

With Vern shepherding them, the cast and crew all filed out, and a frown and a quiet word from the chief discouraged the few who tried to disobey instructions and dart back to retrieve something. From the remarks I overheard, some were grumbling about the interruption to our filming, while others were disappointed that they couldn't stay to watch the search.

"I want to see if *CSI* gets it right," I overheard one guy from the sound crew say.

"I'll stay over there to make sure they don't start talking among themselves," Vern said as he stepped outside to follow his charges to the mess tent.

The chief nodded and looked around.

"I'm a little short on deputies," he said to me. "And this is a sprawling crime scene. Sammy's up at the castle, securing Mr. McIlvaney's personal possessions, and Marge will head out here as soon as she gets back from the dentist. And that's about all the deputies I've got when you count the ones out of town for the holidays and the ones still around but sick in bed with flu. Any chance I could borrow you for a little while to run interference for Horace while he works the crime scene? And then you could send Aida down here to help me search this place."

"No problem," I said. "Once you give them back the tent, they'll want to drag me back here for filming."

"By that time, I hope to have some reinforcements," he said. "I've got calls in with Goochland and a couple of other counties. We'll play it by ear."

So I bundled up again and hiked back to the cow pasture. The hearse from the Caerphilly Funeral Home had arrived and was parked in the dirt lane closest to where Brody lay. Where Brody had been lying—I noticed a gurney with a body bag on top of it slowly making the trek from the pasture to the hearse, with Dad anxiously scurrying alongside it.

The cows were gone, too. Well, not totally gone. Someone had moved them to the farther pasture, the one already occupied by the goats and sheep. I hoped they hadn't left too many cow pies and hoofprints to complicate Horace's work. They, along with the sheep and goats, were all at the fence line, watching what happened at the crime scene.

The hearse left. Aida hurried down to the production tent, glad to be getting out of the cold. I pulled my coat more closely around me and watched as Horace continued to process the scene. He had finished with the area where Brody had been lying and was now methodically searching the pasture, walking bent over, stopping whenever anything caught his eye, sometimes veering aside or backtracking. It reminded me of the ritual Spike and all the resident and visiting Pomeranians performed when we let them out into the yard to answer nature's calls. Sometimes they'd spend ten or fifteen minutes darting back and forth, nose to the ground, as if picking the proper place to pee were a matter of earthshaking importance.

And I suppose to a dog it was. Most of the time it was the most important decision they'd make all day.

And if Horace's minute examination of every square inch of the pasture turned up a valuable clue . . . it wouldn't be the first time.

I spotted one of the ubiquitous black wrought iron benches not too far away, so I hiked over to sit there, making sure I still had a good view of what Horace was up to.

What had Brody been doing out here? Ragnar didn't allow smoking in the castle or even on the terraces, so nicotine addicts soon became resigned to taking a long hike if they wanted a cigarette. But he wouldn't have had to come this far.

A bright spot of color caught my eye. Something red, caught where one of the glossy black fence rails met the post. I stood up and went over to take a closer look. It was a strip of shiny bright red fabric, caught in a slight crack where the end of the rail had split slightly.

"Horace," I called. "Just tell me to shut up if I'm interrupting at the wrong time and breaking your concentration, but could this be important?"

I pointed at the strip of fabric, which rippled slightly as a stray breeze caught it.

The speed with which he trotted over and the cheerful expression on his face told me that I was welcome to interrupt for finds like this.

"Interesting," he said, as he photographed the strip of cloth from every possible angle. "This isn't something Ragnar would have done—I mean, is it possible that he uses strips of bright red silk to mark places where the fence needs repair?"

"I've never heard of him doing that." I pulled out my phone and took a couple of shots of the fabric—after all, it was evidence I'd found. I wanted a souvenir. "And you can show it to Mother to be sure, but pretty sure that's polyester, not silk."

Horace nodded. Then, having finished his flurry of photography, he carefully teased the bit of fabric out of the crack in which it had caught and deposited it in a brown paper evidence bag.

"You didn't happen to see anyone wearing a bright red dress at the party last night, did you?" he asked.

"No," I said. "But that isn't really the sort of thing I'd have noticed unless it was a really cool dress and I envied the owner. Don't remember anything like that last night. Of course, I was dog-tired and went to bed early."

"I'll ask your mother," he said. "I bet she'd remember."

"Definitely," I said. "Especially if it's polyester." Mother was a snob about natural fabrics. I could imagine the faint shudder of distaste that a bright red polyester dress would inspire.

"Keep this under your hat," he said. "The chief may want to make it a hold-back item."

"Roger," I said. "Because if it gets out that we found a strip of red material at the crime scene, whoever owns the rest of the garment will almost certainly get rid of it."

Horace nodded. He began searching up and down the fence, just to make sure Ragnar wasn't in the habit of festooning it with bits of red fabric. Eventually, he went back to plodding methodically up and down the pasture. Watching him, I could easily have fallen asleep if not for the bitter cold.

At one point, when his gradually widening circle took him to my side of the fence, he pointed to something on the ground.

"What's that?" he asked.

I peered down. It appeared to be a small circular brass grate.

"And there's another one two feet away." Horace pointed again.

"I think those are for Winkelman's easel."

"The artist guy?"

"Yes," I said. "He was painting here yesterday morning. I think he puts those down to make sure he sets his easel in exactly the same spot when he comes back to continue his painting."

"Seriously?"

"He's meticulous. Maybe a little obsessive."

Horace took photos of the grates anyway.

"Winkelman was taking pictures of this area yesterday," I said. "I have no idea if any of them would be useful."

"You never know," Horace said. "Where do I find him?"

"He has a studio in one of the towers." I pulled out my notebook. "I'll ask Ragnar where. I could even track him down and get him to give you his photos, if you like."

"That would be great," Horace said, returning to his methodical examination of the immediate world.

I was relieved when I spotted Caroline hiking briskly out toward me.

"Chief's about to let the production people back into the tent," she said when she drew near. "And he figures they'll be looking for you. I'll take over watching Horace's back."

Chapter 22

I thanked Caroline and hiked back down to the tents. Most of the cast and crew were in the mess tent. At one end of it, some kind of filming was going on. Andy was sitting on one of the folding chairs with several lights focused on him. It was curiously reminiscent of a scene from an old B-movie, with the cops putting a spotlight on someone they were interrogating.

Andy didn't look as if he was enjoying this.

I took a seat at one of the picnic tables where I could watch what was going on. Duncan was sitting at the other end of the same table, also watching.

"What's going on?" I asked after Sam yelled "Cut."

"Filming the personal interviews," Duncan said. "We'll all get our turn. Well, except for Brody. They missed their chance with him."

Since he'd brought up the topic . . .

"A shame about Brody," I said. "I know he was a friend of yours."

"He was Alec's buddy, not mine. He wouldn't even be here if not for Alec. He wasn't really in the same league as . . . as some of us."

Interesting. I was wondering how Brody had found his way onto the show. Alec had been vague about it when I'd talked to him yesterday.

"Well, yeah," I said. "But still a friend of yours, too."

"Not really," he said. "Not a close friend. Only met him a time or two before this. Someone to hang out with while I was here, that's all. It's not like there were a lot of choices. He was better than nothing."

I felt sorry for Brody, just for a moment. Even when he was with Brody, Duncan probably hadn't made a big secret of how he felt. Brody had been a jerk, but Duncan was a bigger one, behaving like that.

And I had a feeling Duncan was going to miss Brody more than he realized. He struck me as the kind of guy who needed a sidekick. A minion. Someone he considered weak, to make him feel better about himself.

For that matter, someone who actually wanted to hang around with him. Andy, John, Victor, and I seemed to be falling into a loose sort of camaraderie, putting our competitive natures aside when we were away from the production tent. I didn't see Duncan comfortably falling in with us. Nor could I imagine any of us making more than a token effort to include him. I'd taken a seat at this picnic table for the view of what Andy was going through, not the pleasure of Duncan's company.

"A pity whoever offed him didn't pick someone else, though," Duncan said. "I mean, why did they bother to knock off someone who's bound to lose anyway? Would be nice if they knocked off someone who was a real competitor. Victor or John."

"How unfortunate they didn't ask your advice," I said.

"I bet you thought I was going to say, 'Victor or John or you,' right?" He smirked.

"I'm under no illusions that you're capable of putting aside your misogyny to make an accurate assessment of my work," I said. "Luckily, you're not one of the judges."

"You snowed them with a cute design," he said. "The sword's going to be the real test. We'll see who's laughing when they judge those."

With that, he got up and strutted off.

Cute design? There was nothing cute about my crow-headed

dagger. It was a crow, not a chickadee or a baby duckling. In nearly every culture in the world, crows were powerful. Tricksters. Messengers of the gods. Omens of good or ill. The only bird in the world that will peck at an eagle. Cute, my eye.

And Duncan knew that. He was only trying to annoy me. Or put me off my game. And he could only succeed in doing that if I let him.

Which might happen if I wasn't careful. So I made a mental note that whenever the impostor part of my brain dredged up his "cute" put-down and tried to shake my confidence with it, I'd match it against the uneasy look on Duncan's face when he saw my finished dagger . . . and his look of pure shock when the judges had pronounced it the winner.

Shock and anger.

Sam called for silence and then action. Alec continued interviewing Andy. I settled back to listen, hoping to get a sneak preview of what they might ask me when I had my personal interview, but was distracted when something else occurred to me. What if Duncan was only pretending to be nonchalant about Brody's murder? Pretending to be disappointed that the killer hadn't chosen one of the stronger competitors?

What if Duncan had killed Brody?

If he had, he was being smart not to fake grief. He hadn't even tried to seem heartbroken over the loss of his sidekick, and I didn't think he'd have the acting ability to pull it off anyway. But maybe he was a better actor than I thought.

Still, why would he have killed Brody? Not to improve his chances in the competition. I agreed that Brody was one of the weaker competitors. Possibly the only really weak competitor, given that Andy might not have done as badly in the knife-making challenge if it hadn't been for Brody's sabotage. Considering all he'd gone through, Andy hadn't done a bad job. He'd almost pulled it off.

What if Duncan had also been involved in the sabotage? I remembered seeing him and Brody with their heads together, looking very much as if they were conspiring. What if they'd both been messing with the temperature dials of our forges, and Duncan was lucky enough not to get caught on my camera? Or what if Duncan had come up with the idea of the sabotage and talked Brody into carrying it out? On the one hand, the producers probably wouldn't have wanted to kick out two of the contestants. But on the other hand, they could have kept them both and penalized them so heavily that they had no chance of winning. If Duncan had been involved in the sabotage, or even aware of it, and thought Brody might implicate him, maybe that would give him a motive for murder.

Or what if Brody had tried the same ploy on Duncan as he had on John and me? What if he had pretended to know who had attacked Faulk—and accidentally got it right? It might not ever have occurred to Brody that if he tried to blackmail someone who really was guilty, they might not fall apart and go along with whatever he demanded. Whoever had attacked Faulk probably knew that they could end up serving hard time if they were convicted of whacking someone with a baseball bat. Definitely a motive for murder—at least for anyone capable of breaking another human being's arm and trying to whack them on the head, just to get ahead in a contest.

So what if Duncan had attacked Faulk, who was indisputably a strong competitor, as everyone acknowledged. And what if Duncan thought he'd gotten away with it, only to have Brody come along with his snide, insinuating comments?

I was tempted to call the chief and share all of this with him. But had I learned any new and useful facts from my conversation with Duncan?

Not really. I'd only thought of a new theory. And I was sure the chief had plenty of those.

I didn't even know if Duncan was right about Brody being on the show because he was Alec's friend. For all I knew, Duncan could be lying. He might have recommended or recruited Brody and was now trying to distance himself so no one would suspect him.

Vern appeared at the mess tent entrance. He waited patiently until Sam called "Cut" again, then announced: "We've finished searching the production tent. Y'all can have it back now."

"Thank God!" Sam exclaimed. "Where's Jas—er . . ."

"Roxanne." Roxanne had appeared at his elbow. "But if you forget it, just yell for Jasmyn. I'll know you mean me. Cast and crew to the production tent?"

"ASAP." Sam strode off.

Roxanne went to work. I waved, pointed to the door, and headed for it. As I left the tent, I could hear her calmly asking everyone to return to the set at once. Then she headed outside to hunt down the stragglers.

She was an excellent cat herder. Within fifteen minutes, we were all milling around in the production tent. The production crew members were dragging back the equipment they'd taken to the mess tent and setting up the lights and microphones again. The other contestants were doing the same thing I was— checking our workstations to make sure everything was as we'd left it and starting to arrange them for today's work.

"This is gonna be weird." Andy strolled across the aisle and leaned against my forge. "What are we supposed to say about Brody, anyway?"

"Say about him?" I echoed. "When?"

"When we start filming. You know how they do it on these competition shows. A lot of times they start off a new episode with a sort of postmortem on the previous episode, and the contestants say how relieved they are to be still in, or how mad they are that the judges didn't understand what they were trying to do. And sometimes they show the spot where someone who was just eliminated used to work, and their friends say how much they're going to miss them and all."

Clearly, Andy was a much bigger fan of reality TV shows than I was.

"I expect the producers would rather we didn't say anything about Brody," I said. "Since they're probably going to have to wait until the chief catches the killer before they can figure out how to spin this."

"I'm sure you're right." Andy looked over at Brody's former workstation. "But do you think maybe they should take his forge and stuff away? Or is it just me who can't keep my eyes off of it?"

"I keep staring there, too," I said. "But I don't think anyone who didn't know what happened would find it particularly mesmerizing. The audience won't."

"Poor guy," Andy said. "He was a jerk, but he didn't deserve that."

He ambled back to his space and began tidying his worktable.

Either Andy had nothing on his conscience, or he was giving an Oscar-worthy performance.

"Everyone to the banquet hall." Roxanne was walking up and down the central aisle. "The judges are ready to assign the main challenge."

"Here we go again," Victor muttered.

Everyone was grabbing his coffee mug. I poured my Diet Coke into another of the mugs the boys had given me—this one said EAT. SLEEP. HIT STUFF. REPEAT. I'd save IT'S NOT A HOBBY, IT'S A POST-APOCALYPTIC LIFE SKILL for tomorrow.

We all took our assigned places at the trestle table, though it looked a little unbalanced with just Duncan in the back row.

Alec took a seat beside the two quiet judges at their table. Marco was standing—actually, more like posing—to the left of the table. Evidently, he'd be doing all the talking again.

Alec didn't look resentful, as he had on Monday. More like depressed and miserable. I studied him—covertly, by holding up my phone and pretending to be studying something on its screen while actually looking past it. He had a bleary look, as if he hadn't slept well, or maybe had a hangover. While I watched, I saw him half turn away, so his back was to the two judges, and reach into his pocket to pull out something. A travel-size pill tube, the kind that held only ten or twelve pills. I recognized the distinctive red-and-white Tylenol logo. He shook several caplets into one hand, popped them rather furtively into his mouth, and washed them down with a wince and a gulp of coffee before turning to face forward again.

So, hangover, sleepless night, or grief over Brody's murder? Or some combination of all three? If anyone here was going to be upset over Brody, it would have to be Alec. No one else knew him that well. Although I couldn't really tell how close they were, even after yesterday's conversation with Alec. Would Brody's death really hit him that hard?

Maybe. Or was he looking miserable because he was the one who'd killed Brody? And was worried about being found out?

But no. That didn't make sense. Alec might be the only person here in the tent who was upset about Brody's death. Because even if they weren't all that close, Brody's demise put Alec's pet project at risk. His pet project and his financial future.

Which suggested he'd probably be pretty mad at whoever had bumped off Brody and jeopardized the future of *Blades of Glory*. Mad enough, I hoped, to tell the chief everything he knew. Even if he knew something that implicated one of the other contestants.

Or possibly the producers. They might have had a strong motive for doing in Brody. I glanced around. They were hovering nearby. They looked . . . uncomfortable. Ill at ease. Were those the expressions of men who had committed—or arranged—a murder? Or men who were about to announce that they were shutting down production?

Or maybe just men who had recently been exposed to more Christmas good cheer than their tiny Grinch hearts could handle.

But they didn't make any announcements—they just hovered, like hopeful vultures. They only watched when Sam stepped forward, glowered at us, and held up his hand for silence.

"I want everyone cooperating today," he said. "We lost valuable time this morning, and we're probably going to lose more time as the day goes on and the police want to search things and question people. So no slacking off. We've got a lot of extra filming to do, thanks to this murder."

A murmur ran through the crowd. John was the one who spoke up.

"How is the murder going to cause any of us extra work?" he asked. "Make it harder to get our work done, maybe. But more work?"

One of the Tweedles stepped forward.

"We have to be able to move forward if one of you is unable to continue with the competition," he said.

"What do you think's going on here, anyway?" Victor asked. "You think maybe someone's going to off more of us? Like there's a serial killer out there who has it in for blacksmiths?"

"We have no reason to think that," the Tweedle said. "But there is a very real possibility that one of you might have had something to do with last night's unfortunate events." He smiled without warmth.

"Or that you could fall under suspicion and be arrested," the other Tweedle said.

"In other words, new rule," Sam said. "Any contestant who bumps off another contestant is automatically disqualified. For life. So if the cops figure out one of you's the killer, we're going to need some kind of extra footage we can edit in to show you losing."

"So you're going to film two versions of the judging?" Duncan asked. "One where Marco gives our blades a thumbs-up and another where the judges find some imaginary flaw so they can tell us we've lost?"

"If it comes to that," the Tweedle said. "Let's hope the police find the culprit quickly so we don't have to."

"Let's get started," Sam said. "First up, we're going to shoot Marco assigning the next challenge."

Marco stepped in front of the judges' table and smiled at us. A rather predatory smile, like a cat deciding which mouse to play with.

After a bit of dramatic buildup, Marco announced that our next assignment—the main assignment for this first episode—would be a medieval-style broadsword. Everyone looked pleased at that, probably because we'd all made a few of them in our careers. They sold well at the Renaissance Faires, SF/fantasy conventions, and reenactment gatherings that formed a large part of the modern market for edged weapons.

"Any questions before I send you to your forges?" Marco asked.

"Yeah, I have a question," Duncan said. "We've been told the police are going to want to question all of us. What if they haul us out when we're trying to work? It's not fair for some of us to be penalized just because the police have more questions for us."

"We have no control over who the police want to talk to and for how long," the Tweedle said.

"That's my point," Duncan said. "Some of us are going to lose time, and that's not fair."

"So we keep track of how much time the police spend interviewing every one of us," I suggested. "If they want to interview one of us, they see Roxanne, she notes down the exact minute they interrupt him and exactly how long he's away from his forge."

"Or her forge," Duncan added.

"Or her forge," I agreed. "So if they interview Andy for an hour, and Victor for half an hour, they each get that much more time when the rest of us have to stop."

"Seems fair," John said.

Andy and Victor nodded. Even Duncan frowned and then gave a single curt nod.

"We'll do it that way, then," Sam said. "Jas—er, Roxanne, you're in charge of keeping the records on that."

She made a note on her iPad.

"Now that we've settled that, everybody get to work, dammit." Sam scowled and strode out of the banquet hall area.

Chapter 23

We contestants all trooped up to the table to receive our materials for the competition. A steel bar—a much bigger one this time. And a spec sheet.

I scanned the specs and nodded. Same steel as we'd used for the knife.

Back at my worktable, I took a few minutes to plan what I was going to do. Andy was busily sketching. Some of the others probably were, too.

I've been known to do my share of sketching, but mostly when I was trying to come up with something unusual, like the creepy dagger hilts I'd done for Michael's show. For today's challenge, I wanted something familiar. Tried and true. Something I'd done so often that I could almost do it in my sleep. Because I knew myself. Quite apart from the pressure of being in a competition and having to deal with whatever annoyances and interruptions the camera crew provided, I was going to be distracted by the murder.

Unless, of course, I got so involved with my swordmaking that I forgot all about it. Michael and the boys were always teasing me about how hard it was to get my attention when I was working. Probably not a good idea to get that involved with Brody's killer still unknown and presumably at large. Although I should be fine as long as I was here in the production tent, with not only the other contestants but the entire production crew.

About half an hour after we all started working, Roxanne

showed up and escorted Andy away from his forge to speak to the chief.

Curious how that empty workstation across the aisle from mine seemed to draw my eyes like some kind of magnet.

After a while, Andy came back, and I heard Roxanne telling John it was his turn. At least I couldn't see John's empty space, and with Andy hammering away across the aisle, things started to feel closer to normal.

The camera crews came by occasionally and filmed what I was doing, but they didn't interrupt me. Alec was tagging along with them, but he only looked morose and uncomfortable, as if the camera crew had somehow communicated that they didn't really need him for anything and if he insisted on tagging along he should at least try not to get in their way.

I felt sorry for Alec. I knew how much he'd put into the show—several years of hard work, plus every penny he had or could borrow. And now, first Faulk's injury and then Brody's murder threatened its success. And even if the show did succeed, wouldn't his happiness at that be forever tainted by the injury to one friend and the murder of another?

Of course, I'd have felt more sympathy if Alec hadn't sucked Faulk and Tad into his precarious project. I felt a sudden flash of irritation—not quite, but almost, anger—at Alec.

I paused for a moment to watch as the camera crew filmed what Andy was doing. Andy didn't seem to be bothered by having a camera almost perched on his shoulder.

I focused back on my sword. It seemed to be progressing nicely, but somehow I wasn't enjoying the work. I couldn't seem to lose myself in it as I had with the knife. Rather, I'd start losing myself—getting into the zone—only to have something interrupt me.

Like Sam browbeating the tech crew about things that weren't their fault. Or stomping down the middle of the tent yelling "Where's . . . the new Jasmyn?"

Or one of the Tweedles having a loud conniption fit not far from my workstation.

"What is it with these people? I make a small, simple request and all I hear is 'But it's Christmas!' Do they think their stupid Christmas decorations are more important than our project?"

Actually, yes. A lot more important. And I'd say as much if one of the sound guys stuck a microphone in my face. Where were they when you really needed them?

"It's nothing but a plot to enrich the toy manufacturers and the greeting card printers," the Tweedle went on. "And guilt-trip employers into giving people more time off than they've earned."

He went on for another couple of minutes in much the same vein. I was relieved when Roxanne came over and told him—in a low voice that still carried—that there was filming going on and he needed to be quiet. He spluttered and stormed off to whine somewhere else.

Leaving me in a foul, angry mood. I had taken my roughly shaped sword out of the forge and was about to begin a session of shaping when he'd started his rant. I decided I needed to cool off for a bit before I touched it. The way I felt, I'd probably manage to ruin it.

So I slipped into my coat, called "Fresh air break" to anyone who cared what I was doing, and strode toward the opening in the tent.

"What a Scrooge," I muttered. And then words popped into my head. As usual in December, Michael had been rehearsing his one-man staged reading of Charles Dickens's *A Christmas Carol*. He'd been doing this every December for years, to raise money for local charities, and I'd memorized long passages of it. Including what Scrooge's nephew says when his uncle asks what good Christmas has ever done him:

I have always thought of Christmas time, when it has come round—apart from the veneration due to its sacred name and origin, if anything belonging to it can be apart from that—as a good time; a kind, forgiving, charitable, pleasant time; the only time I know of, in the long calendar of the year, when men and women seem by one consent to open their shut-up hearts freely, and to think of people below them as if they really were fellow-passengers to the grave, and not another race of creatures bound on other journeys. And therefore, Uncle, though it has never put a scrap of gold or silver in my pocket, I believe that it *has* done me good, and *will* do me good; and I say, God bless it!

I said the last few words aloud and followed them with "So there!"

"Sorry—what did you say?"

I had been staring at the ground and scowling. Now I looked up to see Ragnar nearby. He looked uncharacteristically glum.

"Just venting to myself," I said. "What's wrong?"

"Oh . . . it's those producers." Ragnar frowned as if unsure how much more he should say.

"They're annoying," I said. "What have they done now?"

"They want me to take down my Christmas decorations."

"What? But I thought they weren't even filming in the castle. Although I have no idea why—I'd have thought it would have made a much better set than the tent, but then what do I know."

"Yes, originally they were excited about filming in the castle." Ragnar sighed. "At least I got that impression. Perhaps I was wrong. But then they wanted to change everything."

"I remember," I said. "And yes—painting all the walls white. Ridiculous."

"And replacing all my wrought iron sconces with recessed lights. And bringing in more modern furniture."

"They wanted to undo everything you've done since you bought the place."

"Yes, that's just it. So I said no, this is my home, not your set, and if you don't like it, you should film somewhere else. And they were upset by that, so we compromised, and I got the tent."

And I was willing to bet Ragnar was paying for the tent, too. Both tents.

"But since they're not filming in the castle, why do they want you to take the Christmas decorations down?" I asked,

"Oh, they don't mean the decorations in the castle. They haven't complained about them. Although I don't really think they like them very much." Ragnar looked hurt and puzzled.

"They have no Christmas spirit, and no taste, and I hope they say something snide about your decorations in front of Mother," I said.

"Oh, dear!" Ragnar grinned at the thought. "That would be exciting. Perhaps I should tell your mother that they want to take down my outdoor decorations. Her crews started putting them up this morning and have been working very hard now for hours. I think she would have a few words to say."

I nodded my understanding. The outside Christmas decorations Mother had designed for Ragnar were legendary. And she usually arranged to put them up shortly after Thanksgiving, so everyone in town would have plenty of time to enjoy them. People had been asking what the delay was. Once word got out that they were finally up, there would be a traffic jam on the road that ran past his gates.

"And the workers," Ragnar said. "After all they've done, I can't imagine what they would say if I told them to take everything down again."

Mother's crew would be outlining all the fences and all the trees along his half-mile-long driveway with lights. The life-size, slightly luminescent wise men would be riding their glowing camels across the front pasture toward the brightly lit manger down by the duck pond. Some of the braver crew members would be shampooing a few dozen of Ragnar's black Hebridean sheep with what Mother assured me was a harmless, nontoxic, organic luminescent dye, so they'd glow faintly when they were out abiding in the fields with their life-size fake shepherds. I hoped we'd be able to keep the dogs out of the glow-in-the-dark paint this year. And I wondered if Ragnar had finally convinced Mother that it wouldn't be over the top to have a present-laden, reindeer-powered sleigh flying above the castle.

I couldn't wait to see the final results.

"Why would the producers even care about your outdoor decorations?" I asked.

"They have finally decided that they want to film some outside scenes," Ragnar said. "Like the contestants arriving in their vehicles. Or lounging outside on their breaks. They have been here five days, and every day I have asked them if they wanted to film outside and every day they said they weren't sure yet. Yesterday they said they had decided not to, so I told your mother to go ahead with the outside decorating. And now they have changed their minds and they want me to take everything down so they can shoot some scenes outside."

"Tell them no," I said. "You gave them their chance. It's not your fault they're completely disorganized—not to mention massively inconsiderate of other people. And remind them that they're supposedly coming back after Christmas. They can film all the outdoor scenes they want then."

"I told them that," Ragnar said. "All of that. They do not seem happy. I suspect they will continue to harass me about this."

"Tell them if they keep harassing you, they'll have to keep on filming with only four contestants."

"What's that?" I turned to see Andy behind me. "Are we going on strike?"

"I might be," I said.

"Solidarity!" Andy said, raising a fist. "What are we striking for?"

John and Victor arrived while I was explaining the producers' aversion to Ragnar's Christmas decorations.

"That's terrible," Andy said. "Count me in."

"Yeah, me too," Victor said. "Getting tired of those producer dudes making everybody miserable. I was pretty excited when I saw all the Christmas lights and stuff going up. I was going to ask one of you to take some pictures of me in front of some of them so I could send them to my momma and make her feel better about what I'm doing. She's not used to having me away this close to Christmas—you'd think I was five years old instead of pushing forty. I've been flat-out lying to her, telling her that we only work for a few hours and then we run around caroling and sleighing and eating Christmas cookies and such. What's wrong with those jerks, anyway?"

John merely nodded, but it was a firm, determined kind of nod.

"You see." I turned back to Ragnar. "If they harass you anymore, tell them if the Christmas decorations come down, the cast is on strike."

"Well, most of us." With a jerk of his head, Andy indicated Duncan, who had come out of the tent while we were talking and headed toward the mess tent without glancing our way.

"Thank you!" Ragnar looked very affected. "But you do not need to jeopardize your positions on the show. I will put my foot down." He raised his knee slightly, as if to suggest that he might literally use his silver-studded, size-sixteen boots for the purpose.

"Right on," I said. "And if they say another word about taking the decorations down, I will sic my mother on them."

Ragnar laughed and strode off, looking more serene.

"Your mother?" Andy sounded puzzled. "She seemed like a very nice lady when I met her."

"She is," I said. "But don't cross her. Or insult her decorating. Why are we all out of the tent?"

"Lunch break," John said. "Let's not waste any more of it."

So we marched four abreast to the mess tent and joined the buffet line.

Mother had clearly been in the mess tent. She'd obeyed the prohibition against Christmas decorations anywhere the show would be filming, but she'd had tiny speakers installed from which poured a beautiful version of "Veni Veni Emmanuel," sung by a monastic choir. Roxanne was standing just inside the tent. She held her ever-present iPad by her side instead of in front of her face like a clipboard. She was smiling, eyes half-closed, obviously listening.

"And what happens if the film crew comes in?" I asked. "Or the producers?"

She lifted her iPad, touched something, and the music vanished.

"Good planning," I said.

She nodded and brought the music back. People who had looked up, frowning, when it vanished, smiled again and returned to their eating.

"Sorry that I added to your workload," I said. "I hope it's not too complicated, keeping track of how much time each of us loses to the investigation."

"It's the only fair thing to do," she said. "I just hope no one gets nasty when I show up and say 'your time's up for today.'"

I noticed that Horace was sitting at a picnic table in the farthest corner of the tent. Several cardboard boxes full of evidence bags filled most of the table, and what little space remained was occupied by several stacks of paper—probably various forms he had to fill out to submit some of the bags to the crime lab in Richmond. A plate with two sandwiches on it—well, a sandwich and a half—sat on the bench beside him.

I waved, but he was busy studying some bit of paperwork.

I was about to join the chow line when Michael and the boys arrived.

"Why don't you guys grab your food," Michael said to the boys. "And then save places for your mother and me. I'll fill the chief in on what you found."

"What *we* found," Josh said.

"Yeah," Jamie said. "You helped, too."

With that they turned and headed for the buffet.

"And what did you and the boys find?" I asked.

"Let me fill you and the chief in at the same time." He headed for the tent door. "Any idea where he is?"

"No." I followed him out of the tent. "But we can text him. What's up?"

"I already texted him, and— There he is."

The chief was trotting purposefully down from the castle.

"Hope I didn't interrupt anything," Michael called, as the chief drew near.

"Nothing that will suffer from being interrupted," the chief said.

"I have no idea if it has anything to do with Brody's murder," Michael said. "But the boys and I found something a little odd while we were out on our ride."

Chapter 24

"Where?" the chief asked.

"Out in the middle of one of Ragnar's fields," Michael said. "Near a fence separating that field from another field."

The chief looked as if he was expecting more details.

"Also near some woods," Michael added.

The chief frowned slightly.

"Sorry," Michael said. "Rural navigation is not my strong point. We were taking a really long ride, and there's a lot of woods and open fields in this part of the county. I had no idea where we were. When we were ready to come home, we just gave the horses their heads and let them take us back to their barn. But I saved the location in my phone. I could give you the GPS coordinates. And come to think of it, the pictures I took would show the location, too, wouldn't they?"

"Indeed," the chief said. "Show me what you found."

Michael took out his phone, opened up the photo app, and handed it to the chief. I looked over his shoulder.

A picture of some cigarette butts—about a dozen of them, unfiltered, all burned down so close to the ends that I suspected the person smoking them might have scorched his fingers a time or two. They'd all been ground out in a roughly oval bare spot the size of two dinner plates, which suggested that whoever smoked them had at least some appreciation for how flammable the surrounding dead grass could be.

Another picture was a close-up of a sole mark where someone had simply stepped on one of the cigarettes with his shoe, rather than grinding it. Only a partial shoe print—most of the front part of the sole. It was interrupted by the cigarette butt, but you could still see the pattern of the sole pretty clearly.

"Odd that it would make such a clear imprint," the chief observed. "Given how dry it's been."

"Check the next picture," Michael said. "There was a big anthill just beyond what that first one shows. The print was in the loose soil around the anthill."

"Ah." The chief nodded. "Yes, that explains it."

"And then there were the motorcycle tire tracks leading to and from the area," Michael said. "The next picture shows them. From a distance, I'm afraid. They disappeared into the woods. The boys were really tempted to follow them to see where the motorcycle came out, or at least take some photos at closer range, but you'll be happy to know that they've been paying attention when you and Horace talk about the importance of not contaminating evidence. So I saved the location and we headed back."

"Good thinking," the chief said. "I will make a point of commending the boys for their common sense in leaving the scene to the experts. And promising to give them credit if your find proves useful."

Since the chief and his wife were raising their three orphaned grandsons, including Adam, who was close to the boys' age and one of their best friends, he had a very good idea of what would keep Josh and Jamie happy.

"I'd appreciate it if you could forward those photos to me," the chief said. "Along with the location coordinates. Meg, have you seen Horace recently?"

"In the mess tent," I said. "Filling out the paperwork for a bunch of evidence bags."

"Good!" The chief ducked inside, with Michael and me trailing after him.

In the tent, we saw that Horace had cleared away some of his papers and put his plate of food on the table. He was chewing slowly. Ragnar was sitting opposite him, with the anxious expression of a mother whose darling has revealed himself as a picky eater.

"I can bring you some of the soup if you'd rather have that," Ragnar was saying. "Potato leek soup. It's very good, and I could probably find a thermos to keep it warm."

"No, this is fine." Horace noticed us entering and set down the last bit of his sandwich. "Taking a late lunch break."

"Closer to a dinner break, given how early you were out here," the chief said. "Don't stop eating. When you've finished—and I mean finished as in cleaning your plate—we've got another possible scene I'd like you to check out. Michael, could you do the honors?"

Michael pulled out his phone and sent Horace the photographs of the cigarette butts, shoe prints, and tire tracks. Horace studied them, phone in one hand, sandwich in the other.

"Was our victim a smoker?" the chief asked.

"Yes," I said. "I think that was one reason he did so badly in the contest. For insurance reasons, the producers declared the tent a no-smoking zone, and it seemed as if Brody was running outside for a cigarette a couple of times an hour."

"Of course, that doesn't necessarily mean he smoked these," the chief said. "But from Michael's description, it was an odd place for someone to be standing around and smoking a dozen cigarettes. And I tend to pay attention to odd things when they happen anywhere near my crime scene."

"Unlikely that he smoked these," Horace said, through a mouthful of ham sandwich. "These are unfiltered. Camels, I think. McIlvaney smoked filtered Marlboros. Found half a carton in his workstation. Of course, if he ran out of his own brand and got desperate enough, maybe he'd smoke whatever he could find. But—half a pack?"

"And why would he hike way out there—it must be a couple of miles—just to smoke half a pack of somebody else's cigarettes?" Michael asked.

"Looks like what you'd see if the smoker was waiting for someone," Horace said. "To meet someone—or ambush them. Was there any cover nearby?"

"Not really," Michael said. "We found the cigarette butts under a tree, right next to the fence between the two fields. The motorcycle tracks were on the other side of the fence. And there was a wooded area beyond the motorcycle tracks. You could hide in there. No place to hide near the cigarette butts."

"Up in the tree, maybe?" the chief suggested.

"Deciduous tree," Michael said. "An oak, I think. Lots of leaves on the ground around it, but none on the tree."

"So more likely a meeting place rather than an ambush," the chief concluded.

Michael nodded.

"Ragnar, take a look at this." The chief held up his phone. On the screen was a shot that showed the bare tree and the fence. "Any idea where this is?"

Ragnar studied the photo.

"Yes," he said. "I recognize that tree. It's right by the field where I had sunflowers this year. You should have seen how beautiful it was, a whole field full of ripe sunflowers! This year I will plant them closer to the house—you need to rotate them anyway, and—"

"What's the best way to get there?" the chief asked.

Ragnar frowned.

"There is no good way to get there," he said finally. "It is very far from all the roads. You would need an ATV."

"Don't you have one?"

"In the shop," Ragnar said. "But don't worry! I will see if I can find one."

He raced off, cell phone in hand.

"Okay," the chief said. "Ragnar will find us an ATV, and Horace can go out and check the location."

"I still have to examine the victim's room," Horace said.

"Rooms," I said. "They moved him last night to a different room. Farther away from people he was annoying."

"Rooms, then," Horace said.

"I've secured both rooms as well as I could," the chief said. "There's one on the second floor that he'd been staying in, although unfortunately, they've moved someone else in, so I'm not sure there will be anything of his to find. And Ragnar's not sure he ever entered the other one, which is in one of the towers, but all his stuff is there, and you need to check that." He frowned. "No cell phone, though. Did you find one at his workstation?"

Horace shook his head.

"Maybe the killer made off with it," Michael said. "In case it contained incriminating evidence."

"Won't do them much good," the chief said. "I've already got a warrant for his cell phone records. Just waiting on his provider to cough them up. Hiding the actual phone will only delay the inevitable."

Though if any of his suspects suddenly left town, it might be significant. But so far no one had.

"Well, carry on," the chief said. "Do the victim's rooms first. And maybe by the time you've finished them, Ragnar will have found an ATV."

Horace nodded. He had pulled out his phone and was studying Michael's photos.

"We'll leave you to it." The chief nodded to us and strode out of the tent.

I felt a short but intense pang of resentment. If not for the contest—

If not for the contest, I would probably be dashing around, skirting that fine line between helping the chief and butting into his case. Maybe it was a good thing I was tied down to the contest. It would drive me crazy, staying in my forge when all this was going on around me. But it should keep me out of trouble.

"Let's join the chow line," Michael said. "You don't have all day for lunch, and the boys and I have plans for the afternoon."

"Anything I'm going to hate missing?"

"We're going to take Caroline and your grandmother to see the town's Christmas decorations," he said. "Daylight version. We'll save the more exciting nighttime tour to see all the lights until you're available."

"Thanks," I said. "Send me lots of pictures."

We went through the chow line and then joined the boys and my fellow competitors at a nearby table. Today's menu was much the same as yesterday's, which wasn't a disappointment, since I'd filled up yesterday before sampling more than half of the available goodies. The boys were sharing pictures of themselves astride the beautiful black Friesians. Andy, John, and Victor were expressing a satisfactory amount of envy.

"Let Ragnar know if you'd like to go riding," I said. "He's always trying to get people to try it."

Suddenly, the Christmas carols that had been playing in the background stopped, causing more than one person to turn around to see what had happened. One of the Tweedles had just entered the tent.

Roxanne was nearby. I got up and went over to talk to her.

"Isn't it kind of a pain?" I asked. "Having to silence the carols every time Sam or one of the producers walks in?"

"It would be if I had to do it," she said. "But it's started happening all by itself whenever one of them is around. At least if someone else is doing it, I haven't spotted it. I'm beginning to wonder if they're all three wearing some kind of Christmas Cone of Silence."

Puzzled, I went back to the table. And then an idea struck me. I pulled out my phone and texted Kevin.

"So how are you controlling the Christmas carols?" I asked.

I didn't get an answer for at least five minutes. I went back to my lunch, and to listening as the boys reassured Andy that no, the horses might look fierce, but they were gentle giants, and did he want a few riding lessons? But I kept an eye on my phone.

"Christmas carols?" it finally read. If I could have seen Kevin's face, I was sure it would have worn a completely unbelievable look of innocence.

"In the mess tent," I texted back. "Whenever Sam or one of the Tweedles walks in, the carols stop. Just tell me, so I don't have to go taking the speakers apart to find out for myself."

"You're no fun," he said. "I was doing it myself for a while, and it was a lot of fun to watch."

I glanced around until I found the fake carbon monoxide detector near the buffet.

"But now I've automated it," he said.

"Automated it how?"

"You probably don't want the technical stuff."

I rarely did.

"Basically I'm tracking their phones with a GPS program. If they get within twenty feet of the speaker, it shuts off."

I had questions. Many questions. Like how had Kevin managed to track their phones, and what else was he doing with the data, and wasn't this unethical if not illegal?

But then I remembered Sam bellowing at poor Jasmyn over her small effort to bring Christmas cheer to the production tent. And the Tweedles snarking about Ragnar's decorations in particular and Christmas in general. Maybe instead of the Two Tweedles I should start calling them the Two Grinches. Three, counting Sam.

"We could have a lot more fun with them if you like," Kevin texted. "But I figure we should probably wait until the filming's pretty much over."

"I'm not sure I even want to know," I texted back. "And yes, let's not do anything to make them harder to live with until we're nearly finished with the episode."

"But then the sky's the limit, right?"

I didn't answer. But I didn't say no, either. I could always exercise a veto if the producers calmed down and stopped being quite so annoying.

"Attention, please." Roxanne stood in front of the buffet table, holding her iPad. "I have an announcement for the contestants. So far the local authorities have interviewed Andy for thirty-seven minutes, and John for one hour and eleven minutes."

Interesting. I'd have expected them to spend a longer time with Andy. Not that I thought he was all that plausible a suspect, but on the face of it he had a much more understandable motive for doing something to Brody. I eyed John with interest. What could he possibly have had to reveal that took more than an hour?

"We're due to continue filming this part of the competition for the next three days," Roxanne continued. "Rather than wait until the end of that period to give each of you back the time you lost being interviewed by the police, the producers have decided to have the catch-up at the end of each day. That way you won't all be completely out of sync."

Nods and murmurs from my fellow contestants.

"Good idea," Victor said. "Look kind of weird if I was finishing my blade and those two suspicious characters were still starting to shape theirs." He grinned at John and Andy.

"Slow and steady wins the race," John said.

"Not when speedy and steady is part of the competition," Victor countered.

"So anyone who is not interviewed will be knocking off work at least an hour and eleven minutes early today," Roxanne went on. "Possibly earlier if the police find anyone they like talking to even more than John. So finish up—lunch break is over in seventeen minutes."

Chapter 25

We all turned back to our plates. Maybe I wasn't the only one who felt just a bit of anxiety over returning to the contest. I reminded myself not to be silly. Winning the competition didn't matter.

Except maybe it did. I'm not good at doing things halfway.

"I didn't realize I was gone that long," John said. "Does that mean your chief of police finds me a suspicious character?"

"Possibly," I said. "Or maybe just a good source of information."

"That could be." John was playing with—and frowning at—a harmless bit of lettuce that was hanging out of one side of his sandwich. "He had a lot of questions about the bladesmithing community. Was it supportive, was it cutthroat, did it have a lot of organizational politics, did we tend to know the other members that well? Stuff like that."

"Stuff I would have no clue about," Andy said. "I only joined the Society a year ago. Still a journeyman member."

"And I also had to tell him about a weird thing that happened with Brody last night," John went on. "Remember when he came up and said he had to talk to me about something?"

"I remember you didn't seem all that happy to see him," Andy said.

"What did he want?" Victor asked.

"He wanted to tell me that if I helped him talk the producers into letting him back on the show, he wouldn't turn me in for attacking Faulk."

Victor's mouth hung open. Andy, who had been chewing a bite of his sandwich, appeared to choke on it and had to be thumped on the back.

"But you didn't, did you?" Andy asked when he could speak again. "Hurt Faulk, that is."

John shook his head and took a bite of his sandwich.

"Then why'd he think you did?" Victor asked.

John chewed slowly. Deliberately so?

"No idea," he said when he'd finally swallowed. "Maybe he saw me doing something he thought was suspicious. Maybe he saw whoever attacked Faulk and thought it looked like me. Maybe he was just fishing. Obviously, we're prime suspects. Even Brody could see that."

"I vote for fishing," I said.

"Any particular reason?" Victor asked.

"He tried the same thing on me," I said. "And I didn't attack Faulk."

"When did he try it on you?" John asked.

"Maybe an hour or so before he tried it on you."

"How do you know when he tried it on me?" John frowned as if he found my statement suspicious.

"Because I was eavesdropping on your conversation with Brody," I said. "Not intentionally. I was actually eavesdropping on the producers. I was going to come out of hiding after they left, but then you and Brody came in before I had a chance to leave."

"Where were you?" John asked.

"That's a secret," I said. "Ragnar has a place he can hide if he wants to dodge someone. I was in the library when the producers came in, and I wasn't in the mood to deal with them, so I hid."

"Chief know this?" John asked.

I nodded.

"He try this on either of you?" John said, turning to Victor and Andy.

"Hell, no," Victor said. "If he'd tried any of that . . . nonsense on me, he'd have had a black eye when they found him."

Andy just shook his head.

"According to the chief, I might be the last person who saw him." John's voice held a hint of anxiety.

"He probably doesn't count me," I said. "Since my hiding place let me hear but not see. But I am an ear witness to your conversation."

"This makes me feel better," John said. "I mean, for one thing, it was driving me crazy, wondering why Brody thought it was me who attacked Faulk. And for another, I'm hoping having one part of my story confirmed will make your chief more likely to believe the rest. Because I can't prove I didn't kill Brody. After my talk with him, I went back to the dining room, grabbed a brownie and a couple of sodas, and went up to my room. But there's no way I can prove that. No way to prove that after Brody and I left the library, I didn't figure out a way to lure him into a dark corner and kill him."

"I wonder why he didn't try it on Andy or me," Victor mused.

"Maybe he was planning to," I suggested. "Maybe he would have if someone hadn't killed him not that long after he tried it on John."

"Was he?" John asked. "Killed not long after our conversation, that is?"

"I haven't heard the official time of death yet." It was true—I'd only heard Dad's preliminary estimate. His estimates tended to be pretty accurate, but that information wasn't mine to reveal. Still, I could offer my own opinion. And after years of listening to Dad talk about the time of death of both real and fictional bodies, I probably knew more about the subject than the average non-doctor. "If I had to guess, I'd say he was killed closer to when you left him than when Michael and I found him. Rigor mortis takes time to set in, and even in weather like this it takes awhile for a body to cool. Two degrees centigrade the first hour, and then one degree an hour until it reaches ambient temperature."

Maybe too much information. John merely nodded, but Andy and Victor looked uneasy.

"Doctor's daughter, remember," I said.

"And medical examiner's daughter," Andy added.

"I'd be happier if he'd stayed alive a lot longer after he and I talked," John said. "I'd feel less as if I had a target on my back."

"So it would help the police if we could figure out who might have talked to him after John did, right?" Andy said.

"What time were you talking to him?" Victor asked.

John shrugged.

"Around nine forty-four," I said. And seeing John's puzzled frown, I added, "And the only reason I know was that I knew Ragnar was looking for him, so I texted Ragnar that he was in the library."

"That's right," Andy said. "I spent most of the evening in the Great Hall helping wrap toys for that Christmas giveaway thing. Ragnar must have come through half a dozen times asking if anyone had seen Brody. No one had."

"You know," I said, "maybe Brody was trying to find out who attacked Faulk, so he could blackmail them. But I can think of another reason for Brody to try his blackmail scheme on some or all of us."

"We're all ears," Victor said.

"What if Brody was the one who attacked Faulk?" I suggested. "And accusing other people of doing it was his way of trying to divert suspicion from himself?"

John and Andy nodded.

"Yeah." Victor shook his head. "That sounds like just the kind of crazy thing Brody would do."

"And he was pretty desperate to get back on the show," John said. "Too desperate to think straight. I guess it never occurred to him that even if he figured out who attacked Faulk and talked them into backing his attempt to return, he was ticking off the rest of us with his false accusations."

"Lunch break is over!" Roxanne called. "Everyone back to the production tent. Lunch break is over."

We stood up, bussed our trays, and strolled to our forges together.

Back at my workstation, I started setting out my tools for the next stage of work. And one of my tools was missing—a pair of blade tongs that was exactly the right size to hold my sword at this point in the process.

"Did anyone borrow my blade tongs?" I asked.

Andy, across the way, shook his head.

"Not me," John called.

"Me neither," Victor added. "Hope the person who took my cross peen hammer didn't snake your tongs for some nefarious purpose."

"You want to borrow mine for a bit?" Andy asked.

"You'll be using them," I said.

"Not all the time."

"Enough of the time," I said. "I think I know where I left mine."

I made sure my forge was off before leaving the tent and heading for the castle. I had taken some of my mission-critical tools with me when I left the workstation yesterday, and the blade tongs were probably among them. I could check in the suite to see if they'd fallen out of my tote bag. And if they hadn't, I could always run down to the basement blacksmith's shop Faulk and I used. There was probably a pair there.

I was starting to climb the stone steps up to the terrace when I heard a scrap of music coming from somewhere nearby. I paused to listen. There it was again—a scrap of Garth Brooks singing "Friends in Low Places."

It seemed to be coming from the Moon Garden, a fenced-in area at the foot of the terrace where in summer Ragnar planted nothing but white and silver plants, many of them fragrant or night-blooming.

I went back down to ground level and followed the sound. It had stopped by the time I reached the black wrought iron gate to the garden. I opened the gate and winced as it creaked—but I knew it was a deliberate creak for atmosphere. Faulk and I had worked long and hard to perfect the spooky, creaking-gate technology Ragnar had requested.

In summer the Moon Garden would be full of blooms. Their scents would waft up to perfume the terrace above—flowering tobacco, night-blooming jasmine, moonflower, angel's trumpet, night phlox, sweet alyssum, and white heliotrope. Few things were more intoxicating than sitting on Ragnar's terrace, watching the evening primroses bloom and inhaling all the fragrances. There would also be white tulips, white roses, white daffodils, white astilbes, and who knew what else. The only thing visible now were the glossy green leaves of the hardy gardenia bushes, the naked stalks of the hydrangeas, and the graceful bare skeletons of at least a dozen white lilac trees. But it was still a beautiful and ever-so-slightly otherworldly place.

The music had stopped. But I was pretty sure I hadn't been imagining it.

"Friends in Low Places." Hmm.

I pulled out my phone and opened up a saved document—the list of names, phone numbers, and emails of the *Blades of Glory* cast and crew. I scrolled down until I found Brody's number. Brody had come from Murfreesboro, a small town near Nashville. Maybe I was stereotyping, because obviously anyone could choose a Garth Brooks song for his ringtone, and not everyone from Nashville loved country music—but still. It sounded like a Brody kind of thing. I called his number.

"Friends in Low Places" erupted from one of the gardenia bushes.

I ended the call and called the chief instead.

"What's up, Meg?"

"I think I found Brody's phone," I said. "I assume you're still looking for it."

"I am indeed," he said. "Don't pick it up. Just leave it wherever you found it."

"I can't even see it yet," I said. "But I heard it." I explained about hearing the snippet of Garth Brooks, and my suspicion that Brody might be using it as his ringtone.

"Where are you?"

"In the Moon Garden," I said. "Come to the base of the steps leading up to the terrace and then look around for a black wrought iron fence."

We hung up.

I stuffed my hands into my pockets and hunched my shoulders against the cold. Was it really colder here? No reason why it should be—I was on the south side of the castle, and its huge bulk shielded me from the wind. Maybe it was psychological. Seeing the forlorn remnants of what had been a lush summer garden. Hearing a phone ring to alert someone who wouldn't be answering it anymore.

The chief showed up with Horace.

"Now where did you say you found this phone?" the chief asked.

I pointed in the general direction of the musical gardenia bush, and then I dialed Brody's number again.

It took a while, since Horace insisted on taking dozens of pictures of everything before he disturbed it, but eventually, he emerged from the shrubbery with one gloved hand holding an iPhone with a cracked screen.

"Let's take a closer look at this thing back in the mess tent," the chief said.

We followed Horace back to what had become his table. I knew I should be heading over to the production tent, but I lingered, watching as Horace examined the phone.

"Looks as if it's been wiped clean," he said, holding it sideways. "You want me to test it for fingerprints or go for possible DNA?"

"I take it this is one of those cases where trying for one makes it difficult if not impossible to get the other," the chief said.

Horace nodded.

After a technical discussion so lengthy that I almost gave up and returned to my workstation, they decided to try for DNA. I watched as Horace swabbed key areas of the phone, putting each little sterile swab in its own tiny container.

"He's probably got a password," Horace said. "Which means we'll need to see if Kevin can get into it."

"We've already got a request in with his phone carrier for the data," the chief said.

Horace nodded. But then he used one gloved finger and pressed the power button. I expected to see the screen where you entered your passcode. But evidently, Brody hadn't bothered with a passcode. We saw the phone's home screen.

"Holy cow," Horace said. "We just lucked out."

"Check his call history," the chief said.

"Meg?" Roxanne had appeared in the doorway. "They're looking for you."

I muttered a few words that would need to be bleeped out if I said them on camera. Then I resigned myself to the inevitable.

"Got to go," I said.

The chief nodded. Horace didn't even notice I was leaving.

"I marked you as being interrogated," Roxanne said as we walked back to the other tent.

"Thanks," I said. "But that wasn't originally why I took off. I left one of my tools in my room. And I'm going to need it." I turned to head back to the castle.

"Isn't there someone you could send for it?" she asked. "They want to do your individual interview."

"Hang on a sec."

I grabbed a picture of a pair of blade tongs from a blacksmith tool site, texted it to Michael, and asked if he—or the boys—could try to find them, either in our suite or in the blacksmith shop.

"On it!" he texted back.

"Okay," I said. "Bring on the individual interview."

She led me to the banquet hall part of the tent, where they'd set up the lights and cameras.

Chapter 26

I quickly decided that I'd rather make another whole sword than do the individual interview. Alec was the interviewer—at least for the moment. But I was suspicious of the way Sam cautioned me to count to five after each question, to give room for any necessary editing. That meant that they could easily film someone else—Marco, for example—reading the questions and edit Alec out.

I had a feeling that had occurred to Alec, too, making him more nervous and prone to mistakes. And also that he was embarrassed by some of the questions. Way too many of them focused on the fact that I was a woman in what most people considered a man's profession.

"There have always been women blacksmiths," I said after the third or fourth such question. "We have accounts of this going back at least eight hundred years. Granted, in those days, thanks to societal attitudes, women most often entered the profession because they were either the widows of blacksmiths or the daughters of blacksmiths who had no sons. But nowadays a lot of women choose to become blacksmiths."

You'd think once I said that they'd move on. But you'd think wrong. Just about every question made some reference to my sex. I ignored it when I could and dealt with it when I had to. I got in a few digs, like when they asked me what were the disadvantages of being a woman blacksmith.

"No disadvantages that I can think of," I said. "In fact, I can think of one way in which most women are much more qualified than most men."

"What's that?" Alec asked—a little too quickly. I saw Sam frown.

"If we don't know how to do something, we're much better at asking for directions," I said. "And following them."

Alec laughed dutifully at this. But not very convincingly. Poor Alec! I could see why the producers were using Marco more.

I managed to endure the process patiently until Michael and the boys appeared. They waved at me, and Josh waved the blade tongs they'd brought. After that, I could feel my patience rapidly evaporating.

But I persevered and tried not to show how delighted I was when Alec finally ran out of questions and sent me back to my forge.

I had to walk between John's and Duncan's workstations to reach mine. John was hard at work, though he looked up and nodded as I passed.

Duncan's work area was empty.

"You're back on the clock." I glanced up to see Roxanne making notes on her iPad. And then, seeing my glance at Duncan's empty space, she added, "He's been out for over an hour now. Another few minutes and he'll be the record holder."

"Not a record I want to hold," Andy said.

I nodded. And then we both turned back to our forges.

Roxanne took a few steps down the aisle until she was beside Victor's workstation.

"Time for your individual interview," she said.

Victor growled—quite literally—before turning off his forge and following her to the banquet hall.

Victor's voice carried well enough that as long as no one else was actually hammering at the moment, I could hear his side of the interview. Just as my interview seemed too narrowly focused on my gender, Victor's seemed centered around the misguided notion that African American blacksmiths were an oddity. I couldn't hear what questions Alec was asking—and the odds were he hadn't written them anyway—but he seemed to have irritated Victor. I stepped out of my workstation to see what was happening.

"No, the Europeans did not introduce metalworking to Africa," Victor was saying. "There have been blacksmiths in Africa since at least the year fifteen hundred B.C. And in some societies, people thought what blacksmiths did was magic. People feared blacksmiths and did anything they could to avoid their wrath."

His facial expression suggested that Alec wasn't doing a very good job of avoiding the wrath of Victor.

"In Western Africa, for instance, where many of my ancestors came from, most of the cultures worshiped a god of iron and metalworking," Victor went on. "And the blacksmith was a powerful member of the society—almost as powerful as the chief. And in some areas, blacksmiths formed a separate caste. They would only marry within the caste, and even developed a separate language."

Alec said something that I didn't catch.

"Yeah, man," Victor said. "Nobody better mess with a blacksmith."

Then John started hammering, and I couldn't even hear Victor, so I went back to my work.

My sword was starting to look like a sword. Making it wasn't harder than making the knife—same techniques, same problems to be resolved. But there was just a lot more of it. A much longer blade that still had to be smooth, uniformly shaped, and perfectly balanced. And eventually, there would be the challenge of adding a hilt that would provide a comfortable yet reliable way of holding the much heavier blade.

And I needed to concentrate. I took a few cleansing deep

breaths—Rose Noire would be proud of me. I called up my mental image of Brody's body as if on a screen, and then I imagined it disappearing into the distance.

I focused back on my blade.

I managed to get a whole ten minutes of focused work done before losing my concentration. Not my fault, really. The chief stopped by my workstation.

"May I interrupt you?" he asked. "Just for a couple of minutes," he added, seeing Roxanne scurry over.

"You're off the clock," Roxanne said, making some kind of note on her iPad.

"Do either of these phone numbers look familiar?" The chief handed me a slip of paper.

"From Brody's cell phone, I bet. The second one does." I pulled out my phone and retrieved the list of cast and crew information. "Yes—that's Sam's phone. Sam Wilson, the director."

"And the other?"

I scanned the list again, then shook my head.

"Doesn't ring a bell, and it's not on the list."

The chief nodded.

"Just tell me to mind my own business if you like," I said. "But doesn't law enforcement have ways to look up phone numbers? Reverse phone lookup—isn't that what they call it?"

"We do," he said. "But with these two numbers, all we can determine is that they are both inexpensive prepaid phones."

"Burner phones!" I said.

He winced.

"Well, isn't that what 'inexpensive prepaid phones' usually are?" I asked.

"There are legitimate reasons for purchasing a prepaid phone," the chief said. "For example, if someone has bad credit, they might not be able to qualify for a cell phone contract. Or if they're temporarily in an area where their normal cell phone provider doesn't have good coverage."

"But if someone uses a burner phone to call someone who turns up as a homicide victim not long afterward, I bet it looks a lot more suspicious."

"It does indeed. Thank you."

He nodded and left. Roxanne hurried over and made another note in her iPad. I turned back to my anvil.

And heard a snatch of a Christmas carol. Just a few bars of a soft instrumental version of "What Child Is This?" wafting from somewhere nearby.

"Stop that! Who's playing that damn music!" one of the Tweedles bellowed.

"What Child Is This?" vanished. We worked in silence for a few minutes—well, not exactly silence, since up and down the line we competitors were hammering, using our bellows, or just tossing metal tools around. But without a soundtrack. Then the carol erupted again, this time from another direction.

More bellowing from the Tweedles.

And suppressed chuckles from several nearby workstations.

At one point, when Alec and the camera crew were hovering just outside my workstation, the carbon monoxide detector in my workstation came to life with what I recognized as the New Life Baptist Choir, singing a loud and prolonged "Glo-o-o-o-o-o-o-o-o-o-o-o-o-o-o-ria! In excelsis Deo!"

A Tweedle appeared.

"I heard that! Where's it coming from?"

"Heard what?" I did my best to look puzzled.

"That damned howling. You heard it, didn't you?"

He turned to Alec and the camera crew.

"Heard what?" the woman behind the camera said.

"Not picking up anything here," the sound guy said.

Alec's mouth was twitching slightly, but he managed a puzzled frown.

"Sound travels strangely out here in the country," I said. "Especially in winter, when all the trees are bare and you don't get their insulating properties as much."

"Exactly," the sound guy said.

The camera operator nodded firmly. Alec succumbed to a fit of coughing. The Tweedle frowned and hurried off.

Alec and the tech crew went back to filming me shaping my blade. But they seemed to be in a much better humor. I know I was.

As the afternoon wore on, the War Against the Grinches escalated. I began hearing jingle bells coming from nearby workstations. Andy's, definitely. And Victor's. Whenever one of the producers would come anywhere near our workstations, a frenzy of jingling would ring out as soon as their backs were turned, as if several bell-bedecked horse-drawn sleighs were having a drag race nearby. Someone kept leaving tiny candy canes all around the set in odd places, forcing Alec and the camera crew to inspect their surroundings every time they started shooting.

And whoever thought of the Christmas smells was a genius. At some time during the day—probably while we were at lunch—someone had set up several tiny, little electric essential-oil diffusers around the tent. The one nearest my forge was giving off clove and cinnamon scents. Across the way, Andy had pine, and gingerbread was wafting in from somewhere nearby. Since we weren't filming in Smell-O-Vision, the Tweedles had no logical reason to complain about the odors. And yet, as Dad was fond of explaining, odors triggered memories and both positive and negative associations in a much stronger and more visceral way than sights or sounds.

And it was a lot easier to pretend not to notice them when someone complained. Because yes, the Tweedles did complain.

And curiously, all of this didn't distract me from my work. From thinking about Brody's murder, at least some of the time. But I found it remarkably easy to switch from pretending not to hear Christmas music to hammering away purposefully.

Eventually, Roxanne dropped by to tell Victor he was dismissed for the day. Which meant the chief hadn't talked to him for very long. Andy's turn came not much later. And then John's.

I must have spent more time helping on the case than I realized. Longer than anyone's interview.

Except for Duncan, who was still off with the chief.

He walked back in, looking thunderous, about five minutes before Roxanne came to dismiss me.

"When do you need me back?" I asked.

"Not till tomorrow morning," she said. "You're done for the day. Everyone is except for him." She indicated Duncan with a nod. "I was starting to get worried about him. Thought maybe they arrested him and forgot to tell us."

"Let's hope they don't arrest anyone just yet," I said. "Or that might be the end of *Blades of Glory*."

She nodded and strode off. The camera crews swooped down on Duncan, who didn't appear happy to see them.

I didn't stick around to see what happened.

I was about to head up to the house when I spotted the chief sitting in the mess tent and studying something.

"You on break?" he said, looking up as I walked in.

"Finished for the day." I explained how Roxanne was keeping track of how much time we spent being interrogated.

"Good," he said. "I've been a little worried about the idea that I might torpedo someone's chances in the competition."

"Tell me to mind my own business if you like," I said. "But this afternoon it was a little creepy to be standing there hearing my four competitors pounding away on their anvils when I know Brody was killed with a blacksmith's hammer. Have you managed to eliminate any of them as suspects?"

Chapter 27

"Alas." The chief leaned back, took off his glasses, and rubbed his eyes. "All of your fellow competitors are still very much in the running. They all mingled at the party until they decided to go to bed at various times. Unaccompanied, apparently, so none of them have alibis. And they didn't know many people there, so it's hard to find anyone who can definitively vouch for them."

"That's a pity," I said. "Is there anyone you have managed to eliminate?"

"Well, not beyond *all* doubt," he said. "But the show's producers, Mr. Zakaryan and Mr. Duval, are fairly well accounted for. Around ten P.M. they decided it was time to go back to their hotel—they seem to be the only ones staying at the Caerphilly Inn."

"Yeah," I said. "Even the judges are here at the castle—though in a different wing from the contestants. The Tweedles fled to the Inn after one night at the castle. Ragnar put one of them— Zakaryan, I think—in the Robert Louis Stevenson Room and it creeped him out."

"Creeped him out?" the chief echoed. "Was there any particular reason? Or are they just not fond of Ragnar's decorating aesthetic?"

"There's a lenticular portrait over the mantel in that room," I said. "One of those pictures that look different depending on what angle you see them from," I added, seeing his puzzled look.

"When you walk into the room, you see a very conventional picture of Dr. Henry Jekyll, a distinguished, well-dressed, elderly Victorian gentleman. If you hop into bed and glance over at the picture, suddenly you see a really creepy version of Edward Hyde, with a sinister leer and bloody fingers. Makes Hannibal Lector look like a vicar."

"Ah." The chief smiled. "Yes, I can see how much Ragnar would relish that. Neither Mr. Zakaryan nor Mr. Duval strikes me as the sort of gentleman who would be amused by it. At any rate, neither of them has a car—they seem to rely upon the Inn's car service and on Mr. Franzetti to chauffeur them around town."

"Alec's been griping about that," I said.

"He made it plain that he found it annoying. But I imagine he may do a good deal less griping now that his chauffeuring duties have given him, too, an alibi. Mr. Zakaryan and Mr. Duval spent fifteen or twenty minutes in Ragnar's entrance hall, loudly announcing the time and complaining that Mr. Franzetti was keeping them waiting. At around ten twenty-five—give or take a very few minutes according to onlookers—Mr. Franzetti appeared and took them back to the Inn. He then stayed in the Inn's bar for over three hours, first complaining to Mr. Wilson, the show's director, and then to the on-duty bartender. He didn't leave until they closed down the bar at two A.M. So even if he broke a few speed limits coming back here, he couldn't possibly have arrived until two twenty-five—which is more than an hour after your father's best estimate of the latest possible time of death."

I had mixed feelings about this. I was relieved to know that Alec was in the clear. I'd gladly have thrown one or both of the producers under the bus.

"How does Dad feel about his calculations?" I asked. "I mean, I trust him, but he'd be the first to point out that his calculations are only as good as the data he's given."

"He seems fairly confident," the chief said. "Of course, he's still doing more research to see if there are any other factors that could affect his calculations. And his calculations give him a window of between eight P.M. and one A.M. Your sighting of Mr. McIlvaney in the library at nine forty-four helped us narrow down the time of death quite a bit."

"Couldn't one of the producers have done it before taking off for the Inn?" I asked.

"No." The chief shook his head firmly. "Once we recovered Mr. McIlvaney's phone—once you found it for us—we could see his calls and texts. He texted Ragnar at ten twenty-one. Apparently, they hadn't found him to notify him that they had moved him to another room, and he texted to complain that the key code wasn't working on his old room and ask where his stuff was. And at ten twenty-five, while Mr. Franzetti was putting on his wraps—and Mr. Zakaryan was chastising him about how long it took him to answer their request for a ride—Mr. Franzetti received and responded to a text from Mr. McIlvaney."

"And I gather the message didn't say 'Help! Please come and rescue me! I'm about to be brained with a cross peen hammer by— Aarrgghh!'" I clutched my throat and pretended to be falling over.

"Nothing that illuminating," he said with a smile. "A string of badly spelled profanities, accompanied by a plea to get him back on the show. And the three judges are also out of it. Apparently they decided it wouldn't look good for them to be socializing with the contestants, so at around seven the three of them went out to dinner together at the Shack, and stayed on listening to the band until the place closed at two A.M. Of course, we'll be checking to make sure someone at the Shack saw them, but unless they all three ganged up to eliminate Brody, they're probably in the clear."

"I'm sure they're relieved to know that." Of course, I wasn't relieved—I was starting to feel a little worried about how the focus of the investigation seemed to be narrowing down to my fellow contestants. "Too bad the producers are out of the running, because I suspect the show could manage quite well without them. And what if they ganged up on Brody? A really diabolical criminal would have arranged an alternate means of transportation from the Inn back to Ragnar's. One of the producers could stay at the Inn and pretend to be having a meeting with the other, in case a staff member comes by with a message or anything, while the other sneaks through the garage and hikes across the golf course until he reaches the place where he stashed a car so he could drive back to Ragnar's and . . . Sorry," I said, seeing his expression. "I'm starting to sound like Dad, aren't I?"

"Just a little. Actually, we are making sure that's not a possibility. Fortunately, sneaking out of the Inn is rather difficult these days, given the management's increasing concern with its guests' security."

I nodded. My good friend Ekaterina, manager of the Inn, was maybe just a little paranoid about making sure that her guests were safe . . . and that they didn't get up to anything that would generate bad publicity for the hotel.

"So just to be certain, I have Aida over there viewing and collecting video and interviewing the staff who were on duty last night. Pretty sure they're all three accounted for."

"A pity," I said.

I was dying to ask him why he'd taken so long interviewing Duncan, but I knew better. I was still trying to figure out a way to bring up the subject when my phone rang.

I glanced at the caller ID and answered.

"Hey, Ragnar," I said.

"Can you come down to the stables?" he said. "We could use your help."

He hung up before I could ask what kind of help he needed.

"My presence is requested in the stables," I said.

The chief nodded and went back to looking at some papers

on the table in front of him. Just for a moment, I thought of turning back to get just a peek at them.

Not a good idea. Having the camera crew underfoot while I worked was giving me a graphic reminder of how annoying it could be to have other people snooping while I was just trying to get work done. I didn't want to do the same thing to the chief.

As I left the mess tent, I heard a bellow coming from the main tent, wordless but definitely angry. I stuck my head through the tent flap. Duncan was standing there, red-faced and scowling—he looked rather like a cartoon bull getting ready to charge something. Roxanne walked over to him and handed him a ball peen hammer.

"Try not to lose your grip on this again," she said.

Nearby, Vern was frowning as he watched one of the tech crew members sweep up the remnants of a piece of equipment. Yikes. A good thing Vern was there if Duncan had lost his temper so badly that he'd started throwing around three-pound hammers. And also a good thing I was done for the day.

Although it was massively annoying that we had to knock off when we could still be hard at work. And then I shoved the thought out of my mind. Time to think about something else.

The stables weren't far off, so I hiked there as briskly as I could manage. I found Horace and Ragnar in the stable yard, having some kind of discussion.

"You could just drop me off as close as possible," Horace said.

"You'd still be at least a mile away," Ragnar said. "And that forensic gear of yours is heavy."

He gestured toward the two bulging cases at Horace's feet. Horace puffed out his cheeks in obvious frustration.

"What's up?" I asked.

"I need to go out before it gets dark to collect that evidence Michael found," Horace said. "But Ragnar's ATV is in pieces down in Osgood Shiffley's repair shop at the moment, and Ragnar doesn't think a regular car could get there."

"He could get there easily on horseback," Ragnar said. "And one of the Friesians could easily carry him and all his forensic gear."

"I'm not a cowboy," Horace muttered.

"I'd go with him," Ragnar said. "But I've got a million things to do to get ready for tonight's Christmas party. So I thought maybe you could go along. Help him with the horses."

"Sure," I said. "Don't worry," I added, turning to Horace. "It'll be fine."

"Isn't there another ATV somewhere in the county?" Horace asked.

"Not that we can find before dark," Ragnar said. "We've been trying."

"Where's your spirit of adventure?" I asked.

"Lucifer is bringing the horses," Ragnar added.

That sounded alarming, until a slender young man with spiky dead-black hair and an all-black outfit emerged from the stable door, leading one of the Friesians.

"Here we are." Ragnar tossed me a chunk of apple, then gestured to his goth stable hand to lead the horse to me. "You can ride Carmilla. You've met her before."

Carmilla nickered softly, and I fed her the apple. Always a good idea to placate anything that big before entrusting your life to her.

Lucifer handed me the reins and glided noiselessly back into the stable.

"Pretty cheeky, don't you think?" Horace said. "Aren't you afraid King Charles will say 'Off with his head!' if he finds out you've named a horse after his queen consort?"

"*Car*milla," Ragnar said. "With an R. She's named after the Sheridan Le Fanu novel that predated *Dracula*."

"If you say so," Horace said.

"And Horace can have Barnabas," Ragnar said, gesturing to where Lucifer was leading out another black steed even larger than Carmilla, and with even more glossy black hair on his lower legs.

"Collins?" I asked.

"Of course!" Ragnar beamed at me.

"A stallion?" Horace said. "I don't want a stallion. I want a nice, gentle mare."

"He's a gelding," Ragnar said. "Geldings tend to be very gentle."

"You'd think they'd be resentful," I added.

Ragnar laughed at that. Horace was staring up at Barnabas as if Lucifer were trying to hand him the leash of a seriously ticked-off leopard.

"Feed him this," Ragnar said, handing Horace an apple chunk. "No, don't hold it between your fingers—not unless you don't plan on keeping those fingers. His aim might not be that good. Put it flat on your palm."

Horace complied, and Barnabas scooped up the apple with enthusiasm.

"See?" I said. "You've won his heart."

"I've given you saddlebags," Ragnar added. "You can pack all your forensic gear in them."

With a sigh, Horace did so, and then Ragnar gave him a leg up into the saddle.

I could see why Ragnar had chosen Barnabas for Horace. Carmilla was prancing slightly as if excited by the prospect of taking me somewhere. Barnabas stood as steady as a statue, with a look of patient stoicism, as if resigned to his fate as the horse who got all the newbies and scaredy cats. And when I nudged Carmilla forward with a slight pressure from my legs, Barnabas slowly followed us, moving with ponderous grace.

Ragnar followed us to the stable yard gate and opened it for us.

"Have fun!" he called as we ambled down the dirt lane beyond.

Horace sighed audibly again.

I pulled out my phone, opened up the GPS app, and steered

Carmilla in the direction the coordinates indicated. Eventually, we encountered a fence separating us from a pasture. I glanced up and down the fence until I spotted a gate, then turned that way. We crossed the pasture, eventually encountering another stretch of fence, and plodded up and down its length until we found the next gate.

This wouldn't be a speedy trip. But it was relaxing. And I couldn't help thinking that we were proceeding much as the wise men had traveled to Bethlehem, with no idea where we were going or how much longer it would take. Nothing to do but trust our guiding star.

Of course, I had to be careful not to lose my grip on the small electronic device in which our guiding star lived. We'd be out of luck if one of Carmilla's huge hooves landed on it. And I hoped our journey didn't take so long that it would drain my phone's battery. Which meant it probably wasn't a good idea to use up power by playing Christmas carols while we traveled. A pity. But I could hum instead.

Horace actually waited a full ten minutes before asking for the first—but not the last—time, "Are we nearly there yet?"

I tried to shove the contest out of my mind. To stop thinking about my sword, and what I needed to do when I got back to the contest tomorrow. To forget all the comparisons my mind was making between my blade and the ones the others were making. To damp down my worry about whether Duncan, back in the production tent, was having a temper tantrum.

Although I did succumb to the temptation to send Vern a text.

"Keep me posted if anything exciting happens in the contest," I said.

"Roger," he replied.

After that, I had more luck forgetting about what was going on back in the production tent and enjoying the ride. The landscape changed from pasture to woods, and then back to pasture again. The fences changed from wood that was painted glossy black to wire fences, with or without a top strand of barbed wire. The farther we got away from the castle, the hillier and more rugged the terrain grew. I could see why doing this with a regular vehicle, even one with four-wheel drive, would be dicey.

A small honor guard of crows accompanied us, wheeling overhead as we plodded along. I soon figured out that the crows knew where the gates were—and that we earthbound creatures needed to use them. After the first couple of gates I learned to look up at the crows whenever I spotted a fence, so I could let them lead us to the nearest gate.

"We're nearly there," I was finally able to tell Horace. "See that big tree ahead?"

I reined in Carmilla. Barnabas and Horace came up beside me. Ahead we could see the landmarks I recognized from Michael's photo—the enormous bare oak and the wire fence running beside it.

"Maybe we should park the horses here," Horace said. "We don't know how far out the crime scene extends—assuming it is a crime scene. We don't want to contaminate it with hoofprints."

"I figured as much," I said. "That's why I gave you the heads-up."

"Will they stay put if we leave them here and walk the rest of the way?" Horace asked,

"Probably," I said. "But just to play it safe, let's tie them to the fence."

We ambled over to the fence, staying a good hundred yards from the tree. We dismounted and tied the horses' reins to one of the fence posts. Then we fished Horace's forensic gear out of Barnabas's saddlebags. Ragnar had tucked in a few more chunks of apple, so I rewarded the horses and then followed Horace as he began slowly making his way to the big tree—slowly, because he was bent over nearly double, scrutinizing every inch of the path ahead for . . . whatever he was hoping to find. The cigarette butts, of course, and footprints, and anything else that you wouldn't expect to see this far out in the middle of nowhere.

The crows all settled either on the fence or in the leafless oak, and seemed to be watching what we were up to with great interest.

"Aha!" Horace finally muttered.

He had arrived at the little bare spot with the cigarette butts and the footprint. He took what seemed like a thousand photos of these—a good thing he'd gone digital, or the film he used up on this case alone would break the chief's annual budget. Then he began collecting the cigarette butts.

"Do they really each need their own separate little evidence bag?" I asked.

"We don't know for sure that they were all smoked by the same person," he said. "Makes for a cleaner process if we end up having to test them for DNA."

We also didn't know if they had anything whatsoever to do with Brody's murder, but he knew that. So I just nodded. I held the top and middle wire strands of the fence apart so I could slip through it—still keeping a good distance from the tree—and scanned the ground on the other side. About ten feet or so from the fence, a tiny stream trickled along, and beyond that, open pasture gave way to woods.

And yes, there were motorcycle tire tracks in the slightly damp ground on either side of the stream.

Knowing how Horace preferred to concentrate on one part of a crime scene at a time, I decided to wait until he had finished with the cigarette butts before pointing this out to him.

My phone dinged with a text from Vern. No words—just a picture of Duncan, waving his half-finished broadsword in the air, looking like some berserk Viking warrior storming a city. And then a picture of him at his anvil. His left hand held the blade, ready to be hammered, but his right arm, with the hammer, was limp, as if he couldn't be bothered to lift it.

What was going on with him? He didn't seem to be that broken up by the loss of Brody. Was he that irritated merely because the chief had interrogated him? Or was all this temperament the sign of a guilty conscience acting up?

And what was it going to do to the contest? Yes, Roxanne was keeping a record to make sure we all had the same amount of time to work, but she couldn't give us equal focus and concentration. By the look of it, Duncan was in a thoroughly foul mood. When that happened to me, I knew I needed to put my blacksmithing work aside before I ruined it. Duncan didn't have that luxury.

What if he couldn't hold it together, ruined his sword, and came in dead last? Would they eliminate him? Or would the fact that they'd already kicked Brody out mean that they could keep him around—maybe even needed to keep him around? And if he lost due to all the distractions of the murder investigation, wouldn't he have a valid complaint that it was unfair?

I decided to talk to Andy, John, and Victor. Suggest an informal pact—if the producers tried to send anyone else home this week, we'd down tools, because whoever came last could make the argument that the murder and subsequent investigation had thrown them off their game.

Unless, of course, Duncan—or any of the other competitors—turned out to be Brody's killer. If that happened, we'd soldier on with only four.

Horace stood up and stretched his back. Evidently he was finished communing with the cigarette butts.

By this time, I'd noticed that someone had placed two large fallen logs right beside the fence and at the foot of the big tree—one on each side, so you could use them to get over the fence instead of crawling between the wires. I pointed them out to Horace. He joined me on the stream side of the fence and then documented the tire tracks with another few hundred digital photos.

"Probably Dunlops," he said.

"Is that useful?"

"No," he said. "Dunlop tires are really popular. But one of these has a nice, distinctive little slash in the tread. That's useful. I'd know it if I saw it."

Some of the crows had followed us, stopping to sip from the little stream, and then flying ahead of us into the woods. Horace glanced after them and sighed.

"Wish we knew where it came from," he said.

"We could backtrack it," I suggested. "I think the crows are expecting us to."

"Can you tell them we might need Vern for that?"

"Let's give it a try."

Thanks to little bits of mud that had obviously fallen out of the tire treads, we were eventually able to figure out where the motorcycle had entered the woods. Vern would probably already have followed the trail all the way to whatever country lane or gravel road it had entered the woods from. We were about six feet into the woods, eyes glued to the ground, and not finding any more clues about which way to go.

"It's hopeless," Horace said. "We can send Vern out tomorrow if the chief thinks it's important. Let's head back to the castle."

I stood up, eased my back, and looked around.

"Don't you want to examine the motorcycle itself before we go?"

Chapter 28

"Motorcycle?" Horace jerked his head up and followed my pointing finger. A motorcycle was leaning against a tree, with a large dead branch pulled in front of it to provide a little bit of camouflage. Not very effective camouflage. The bright red gas tank stood out vividly against the dull grays and browns of the forest, and it was hard to miss the big Harley-Davidson logo. Even if the motorcycle had been better hidden, we'd probably have noticed it when the crows began landing on it. But it was far enough into the woods that we hadn't spotted it across the fence.

After the requisite amount of forensic photography, Horace approached the motorcycle.

"Yes," he said, bending to the rear tire. "Same distinctive little slash."

He'd been using his digital camera for the photos. Now, he pulled out his phone, took a picture of the motorcycle's license plate, and then did something with it. Sent it somewhere for identification, I assumed.

In the distance, one of the horses neighed.

"Is it okay, leaving them where we did?" Horace asked.

"They should be fine," I said.

"There's nothing out here that could hurt them, is there?"

"Not unless Grandfather's had a security breach at the zoo and some of the wolves or big cats have gotten loose," I said. "And I think we'd have heard about it if that had happened. It would take a pretty sizable predator to attack horses that big."

Then both horses neighed. It didn't sound like happy neighing.

"On second thought, maybe we *should* check on the horses," I said. "See what's making them restless."

We turned and headed back to where we'd left the horses. I noticed that Horace seemed . . . tense wasn't quite the word. Alert, maybe. Vigilant. And he had adjusted his coat so his hand had a clear path to his service weapon.

When we emerged from the woods, we both paused at the sight of a human figure standing by the fence on our side of it, about ten feet to the right of the horses. A relatively small human figure, and he didn't seem to be bothering the horses— just staring at them with his head cocked to one side as if puzzled. The horses didn't seem to like him. They shifted restlessly from foot to foot and craned their necks to look at him.

"Oh, great," Horace muttered. His body language had changed from alert to annoyed. He walked forward until he was right behind the man.

"Hey, Rodney," he said.

Rodney started and turned around.

"Hey, Horace," he said, his tone unconvincingly casual. "What's up?"

"I could ask you the same thing."

Rodney was a short, slight, pale man, probably in his thirties, with thinning dark blond hair and a pencil-thin mustache so sparse and nondescript that I had to wonder why he bothered.

"Oh," Rodney said. "I'm just out here . . . you know . . ."

"Just waiting for a rendezvous with one of your customers?" Horace asked.

Rodney pressed his lips together as if signaling his intention to remain silent.

"So who is our suspected horse thief?" I asked.

Horace turned to me.

"This is Rodney Peebles," he said. "One of our neighbors

from Clay County. You might not have met him before, since until a few months ago he was enjoying the hospitality of the Virginia Department of Corrections. Up in Coffeewood, wasn't it, Rodney?"

Rodney pretended a lofty disdain for this topic, reaching into his shirt pocket and pulling out a pack of Camels. He fished out a cigarette and began patting various pockets, presumably searching for matches or a lighter.

The crows had followed us back and were settling on the fence again, clearly interested in whatever we flightless creatures were up to.

"Rodney's quite the entrepreneur," Horace went on. "Unfortunately, his product line's mostly illegal substances. I figure you're probably out here to meet Brody McIlvaney, right?"

Rodney feigned disinterest and continued patting pockets he'd already patted.

"I hate to be the bearer of bad news," Horace continued, "but I don't think Brody's going to show up."

"You run him in for something?" Rodney said, through lips compressed to keep the cigarette from falling out. It bounced comically as he spoke. "This Brody guy you think I know?"

"Someone killed him," Horace said.

Rodney's mouth fell open and his cigarette tumbled to the ground.

"And I think the chief would like to talk to you," Horace told him.

"I don't know anything about it," Rodney said.

"Good to hear it," Horace replied. "The chief would probably rather you told him that firsthand."

"How are we going to get him back there?" I asked, gesturing at the horses.

Horace frowned and glanced around as if he'd momentarily forgotten that his cruiser was back at the castle.

"I've got my chopper over there," Rodney said.

"Yes," I said. "We found it."

"I can just ride it back to the road," Rodney said. "Meet you down at Ragnar's house."

"Yeah, right." Horace frowned. "We could call Ragnar. Maybe he could send someone up with another horse."

"I'm not getting on one of those things," Rodney warned, taking a half step away from Carmilla and Barnabas.

"If Rodney came here by motorcycle, he probably knows the way back to a road and civilization," I pointed out. "If we can find a gate to get the horses on the other side of the fence, maybe we could lead the horses and wheel the motorcycle along with us."

"Not seeing any gates," Horace said.

"Haven't run into one myself," Rodney said.

"Well, then let's start walking back to the castle," I said. "And I'll call Ragnar to see if he can meet us partway with some kind of transportation."

"Do you actually know the way back?" Horace asked.

"Probably not," I said. "But I saved the location of the castle in my phone before we set out."

"Sweet," Horace said.

Just then Rodney took off running. He made use of the fallen logs to vault over the fence, back to the side the horses were on, then veered left and kept on going—which meant he was getting farther and farther from his motorcycle. Still, he was making good time and was probably hoping to circle back and reclaim his transportation.

The crows took flight and began flying around over Rodney's head, as if trying to make sure we knew where he was going.

Horace groaned and pulled out his phone.

"Aren't you going to chase him?" I asked.

"Dude made all-state back when he was on the Clay County High School cross-country team," Horace said. "And from the look of it, he can still run like a cheetah. I know my limits. Calling it in. We can put out a BOLO for him and— Hey, Debbie Ann. Got a situation here."

"We can do better than that." While Horace briefed Debbie Ann, I went over the fence, untied Carmilla, climbed aboard, and set off in pursuit of Rodney. Horace was right—Rodney was fast. But not fast enough to outrun a horse. Especially once the horse decided what we were doing was a lot of fun. We caught up with Rodney and fell in beside him, alternating between a trot and a canter.

Rodney pretended not to notice us. But I could tell Carmilla made him nervous. He flinched every time she snorted.

I wondered, briefly, if chasing Rodney was wise. What if he pulled a gun? But Horace wasn't shouting at me to stop, come back, and stay away from him. And Horace had relaxed when he recognized Rodney, rather than becoming tense and warier. I was probably okay.

"You might want to rethink this," I said. "Cops get annoyed when you run away from them. Why not go back and let Horace take you to talk to the chief? Get it over with."

Rodney kept running. He'd slowed down quite a bit, though, exchanging his first frenzied sprint for a steady ground-eating pace. He'd probably run some longer distances in high school.

But he hadn't done it recently. His pace was slowing and his breathing was getting heavier.

We'd been traveling parallel to the barbed wire fence. Suddenly Rodney put on a burst of speed and veered sharply left, heading for the fence.

Carmilla accepted the challenge and gave chase. And while the Friesians were usually docile and obedient, she paid no attention to my tugging on the reins. She was running straight at the fence.

Evidently, I was about to find out if my horse could jump the fence. No, actually, I had no doubt she could. The burning question was whether I could stay in the saddle while she did it.

Rodney sailed over the wire fence with ease and fairly impressive form—Horace should have mentioned that he'd also done hurdles in high school. Carmilla's stride changed as she gathered her legs beneath her and sprang into the air. I felt a mix of exhilaration and sheer terror. But I kept my seat and breathed a sigh of relief when we landed. Carmilla didn't resist my efforts to steer her in a wide circle back to the fence, where Rodney was struggling to free the back of his pants from the strand of barbed wire on which it had snagged.

I decided not to help. Rodney was still flailing around when Horace trotted up.

"Freeze." Horace pulled out his gun and held it at the ready. "Put your hands on your head."

Rodney obeyed. A few seconds later, we heard a loud ripping sound as the fabric of his pants gave way and he landed on the ground with a gaping hole over his backside. Luckily he was wearing underwear—although I was surprised to learn that they made Spider-Man briefs in adult men's sizes.

I suppressed the laughter this inspired. I didn't think either of the men found the situation amusing.

"Vern's found himself an ATV," Horace said, through clenched teeth. "He's on his way."

I wondered if this meant that Duncan's catch-up time was finished or if he was still hammering away in the production tent. Then I shoved the thought aside. I'd find out later.

"Good," I said. "You can go with Vern and Rodney in the ATV. I can lead Barnabas back."

As I expected, the thought of parting with Barnabas considerably improved Horace's mood.

"Of course, we have to figure out how to get Carmilla back on the other side of the fence," I said.

"You could ride her over the fence again," Horace suggested. "Now that you know she can jump it."

"Once was enough," I said. "But I have an idea. Let's head back to where Barnabas is."

"Let me handcuff our prisoner first."

"Prisoner? Me?" Rodney's tone held a note of gentle reproach. "Horace, you know me."

"I know you just tried to run away," Horace said, as he fastened the handcuffs around Rodney's wrists.

Rodney sighed as if deeply disappointed by Horace's lack of trust.

When we returned to the big oak tree, I looped Carmilla's reins over the saddle and used the logs to climb over the fence. I fished a couple of apple slices out of the saddlebags and fed one to Barnabas.

Carmilla was definitely paying attention. So were the crows, but I wasn't sure I had apples enough for all of them.

I walked along the fence until I was about ten feet away from Barnabas and held up the apple slice.

Carmilla's ears swiveled forward.

It took a few tries, first feeding her a couple of apple slices over the fence, and gradually moving farther away from it, so she had to stretch out her neck. Finally, when the hand holding out the apple chunk was definitely out of reach, she got the hint and jumped over the fence with neat efficiency.

"Good girl!" I exclaimed. I gave her another bit of apple, and then scattered a handful for the crows.

"Vern says he's about ten minutes away," Horace said.

Suddenly the sound of a laughing hyena startled us. All of us, especially the horses.

"What's that?" Horace snapped.

"Just my phone," Rodney said.

The hyena laugh sounded again.

"You want us to answer it for you?" I asked.

"Nah. Won't be anything important," Rodney said. "I'll just let it go to voicemail."

The hyena laugh repeated two more times. The horses seemed a lot happier when it stopped.

An idea struck me. I pulled out my phone and thought back to the two phone numbers the chief had shown me. While scanning the cast and crew directory to see if it matched any of the numbers there I'd recited the second number—the one that wasn't Sam's—multiple times. Could I remember it accurately? I closed my eyes and tried to put myself back in the moment. The number—at least what I thought was the number—sprang to mind. I dialed it.

The hyena laugh rang out again.

"You're popular today," Horace said to Rodney.

"That's me, actually," I said. "Calling that phone number the chief wanted to identify."

Horace looked at Rodney with new interest.

A few minutes later Vern showed up in the ATV.

"Now that I've got you for backup, let's pat him down," Horace said.

"You already had Meg for backup," Vern said. "No need to wait for me."

"I don't give you permission to search me," Rodney said.

"So noted," Vern said. "But you know as well as we do that we're not going to get in a vehicle with you until we're sure you're unarmed."

Rodney submitted to the pat down with the same sullen, uncooperative air my sons would have displayed if I was trying to make them look presentable after a good wallow in a mud puddle. Then Vern and Horace loaded both Rodney and his motorcycle in the ATV and took off.

After flying back and forth between the ATV and me for a few minutes, the crows decided to join forces with me.

I plugged the coordinates for the castle into my phone's GPS app. Then I untied the horses, climbed back into Carmilla's saddle with Barnabas's reins in my hand, and headed for the castle. After a while, the horses got the message that we were heading back to their barn, and I could sit back and let them do the navigating.

Unfortunately, that left me plenty of time for thinking. I alternated between worrying about how Duncan was doing with his broadsword and trying to sort out how Rodney fit into the picture.

Rodney had seemed genuinely surprised when Horace had told him Brody was dead. But what if he was merely a very good actor? Had Brody been on his way to a rendezvous with Rodney when he was killed? That would account for where he'd been killed. We'd detoured around the crime scene on the way here. Someone walking this way would probably have cut straight through it. But if Rodney were the killer, why would he come back to—well, not exactly the scene of the crime. That was a couple of miles away. But back to Ragnar's property. Back to a place where he'd probably spent some time waiting last night. Presumably waiting for Brody.

I puzzled over this new piece of the case all the way back to the castle, without coming to any brilliant conclusions. When we arrived at the stables—even Barnabas managed a brisk trot for the last stretch—Lucifer helped me dismount. He didn't say anything about the fact that we'd returned one rider short, but when I left the barn he was examining the horses, inch by inch, as if trying to reassure himself that they'd come to no harm while in my care.

I stopped by the production tent to check on how Duncan was doing. His forge was empty—well, empty of Duncan. He'd left rather a lot of stuff lying around on the floor and on his worktable. I didn't leave my forge that messy in normal times, much less when I knew it would be on camera. Was he just a slob? Or had he, perhaps, stormed off the set in a temper when Roxanne told him his time was up?

I'd ask Roxanne later. For now, I headed for the castle. On top of my long day of blacksmithing, my ride on Carmilla had called on muscles I didn't often use. Maybe I could commandeer the bathroom and take a long, hot, soaking bath before dinner started.

Though a long, hot, soaking bath would be incomplete without some kind of soothing bath oil. Preferably one of Rose Noire's organic lavender concoctions.

I texted her.

"Did you bring any bath oil with you?"

"Of course!" she texted back. "Come down to the kitchen."

So I went in through a side door that let me into the house on the basement level, not far from the kitchen. Much as I enjoyed Ragnar's social events, I didn't want to get sucked into this evening's event just yet. Or, more likely, into preparations for this evening's event.

Down in the kitchens, Alice and her team—which now seemed to include Jasmyn as a gung ho participant—were baking gingerbread. Gingerbread persons, gingerbread animals, and sheets and sheets of flat gingerbread pieces that could be assembled into gingerbread houses.

Alice looked uncharacteristically frazzled.

"We're already running late with the gingerbread houses," she fretted. "And with such crowds to cook for, I have no idea how we're going to get them all assembled and decorated."

"Use the crowds," I suggested. "Instead of making the gingerbread houses another major project on top of all the others you have to do, turn them into a fun, family-friendly Christmas activity. Set up all the materials in the dining hall and announce that everyone is invited to help decorate gingerbread houses after dinner."

"Meg! That's perfect!" Alice exclaimed. "Why didn't I think of that?"

"Because you've been working too hard." I claimed a small gingerbread person as my reward for coming up with a good idea and strolled over to where Rose Noire was cutting out cookies.

"So, can I hit you up for some bath oil?" I asked.

"Of course." She looked around at the dozen or so people

dashing around the kitchen. Then she grabbed her purse and headed for the door. "This way."

She led me out of the kitchen and down the hall. We ended up in what Ragnar referred to as the pantry—actually a cavernous storage room in which he kept all the non-refrigerated foods and other household supplies. Someone—Alice? Rose Noire herself?—had brought in an aging red velvet sofa and half a dozen black and purple yoga mats, making a small lounging area in one of the far corners.

A good choice for a private conversation. I was reasonably sure that, unlike the library, it didn't contain any secret rooms or passages.

"Is there a reason we're doing a clandestine handoff of the bath oil?" I asked.

"Of course not." She reached into her purse and pulled out several small bottles. "Do you want rose or lavender?"

"Yes," I said. "You know I'm a sucker for both."

"I know." She smiled as she handed me the bottles. "I wanted to ask you something without everyone listening in. It's about Jasmyn." She took a seat on a box of commercial-size cans of tomato sauce. "I'm worried."

Chapter 29

"Worried? Why?" I was tempted to say, "What now?"—but that would have been rude. After a wistful glance at the sofa, I pulled up a nearby rolling step stool and sat across from her.

"Remember what I told you yesterday?" Rose Noire clasped her hands as if keeping them still helped her stay calm.

"That Jasmyn seemed haunted by something," I said. "And seemed to be clinging to you as if for protection. Has it gotten worse?"

"No." She pursed her lips as if trying to keep something in. "She's fine today."

"Well, that's good. Right?"

"It's as if whatever was worrying her or threatening her or haunting her is . . . gone."

Uh-oh.

"She seems quite calm," Rose Noire continued. "Almost happy."

"Obviously she's heard the news that Brody was killed," I said. "And however sad she might be at the violent, untimely death of another human being, she probably feels safer now."

"Ye-es."

There was more. I waited as patiently as I could.

But patience was never my strong suit.

"You're not suggesting she did it, are you?"

"Not exactly. But . . . should I worry that she doesn't have an alibi?"

"A lot of us don't."

"You do," she said. "You have Michael and the boys. And I do. Alice and I brought a TV into the kitchen and stayed up much too late, baking and watching movies. We watched *The Bishop's Wife,* and *Love Actually,* and *The Shop Around the Corner,* and *Miracle on 34th Street,* and *The Nightmare Before Christmas.* I think that was all. No, we also watched *How the Grinch Stole Christmas.*"

"You must have been up all night."

"Pretty much." She chuckled. "After a while, we decided to pull an all-nighter, take a break from baking to fix breakfast, and then take naps. Which is what we did. At least I did—I hope Alice was able to. Anyway, I told Jasmyn what we were planning, and I thought she sounded interested, but when I knocked on her door, she didn't answer. Of course, she was tired. Maybe she was already asleep."

Exactly what I had been opening my mouth to suggest.

"But I tried at around seven, when we were getting started, and again at about ten, when we took a break, and then again just before midnight. Of course, I knocked very softly that time."

"She probably was asleep," I said. "She's been putting in some really long days."

"But they're going to suspect her." Rose Noire looked almost tearful. "Everyone knows Brody was harassing her."

"She wasn't the only one Brody was harassing," I pointed out. "And remember, it's usually the people who are up to something who try to arrange alibis for themselves. Ask Dad." There might be mystery books on the planet that Dad hadn't read, but he was working hard to fix that. "And I don't think this is a case that will be solved on alibis," I added.

"I just wish I understood why she seems so calm. And happy."

Her voice held a note of doubt. I suspected she'd be studying Jasmyn's aura with a new intensity, trying to figure out if she'd been fooled before.

"And maybe this is a little odd, but she's been showing an interest in the show again," she added.

"Does she want her job back?"

"Oh, no." Rose Noire shook her head vigorously. "She's happy to be done with that. But she has been talking about how it would be nice to see some of the people."

"They'll all be here in the castle tonight."

"Yes—I reminded her of that." She frowned slightly. "She seemed excited. I think she might be . . . interested in someone. One of the competitors, I think."

"Do you know which?"

"No." She shook her head. "I don't think she trusts me well enough to confide in me just yet."

Even Rose Noire couldn't always work her empathetic magic overnight. I tried to remember if I'd seen Jasmyn interacting with any of my fellow competitors. Andy and John had seemed concerned when she'd fled the production tent, but that didn't necessarily mean anything. And I could see someone finding any one of the four attractive. Even Duncan, annoying as I found him.

"Just keep an eye on her," I said.

"In case she does anything suspicious?"

"Or in case she suddenly realizes she's a suspect and plunges back into the depths of despair. Or in case we figure out whoever she has a crush on is turning out to be the chief's main suspect."

She nodded absently.

"I don't want it to be her," she said finally.

"Neither do I," I said. "Let's hope it's not her. Or whoever she's interested in."

"But what if it is? What if Brody . . . what if she was driven to kill him by something he did?"

"Then we find her a good defense lawyer," I said. "We've got several in the family, you know."

She nodded again.

"Thanks," she said. "I hope the chief figures this all out soon. We don't want this cloud still hanging over us at Christmas."

I hoped the same but wasn't optimistic.

"I need to do a cleansing," she said. "I'll get on it first thing tomorrow."

"A cleansing of what?"

"The castle and the grounds," she said. "I'll use sage, to clear away negative energy. And rosemary, to promote clear thought."

Since Rose Noire's cleansing ceremonies usually involved marching clockwise around whatever thing or place she was trying to heal, she was probably in for a long walk and a strenuous day. I was relieved to realize that I didn't have to think of an excuse not to join in—I'd be down at the production tent, working.

She stood up, looking calmer, and led the way out of the pantry and back to the kitchen. I snagged a gingerbread llama for the road and headed back upstairs, using the back stairs that came out near the library.

Upstairs I could see that tonight's festivities were already gearing up. Ragnar's helpers—I could never tell which were paid staff members and which were long-term guests, volunteering in lieu of rent—were carrying buffet tables down the corridor toward the Great Hall. To make room for the gingerbread house decorating in the dining hall, I assumed. The little speakers hidden in the garlands were pumping out a lively playlist of rock-and-roll Christmas carols. Bruce Springsteen's "Santa Claus Is Comin' to Town" was playing at the moment, and I knew Ragnar had enough material to keep the theme going for hours. He'd inveigled most of his bands into recording at least a couple of Christmas songs and had recently been working with Rancid Dread, Caerphilly's own homegrown metal band, to record even more.

My first thought, when I saw all the activity, was that I should pitch in and help. I could feel the pressure to do it, like a strong tide trying to sweep me away.

I reminded myself that I'd gotten up way earlier than usual

and divided my day between hard physical labor and dashing around trying to help the chief with his murder investigation. Surely if anyone deserved a brief respite from doing something useful, I did.

Although there was at least one useful thing I wanted to get done. I'd meant to tell the chief about how Winkelman had been painting the crime scene before it had even become a crime scene—and might have photos. I pulled out my phone to check the time. Still a while before dinner. I could tackle Winkelman myself. The only question was where I could find him.

I strolled around until I found Ragnar in the entrance hall.

"Any idea where I could find Winkelman?" I asked.

"At the top of the North Tower." He sounded distracted—and looked worried.

"What's wrong?" I asked.

"Everyone is coming again tonight, but—well, Rose Noire thought we should cancel the party. Or change it into a memorial event for Brody. I thought this was a little much but—well, what do you think?"

I pondered for a moment.

"Mother's the etiquette guru," I said. "But if you ask me—"

"I do."

"It's Christmas," I said. "A time for getting together with friends and family. And most of the friends and family here never even met Brody, so I can't see that it would be disrespectful to go ahead with dinner and a low-key gathering for them. And those who did know Brody well or just don't feel comfortable with the idea of the party can do their own thing. Remember in *A Christmas Carol* how the Ghost of Christmas Present shows Scrooge that even in the holiday season, suffering still haunts the world—but that doesn't mean people shouldn't celebrate—only that along with the celebrating they should do what they can to alleviate the suffering."

"Yes." Ragnar's face cleared. "We do everything we can to bring Brody's killer to justice—and then we celebrate with a clear conscience. But we keep it a little low-key, for now, out of respect."

Just then the speakers blared out the opening guitar riff of Chuck Berry's version of "Run Rudolph Run." Both of us looked up and smiled appreciatively. Then Ragnar's face fell. Low-key and Chuck Berry didn't exactly go together.

"Maybe just change the soundtrack a little," I said. "Love the rock carols, but maybe when you get a chance, change it to something a little more . . . subdued. Just for today."

Ragnar frowned and nodded. He looked puzzled for a few moments. Then his face cleared.

"I have it!" he said and dashed off.

I headed for the North Tower. Although, since I was passing by the library, I decided to drop in and see if I could find something to read during the long, hot soaking bath I had planned for later. Ragnar had an entire bookshelf dedicated to what he referred to as "picnic books"—inexpensive paperbacks that people were welcome to take with them for reading outdoors, or with a meal, or even in the tub.

The speakers in the library were at a lower volume, though they were still pumping out the same lively rock-and-roll Christmas music. I spotted Victor, sitting in one of the library's comfy chairs, reading Chester Himes's *The Real Cool Killers* and tapping one toe in time to "Run Rudolph Run." He looked up when I came in.

"Needed to get away for a while," he said.

"Kick me out if I'm bothering you," I said.

He shrugged.

I headed over to the picnic book section and scanned titles, trying to figure out what I was in the mood to read.

"Can I ask you something?" he said.

"I think you just did," I said.

"Something else," he said, with a chuckle.

"Go for it."

He pulled out a bookmark—an actual, honest-to-God book-mark rather than a sales receipt or a napkin—and marked his place in Himes.

"You can tell me I'm full of it," Victor said. "And maybe I am. But I worry, you know?"

"About what?"

"Caerphilly's a really small town," he said. "Don't get me wrong. Seems like a nice place. But . . . your cousin's the CSI. Your dad's the medical examiner. And this police chief of yours . . . um . . ."

"Not actually a blood relative," I said. "At least not that we know of."

He chuckled at that.

"Although one of the orphaned grandsons he and his wife are raising is my sons' best friend, so I see a lot of him," I added. "Yes, it's a small town."

"So how many murders have your cops actually seen?" Victor asked.

"You'd be surprised," I said. "Too many for the chief's taste."

Victor nodded as if to say, "I told you so."

"But then, after fifteen years as a homicide detective in Balti-more, he's seen a heck of a lot of murders. More than most cops."

"Seriously?" Victor looked surprised.

"Seriously. I think when he took the job here he was hoping he'd seen his last homicide. Hasn't quite worked out that way, but maybe that's good. We see a lot less major crime than Baltimore does, but it's still plenty to keep his detective skills sharpened."

Victor nodded. He didn't quite look reassured, though.

"And in case you're worried that in a small town, the cops would be trying to pin the murder on an outsider—not Chief Burke. You'd be amazed how seriously he takes it when he sus-pects one of *his* citizens has committed a crime in *his* county. I think he's harder on us locals than outsiders."

"You can understand why I'm worried," Victor said. "The four of us—John, Andy, Duncan, and me—we probably look like the best suspects."

"I think anyone who ever met Brody would look like a suspect," I said.

"Yeah, Mr. Personality he wasn't." Victor shook his head. "But what I mean is, the chief's not just asking about last night. He's also asking about Sunday night. Like he thinks maybe the same guy mugged Faulk and then killed Brody."

"Sounds plausible to me," I said.

"To me, too. And that bothers me. Because none of us would have any reason to off Brody. But Faulk—I can see how someone who's dead set on winning and maybe knows he doesn't have much chance might be happy to see Faulk out of the competition."

"Definitely," I said.

"But the only person here who fits that description would be Brody," Victor said.

"You see the chief's dilemma."

"Jingle Bell Rock" gave way to a loud, heavy-metal rendition of "O Come, All Ye Faithful." Victor's head snapped toward the speaker.

"Undergangens Skogkatter!" he exclaimed.

I resisted the temptation to say "Gesundheit," since I knew what Undergangens Skogkatter was.

"That's who's playing," he explained. "Undergangens Skogkatter is this really cool Norwegian metal band."

"I know," I said.

"Are you a metal fan?" he asked.

"No," I said. "But I know who Undergangens Skogkatter is. Ragnar used to play the drums with them."

"Seriously?" Victor's jaw dropped. "Oh, my God—no one really introduced me to him—he's actually Ragnar *Ragnarson*?"

I nodded.

"This is amazing," he said. "I love that band. They're so . . . awesome!"

I nodded and managed not to laugh. The band's name sounded fully bombastic and Scandinavian enough for an edgy death metal band—or maybe it was black metal. I never could remember. But it was hard to keep a straight face once you found out that Undergangens Skogkatter was Norwegian for Forest Cats of Doom.

"Keep your ears open," I said. "He does concerts every so often with a local heavy-metal band called Rancid Dread."

"Rancid Dread? I think I've heard of them." Victor looked thoughtful. Then he snapped his fingers. "Yeah! They did 'Rumble to the Leech.' Not bad. Not on the same level as Undergangens Skogkatter, of course."

"I'm just amazed that you've heard of them at all," I said. "I've been hearing them play since they were in middle school."

"Definitely an interesting place, Caerphilly," he said.

"Aha!" I exclaimed.

"Found something you like?"

I held up the battered paperback of Charlotte McLeod's *Rest You Merry*. "One of my favorite Christmas books. I'm going to relax and read a little before dinner."

"Sounds like a plan. Good book?"

"Very." I held up the cover so he could see it, and he pulled out his phone and tapped in a note.

I turned and headed for the library door. Suddenly Undergangens Skogkatter was replaced by a Gregorian chant version of "Veni Veni Emmanuel."

"What the devil?" He frowned up at the speaker.

"Ragnar decided to set a more contemplative tone for this evening's gathering," I said. "To fend off any accusations that we're having an inappropriate amount of fun too soon after the murder."

"Ah."

"By the way," I asked. "Speaking of accusations—remember what I told you about earlier? About how Brody tried to accuse first me and then John of attacking Faulk?"

"Yeah. Never tried it with me. Of course, I was kind of avoiding having any kind of conversation with the jerk. Why?"

"Did you hear about him trying it with anyone else?"

"No one's mentioned it to me. You think it had anything to do with his murder?"

"No idea," I said. "I'm just curious, now that I've figured out what he was up to."

"Blackmail, maybe?" He said it softly, and from his frown, he wasn't kidding.

I nodded.

"Police know?"

I nodded again.

"I'm going to tackle Alec about it, too," I added. "And anyone else he might have tried it on."

"Good plan."

He went back to his book while I tucked mine into my tote and left the library. Time to see if I could find Winkelman.

Chapter 30

Outside, the crowd of guests was growing, and I could hardly take two steps without stopping to explain that no, I wasn't playing hooky from the contest, since it was finished for the day. I wound through the halls until I reached the ground floor of the North Tower and took a deep breath before starting to climb.

The North Tower was both the tallest and the thinnest of the castle's towers, and unlike some of the larger towers, had no elevator. A circular stairway wound through its middle like a stone corkscrew, opening up every fifteen feet or so to reveal another doughnut-shaped room. Thanks to large stone windows, the rooms were full of light, and they were popular as studios for resident artists and musicians. Winkelman, who'd now been at the castle longer than any of the other artists, had claimed the most desirable studio, on the tenth or top floor, with its panoramic view of the surrounding countryside.

And long before I reached his floor, I found myself filled with admiration for the stamina it must take to work up there every day. By the time I drew near his aerie, I was starting to feel slightly winded by the climb—and slightly dizzy from going around and around in the tight, circular stairway.

As I started the climb from the ninth to the tenth floor, I heard scuffling overhead.

"Who's there? And what are you doing here? I'm working!"

Oh, dear. I seemed to be getting off on the wrong foot.

"It's Meg Langslow," I called out. "And if now's a bad time, just tell me when it would be okay to come back."

"Oh, it's you." I could see the doorway at the top of the steps now. Winkelman was peering out. He had a bad case of hat hair, with his long salt-and-pepper locks sticking out in all directions, and there were spatters of red and green paint on his glasses.

"I'm not interrupting?"

"I need an interruption!" he said. "I need someone to tell me to stop before I ruin what I'm working on. Come on up. I'll put the kettle on."

I finished my climb and collapsed onto an ancient sofa whose black wide-wale corduroy upholstery sported a regular mosaic of paint and food stains. I was about to tell him not to bother with tea, but by the time I'd gotten enough of my wind back to say it, he'd already filled a battered kettle and set it on a hot plate to boil. And I realized that a cup of tea would be rather nice, to say nothing of helping conversation flow more easily.

I glanced around, enjoying the chance to look at Winkelman's latest paintings—both the finished ones hanging on the walls or leaning against them and the half dozen in progress on various easels. Moody winter landscapes, most of them, sometimes featuring a handful of black cows or sheep, and always with a beautiful or dramatic sky. Many of his paintings were more than half sky. He'd never met a gnarled dead tree or a patch of fog he didn't like. I could tell he was feeling the lack of snow, though. One easel showed a painting in progress of an old barn in the snow, with half a dozen photos of snow scenes taped to a nearby wall for reference, but he hadn't gotten far with it. Maybe it was hard to get inspired when Caerphilly was in a snow drought.

And he had several pictures that included crows. Distant crows, little more than silhouettes, sitting on the branches of a stark, leafless tree. A closer look at half a dozen crows drinking from a puddle on the wet stone of the back terrace. A small canvas showing a crow in close-up, head cocked as if to ask "Are you nearly finished? Do I have to sit here much longer?"

"Sorry I sounded so inhospitable when I first heard you," he said. "I was afraid it was Ragnar. I have warned him not to come up just now, because I'm working on his Christmas present, but he forgets sometimes. Want to see it?"

"Do you need to ask?" I said.

He chuckled, strode over to an easel, and whisked away its cloth cover to reveal a portrait of Ragnar. But not the ordinary, everyday Ragnar, clad in jeans and a black T-shirt with the fading logo of one or another long-defunct band on it. And not even the festive Ragnar of feast days, clad in leather and chain mail and a horned Viking helm. This was Ragnar as the Ghost of Christmas Present, straight out of *A Christmas Carol.* Just as Dickens described, he wore a dark green velvet robe with white fur trim. On his head was a holly wreath, trimmed with tiny icicles, and he held a blazing torch in one hand and a pewter mug in the other.

"Do you think he will like it?" Winkelman asked in an anxious tone.

"Like it? He'll love it."

"Not too colorful?"

"It's perfect." The wall and hearth behind the painted Ragnar were hung, much like their real-life counterparts downstairs, with dark green garlands of spruce or fir, decorated with red ribbon and gold tinsel. And the floor at his feet was covered, as described in the book, with the makings of a Victorian-era feast—turkeys, geese, ducks, joints of beef, sausages, and mince pies, along with a few anachronistic items like shish kebabs, pizzas, and pigs in a blanket. A feast even Alice might envy.

"And it seems to me that Ragnar fits in well with a Dickensian Christmas," he said. "He's such a fan of Christmas."

"'It was always said of him, that he knew how to keep Christmas well, if any man alive possessed the knowledge,'" I said, quoting one of the closing lines of Michael's one-man show. Okay, the line was about the reformed Scrooge, but it still fit Ragnar. Every year, while the rest of us were still in our Thanksgiving turkey comas, Ragnar was already in high gear preparing for Christmas with an orgy of decorating, caroling, shopping, wrapping, feasting, and giving to every seasonal charity he could find. He'd be in the front row at every performance of Michael's one-man staged reading of *A Christmas Carol* surrounded by seniors from the Caerphilly Assisted Living home, for whom he'd bought tickets. He never missed a school Christmas concert, a church nativity pageant, or a trip to carol up and down the halls of the hospital. And he'd be spending Christmas Eve delivering turkey dinners with all the trimmings to families that might otherwise be tightening their belts instead of feasting on the big day.

"Yes." Winkelman nodded. "Part of me thinks the darned thing is finished, and part of me wants to keep fussing with it. Add a few more bits of food. A little more tinsel."

"I know the feeling," I said. "I think it's finished."

"The problem is that I don't know what to work on next. I don't want to go back to that one." He gestured at the painting of cows in their pasture that I'd seen him working on outside. "Not until some time has passed and I can forget that it was the scene of a murder. And I'd like to work on that snow thing, but you can only go so far with just photos."

"Speaking of photos," I said, "I actually came up to ask you about some of yours. You were painting out there Monday, right?"

He nodded.

"And took some photos."

"I usually do when the sky's that beautiful."

"May I see them?" I asked.

"Why do I suspect that your motives are forensic rather than aesthetic?" he said. But he was smiling as he rummaged in the clutter around him, found his digital camera, and handed it to me.

I started with the most recent pictures—of two crows sitting in one of the open tower windows, eating something or other. Heartening to know that Winkelman also fed them. I kept clicking through the shots until I was back to Monday's photos. A lot of beautiful shots of the sky. Some close-ups of the cows. And the crows. And yes! A crow sitting on the post where I'd found the strip of red fabric. I could actually see the black-painted rail with the slightly split place in which the fabric had caught. No splash of red in Winkelman's picture. And yes, it was the same fence post. Both Winkelman's shot and mine showed the top of a dried allium flower—there had been a clump of them rattling against that fence post when the breeze blew, but I didn't remember seeing alliums by the other nearby posts.

"Would you mind if I took this to my cousin Horace?" I asked.

"The CSI guy? No problem," he said. "Do you see something that could be a clue?"

"Not really," I said. It wasn't a lie—the clue had arrived after he took his picture. "But you shot a whole bunch of pictures of a place that became a crime scene less than twenty-four hours later. An area Horace has been going over with the proverbial fine-tooth comb. It would be useful to see if he notices any difference that could be significant."

"Pop out the data card," he said. "I've got others."

I did and tucked the card safely in my pocket.

"Do you still have time for tea?" He looked hopeful, as if he didn't get all that many visitors to tea. Understandable, given what a climb it was to get here. And I confess, my first impulse was to dash off to deliver the data card to Horace.

But the world wouldn't fall apart if I stayed for a cup of tea.

"Just let me text Horace to let him know that I have something for him," I said.

So while Winkelman made the tea and put out a plate of cookies—probably some of Alice's baking—I texted Horace.

"I have a data card with some photos that show the red fabric wasn't stuck in the fence Monday morning," I said. "Can bring it to you soon."

Horace texted back "Great!" and I stuck my phone back in my pocket and focused on being a gracious guest.

Although evidently, I wasn't entirely successful.

"You're worried about something," Winkelman said during a pause in our conversation.

"This murder could torpedo the TV show we're filming," I said.

"I thought the victim had already been eliminated from the competition."

Clearly "what happens in the production tent stays in the production tent" wasn't working very well. The progress of the contest was the worst-kept secret in Caerphilly.

"Yes," I said. "But his murder means they can't get him to do any retakes or outtakes or whatever else they need. It may be reality TV, but it's not necessarily spontaneous and unrehearsed. And worse, the other competitors are prime suspects. If one of them gets arrested for the murder, that could be the end of *Blades of Glory*."

"Ragnar's blaming himself," Winkelman said. "I'm not sure why. He can't possibly watch every single one of his guests every minute."

"True enough," I said. "And—"

Just then we heard a rattling at the tower window. I glanced over to see a crow peering in.

"My other guests have arrived." Winkelman hurried over to the window. I followed, curious to see what he was doing.

The crow was peering in the window over a worktable cluttered not just with paints and brushes but also with tools and bits of hardware, suggesting that Winkelman either dabbled in some kind of metal sculpture or doubled as a handyman.

He reached under the table and opened up a small refrigerator—one of the half-size kind popular in dorms—and took out several plastic containers of fruit—grapes, apples, oranges, cantaloupes, and honeydew melons. He opened the window—slowly, to avoid dislodging the several crows who were sitting there. They fluttered into the air to dodge the window frame and then settled down again. Winkelman began spreading handfuls of fruit from the plastic container onto the wide window ledge.

"There's a bag of nuts over there on the shelf," he said. "Mind grabbing that and putting some out?"

I did so, and then we both brought our chairs and our teacups over to the window so we could watch the crows eat and replenish their banquet from time to time.

"I think that should keep them going," he said after a while. Many of the crows had gorged themselves and flown off, and the few remaining were picking over the food, selecting their favorite bits—filling up the corners, as the hobbits would say.

Then one particularly large crow fluttered down right in front of the open window and dropped something bright and shiny just inside before flying off.

"Payment for services rendered," Winkelman observed. He shut the window—again, carefully, to avoid inconveniencing the remaining crows. And then he picked up the shiny object. A bit of brass—probably a piece broken off of some machine.

"Another addition to my tree." He rummaged through the clutter on his worktable. Eventually, he found what he was looking for—a spool of thin copper wire. He cut off a length of it, wrapped it around the little brass object, and hung it on the Christmas tree that occupied the far end of the bench.

An unusual Christmas tree, even here at Ragnar's castle. I deduced that the ornaments were all objects the crows had brought him as gifts. Shells. Pebbles. Feathers. Bits of metal. Broken shards of glass or mirror. More than a few strands of tinsel. A tiny blown-glass Christmas ball. A dog's ID tag. And an inch-high miniature wise man, lost or stolen from someone's nativity set.

"The tree gets better every year," he said, noticing that I was studying it.

We finished our tea, and I said goodbye, patting my pocket as I did to make sure the data card was still there. Then I hiked back down to ground level and found my way to the back stairway. Using that to go up to the suite would mean less chance of running into anyone who might try to rope me into a project—and if I could avoid that, I might still have time for a relaxing hot bath before dinner.

But the data card was burning a hole in my pocket. I should turn it over to Horace. So I headed for the Great Hall.

As I was on the way, my phone dinged with a text from Michael.

"Taking Caroline and your grandmother to the meadery on our way home," he said. "Want anything?"

"Do you even need to ask?"

The Gregorian chants did add an air of elegance to the gathering. And the crowd was . . . subdued. Not so much sorrowful—after all, none of them knew Brody. Appropriately respectful that a sorrowful event had happened.

Which actually fit my slightly melancholy mood a lot more than a livelier party would have. I drifted through the Great Hall, greeting friends and relatives, and gave in to the temptation of helping myself to a few delicacies from the buffet dinner.

I eventually found Horace, sitting in the far corner of the room with a plate on his lap. He was chewing slowly with his eyes closed, and I wondered if he was about to fall asleep.

I went over and perched on the arm of his chair. He looked up and nodded at me.

I glanced around to see if anyone was near enough to eavesdrop on our conversation.

"Here," I said, handing him the data card. "Winkelman took a bunch of pictures Monday morning of what later became your crime scene."

"Cool." He pocketed the card. "Anything interesting?"

"No red fabric stuck in the fence," I said. "Kind of narrows down the window for when it could have been left there."

"Excellent."

"Any luck finding out who the fabric belongs to?" I asked, sotto voce.

Horace shook his head.

"Your mother said you're right, it's polyester, not silk," he said. "She seemed surprised and pleased that you knew the difference. And she also said it was the sort of fabric you'd most likely see as the lining to a garment, rather than the garment itself. A coat, a jacket, or even some dresses."

"That makes sense," I said. "But it makes finding the owner harder, I gather."

"Yeah." He took a sip of his cider. "Can't exactly go around asking everyone to show me the inside of their clothes. Especially not the women. And I gather just because the lining's red doesn't mean the whole garment is."

"True," I said. "One of Mother's favorite suits is made of off-white linen—very demure-looking, unless she unbuttons the jacket to reveal the vivid fuchsia lining. But I don't think linings are as big a thing in women's clothing anymore. You mostly see it in tailored things, like blazers, suits, and fairly structured dresses. And I don't really remember seeing a lot of women wearing that kind of clothes to Ragnar's party—not even Mother. But she could give you a better idea about that than a fashion dropout like me."

"Yes." He puffed out his cheeks and blew out his breath. "She said something of the kind—about there not being all that many lined women's garments these days. She thinks this means the killer is probably a man."

"If you assume that the scrap of red fabric was left by the killer, she's probably right."

"Nothing's certain," Horace said. "But it does look suspicious, that fabric. So I've been looking everywhere for red-lined garments. We've been searching people's rooms, you know."

I nodded.

"No red linings, though." He picked up a ham biscuit and studied it for a moment before nibbling at it.

"Not surprising," I said. "If I were the killer and noticed the morning after the murder that my jacket lining had a big old rip in it, and maybe a missing strip of fabric, I'd make sure the thing never saw the light of day again."

He nodded gloomily. Maybe I should change the subject to something that was less of a downer.

"So what happened to our friend Rodney?" I asked.

Chapter 31

"Rodney's in jail." He looked a little more cheerful, which struck me as a bit hard on Rodney.

"That's too bad," I said. "Not that he's in jail if he belongs there, of course, but I suppose even drug dealers have families who'd like to have them home for Christmas."

"He did say if he had to be in jail, at least he'd rather have it be here than in Clay County. Or most anywhere nearby."

"He's a connoisseur of local jails, then?"

"Frequent flyer in both counties," Horace said. "Or as your dad puts it, a hardy perennial. Keeps coming back year after year. But if Rodney plays his cards right, he might get out in a day or so."

"I assume that means he's cooperating with the investigation."

"Well, he didn't want to at first. But once we knew he was the owner of the burner phone that was texting and calling back and forth with our murder victim—thank you for that—we were able to put a little pressure on him and get him talking."

"'We' meaning you and Vern?" I asked.

"Yup." He grinned. "Had him singing like a bird by the time we turned him over to the chief down at the station. Confessed that yes, he sold cocaine to Brody a couple of times, but he couldn't possibly have killed him because he was too scared of Ragnar to come any closer to the castle than where we found him."

"Scared of Ragnar?"

"Last time Ragnar caught a dealer at one of his parties, he locked the guy up in some kind of dungeon and played polka music at about a million decibels until we could get out here to collect him."

"I can see why Rodney was worried."

"Even for a second offense, possession with intent to distribute's not quite as heavy as murder. Rodney was begging us to look at his phone, to show us that he was still trying to get in touch with Brody this afternoon. Because, as he put it, how could he expect to get any money out of a dead guy?"

"Not exactly ironclad proof that he's innocent."

"No." He grinned. "But darn close for a burnout case like Rodney. The poor guy's only got about three brain cells left. Maybe you or I would think of continuing to call Brody to make it look as if we hadn't killed him. Rodney . . . the elevator doesn't go that high."

"So is Rodney going to be a guest of the state again?"

"Maybe. He might just be doing some months here in his favorite jail if he listens to his lawyer and gives us the information we want."

"Which is? Or am I being too nosy?"

"Someone put Brody in touch with Rodney. A local, or at least someone who's been here long enough to know where to find someone like Rodney. You can't just turn up in a strange town and look up drug dealers in the Yellow Pages. And from a hint Rodney let slip, the same someone may even have served as a go-between on Monday, when Brody couldn't easily sneak away from the filming for long."

"Still a distance from being the go-between to killing Brody," I said.

"Yes, but how many people here would have any reason to expect Brody to be sneaking out of the house in the middle of the night for a long walk?"

I nodded. I wondered if he might even have uncovered another possible motive someone might have for murdering Brody. What if he'd been planning to turn someone in—not for attacking Faulk but for buying drugs? What if Brody tried to arrange another buy from Rodney and set up the go-between to take the fall? Although Mother would have chided me gently for speaking ill of the dead if I said it aloud, I couldn't help thinking that it was just the sort of spiteful thing Brody might do.

"I'll leave it to you and the chief to sort that out," I said. "And let you eat in peace."

He smiled a little wanly and leaned back in his chair.

I strolled around the room for a while. I'd gotten my second wind while talking to Horace and decided to save Rose Noire's bath oil for later. Instead, I could see what was happening with the gingerbread houses. In the entrance hall, I ran into Roxanne. Or the new Jasmyn, as Sam called her.

"How's it going?" I asked.

"Michael warned me that this might not be exactly a typical TV production experience." She rolled her eyes—no doubt an editorial comment on Michael's talent for understatement.

"Is that what he said?" I asked. "Or did he actually come right out and tell you that we have no idea if these guys are legit or not?"

"He did rather hint that this might not be something I actually want on my résumé," she said. "But he also said that it might be an interesting experience anyway, and he'd give me some production credit for it, and that if nothing else, having a reason to spend time out here at Ragnar's castle was worth it."

"Glad he warned you."

"By the way," she said. "I've been meaning to ask you something."

"Ask away."

She glanced around and frowned slightly. Okay, evidently she didn't want the whole world to hear her question.

"Let's see if the game room is free."

It was—not only free but likely to remain so since someone had hauled most of the game tables elsewhere. To the dining hall, I suspected, for the gingerbread house project. We ducked inside and shut the door.

"So what's up?" I asked.

"Do you happen to know who had my room before I got it?"

"Not offhand," I said. "Unless—"

I suddenly realized that maybe I did know.

"Unless what?" she asked.

"Do you remember the name of your room?" I asked.

"The Pointe du Lac Room," she said. "It's on the second floor, a few doors from the stairs."

"I think that used to be Brody's room."

"The dead guy?"

"Yes," I said. "But he didn't die there."

"Don't worry." She smiled. "I know. And I'm not superstitious. But that could make giving this back to its owner a little . . . embarrassing."

She reached into her purse and held up a ziplock plastic bag containing a small wisp of pink satin and lace. A bra. Not one I could ever fit in, and I doubted if it was Roxanne's, either.

"I mean, I can't just wave the thing around and ask who left it in Brody's room."

"Where did you find it?"

"Under the bed. When I got there, I sat down on a chair just beside the bed and kicked my shoes off. One of them landed halfway under the bed, and I decided to fish it out before I forgot where it was. And I found this there—sheer luck. Was this Brody guy . . . seeing anyone here?"

"Not that I know of," I said. "And not from lack of trying."

"Is there something like a lost and found where I could leave this?" she asked. "So whoever lost it can claim it without too much embarrassment?"

"There is," I said. "But maybe you should take that to the chief instead."

"Oh!" She frowned slightly. "I'd hate to get anyone in trouble."

"Even if they might have killed someone?"

She winced slightly and nodded.

"You're right," she said. "You know where he is?"

"I can find out."

I pulled out my phone and texted the chief.

"In game room with someone who may have a piece of evidence for you," I said.

It only took a few seconds for him to reply.

"On my way."

"He's coming here," I said to Roxanne.

"Thanks."

"When did you find it?" I asked.

"Last night, when I first got to the room," she said. "Kind of late—they said someone else had just vacated it, and they had to change the sheets and such. And I figured I'd take the bra downstairs in the morning and see if there was anything like a lost and found, so I put it in my purse to make sure I didn't forget."

"Ah," I said. "That explains why Horace didn't find it when he searched the room."

"If he had found it, he'd probably have assumed it was mine," she said.

"Probably," I agreed.

Someone knocked on the door.

"Come in," I called.

The chief.

"Possible evidence." I handed him the bag, since I happened to be holding it. "I'll let Roxanne explain where she found it."

With that, I left them. But I stopped just outside the game room door and typed out a text to the chief.

"I didn't say this to Roxanne, and it's only a guess, but I suspect the bra belongs to Jasmyn."

I stared at the words for a few minutes. I liked Jasmyn. But what if she'd killed Brody?

If she'd killed Brody, it would probably be because he'd been harassing her. Or worse. So we'd get her a good lawyer, one with experience defending women who'd fought back against their harassers. Or assailants.

I hit SEND. And then I headed for the dining hall. Maybe watching the gingerbread house construction would improve my mood. And if they needed help disposing of any building materials that happened to get broken . . .

The party might have been low-key in the Great Hall, but things were hopping in the dining hall. A loud buzz of conversation almost drowned out the Gregorian chants, and the room was full of tables covered with red and green plastic Christmas tablecloths.

"Meg! There you are!" Ragnar shouted across the room. "You can have this place."

"No, you carry on," I called back. "I've been working hard—I want to be a spectator for a change."

"That's fine!" he boomed. "Come and see what Josh and Jamie are doing. It is amazing!"

I began working my way over to that side of the room, but it was slow going because I had to stop and admire every other house that was being built. Apparently, the volunteers had started off making classic gingerbread houses—quaint, cozy cottages that looked as if any minute Hansel and Gretel would begin nibbling on a shutter to summon the Wicked Witch. There was a whole line of them along one side of the room. Then someone had built a gingerbread A-frame. Someone else had created a gingerbread split level. Next, apparently in response to a request by Josh and Jamie, Alice had produced sheets of translucent candy glass and an architectural frenzy followed. Josh and Jamie had collaborated on a gingerbread Fallingwater, complete with a graceful waterfall made of rock candy, and a gingerbread Monticello, for which Alice had produced quantities of white icing. Now Josh was working on a gingerbread Taj Mahal, while Jamie countered with a gingerbread Chartres Cathedral. Their friend Adam Burke was working on a gingerbread Camden Yards. Across the room were two-story gingerbread Colonials and sprawling southwestern-style gingerbread haciendas, along with gingerbread Victorian mansions, gingerbread painted ladies, gingerbread high rises, and gingerbread castles. The White House, the Empire State Building, the Flatiron Building, the Chrysler Building, the Sydney Opera House, the Leaning Tower of Pisa, the Roman Colosseum, St. Basil's Cathedral, the Great Pyramid of Giza, and Norman Bates's house from *Psycho*—iced with chocolate—were all taking shape on one or another of the long tables.

And the whole room smelled divine.

"This is amazing," I said. More than once.

Every so often Alice, Jasmyn, or Rose Noire would dash in, and the builders would mob them to get their share of new building supplies. More sheets of gingerbread and candy glass. More bowls of icing, both vanilla and chocolate. More peppermint sticks, gumdrops, lemon drops, candy canes, and cinnamon hearts.

And every so often, one or several of the kids would race to a window, peer out, then return to the worktables looking disappointed—but only briefly. A few minutes later, someone else would repeat the process.

"Has the weather service predicted snow?" I asked.

"Not yet," said Vern Shiffley, looking up from the gingerbread barn he was covering with bright red icing.

"Alas," I said.

"But Judge Jane Shiffley's left knee definitely says snow," Vern added. "And so does Great-Uncle Jasper's shoulder. So I figure the weather service will be getting a little holiday surprise some-time before morning."

I wasn't going to bet against Judge Jane Shiffley's left knee.

I stayed for a while, kibitzing as the boys worked on their gingerbread masterpieces. I was feeling relaxed and cheerful when—

"What is all this?"

Chapter 32

I looked up to see Duncan standing at my elbow.

"Local tradition," I said. "Every year, Ragnar's cook makes dozens of gingerbread houses and gives them away to deserving families."

I offered him a roughly cookie-size shard of gingerbread.

"No, thanks," he said. "Any chance you could show me where that lost and found is?"

If he'd asked me a couple of hours earlier, I probably would have pointed out, perhaps a bit testily, that I'd given him perfectly adequate directions. But the last several hours had mellowed me.

"Back soon," I said to Michael and the boys. I led Duncan back to the entrance hall and pointed to the picture of St. Anthony. A relatively flattering picture, if you asked me. Most painters depicted him as if he were entering a contest for the monk with the most extreme tonsure. I suspected Winkelman had painted Ragnar's version, which used a dark, moody color palette that fitted perfectly into the décor. It showed the saint wearing a hooded monk's robe, which struck me as a lot more elegant than the acre of bald scalp shown in most portraits.

Then, seeing Duncan's puzzlement—okay, maybe the knob was a little hard to see—I opened the door and gestured him in with a bow.

He strode in.

"Bingo!" he exclaimed, almost immediately. "It's hanging right here."

He reappeared, carrying the jacket, and checking it to make sure it was in good shape. I could see why he'd been upset at its possible loss. Clearly an expensive jacket, with soft, supple leather.

And a bright red lining.

"Damn," he said. "Someone's been messing with it."

"What's wrong?" I asked. But I had a feeling I knew what he was about to say. I pulled out my phone and texted the chief, saying "Come to the entrance hall ASAP."

"The lining's ripped." He frowned as he examined the tear. Yes, I could see that a section of the lining was hanging loose rather than attached to the leather at the bottom of the jacket, and its edge was slightly frayed.

I sent Horace the same text I'd sent to the chief.

"Let me take a look," I said.

He held up the jacket, red lining toward me, and scowled petulantly.

"Oh, that's too bad," I said. "But my mother knows a seamstress who can probably fix it."

"It's all ripped," he said. "Not sure how you can fix that."

"She could put in a completely new lining," I said. "Mother's had her do that more than once."

Just then Horace popped in from the Great Hall. He stiffened and stared when he saw the red lining.

"Cost a lot, I bet," Duncan said.

"Nowhere near what it would cost in Los Angeles," I said.

Horace stepped forward.

"May I see that, please?" He held out his hand.

"It's my jacket," Duncan said. "Been looking for it all day."

"I'm glad you found it," Horace said. "Mind if I take a quick look at it?"

"Maybe Horace can figure out who ran off with it and ripped

it and then tried to cover up the theft by dumping it in the lost and found," I said.

"If you don't mind." The chief had entered the entrance hall and was looking at Duncan with a steady, searching gaze.

"Whatever." Duncan shrugged and handed over the leather jacket.

Horace and the chief examined the jacket. They exchanged a nod, and Horace ran out of the entrance hall.

"When did you notice its loss?" the chief said.

"Yesterday afternoon," Duncan said readily. "I put it in my locker when I arrived at the production tent, and it was gone when I went to get it at the end of the day."

Horace returned with a brown paper evidence bag. He handed it to the chief while he put on gloves. Then he opened the bag and took out the red fabric strip. The chief lifted up the jacket and Horace held the fabric strip up to the torn lining.

It matched. They both lifted their heads and looked at Duncan.

"Does this mean you know who stole my jacket and ruined it?" Duncan asked.

"It means I have a great many questions I'd like to ask you," the chief said. "And we'll have a lot more privacy down at the station. If you'd come with me, please."

Duncan didn't look guilty or stricken. He mostly looked annoyed, especially when Horace and the chief told him that no, his leather jacket was evidence, and he couldn't have it back just yet. Ragnar located a coat big enough to fit Duncan, and after he put it on—not without a good deal of grumbling—Horace and the chief led him out. A good many of the party guests followed them out onto the front terrace to watch as they made the long journey down the marble steps.

I went back to the gingerbread construction site, in the hopes of recapturing my good mood.

Word of Duncan's—well, not exactly arrest, though that might follow. Duncan's trip downtown to be interrogated—

was spreading through the room. I noticed Vern checking his phone.

"Technically I'm finally off duty," he said. "But I'm tempted to head downtown. See what I can find out. And—"

"Nooooo!" The shriek rang out, accompanied by the noise of something breakable hitting the dining room floor. "He didn't do it."

I turned to see that Jasmyn was standing in one of the doorways, with both hands clapped over her mouth. Rose Noire was gently urging her out into the hallway.

And yes, I'm nosy, so I headed that way. I noticed Vern was following me.

"He couldn't possibly have done it," Jasmyn was saying.

"There, there," Rose Noire said as she patted Jasmyn on the shoulder. "If he didn't do it, the chief will figure that out."

"Someone must be trying to frame him," Jasmyn said. "He couldn't possibly have done it. I know that."

"Just how do you know it, miss?" Vern asked.

Jasmyn looked up, and for a moment she looked wild-eyed and terrified. And then her face hardened.

"Because he was with me."

She looked at us defiantly.

I didn't believe her. Glancing over at Vern, I could tell he didn't, either.

"Funny he didn't mention that when the chief took him down for questioning," Vern said.

"He wouldn't, of course," Jasmyn said. "He's too much of a gentleman."

Not the Duncan I knew.

"If that's so—" Rose Noire began.

"You're just down on him!" Jasmyn snapped. "He would never do anything like that."

I could tell from Rose Noire's face that even she didn't believe Jasmyn.

"Maybe you could come down to the station with me," Vern said. "And you could tell all this to the chief."

"That's a good idea." Jasmyn lifted her chin in a way that reminded me of what I thought of as Mother's Joan-of-Arc look. "And then he'll have to let poor Duncan go."

She began striding down the hallway toward the entrance hall, head high.

Vern glanced at us, then shrugged and followed Jasmyn.

I decided to trail after them.

By the time I reached the entrance hall, Jasmyn was bundled up in a coat she'd borrowed from Rose Noire, having arrived from Los Angeles with nothing heavier than a blazer. One of the Tweedles—presumably Mr. Zakaryan, her uncle—was arguing with Vern.

"But this is ridiculous," Zakaryan was spluttering. "She can't possibly be mixed up in any of this."

"I could, too," Jasmyn said. "You never give me any credit."

"Sir, your niece has said she wants to go down to the station and talk to the chief," Vern was saying as he ushered Jasmyn out the door. Zakaryan uttered a few words that would have gotten his mouth washed out with soap if Mother had heard them, and then turned around and began bellowing.

"Alec! Where is that idiot Alec?"

"Right here, B. J."

Yes, Alec had been standing nearby, watching. Half of the guests were crowded into the entrance hall, watching the action.

"We're going down to the police station." Zakaryan strode out of the front door. Alec scurried over to the coat closet and then raced outside, struggling to put on his coat without dropping Zakaryan's.

A few moments of silence followed their departure. Then the hum of conversation burst out, as everyone began discussing and debating what had happened in the last few minutes.

I was in no mood to join in, so I took refuge in the library, where I found that Sam, and the other Tweedle—Duval—had taken refuge. Convenient. I was curious to hear their reaction, and if they kicked me out I could always use the secret passage to eavesdrop on them. But they barely seemed to notice my arrival.

"What are we going to do?" the Tweedle was moaning. "They've arrested one of our contestants!"

"I don't think they've actually arrested him," I said. "Just taken him down for questioning."

"The chief of police seemed very keen," Sam said. "If they haven't arrested him yet, I bet they're going to."

Did he realize this wasn't helping?

"Of course, maybe they'll decide B. J.'s niece did it," Sam went on. "They arrested—sorry, took her down for questioning, too."

"And they'll probably arrest B. J., too," Duval said. "You know how overprotective he is of her. He'll probably make a fuss and get arrested. What are we going to do?"

"Let's see how things look in the morning," I said. "If they do arrest either of them, we'll make sure they get a good lawyer. In fact, I'll arrange that right now. The police don't exactly arrest you one day and pop you into prison the next, you know. It usually takes a long time to prepare for a murder trial. With a good lawyer, we can probably get both of them out on bail—assuming someone can come up with whatever bail the judge sets. And then we can keep on with the filming. Not just this week, but after Christmas, too."

"You really think so?" The look of anxious dependency on Duval's face was unsettling.

"We won't know till we try," I said. "Let me go see what I can figure out."

Actually, I could have called from right there, but I wanted more privacy. I walked down the corridor until I was sure I was out of earshot, and then called my cousin Festus Hollingsworth. Although his specialties were suing evil corporations and getting wrongful convictions reversed, he was generally my first stop whenever I had a legal question or problem. He always gave good advice, and I knew if it wasn't something he could handle himself, he'd put me in the hands of the most qualified expert he knew.

"Yes, I'm going to drop by Ragnar's sometime soon," he said as he answered the phone. "Probably not tonight, though."

"Long day in court?" I asked.

"Long day in the conference room," he said. "Negotiated a good settlement, which is nearly always better than going to court."

"Not as much fun for you, though," I said. Festus was a feared courtroom opponent. I had a moment of doubt. Did I really want Festus—or whatever defense attorney he'd recommend— representing Brody's killer?

Yes. Because there was always the possibility that Duncan wasn't the killer. And whether or not he was, he needed a lawyer, and the chief wouldn't resent my helping him find one.

"Alas," Festus said. "No big trial next month. I'll live with the dis- appointment. If you're not calling to invite me out to the party— what's up? Anything to do with your murder?"

"Not my murder," I said. "I only found the body. But yes, it's about the murder. The chief has taken two people in for ques- tioning, and I think maybe they need attorneys."

"You think they're both innocent?"

"Pretty sure one of them might very well be guilty," I said. "But I'm hoping an attorney can keep them both out of jail for the time being in spite of that. Especially the one who might be guilty, strange as that sounds."

I explained, as succinctly as I could, about *Blades of Glory,* to- night's discovery of the leather jacket with the torn lining, the financial peril Faulk and Tad faced if Duncan's arrest brought the filming to a sudden halt, and Jasmyn's dramatic though not entirely convincing attempt to alibi him.

"I'll make a few calls," he said. "And in the meantime, I'll head downtown myself, just in case. Shouldn't be too hard to get the young lady released, even if the chief thinks she's lying. The other one—does he have a clean record, this possibly homicidal bladesmith?"

"No idea," I said. "If this were a really professional production, they'd have done a background check on him. These clowns probably only cared that he'd look good on camera."

"I'll see what I can do. Unless he's a known troublemaker, the local judges would probably go for letting him out on bail with an ankle monitor. They'd probably also impose house arrest, but that shouldn't be much of a hardship out at the castle. Am I doing this pro bono, or is there anyone likely to foot the bill?"

"Jasmyn's uncle will probably foot the bill for her. And if Duncan can't afford it, the producers might be willing, and Ragnar's pretty keen to keep the show going."

"So maybe. Ah, well. What can you expect on the feast day of St. Thomas of Dover?"

"Still using that saints' calendar Aunt Hildegard sent you from the convent, I see. What's he the patron of?"

"Doesn't say. Only that he was murdered by pirates. If I were him, I'd have taken that as my cause when I became a saint. Saint Thomas of Dover, Scourge of Pirates. I'll keep you posted."

We hung up, and I returned to the library. Duval was still there, looking ashen. Sam looked more cheerful than I'd ever seen him.

"I've arranged for an attorney to go down to the police station," I said. "With luck, he can get Duncan out on bail long enough to finish filming. And Jasmyn, too, assuming Mr. Zakaryan is okay with it."

"But what if Duncan actually did it?" Sam sounded as if he found the idea rather interesting.

Duval groaned and buried his face in his hands.

"Then we roll with it, and turn this into a true crime show," I said.

On that note, I left them to fret by themselves.

I thought of going back to the dining hall to watch a little more of the gingerbread project. But I wasn't sure I was still in the mood. And besides—

"Mom! It's snowing!"

"Yay! White Christmas!"

Josh, Jamie, and Adam came dashing into the entrance hall. And then through the Great Hall onto the back terrace.

I followed them outside. Yes, the snow was indeed falling. And not the kind of big, wet flakes that wouldn't even stick on the ground, much less the roads. These were the tiny, determined little flakes that suggested they were in for the long haul.

The party fell apart, as people who were staying in town made haste to get there before the roads got too bad, while those who were staying at the castle put on their wraps and went out to watch the snow or join in the snowball battle raging down in the goat pasture.

I watched for a while, then gave in to exhaustion. It had been a very long day. I crawled into bed and was fast asleep long before Michael and the boys returned from their snowball battle.

Chapter 33

"Mom? You awake?"

I resisted the temptation to growl, "No." And then realized that I didn't feel like growling. The boys had let me sleep until nearly nine, and I felt rested. Cheerful.

Not quite ready to tackle *Blades of Glory*, but then with luck I wouldn't have to quite this early.

"Breakfast is being served in the Great Hall," Michael said. "After which the boys and I plan to do some sledding. Ragnar's given me directions to a prime sledding hill. Want to come along?"

"Sounds good to me," I said. "Provided I'm not needed in the production tent."

"No filming this morning," he said. "I already checked with Roxanne. Word is that Duncan has an early bail hearing. If they let him go, the production can probably restart this afternoon. But for the time being, you're free. Oh, and Jasmyn's back, still trying to give Duncan an alibi he doesn't seem to want."

Breakfast was subdued. I had a feeling a lot of people stayed up way too late, either gossiping or snowballing. And the snow was still coming down; not as heavily as when I'd gone to bed, but still—there were already six inches of the stuff on the ground. It would take a while to clear the roads. The usual crowd of visitors from town wouldn't be arriving just yet.

So after a hearty breakfast—so much more enjoyable when I

was fully awake—we collected a few sleds from Ragnar's sports closet and set out. Josh, Jamie, and their friend Adam Burke dashed ahead with the sleds while Michael and I marched behind, enjoying the scenery.

We followed one of the farm's gravel roads—someone had plowed it an hour or so earlier, so we were walking on an inch or two of snow rather than floundering through drifts. We passed several fields, then a short stretch of woods, then more open fields. At last, we reached Ragnar's favorite sledding hill—easy to find because he'd arranged to have one of his black-and-red dragon banners set up to mark the spot.

And a perfect spot it was—the top of the hill, where we were, curved around like a horseshoe, and the slope varied greatly, from a wide, gentle slope at our end of the horseshoe to a periously steep one at the far end.

The boys had dragged along four sleds—one for each of them, and one for Michael and me to share. So Michael and I took turns near the gentle end of the horseshoe and kept an eye out to make sure the three boys weren't getting too near the almost perpendicular far end.

As I was trudging up the hill after a particularly satisfying ride, I felt my phone buzz in my pocket. I waited until I reached the top of the hill to check it. From Roxanne.

"Damn," I said when I'd read her message. "They're going to start filming again. I need to head back."

"Want us to come back with you?" Michael asked.

"Of course not," I said. "I'm sure the boys want to keep sledding—why waste what might be the best snow we get all winter? I'll let Roxanne know where I am and that I'll be walking back, and with any luck she'll find a snowmobile or something she can send for me."

So after watching the boys launch themselves down the slope again, I climbed down to the road and began hiking toward the castle.

I was in a cheerful mood. We didn't yet know for sure that Duncan had killed Brody, but I was sure the chief would find out sooner or later. The fate of *Blades of Glory* was still up in the air, but if it failed, I'd know I'd done everything I could to keep it going, and I'd already thought of half a dozen ways to help Faulk and Tad out of their financial bind. And if we were restarting the show now, maybe we'd manage to finish shooting the first episode on schedule, so everyone could go home and enjoy the Christmas season.

So I hiked along briskly, enjoying the bright sunny weather, the crows cawing nearby, and the view of field after field covered with snow, with only a few animal tracks to mar their smooth surfaces. Their smooth and uncomfortably bright surfaces. Next time I came out, I'd bring my sunglasses. It was actually a bit of a relief when I reached the point where the road led through a stretch of woods. Although it was also colder out of the sun. I picked up my pace.

"Hey, Meg," came a voice from behind me.

I turned to see Alec stepping out from behind a tangle of thorny shrubs.

He was holding a gun.

Chapter 34

"Hey, Alec." I kept my voice cheerful and decided to pretend not to notice the gun. Because I had the sneaking suspicion he wasn't there to see me safely back to the castle. Just turn around and keep walking. "Did you get the word that they're starting up the filming again?" I said over my shoulder. "We should hurry back."

"Guess they'll have to do it without you," he said. "Stay where you are. Stop! Now!"

Okay, pretending not to see the gun wasn't working well. And I was starting to get the sinking feeling that maybe the chief had been wasting his time interrogating Duncan.

"What's wrong?" I asked. "And why are you waving that thing about?"

"You had to keep snooping, didn't you?" he said. "Throw your cell phone over here."

"Actually, I haven't had much time for snooping," I said.

"You had to go and dig up Rodney. I mean it. Cell phone."

"Rodney the coke dealer?" I wasn't sure where this was going.

"And he told you. I mean it. Cell phone, now."

"He didn't tell me anything." I pulled my phone out of my pocket and tossed it toward Alec. "He hasn't even told the chief very much yet. And how do you know Rodney, anyway?"

"Long story." He scooped up my phone and stuck it in his pocket. "I knew I needed to find someone like him if I wanted to keep Brody happy. Guess I should have kept trying to find a blacksmith who wasn't a druggie. How did you figure out it was me who killed him?"

"Actually, I hadn't," I said. "And if this is some kind of practical joke, it's not very funny."

I needed to get him talking. Keep him talking until either someone showed up or I could find a chance to get the drop on him. Which should be doable. If I could just get him bragging . . .

"So if you killed Brody, why?" I asked.

"Duh. He saw me whack Faulk."

My temper flared at his matter-of-fact tone.

"And that was pretty low, if you ask me," I said. "Faulk's your friend. He taught you blacksmithing. Lent you money he couldn't afford to keep the show going. And you go and whack him."

"I never meant to whack Faulk," Alec protested. "I thought he was Brody."

"Seriously?" I muttered. He might actually be telling the truth.

"I needed to get one of them out and you in," Alec said. "The producers were driving me crazy complaining because I hadn't been able to find a woman competitor. I figured you'd do it if Faulk needed rescuing, and if he didn't tell you he had money in the show, I'd make sure you knew. And it worked! Everything was going great until I found out Brody had seen me and was going to turn me in unless I did what he wanted."

"Which was?"

"To get him back on the show." He shook his head. "And I knew the producers wouldn't go for it. I didn't have a choice. I had to get rid of him before he told."

"So how did you lure him out to the cow pasture?" I asked.

"You helped, you know." He grinned mirthlessly. "You told me he was in the library."

"I also told Ragnar."

"Luckily I was closer. I caught Brody just as he was leaving the library. Didn't have any trouble luring him out of the house—I reminded him about those spy cameras you used to catch him messing with your forge, and then I pointed at one of the garlands that obviously had a hidden speaker in it, because you could tell that's where the carols were coming from, and I asked how we'd know there wasn't also a microphone in them. It worked. I led him out one of the side doors, so no one would see us leave."

Yes, Alec had been spending enough time out here at the castle. He'd know some of the less traveled routes. Keeping him talking was going well. Getting the drop on him, not so much. And I was starting to get pessimistic about the odds of someone coming along. Not a soul in sight except for Alec, and me—well, except for a couple of crows that had followed me all the way from the sledding hill.

"Going outside is one thing," I said. "How'd you manage to lure him all the way to the cow pasture?"

"I kept pretending to see or hear people nearby. He was so gullible. The more eager I seemed to make sure no one overheard us, the surer he was that he had me."

"So you led him out to the cow pasture," I said. "And you just happened to bring along Victor's cross peen hammer? And Duncan's jacket?"

"I was still carrying them around in my backpack, trying to figure out good places to hide them. I lifted them from the workstations after everybody left. Wasn't planning to use the hammer as a murder weapon. I just thought having it disappear would cause more drama. Victor can be a bit of a hothead—I figured if he thought someone stole one of his favorite tools, he'd pitch a fit. And Duncan was the same about that jacket of his—thought it made him look like such a stud. So they'd both pitch fits and the producers would like that. They really liked Brody getting caught sabotaging. That was one of my better ideas. Wish I'd thought of those hidden cameras you used. That was brilliant."

"You put Brody up to the sabotage?"

"You didn't think he had the brains to come up with it himself, did you?"

Actually, I'd thought it was exactly the kind of stupid trick Brody could have thought up all by himself. But I decided this was not something I wanted to say to a man who was holding me at gunpoint. When he got tired of bragging about talking Brody into sabotaging the rest of us, maybe I could confirm my suspicion that, along with stealing Victor's hammer and Duncan's leather jacket, he'd filched Jasmyn's bra and planted it in Brody's old room.

"And it was a real hassle," Alec went on, "keeping the camera crews from spotting him, given how bad he was at sneaking around. What a loser. I felt bad about getting rid of him, because I knew it could cause some problems with the show—I mean, what if they needed Brody for some kind of retake? But I couldn't take the chance of him turning me in."

"But Chief Burke seemed to think you had an alibi," I said. "How'd you manage that?"

"Now that was brilliant," Alec said. "You see, B. J. and Pierre had started texting me to meet them in the front hall 'cause they were ready to go back to the hotel. They were always doing that—like I was their personal assistant or something. Pick them up at the hotel at eight, take them back to the hotel for lunch, drop off their dry cleaning, stuff like that. They were a pain—but I figured I could use them as an alibi if I could just figure out some way to make it look like Brody was still alive when I left with them. So I took Brody's phone with me. I knew he didn't have a password on it because he couldn't remember passwords for beans. And I went back to the castle, and on the way in I put my backpack down on the terrace. And I went up to B. J. and Pierre and let them yell at me and told them I'd bring the car around. And then I said, 'Whoops! Left my backpack on the terrace.' I ran outside, sent a text from Brody's phone to Andy and another one to myself. And then I hurled the phone off the side of the terrace, as hard as I could throw, and ran back inside with the backpack. I made sure B. J. and Pierre both saw me get the text from Brody and answer it. So I had two witnesses that I was either in the castle or driving them back to the hotel from ten thirty onward. I even stayed in the bar with Sam for a couple of hours, letting him vent to me about how they didn't respect him, and hearing all his stories about important things he'd directed."

"You fooled us all," I said. "But how did Rodney fit in?"

"I was supposed to meet him," Alec said. "Do a pickup for Brody. Only there was no way I could get there. So I had to cancel, and I figured when he heard someone had killed Brody he'd figure out I did it."

"How?" I asked. "You could have given him the same alibi you gave the chief."

"Well, he could still turn me in for the drugs."

"Not without implicating himself. And just what makes you think I figured it out?"

"I overheard you telling someone. You need to tell me who."

"Overheard me telling someone? Alec, I had no idea. I was trying to figure out if it was Duncan or Jasmyn."

"I heard you." His voice took on a stubborn, sullen tone. "You said, 'I figured out what he was up to.' And then the other person said something, and then you said, 'I'm going to tackle Alec about it.'"

"You're an idiot." Maybe it wasn't the smartest thing to say to someone who was holding a gun on me, but I couldn't help it. "Do you really think doing something to me will help you cover up what you've done? Rodney will spill the beans and connect you with Brody's death, and Horace has probably already got enough forensic evidence to nail you. And just so you know, I hadn't figured out who killed Brody. I only figured out that he had no idea who attacked Faulk. He just went around telling people he'd seen them do it, figuring if he accused the guilty party they wouldn't know he was bluffing."

"You don't know that," Alec said, but his voice didn't sound at all sure.

"Yeah, I actually do," I said. "Because he tried it on me, and then I overheard him doing the same thing to John. That was what he was doing in the library when I texted you and Ragnar. After John told him to go to hell and stormed out, Brody just said, 'Ah, well. Next target.'"

"You're lying." He took a couple of quick steps forward as he said it—to confront me? Retaliate? Either way, he put himself close enough that I thought it was worth making a grab for the gun. I missed—but just then one of the crows swooped down and pecked savagely at Alec's head. Alec struck out with both arms and managed to keep the crow from landing the blow, but in doing so he lost his grip on the gun. It went sailing away into a snowbank.

I dived for the gun. So did Alec. Unfortunately, we located it at about the same moment. I got my hand around it first, but Alec grabbed my wrist, leaving us locked in something that resembled arm wrestling.

I'm good at arm wrestling. Thanks to my blacksmithing, I could probably win a contest against most people. But Alec wasn't most people. He was a fellow blacksmith. And while he wasn't as good a blacksmith as I was, he was bigger and had more muscle, and I had the sinking feeling he was going to win eventually. In fact, pretty soon.

Where was that damned crow when you needed him?

And no sooner had that thought crossed my mind than I heard the cawing as not one but a dozen crows began flapping around us and dive-bombing Alec. I felt him flinch as one of them struck him. And then another.

They were aiming for his eyes, I realized. Just then he figured out the same thing. He let go of my wrist and threw himself face down into a snowbank with his arms over his eyes.

I took a few steps away, partly to make sure he couldn't leap up and grab the gun, and partly to give the crows a better shot at him. Annoying that he still had my phone in his pocket. Would the crows back off briefly if I tried to reclaim it? Or should I head for the safety of the castle and leave him to the crows? I could even fire a shot in the air, to attract the attention of anyone nearby—but no. Since we were right in the middle of deer hunting season, anyone who heard shots coming from the woods would just assume it was hunters. Heading for the castle was probably the smartest thing. And—

"Meg! Are you all right?"

Startled, I turned my head and saw a pair of black Friesians galloping down the path. Ragnar was mounted on one of them, and the other was either riderless or had a rider so tiny as to be concealed by the horse's long, flowing mane.

"I'm fine," I said. "No thanks to Alec."

Ragnar leaped down from his horse and dropped the reins. The horse—both horses—stood stock-still, though they snorted in a way that suggested they were hoping this boring stop would end soon so they could have another gallop.

"I was coming to bring Carmilla so you could ride back to the castle," he said. "Why are you holding that thing?" Ragnar pointed to the gun.

"I took it away from Alec," I said. "Would you like it?"

"No, thank you," Ragnar said, with a grimace of disgust. "I do not approve of firearms. What has he done to annoy the crows?"

"I think they figured out he was planning to do away with me," I said. "And they're probably also upset that he injured Faulk. I should think they were asleep when he killed Brody, but you never know. Crows have a way of finding things out."

"Oh, dear." A pained look crossed his face. "And I thought

he was one of the good guys. Well, Chief Burke will be very distressed if we let the crows do too much damage to him."

He waved one arm over his head as he strode toward Alec, and the crows stopped attacking—although they continued to circle overhead, cawing triumphantly. Ragnar put his foot in the middle of Alec's back, in much the same way old-time big-game hunters used to pose to have their picture taken with their prey.

"Why don't you call the chief?" Ragnar suggested.

"Alec's got my phone in his pocket," I said.

Ragnar reached down and patted Alec's pockets until he found the phone. He tossed it to me.

"Before you call, let's tie him up." Ragnar gestured to the horses. "There should be some rope in Carmilla's saddlebag."

I fetched the rope and kept the gun handy—though pointed at the ground—until Ragnar had trussed up Alec with a length of the rope.

Then we mounted the Friesians, and while I made my call to the chief we headed for the castle, with Alec marching glumly in front of us and an honor guard of crows wheeling overhead.

Chapter 35

"And now for the winner of this first main challenge." Marco posed elegantly beside the judges' table that now held our five broadswords. Looking at him, you'd never have guessed how dog-tired he was. We were all tired at the end of this fifth long day of shooting, but Marco more than any of us. Sam had kept him busy all week, shooting new versions of every single scene in which Alec had appeared. They'd even managed to re-create a couple of scenes in which Alec had been interviewing Brody, using Faulk as a stand-in and shooting Marco over his shoulder.

I stole a glance over to the sidelines, where a small audience was gathered—including Michael and the boys, who'd been allowed in the tent to watch the finale on condition that they stayed out of the tech crews' way and didn't utter a peep. Michael gave me a thumbs-up. Jamie waved. Josh was chewing a knuckle and staring intently at the swords.

"Victor's blade was the sharpest," Marco proclaimed. "Cutting completely through the rope with both edges."

Yes, but mine was almost as sharp—it cut completely through with one edge and only left a few strands with the other.

"And all of the blades passed the strength test," Marco went on.

Yes, but whose blade passed it most easily? Mine had cut into the slightly rusty barrel as if it was made of butter, not only making a hole going in but actually denting the far side of the barrel. None of the others had done that.

"And all of the swords are excellent weapons," Marco continued. "Historically accurate, aesthetically pleasing."

Just get it over with, I wanted to say. But I kept my face calm and neutral. At least I hoped I did.

Marco hovered over the swords, touching first one, Victor's, then another, John's. He ran his fingers over the polished bone handle of Andy's sword, and down the blunt, heavy blade of Duncan's.

Then he picked up one of the swords and turned around.

"Meg Langslow," he said. "You are the winner of the first main challenge."

I heard slight squeaks from the boys, but they were lost in the cheering from the crew. And from my fellow competitors.

"Congratulations," Andy said, giving me a high five.

"Well deserved," John said.

"Enjoy it while you can," Victor said. "We'll be coming for you next time."

"Bring it on," I said.

Duncan only nodded and applauded with the rest.

We shot a brief presentation ceremony, with Marco handing me a certificate that gave me immunity from elimination in the second round of the contest. Shot it five times, just to make sure Sam had enough footage to work with when they went into the editing room.

"Okay," Sam said finally. "It's a wrap."

Spontaneous cheers broke out from cast and crew, and Michael and the boys raced over to congratulate me.

"All hail the winner!" Josh shouted as we headed for the castle.

"Go, Mom!" Jamie added.

"Good job!" Michael exclaimed.

"Only the winner of the first episode," I said. "Four more to go, remember."

"You'll skunk them," Josh said. "Wait and see."

"Think positively," Jamie said, as he patted me encouragingly on the shoulder.

I decided not to mention that my version of thinking positively probably differed from theirs. I couldn't help hoping something would happen to prevent my having to participate in the remaining four episodes. At the same time, I knew it wasn't in my nature to slack off and let one of the other four win. And I couldn't hope that the producers would cancel the show without filming the rest of the episodes because that would hurt Faulk and Tad. I had settled for hoping that the Tweedles would decide that they didn't need to hang around for the rest of the shooting. They were definitely the most annoying aspect of the production process.

But I didn't have to see them for a whole week—that alone made me cheerful. My real Christmas season had finally begun.

"Congratulations!" Ragnar strode up, beaming. "Now, back to the castle! You must be starving."

"Mom! Look!" Josh exclaimed as we stepped out of the tent. "Cool!"

"It's snowing again!" Jamie elaborated.

Yes, tiny snowflakes were beginning to fall. The weather forecasters had predicted scattered snow showers this evening and tomorrow. More reassuringly, Judge Jane Shiffley had consulted her knee and pronounced that it might be pretty, but it wouldn't amount to much. I was relieved—we had quite enough snow for the time being, thank you very much.

"An even whiter Christmas!" Jamie said, with visible satisfaction.

"Laters," Josh said. He and Jamie ran off toward the castle. Probably planning to visit Alice in the kitchen, to beg for more hot chocolate and gingerbread to replenish their energy after a day of sledding, snowballing, and cross-country skiing. They were determined not to waste a single minute of our rare snowy weather.

"Don't be long," Ragnar called after them. "I have a surprise for you!"

The boys turned to give him a thumbs-up before racing up the steps to the terrace.

"I'll go make sure they don't spoil their dinner," Michael said, and strode off after them.

"Of course, who knows if the show will ever be broadcast," I said, as Ragnar and I followed—though at a more sedate, grown-up pace. "Somehow I get the idea that the Tweedles—sorry, Mr. Za-karyan and Mr. Duval—aren't all that keen on the project any-more."

"No, they're not," Ragnar said. "I overheard one of them talking on the phone to someone—I think it was his accountant—about getting the maximum possible write-off for their losses if they cancel the production."

"I'm not that surprised."

"And I thought it was a real shame," Ragnar said. "Filming this first episode was such a lot of fun. And I'm looking for-ward to seeing the finished product. I hate the idea of every-one's hard work going to waste, and besides, I want to see more of it."

I nodded.

"So I bought it."

"You what?" I turned to look at him.

"I bought it." Ragnar beamed at me. "*Blades of Glory.*"

"It's very nice of you to bail Faulk and Tad out," I said. "But you didn't have to go that far."

"Oh, I am not bailing them out," Ragnar said. "They are still investors, but the finder's fee I paid them for making me aware of the deal should help take care of their current financial dif-ficulties."

I'd be willing to bet the finder's fee approximated the amount Tad and Faulk stood to lose if *Blades of Glory* tanked. Or possibly the entire amount of their debts.

"So now I am the producer!" Ragnar exclaimed, puffing out his chest.

My face probably betrayed what I was thinking.

"And no, I don't know anything about being a producer and selling a TV series," Ragnar said. "But that's okay. I can hire people. I know someone who is a director and a producer and also a major fan of Undergangens Skogkatter."

Amazing how many people still loved that particular band. I made a mental note to look up some of their music. Maybe I was missing something.

"He made several low-budget documentaries about the band when he was just getting started," Ragnar went on. "And one of them got an honorable mention at the Sundance Film Festival, and that was the start of his successful career."

"You think he might be interested in *Blades of Glory*?"

"Oh, I know he is." Ragnar beamed. "We have already talked about it. He shares my excitement. And he thinks there is no reason not to film in the castle. We keep doing the blacksmithing in the tent for this first season, but we do all the interviews and the judging and the candid moments in the castle. It will be much more fun."

"I'm sure it will be."

"And of course, I will be rooting for you to win," he said. "But if you do not win, you can come back in a future season and try again."

He looked so happy that I wondered if I'd ever manage to convince him that no matter how well or badly I did this season, I intended to retire on my laurels. I loved blacksmithing, but I preferred to do it in my own forge, on my own schedule, without cameras hanging over my shoulder.

We had arrived at the top of the steps and found Faulk standing on the terrace. He was wrapped in an elegant black wool cloak—probably something he'd borrowed from Ragnar until his arm was out of the cast and regular outerwear would fit again.

"Congratulations!" he said.

"A lot of the credit goes to you," I said.

"A little of it, maybe," Faulk said. "I gave you the tools, but you were the one who learned how to use them. Not everyone does that—look at Alec. I'm not bragging about having taught him."

"Don't blame yourself," Ragnar said. "It's not always possible to understand why people turn to the dark side. And, Meg, in case you were worried, I have bought out Alec along with the producers."

"Good," I said. "He probably needs the money to pay for all the legal fees he'll be racking up."

"And we will not have to see any more of him," Ragnar said. "But let us talk of happier things. Faulk, have you scheduled the moving van yet?"

"You're moving?" I asked. "Is this a good thing or a bad thing?" I knew Faulk and Tad had been complaining about how much the rent had increased on their small house. But I hoped they weren't having to cram themselves into a run-down dive.

"It's a very good thing!" Ragnar exclaimed. "I talked Faulk and Tad into house-sitting for me!"

With that, he dashed off.

"House-sitting?" I repeated. "Is Ragnar going someplace?"

"No," Faulk said. "What he calls house-sitting is actually letting us live rent-free in one of his cottages until we get back on our feet financially. We're going to insist on paying some kind of rent, though, even if it's below market."

"Get Tad to take care of all Ragnar's computers and other electronics, the way Kevin does for us," I suggested. "That would be better than paying rent. I dread the possibility that Kevin might eventually find a place of his own and leave us to take care of our own computers and routers and such."

"I'll keep that thought in mind," he said. "But now I'm going back inside. Fresh air is overrated when the temperature's this low, and Tad's looking for me."

I followed him into the Great Hall.

We were in a relatively quiet time here at the castle—that point in the late afternoon or early evening when the day's filming was over and most people retreated to their rooms or some other quiet place to rest before the evening's festivities. Only a few people were here in the Great Hall. I nodded to a couple of aunts who were knitting together in a corner and three cousins who were sitting with their backs to each other, wrapping presents.

And off in a corner, Duncan was sitting in a red velvet armchair with a look of bewilderment on his face. Jasmyn was perched on the arm of his chair, holding a cup of tea in one hand and a plate of cookies in the other.

"How can they expect you to focus on anything after what they put you through?" she cooed. "You'll do great in the next challenge."

Duncan's face suggested that he wasn't sure whether he appreciated the sympathy or resented being reminded that he'd come in dead last in today's judging. And was it only my imagination, or did he have the look of someone who'd rather have a stiff drink than all the tea and sympathy in the world?

"Think that will last?" Faulk asked when we'd left the Great Hall for the Entrance Hall.

"Your guess is as good as mine," I replied.

"Meg! Faulk!" Ragnar raced in from the front terrace. "You are just in time! Come outside and see."

"I need to find Tad first." Faulk headed for the elevator.

I followed Ragnar out onto the front terrace.

"What's up?" I asked.

"Our evening's entertainment is about to begin!" he said.

I heard jingling noises approaching. I walked to the edge of the terrace and looked down. A sleigh drew up at the foot of the steps. No, half a dozen sleighs, pulled by pairs of glossy black Friesians. And they were the special sleighs Mayor Randall Shiffley had invented to make sure the Caerphilly Christmas parade could go forward whether or not there was any snow—they could be quickly and easily converted from wheels to runners and back again. The bodies of the sleighs were decorated with enough tinsel and lights to make their headlights redundant, and enough jingling sleigh bells on both sleighs and horses that there was no way they'd ever be able to sneak up on anyone.

Now more sleighs were arriving—the newest ones pulled not by Friesians but by other equally large and powerful horses. Ragnar must have commandeered every wagon and every draft horse in the county.

"So we're all going for a sleigh ride in the snow?" I asked. Okay, the sleighs were in wheel mode at the moment, but they were still sleighs.

"A sleigh parade in the snow!" Ragnar exclaimed triumphantly. "Once we get everyone loaded up, we're going to head into town. Tour all the light displays and entertain the tourists at the same time."

"I think they will be entertained when they see this," I said.

"And when they hear us," Ragnar said, "there will be music!"

I winced. Ragnar's definition of music and mine weren't exactly equivalent. What if he'd recruited Rancid Dread to play in his parade? However proud I was of our local heavy metal band in theory, I wasn't all that keen to have them serenade me for several hours. And what would the tourists think?

But I tried to keep my face from showing my reaction.

"Which sleigh do you want us in?" a voice behind us asked.

I turned to see Minerva Burke, the chief's wife, and the musical director of the New Life Baptist Church choir. She was wearing one of the choir's red, green, and gold Christmas robes—though she looked bulkier than usual, so I suspected she was wearing several layers of wraps under it.

"In one of the middle sleighs, I think," Ragnar said. "So everyone in the parade can hear you."

I looked behind her and saw another dozen choir members. Evidently, Ragnar had arranged for one of the choir's small a cappella groups to provide the evening's musical accompaniment.

"Are we ready to take off?" Minerva asked.

"Almost." Ragnar was peering down. "We're just waiting for— aha! Here they are!"

He began half running down the steps. I followed him, more slowly.

An SUV had pulled up in the driveway, right beside the lead sleigh. My brother, Rob, leaped out of the front passenger seat and hurried to open the back passenger door and help my grandfather down. Delaney, Rob's wife, waved from the driver's seat.

"Welcome back!" Ragnar said. "You can just get right into one of the sleighs."

"Give me a couple of minutes to park the car," Delaney called back, and took off toward the parking area.

"Welcome home," I said, giving first Rob and then Grandfather a hug.

"How's that damn fool contest of yours going?" Grandfather asked.

"I won the first round," I said.

"Good." He nodded as if this result didn't even surprise him. "See that you keep it up."

"Way to go!" Rob gave me a high five.

"Time to load the sleighs!" Ragnar bellowed up at the terrace.

People began streaming out of the castle and toward the sleighs.

Minerva and the a cappella choir—including my honorary niece Kayla, Aida's daughter. Aida trailed close behind them, taking video with her cell phone camera.

Posses of tech crew members—did the sound, camera, and lighting crews always stick to their own kind? I made a mental note to see what I could do to change that when filming began again.

Faulk, swathed in blankets, visibly restraining his impatience at the way Tad was fussing over him.

Delaney, dashing back from the direction of the parking area, with Kevin trailing behind her.

Horace and the chief, looking more relaxed than I'd seen them in days.

Jasmyn and Duncan, arm-in-arm. Jasmyn looked deliriously happy. Duncan . . . less so.

Marco, who looked annoyed—perhaps because he was not at the head of the procession. Or did he have his own designs on Jasmyn?

Rose Noire, Alice, and several of their kitchen helpers, carrying thermoses and picnic baskets.

John, Andy, and Victor laughing merrily over something with Vern.

Mother and Dad, arm in arm. Mother was looking resplendent in a deep green coat with red trim, and evidently she'd talked Dad into putting on enough wraps for a change.

Josh, Jamie, and Adam Burke. They detoured around the slow-moving adults to make a beeline to the first sleigh, where Rob was helping Grandfather settle in.

And finally, Michael, who had a pile of blankets over one arm and had given the other to Caroline to help her safely down the stairs.

"I've got all our stuff packed in the Twinmobile," he said, as he helped Caroline into the first sleigh. "Much as we've enjoyed Ragnar's hospitality, after the parade it will be time to go home and concentrate on our Christmas celebrations."

"But you'll be back in a week's time," Ragnar said, as he helped me into the sleigh. "And in the meantime—let's start the parade!"

Ragnar took his place in the driver's seat and shook the reins. The Friesians took off at a brisk trot. The choir began singing "Jingle Bells" and we all joined in.

And the first annual Ragnarshjem Christmas parade began dashing through the snow toward town.

Acknowledgments

Thanks once again to everyone at St. Martin's/Minotaur, including (but not limited to) Claire Cheek, Hector DeJean, Stephen Erickson, Nicola Ferguson, Meryl Gross, Paul Hochman, Kayla Janas, Andrew Martin, Sarah Melnyk, and especially my editor, Pete Wolverton. And thanks also to the art department for another beautiful cover.

More thanks to my agent, Ellen Geiger, and all the folks at the Frances Goldin Literary Agency for taking care of the business side of things so I can concentrate on writing.

When I describe Meg's blacksmithing anywhere in this series, I'm probably thinking of the wonderful ironwork of Dan Boone VII. Over the years, Dan and his wife, Judy, have answered countless questions about blacksmithing. Anything I got wrong would have to be something I didn't ask them about.

Many thanks to the friends who brainstorm and critique with me, give me good ideas, or help keep me sane while I'm writing: Stuart, Aidan, and Liam Andrews; Deborah Blake; Chris Cowan; Ellen Crosby; Kathy Deligianis; Margery Flax; Suzanne Frisbee; John Gilstrap; Barb Goffman; Joni Langevoort; David Niemi; Alan Orloff; Dan Stashower; Art Taylor; Robin Templeton; and Dina Willner. And thanks to all the TeaBuds for two decades of friendship.

Above all, thanks to the readers who make all of this possible.